Mirrors on which

dust has fallen

Jeff Bursey

Mirrors on

which dust

has fallen

Jeff Bursey

Verbivoracious Press

Glentrees, 13 Mt Sinai Lane, Singapore

This edition published in Great Britain & Singapore

by Verbivoracious Press

www.verbivoraciouspress.org

ISBN: **978-981-09-5437-6**

Printed and bound in Great Britain & Singapore

Introduction

CHRISTOPHER WUNDERLEE

You are a reader[1] . . . I know this for obvious reasons but also for less obvious reasons. The latter is interesting.

You are a reader because you're holding this book, but more importantly, because you are holding *this* book.

Not all readers are indeed 'readers'. Most are not in fact. They are consumers. They seek out entertainment, express stimulation, fleeting amusement.

You – to your credit – are a reader[2]. You browse bookshelves examining titles, searching for that book that will kidnap you[3], that book that will reign over you, that book you will bring up whenever the chance arises – the one that will cause your spouse to beg you to shut up about, the one that you'll refuse to loan to anyone despite constantly praising it – that book that will alter something about you and require you to consider it at random moments for years to come[4].

It's a tall order, but that's who you are – that's the kind of reader you are. You have every right to expect it because you've experienced it be-

---

1 "No part of a book is so intimate as the Preface." Introductory Note, *Prefaces and Prologues to Famous Books with Introductions, Notes & Illustrations*, by Charles W. Eliot.

2 "Introductions are acts of persuasion", 'Introductions: A Preface', Michael Gorra, *Swanee Review.*

3 "I wanted the reader to be kidnapped, thrown ruthlessly into an alien environment as the first step into a shared experience with the book's population—just as the characters were snatched from one place to another, from any place to any other, without preparation or defense." Introduction to *Beloved*, Toni Morrison.

4 "When a reader falls in love with a book, it leaves its essence inside him, like radioactive fallout in an arable field . . ." 'Books vs. Goons', Salman Rushdie, *LA Times.*

---

fore. You say the name of these titles as if talking about a recent saint or wise deceased mentor.

For me, these venerations trace how I learned to experience literature (among other ways[5]). Starting humbly (*The Little Prince* to Mark Twain to *The Hardy Boys* to S.E. Hinton to Steinbeck) and maturing (*The Catcher in the Rye, Frannie & Zooey, On the Road, Tropic of Cancer*) as I moved through the canon (*The Sun Also Rises, Mrs. Dalloway, To the Lighthouse, The Waves, Portrait of the Artist as a Young Man, Ulysses, Dubliners, The Stranger, The Trial, Swann's Way, Lolita, 100 Years of Solitude, Love in the Time of Cholera,* etc.) and came into my own (*A Frolic of His Own, The Recognitions, Gravity's Rainbow, V., The Crying of Lot 49, Under the Volcano, Ada or Ardor, Wittgenstein's Mistress, At Swim-Two-Birds, The Third Policeman,* etc.).

Because you've experienced this overthrow from a book, you feel a need to have it happen again. People say it's an addiction[6], but that is too simple. It is a magic act – it is being the volunteer called up on stage to experience the illusion, only to still have no idea how it was done. You've been snatched; you've been kept; you've been found and lost again; you've been in that slip between the word-tempest of the page and the lodging voice in your ear, and you intend to return.

Most likely, you're holding this book in a carefully lit, well-arranged bookstore while you peruse the contents to determine if you should purchase it. You should.

If you cannot afford it, let me urge you to slip it into a covert pocket or dash it into a bag from another store or depart to the services and stuff it in between your trousers and your shirt. You will probably be caught, but let me assure you it is worth the risk.

I don't often suggest shoplifting (especially if not only from a bookstore), but here we are . . .

---

5 "I spent a lot of time in jazz clubs, nursing the two-beer minimum. I put on hornrimmed sunglasses at night. I went to parties in lofts where girls wore strange attire." Introduction to *Slow Learner,* Thomas Pynchon.

6 "[Reading] was like an addiction; I read while I ate, on the train, in bed until late at night, in school, where I'd keep the book hidden so I could read during class." *South of the Border, West of the Sun,* Haruki Murakami.

If you are to be kidnapped, there is always the ransom. If you can't pay it, well then, something bad happens.

Something bad happens is pretty much the outline of a plot of a story[7]. However, because you are a reader, this is too much of a simplification. The story is more than its plot, its devices.

It has escaped no one that the word 'story' shares its derivation with the word 'history'. The two terms share more than etymology however, literature is the language of experience – it is the primary source of the record[8].

Jeff Bursey is quite well aware of this. If you've cared to notice, Bursey's previous book, *Verbatim: A Novel,* is the historic record of an invented Canadian province. Based on transcripts, memoranda, and all the other bureaucratic minutiae of a governing body, the novel revels in the paradox of presenting historical accuracy as fiction.

And how narrative – or the constructs of it – is employed to record facts. Story after all is a clouded Greek, bastardized Latin, contorted Old French, Middle English word that cannot be cleaved from its doppelganger[9].

While 'history' (at least the way we now use it) was saved (mostly) by Francis Bacon, and we now delineate between the two, the etymology does a fine job of reflecting just how shifty the line between them really is[10].

Bursey's account in *Verbatim: A Novel* gives this strained relationship a postmodern twist – that is to say, how the history is recorded is the story (and the story is the history). We have a fictionalized historical record as

---

7 "Be a sadist. No matter how sweet and innocent your leading characters, make awful things happen to them – in order that the reader may see what they are made of." Introduction to *Bagombo Snuff Box,* Kurt Vonnegut.

8 "All we can say of it is that it [the novel] is bounded by two chains of mountains neither of which rises very abruptly – the opposing ranges of Poetry and History . . ." Introduction to *Aspects of the Novel,* E.M. Forster.

9 "It takes a great deal of history to produce a little literature." *Hawthorne,* Henry James.

10 " . . . fiction is both artifice and verisimilitude, and that there is nothing difficult in holding together these two possibilities." Preface to *How Fiction Works,* James Wood.

a novel in which even how the historical record is chronicled is unreliable (and to make matters worse [or better {depending upon your perspective}] there are the Hansard editors in a bitter debate about just how the record should be presented, which is also recorded)[11].

Verbatim is therefore true satire in that it mocks a significant topic; however, not the one a non-reader might presume. One can read the novel as simply a great pretence, the slight of hand of an illusionist doing street magic (very well); however, the real trick is the trick itself – that it *can be* pulled off[12].

And this is how literature works – by creating mind-theatre. Experimental fiction has been criticized for failing at this because the reader focuses too much on the craft and too little on the construction – the invented stage[13]. In realism or naturalism, so goes the assessment, readers are drawn in, forgetting that this is not reality[14]. While other (experimental) forms can never shake the feeling, the impression is that you are reading a construct developed by clever mechanisms[15]. As a reader, you focus on the writing not the storytelling.

But with Joyce and Proust and William Gaddis (and others), there is even greater trickery. This is the magic of the illusion happening before your eyes as an illusion while reminding you that you are staring at an il-

---

11 " . . . even as a poet he likes the role of editor and archivist, the game of masquerade behind the guise of one who 'brings to light' other people's papers." Introduction to *Demian* (Hermann Hesse), Thomas Mann.

12 " . . . when I read fiction, I want to be tricked, I want to be beguiled." Introduction to *The Novel: An Alternative History*, Steven Moore.

13 "Mr. Difficult: William Gaddis and the Problem of Hard-to-Read Books" by Jonathan Franzen, *The New Yorker*

14 "Realism, n. The art of depicting nature as it is seen by toads. The charm suffusing a landscape painted by a mole, or a story written by a measuring-worm." *The Devil's Dictionary*, Ambrose Bierce

15 "One of the awkwardnesses evaded is precisely an awkwardness about the possibility of novelistic storytelling. This in turn has to do with an awkwardness about character and the representation of character. Stories, after all, are generated by human beings, and it might be said that these recent novels are full of inhuman stories, whereby that phrase is precisely an oxymoron, an impossibility, a wanting it both ways." 'Human, All Too Inhuman' by James Wood, *The New Republic*

lusion[16]. The trick of the trick is the trick.

Bursey pulled this off in *Verbatim: A Novel* splendidly. The story of the history is the illusion; the illusion that the history is a story. It's meta-mind-theatre inside mind-theatre. The levels of it are labyrinthine.

In this book, the one you are smartly holding in your hands ready to pay top dollar for or risk severe criminal penalties to procure, Bursey winks at Gaddis and Joyce (as well as others)[17]. It is experimental – Bursey employs a Gaddisian myriad of voices who shift in and out based on the transitioning scenes (with constrained narration), and the Joycean internal monologue to afford his characters their unique reflection upon the dialectical theatre.

Mirrors on which dust has fallen is that artifice providing a reflection that is unclear, obscured, unreliable, making the fact that it is a reflection apparent[18]. The trick of the trick is the trick.

In this novel we stare back into a fictionalized Canadian town. Like Joyce's Dublin, Bowmount is the seat of a collection of ventures, enterprises, rivalries and relationships. It is not large, and so the myriad of characters collide into one another at the local pub or at church or in the bedroom, they have entangled histories and hidden knowledge of each other, they shift and scheme and fail.

Tingeing the host and its inhabitants are key events occurring prior to the opening pages – a hostage situation and an explosion at a pet shop, sexual assault investigations into the local Catholic church, and major social upheaval erupting into violence in the gay community. These incidents affect the narrative as murmurs, mere mentions, just under the surface; however, their effect is profound in its latent ubiquity.

A local radio station seeking to introduce a new system that will make

---

16 "It can be said that all prose fiction is a variation on the theme of *Don Quixote*," i.e. "the problem of appearance and reality", *Liberal Imagination* by Lionel Trilling.

17 "It is because we have had such great writers in the past that a writer is driven far out past where he can go, out to where no one can help him." 'Banquet Speech for the Nobel Prize in Literature', Ernest Hemingway.

18 "[A] novel is a mirror carried along a high road. At one moment it reflects to your vision the azure skies, at another the mire of the puddles at your feet." *The Red and the Black*, Stendhal.

DJs obsolete, a painter whose art outrages the town's sensibilities and causes rifts within his own community, a romantic who tiptoes near incest, a believer scandalized by his church's conspiracy, and a local government infested with disruption and discord – the range of the novel reflecting in its varying character studies, the multiplicity of themes attached to its devices offers a construct in which Bursey's technique complements and the word-works play out in the Chorus at center stage[19].

The minute dramas of the everyday and how they can be magnified (and quickly discarded), how they can be tragic and humorous, how they can lead us down the wrong path or detonate into life changing events – this illusion of the moment commotions in *Mirrors on which dust has fallen* is its foundation[20].We become invested in the moral dwindling, the control mêlées and influence struggles, the spiritual and aesthetic values, the lust and debauchery of the characters by having fleeting glimpses into their conversations and their thoughts.

We come to know them – these characters – because we witness their pettiness, their anger, their honor, their individuality through brief vignettes of direct discourse both from their invented mouths and the spoken thoughts and commentary of those around them[21].

They are not known to us because Bursey provides their measurements and biographies, but because he constructs for them a unique voice, and provides an echo of their personality in the gossip and commentary and interpretation from other characters[22].

---

19 "I shall resist the temptation to say what first made me gape, grin, laugh out loud, shake my head in wonderment. Better let the reader make the discovery on his own." Introduction to *A Confederacy of Dunces* (John Kennedy Toole), Walker Percy.

20 "The material that makes up a story . . . must be epiphanous, yet remain an enigma. Its shortness must have a formal function: the deepening of the understanding, the darkening of the design." Preface to *In the Heart of the Heart of the Country*, William Gass.

21 "In its subject matter, the book invades our privacy. The characters too are reconceived: they offer new blends of heroism and mock-heroism. Their thoughts are disclosed in internal monologues that register the slightest waverings of consciousness of the world that surrounds consciousness." Preface to *Ulysses* (James Joyce), Richard Ellmann.

22 "Ultimately, a novel in which language abounds and yet fails is a novel about how feeling, emotion, mutual response no longer function." Introduction to *JR* (William Gaddis), Frederick R. Karl.

This conceit by Bursey makes them seem more real because it mimics the way we interact with people in our lives. It is this illusion that completes the larger illusion of the novel.

That many of the characters seem to be on a trajectory, only to have it diverted or never realized, and that the linear movement of the novel is complicated by the reflections, asides, and entanglements of the voices furthers how the craft contrasts with the paradigm – the relationship of language to its subject[23].

So we have *how* Bursey wrote the book complementing its structure while at the same time obstructing it, and this is very apparently purposeful[24].

As readers, we[25] want this dichotomy, we want this punctuated equilibria of characters and structure, we seek voices that both recreate reality and artfully reflect upon it, we want to be tricked – to be taken in by the illusion – and it's all the better when we don't realize the real trick is not the magic, but the fact that we are watching the trick trick us, and we can't figure out how.

---

23 "The struggle of literature is in fact a struggle to escape from the confines of language; it stretches out from the utmost limits of what can be said; what stirs literature is the call and attraction of what is not in the dictionary." *The Uses of Literature*, Italo Calvino.

24 "Every novelist's work contains an explicit vision of the history of the novel, an idea of what the novel is." Introductory note to *The Art of the Novel*, Milan Kundera.

25 "Reader, fuck you! . . . You think I give a shit whether or not you've read this book?" Afterword to *Journey to the End of the Night* (Céline) by William T. Vollmann.

Mirrors on which

dust has fallen

For our only terra firma in a boiling and shifting world is, after all, our "self."

Wyndham Lewis

We are all in secret fighting for our sanity.

John Cowper Powys

Sweat

April 21, a Friday, marks the beginning of this story, set in Bowmount, and a few introductory words about this setting are necessary. Many of its loyal citizens are adamant about the importance of their City (as they write it) and its status as entrepôt for the entire province, situated as it is on Bowmount River. Tremendous quantities of goods are shipped through Bowmount up and down the river, or along the railway lines crisscrossing the land, and any one of her many proud residents would quickly tell a stranger how vital the River, the Port, and the Railway have been in Bowmount's brief, glorious life. Without much provocation a Bowmountian would further relate the adventures, mercantile and otherwise, of the country's pioneers who from the first attached more importance to the deep, sluggish River than to the land, leaving the hills beyond to the labourers, who always trail the entrepreneurs. The only acreage that had interested the first men surrounded the waterfront, and this quarter became the site of shipping and commercial businesses, with a handful of grand houses installed at its outskirts. If the stranger, by now unwilling or unable to withdraw from the firm grip of his host's monologue, listened further he would be told that Old Bowmount was born on that land, and New Bowmount is everything else – the hills and valleys east and west of the River. Rattling through a short yet overfilled history the narrator might not notice that very little of what he said meant much to the visitor, who had only inquired of a passing individual as to a certain address in the twisting streets which made up most of the city, or else had wondered aloud where the hotel, advertised as within walking distance of the railway station, actually was located. At some point civic pride would relax long enough for the resident to pay stricter attention to the stranger, and in the most helpful manner, treat him or her to the province's fabled hospitality. This initial encounter, added to subsequent ones during the tourist's stay, would reaffirm what Bowmount and its sister cities Carlyle and Crescent City were known for throughout the nation: affability, pride, and garrulousness.

Yet the City Fathers, as some people referred to the City Council (at the time of this story an entirely male environment), knew that not every taxpayer appreciated the commercial aspect of constant amiability. Reluctantly, they concluded, there would always be some people who besmirched Bowmount's name by obstinately refusing to provide what Bowmount required to maintain its friendly reputation. None of these people were truly loyal to the spirit of the place, embodied best in boards of trade and commerce, Rotarians, and other socially-minded citizens. This element, an ugly word, the Fathers knew, but accurate, comprised the apathetic, the pathetic, the atheistic, and many were neither Christians nor originally from Bowmount. Criminals formed a part of this other society, as one sociologically-minded councillor phrased it, but did not comprise the most part.

No, the troublemakers, the poisoners of public initiative, were those who never gave Bowmount anything but a passing thought, whose contribution began and ended with their taxes. In an address to the banking and investment community, the Mayor made it plain that he viewed such an attitude as especially selfish in these mean economic times and that all hands were needed on the deck of the ship of state for success to be assured. Clearly, for those alleged troublemakers Bowmount was not a community but a point on a map, not a City rich in varied history but a town with a grandiose self-conception. At the deepest level, the real charge laid against these idlers by the Fathers was that they took no part in the fight for City greatness. All these inhabitants cared about was saving money and getting by, never showing confidence in Bowmount by establishing factories, running for school boards or other political positions, nor beating a drum about the wholesomeness of life in the City, the province generally, to entice investors. That such a motley collection of men and women from all strains, ages and affiliations could show such contempt for this wonderful, glorious metropolis of nearly 200,000 souls (when Inner Bowmount, that is to say Old and New Bowmount, was added to Greater Bowmount and environs) scored an unforgivable insult on the sensitivities of those who possessed confidence and faith in industry, financial houses, government, public service, proper religious conduct – or, to use an overarching description, in the going enterprise called the City of Bowmount. If those people had been employees they would have been fired.

It is mainly with that despised group of non-believers that this narrative is concerned. Not being boosters, they do not appear at rallies for the city, or vote much of the time; not rich, they do not press their viewpoint on anyone through newsletters, and have no guild or association looking out for their interests; unaware of the importance of faith, they do not respond to public calls for their support, concentrating instead on making it through a day and a night without losing too much hope that tomorrow might not be as bad, all the while praying, sometimes consciously, for a different future if a better one is not possible.

One of these people not susceptible to re-education is a twenty-three year old named Loyola Holden. On the morning of this warm April day, snow melting from the mountains in the freakish weather, he ascended Elephant Hill, his face damp with sweat and his mind centred on amorous adventures. The gods smiled on me last night, that girl Jennie was ready for it, like she hadn't had sex in years. Barely kept back till I wanted to come, she had me so hot. Those beads, where'd she come up with that? Loyola wiped his forehead as the sun radiated with unseasonable intensity, making the road, buildings, vehicles shimmer. Never heard of that before, beads, jelly on them, putting them up my ass. Didn't know what she was up to. When she pulled them just as I was ready to come I felt like my ass was going out of me, but so fucking fine, so . . . His face darkened while passing through the shadow cast by the immense white cross dominating Elephant Hill and the graves arranged around its base. Sunlight glinted off the Crucifix on the Hill, off split, whitened headstones, numerous Madonnas, angels and urns, shattered marble and uprooted final markers of the lower- and middle-classes. Often he stopped at this precise point to observe the city below and around him. Prominent in this landscape if he faced south were the churches of St. Adamnan, St. Lawrence, and most notable, St. Finnian. Its two bell towers, obscured by scaffolding and rough fabric while workmen cleaned their exteriors, made Loyola think that they resembled a homeless guy's trouser legs. Dreary memories surfaced of his mother forcing him year after year inside that dank, drafty place during Lent for confession and prayers. Loyola shook his head, dull anger rising in him at the wasted time spent on teaching what he determined later was false. He stood with the cemetery behind him, drawn by the view again, simultaneously recalling last night's details to prolong his ecstasy, failing to notice in the graveyard the white cross standing purer than the previous day, scrubbed diligently last evening to remove stains left by the most recent vandalism. His mind fixed on Jennie crying out as one after another orgasm uncoiled inside her and his left hand in his trouser pocket felt thickening against his fingers. He refrained from touching himself under the influence of the gentle pulsing and the early morning sun, its warmth tempered slightly by the breeze.

Popping and rippling sounds accompanied by delighted squeals diverted his attention. Across the street lay a parking lot in front of an apartment building where welfare families lived. Avoiding potholes and jagged chunks of asphalt in the tiny lot skipped a blond girl of ten or eleven enjoying the Easter break, a plastic supermarket bag held open in the air over her head as though it were a balloon. A third party viewing this scene might have first remarked on the little girl's delight as she frolicked, before observing the young man's intense stare. Over these two figures on this momentarily quiet street towered the Crucifix, or more accurately its shadow, its arms spanning the length of the parking area, while its thick vertical shadow absorbed Loyola's meagre one. Shopping bag, what, no toys? Loyola advanced to the edge of the sidewalk for a closer look and a car horn cut the peaceful air. He jerked back blurting incoherently in the vehicle's wake, the girl now regarding him, a hand above her eyes, the shopping bag hanging to one side. He suddenly felt too afraid to even nod. As he hurried to work past the graveyard he heard the child running on the lot, free from the embrace of his look.

In the workroom of the Moscati-Mann Clothing International warehouse Loyola removed his thin coat. After pulling a gray, stained sweater over his head not a trace of last night's jubilation remained on his features. Pity for the child, as well as an irrational fear she would alert her family to his attention, sank to a dim corner of his mind and rooted, spreading tendrils and blossoming. What if she'd called her folks and the old man had come out? Called the cops? Way it is you can't look at a kid playing but they say, what is it? as he picked up a two-day old *Bowmount Courier* with the headline **LEWIS HAD EYES OF RAPIST SAYS JUROR**. Just looking at him, what the hell does the juror know? There I was thinking of Jennie and . . . an erection, suppose she could tell? Then they'd say, where, here, **LUSTFUL INTENT OF CHILD ABUSER CELAR**. What? Clear, they must mean. That could be me, if that kid . . . Get a hold of yourself. Holt, as Bart says, get a holt of myself, oh, and he's the guy who should know, what with him getting arrested for – why'd I think of him? Starlene Barker's New Zealand twang reached out to him from the stockroom.

—Loyola! Loyola! Where were you? Asleep? You have to do -

—I'm here, it's not even 9:00, what's, what's the matter -

—better than that, didn't I tell you. Don't argue, I don't need an argument this morning with my headache. A delivery, I told you yesterday, it could have come in any time after 8:30 and I come out here and find you reading the paper. Look at you, a mess, can't even comb your hair! You could wash that sweater too. A bell rang in the loading area adjacent to the workroom. —See? Get going, none of your excuses, I know what you're going to say, you get all defensive and I'm not interested, all right? Come *on*, help me get the garments in. Hurry up! Mike's waiting out there. Loyola followed, experiencing the familiar fear of losing this job because he would one day snap and say —You dumb kiwi bitch, you don't know anything about me, you never talk to me, so stop telling me what I am! One of his father's phrases came to mind, the stuffing knocked out of you, usually uttered after a hard day at work, and already the morning's walk, usually relaxing, had dimmed the previous evening's glowing memory and set this day in its relentless groove. He scratched his chafed backside discreetly and began hoisting clothes out of the Quigley Myers Trans-Shipping truck and onto racks. Starlene's barbed comments accompanied his every action, broadcast down the length of the back street, amusing Mike the driver. Apart from her shit it's a great fucking day.

Alone on the street rolling the last of the men's mohair suits towards the loading doors he swore at —Shits parking their cars right in front of **NO PARKING – DOORS IN USE**, what do they need to understand? Ought to smash their windows in, get the idea across. His attention switching from the cars to the street, he noticed once more the filth of Prospect Avenue, which served as the loading route for other wholesalers beside Moscati-Mann, such as Pierce, Frisk and Coughlan, Zeppelin! Dressware, H.S. Mauberley Dry Goods, a computer company and a mongrel assortment of small businesses. Garbage and bird dung on the road and sidewalk when mixed with the sewer's emanations on humid days produced an overpowering stench. Not as bad as it could be, but another great morning ruined by this smell, and he inhaled to verify it as he lifted the heavy rack over the sidewalk prior to wheeling it inside. Sunshine and that rotten smell, like some – but the simile lodged unfinished in his throat as the thick metal pipe of the clothes rack tipped, crushing his neck. Loyola staggered under the impact and the gross weight, yellow plastic wrappers over the suits covering his face, getting inside his mouth, the smell of polyethylene obscuring faeces, guano, discarded food, paint cans left for the garbagemen. Got to save the suits, they'll kill me, and he struggled upwards blindly holding pipes that might keep the rack perched on his reddening neck until he set the wheels on the sidewalk, making sure no clothes touched the ground. When he entered the loading area he heard —What's the matter with you, you're so slow, we'll never get this done and Mike's waiting. There, roll it over there, I'm not counting those yet. Get counting. Not that one, those ones. Where was I?

Rubbing his neck, Loyola enviously regarded the driver's role in the monotonous procedure of accounting for every piece of clothing. He just has to wait it out until the number of garments counted match the delivery slips, then he's free to bugger off from this four-man nuthouse. While Mike stood drinking Moscati-Mann coffee with a grin on his face Loyola's fingers raced along the hangers, his neck beginning to ache. All the time he's standing there that kiwi keeps on and on about making sure I counted this and that, interrupting me when I count, but me interrupt her? No way, and he's getting a great laugh like he always does, doesn't pay any attention to her, why the hell can't I be like that? There were to be six suits in each yellow bag, six jackets in each yellow bag, eight bags per rack; with trousers there were to be ten in each yellow bag, sixty on a rack, all in good condition. However, there were often times when the trousers of suits, despite the opaque plastic clips that kept them on the black hangers, were found at the bottom of a bag. —One hundred and eleven, one hundred and twelve, one look at the pants there, what happened Mike did you spill all this in the – one hundred and twelve, one hundred and thirteen. What's this? For crying out loud Mike, what speed were you doing? The driver smiled and kept drinking. —Pants everywhere, bottoms of – that's why the count, Loyola did you notice this, were they like this when you took them out of the truck, are you sure, is so slow, that and – Loyola! Are you finished? Then don't stand there, unwrap them, you know what to do, bring the mohairs into the stockroom, wools next, jackets, then trousers, put them on the rack out there are you listening next to the cotton ones do you understand, not above them, next to, her voice escorting him as he trundled out of the loading room, —Honestly! flung at his retreating figure.

The stockroom was a dim place, long, wide and high, decorated in the mid-1980s in chocolate and cream, containing two wooden desks with matching chairs, two telephones, an electronic typewriter on a table, and a small vinyl couch with split cushions. The rest of the room consisted of long racks, four rows across, each with three levels, the highest rack twenty feet from the floor. Along one short wall two short racks with double rails had been installed to store white dinner jackets, sport jackets, and returned goods. On days like this, as he stood sweating under the naked fluorescent lights on the slender, swaying aluminum ladder, heavyweight suits hanging on the side of one hand while with the other he pushed aside old stock to make space for the new arrivals, Loyola contemplated quitting, walking out as easily as he had walked into this position. —I should have stayed in college, was how the fantasies began, or resumed, and he shook his head, knowing he would have done no better in geography, science, mathematics, whatever he had eventually decided to devote himself to, than he had in English and folklore courses. Never able to stay interested in any topic he had remained as mediocre a student when he abruptly left last year as when he entered. All college had done for him was reveal his defects and weaken his resumé, declaring him a quitter as well as undereducated. Employers now wanted computer or communication skills. He caught himself as the ladder started to wobble, noticing the dull pain in his chest and side muscles where they had become inflamed again. Groaning he thrust the last of the suits onto the rack, wiped his forehead, and descended to the stockroom floor.

—What were you doing, talking to yourself? Now, there's suits out there that have to be boxed and shipped, why you didn't do it yesterday I don't know, you were here till 5:30, and I suppose you think – well?

—We get off at 5:30.

—No. You get off when the last garments are boxed. Understood? I'll have more ready for you in a few minutes, we got a lot to get out, those mohairs you just put up, for instance, so I hope you've done them like I said you had to. Oh, Anthony, can you spare Doug, we have a lot of suits to sort -

—Starlene, I've Mr. Bodrik on the line, Bodrik Fashions For Men, he says we didn't send him the suit he requested, a 50R. Do you know anything about a 50R?

—Number?

—50R.

—Suit number.

—Yes, 51226/03, last week, he spoke -

—Did you take that call, Loyola?

—to you he said, the woman.

—My name is Starlene, I'm not some woman. I'll check my book, and Loyola, check your posting books, was it regular post, did he want it, why are you standing here check it out, by regular post or special delivery?

—Regular. Anthony's left loafer dropped to the floor as he bent one leg up to the other repeatedly, one gray sock with a faint pattern slipping in and out of the shoe. —He's not very happy it hasn't arrived, hee-hee. Particularly since he has the bill already.

—Put Bodrik through here, will you?

—Certainly. I told him it had probably been sent. Flipping through postal books Loyola waited to be told he was taking too long, or to find out he had not sent the parcel. Look, there it was, mailed Monday, number such-and-such, that bitch got me rattled. —Starlene? We sent it out Monday.

—You sure? Are you - damn it, I know he can hear me. Cripes, what - Mr. Bodrik, hello, Starlene Barker here, stock service manager, good morning to you. It's a beautiful day, isn't it? Shame to be working, hope it'll be a great summer. Now I understand from Mr. Coish you haven't received a 50 reg pinstripe? We sent it the day you called, Monday. We're quite sure, our stockroom boy's checked his records, it went out that afternoon about 1:00. I'll hold. Fingernails drummed on the smoke-stained desk next to day-old tea in a mug where the drawing of a plain-faced woman asked **WHY DOES THE RIGHT MAN ALWAYS COME ALONG – ON THE ARMS OF THE WRONG WOMAN!?** Past the narrow window which opened out on a well a pigeon clucked and swaggered in mating dance at another pigeon, the male's swollen neck and amorous cooing wasted on a corpse. —Yes, I'm here, what was that? The suit arrived just now. Well, that's fine, you see, so . . . Yes, I'll hold. Of course the suit arrived, twitchy bastard. Doug, hi, sorry to take you away from the accounts, it won't take long.

—Just filing, nothing important.

—Don't let Anthony hear you say that. Take this list, see, where it says

51112/01? Pull out the sizes indicated, the suits are on that lowest rack if he put them where he should, and put them on this portable rack. Thanks a lot, it's appreciated. Hello again, Mr. Bodrik. What? Yes, the price is 10% more because the suit is a large size. Didn't write it down? You don't want to pay, I see, because it wasn't written down. What delivery note number – just a sec. Yes, okay, I got our copy. No, I didn't write it down. Yes, I do sometimes, not always, sometimes. You won't pay because – well, look at the box at the bottom of the delivery note, see the tiny print where it says suit sizes over 48 reg, add 10%? Yes, that's it. What? Of course we expect our customer to read the invoice, it's – certainly, contact your sales rep, Mr. Delaney's there to help. Hello? Hello? She slammed down the handset. —The delivery note says it, and the post got it to you after all you rotten bastard!, taking up my time. She ran out of the stockroom calling —Anthony, Bodrik doesn't want to pay the 10% because it wasn't written in ink, can you believe that, we're not going to let him get away with that are we? The telephone on his desk rang.

—Moscati-Mann, Anthony Coish speaking. Hello, Mr. Bodrik sir, how are you? The invoice, 10%? It is the custom, hee-hee, and if Starlene didn't write it by hand, it is written down there. Yes sir. That's understandable. Contact head office, very well, I shall be speaking to them shortly myself. Good-day. Anthony's hand touched his moustache and came down to grip a fountain pen. —I want you to call Mr. Simpkins to tell him Mr. Bodrik is annoyed he has to pay the full price, and explain why.

—He's going to pay it though, you aren't going to let him -

—I do what I'm told to do, and you know, or ought to know, head office likes him. He buys there when he visits, and he buys big, big, hundreds of thousands of dollars a year, for all his stores, and if he wants it he'll get it.

—We can't let someone tell us what they'll pay -

—It wouldn't have happened if you hadn't started writing it down for them, would it? I told you, I said -

—You said what? No such thing -

—that it would lead to – and what do you call this? Hello, Anthony Coish speaking. Good morning, Mr. Simpkins. Yes, she's in the stockroom,

I'll transfer you.

—Already?

—It must be something else. Fix this up, Starlene, right hand stroking the left side of his moustache, —figure out a way to make sure this doesn't happen again. Head office doesn't want unhappy clients, they don't buy enough as it is.

—Thanks, Anthony. Loyola, why aren't those suits boxed? How's it going, Doug?

—Fine, Miss -

—Starlene, call me that, Doug, her hand stabbing at the telephone.

—It's going all right. Can Loyola give me a hand if he's not -

—If he knows where one is, Mr. Simpkins? Yes the clothes arrived this morning, that's what you called about? And something has come up, here. I'll hold. She looked absently through the glass separating the stockroom from the packing room, fingers tapping the mug where, on the other side, a vulgarly painted and attired woman advised, **FORGET WHAT MOM TOLD YOU - BE A WRONG WOMAN TOO!** The object of her blank stare bustled around in his workroom, murmuring —That bitch, that bitch, as he jammed paper inside the arms of jackets, folded pants, sealed boxes with tape before addressing them with labels written in his manager's solid hand, stamped "Moscati-Mann" in the top left-hand corner, lastly adhered a postal identification sticker in the right-hand corner prior to tossing the boxes, which mounted as morning slid into afternoon, in a corner from where the postman picked them up at 2:00, freeing Loyola for lunch.

In some ways afternoons were easier, though Fridays meant customers' last-minute demands and consequently rushed postings. This day, however, time afforded Loyola a few minutes outdoors after sweeping the loading area and folding the yellow clothing bags, putting them in a large cardboard box for later use lining garbage bins. Opposite the loading doors was a small green area, considered by some local residents a garden, others a park, with flowers growing along its far side. In the middle, surrounded by grass reviving after the brutal winter, stood a tree, which Loyola did not know was a copper beech. Underneath it, needing a fresh coat of paint and new slats, a sea-green bench, upon which Loyola carefully settled, positioned between splintered wood and bird droppings. He took off his sweater and squinted at the sun. You're what I need, nothing else. Maybe after work I'll sit and get some rays. He considered the small balcony attached to his apartment. I have sun, even if I don't have money like most people. Or freedom. He tried to calm himself. This hidden square of greenery at times helped Loyola escape from thoughts of work. In the approaching summer he would eat lunch surrounded by the essence of flowers and rich earth, free from the cramped, airless packing room and what he considered Starlene's double-hinged tongue. Once more he wondered what made her tick, why she talked normally to the surveyors in the nearby office building, or the people who worked in the computer software firm. What's that red-headed slag got against me, ever since I came here, because I took the place of that idiot she liked? Always talking about how smart he is and how he should have gone to law school, but he didn't have any organization, the packing room was a mess, I cleaned it up myself, think she notices? She missed talking to him, so took it out on me, at the start, and by now . . . Not fair, not fair.

Occasionally when Loyola sat in this square of nature he brooded on work and the future, unable to reroute his emotions away from some troubling pathway to a more cheerful course. Even last night's memories proved feeble against today's unrelenting impulse to quit, for by now he was unable to recall clearly what he had truly felt after leaving the girl. Happy, blown away, numbed, sickened? Why was it so difficult to be sure how you were feeling? Even her face is getting hard to describe. What she did to me, was that normal? Could that hurt me, or make me some pervert? Is she laughing with those stupid friends of hers she was with, saying, He's a fag? If she tells anyone I'll, I'll . . . Shifting on the bench he scrutinized his hands. They look like Dad's right before he hurt his back. Raising his head he took in the blue sky dotted with white clouds, letting his gaze follow a formation of birds soaring away. Dad always said any job you hate takes the heart's blood out of you, unless you got dreams. He's always saying nobody at the railway had anything in them after a while, after doing the same thing day in and day out, worried about money and your health all the time. Bills, job, family, house, food. Jennie, or Krysta or Merilee, the same, everything's the same shit when you have no way out. All Mom's prayers and talk about a soul and God, pure Catholic shit, didn't keep her from burning to death, keep Dad from hurting himself. Heart's blood, like Dad said. Maybe now I see what Dad meant. This revelation squeezed from misery silenced him for a few minutes.

Doug stepped out of the loading area, squinting in the bright light as he looked around. There's a bright little prick, business school, younger, makes more than me and hasn't worked here three weeks. Doug called out too loudly for this quiet street, —Miss Barker's looking for you. Nodding, Loyola turned his head, waiting for the accounts clerk to withdraw. Can't get a break without her after me, surprised she lets me piss on company time. His watch read 3:00 and he slowly stood up, concentrating one last time on the garden. What a paradise it seemed, especially on summer days, the tang of newly-mown grass mingling with the beech and the perfume of colourful flowers whose names he did not need to know in order to admire them. Sometimes he picked a wild rose or lilac, guiltily, crushing the flower against his nose, inhaling deeply and losing himself in its moist softness. At unpredictable moments this action made him recall the half-dozen English courses he had taken, and the scraps of poetry that had stayed in his mind and at times encouraged women to talk further with him. He hated leaving this spot for Moscati-Mann where no breeze stirred the dusty air or relieved the closeness, and all one could look at were men's outfits of mohair, polyester, wool, cotton, linen, satin finishes, overlaid with plastic. —I could tell them I hate this and walk out, came whispering through a grimace. What bothered him most was the possibility that there existed in the world a better situation he would never experience, because in the end, no matter how insufferable this work was, he could not utter a bold proclamation and leave. To clear his head he closed his eyes, drawing in long breaths, the beech and flowers, the grass, their distinct scents forming a thin poultice which acted like balm on his heart's wound, but underneath this fragile dressing like blood under skin lay mildew, fungus, rotting fruit, sour milk, decaying carcasses. —Excuse me, but Starlene sent me. Doug's voice woke Loyola from his daze, the magical garden swiftly transforming into a plot of land that deceived him with a false promise of ease.

—Where were you, we have work to do, Loyola!

—I've packed everything there -

—Don't interrupt, we got to do a stock list. You know what to do. And listen, if Bodrik calls don't speak to him, hand him to me all right? Not a word to Anthony. More to herself, —If that glorified accountant meddles in my business I'll give him an earful, thinks he knows something about the stock well he doesn't, and he won't so far as I can help it are you still standing there?

—I thought you were talking to me.

—No, go on, get to it, her hand raised in vague dismissal revealing next to stagnant coffee completed crossword puzzles from the day's papers. That hand remained poised in a position resembling those of sophisticated ladies, seen exclusively in magazines, waiting for a suitor's firm grip to lead them to a dance floor, a table in a restaurant, a secluded room in a private resort where the hand could finally drop to etch hieroglyphics in carmine across a hirsute back, re-enacting its brief elation the next morning in a paroxysm of identical satisfaction, before landing on a phone to order —That shipment to be sent to Robinson & Robbin, the Wicker Street store, Tuesday, not sent here, all right Tammy? No they'll be expecting it, I've called them. The morning? Fine. Listen, Mike was saying Quigley Myers might be moving, is that right? Who knows, you guys might get a better office out of it. See you. These friendly words reached Loyola as he checked how many navy and black pinstripes were in stock, his hands blackening from their transparent covers. She thinks she's going to get this done and in the mail by 4:30, she's crazy, she's just making me sweat, do something, while she sits there. The telephone rang, and rang, and rang, finally prompting —Loyola, get out here, Cranford Clothing, three suits, all 44 reg, 51110/01, 51210/04, 51870/02, bring them up, they'll go registered post, you have time haven't you. Then there are these other suits just called in, I'm doing the slips, hurry up, make sure they go out special delivery, the stock list can wait.

At his workbench Loyola regarded the suits and jackets, measuring labour against time. Snapping on the radio he buried himself in the work, wrenching a flat piece of cardboard into the shape of a box, layering it with tissue paper also used to protect trousers, filling out forms to be photocopied, scrawling details in postage books, whipping the tape gun across, over, down the box, stamping them, then throwing each into a corner where six boxes of various sizes would eventually rest. Goddamn her, she knew this, had those suits from the first phone call, but she didn't tell me, and why not? Bitch, they're all bitches, even what's her name with her fancy screwing games. They're out to suck everything out of me. The rest of Loyola's thoughts were smothered by a red mist inside his head and the final blaring of horns and voices in "My Little Town" emanating from Bowmount's top-rated radio station. Bright moog music cut off Simon and Garfunkel, the news fanfare's stinger fading under an earnest voice betraying excitement.

—Good afternoon, it's 4:30, the temperature is 22, and I'm Brad Dombrowski with the Tuckman Motors Mid-Afternoon News Bulletin, only on CCII-AM. These are the headlines we're following, with more details at 5:30. Police free seven hostages held by a radical animal rights' group at a local pet shop but, tragically, lose three of their finest. The officers, whose identities have not yet been released, had volunteered to swap themselves for the captives. The hostage takers agreed. An explosion in the shop, possibly caused by an explosive device, killed the officers and the activists. Investigators are on the scene. As for the pets, most were killed in the blast, but some are thought to have escaped from their cages. Residents of the area are advised to be on the lookout for snakes, turtles, lizards and spiders, many dangerous to children. In other news, it seems no one is eager to claim responsibility for an underground publication called *Medic Alert: Who's Good and Who's Bad.* In brief remarks the anonymous writer ranks Bowmount doctors according to how many drugs they dispense, how they treat patients, and their level of expertise, based, so the book's introduction says, on overheard and unsolicited anecdotes collected from many unnamed patients. The book has been found throughout the City in public places such as telephone booths, washrooms, clinics and bars. Some City physicians have issued a statement criticizing the publication as a wanton act of libel, slander and malicious damage to physicians in the community, and not the work of a philanthropist, as some letters to local papers claim. Today, Olive Bancroft is $270,000 richer thanks to a lucky lotto ticket she almost lost. Seems last night she mistook a ticket which won in Monday's draw, but which she thought she'd lost, for a napkin, wiped her mouth with it, and tossed it in the garbage. When she emptied the kitchen trash this morning because her son's school was on a bottle drive, there lay the ticket. Despite stains, it clearly showed the six winning numbers. Good thing the boy found it, as Olive says she's been saving for his college education. Maybe he'll be a sanitation inspector. In sports, the local sensation, T'Keitha Lynne Shugge, a whirlwind on the track and a favourite with fans, has been found dead from a heroin overdose. She was sixteen. At this hour details are sketchy. In Tuckman Motors' weather, sun will persist, with temperatures reaching 25 tomorrow, as a high pressure system covers the region. We'll have the extended forecast on our major newscast at 5:30, as well as more news and sports, with the CCII-AM news team. For all of us here, I'm Brad Dombrowski. Good afternoon.

—What, heroin?

—What? and the headset slipped on again. —Kevin?

—Brad, you say heroin?

—So?

—Saw her last night on t.v., looked fine. When'd she die?

—Taped broadcast. Don't know, maybe two days, she'd holed herself away from her family, a deserted apartment building. Her mother looks like a dragon. She left a note, can't read it because they can't make out her words.

—Bitch about those cops, hey? Not a good-news day.

—What do you mean, it's great. See you at 5:30, Kevin, the news booth door closing as Brad pushed through Production Room 1's door. —Harvey, hi, you free?

—Come in, Uncle Lou.

—It's Brad.

—How many days?

—This is the end of my first week. I came to -

—Think you'll like it? Newsroom, not the week. Different from where you were before, isn't it? Hold it. A finger depressed a button. —Mitch, good to see you, I got spots, you free? In the recording room opposite, a sullen and unshaven young man in jeans and a t-shirt regarded the glass separating the two rooms as he absently pressed down a corresponding button. —That's why I'm here. What you got?

—Nickel-and-dime stuff, big sales, promotions, the whole scoop. All new in boxes.

—I'll get it from Continuity.

—Harvey, if you -

—Hold on now, I gotta get this together and in the slot. Mitch's a nice guy but not patient, you met him yet? Course you have, what am I saying, everybody meets everybody. You're looking for carts. Brad eyed the semi-transparent plastic tape containers next to a degausser.

—Yeah, the newsroom -

—Check with Frank, the supply manager, he has some. I can't give any away, got all these spots. He'll help you out. Newsroom always sends the new guys asking for carts when they know I need 'em for commercials. They don't grow on trees, you know. Would be kind of freaky if they did, a - hold on. Mare! Harvey called through a slot in the wall separating Production from Copy and Continuity.

—What? came the response from an attractive woman in her mid-twenties whose hand held white sheets and yellow sheets with numbered tags clipped to them. Brad looked sideways at her figure through the glass that made up most of that wall. Crouching, Harvey addressed Mare's right hand, the only part of her to be seen through the slot in the wall separating the rooms. —Ask Mitch to read Formal Wear for Informal People first, then the beer tag, okay?

—Mitch is doing these? Since when?

—What do you mean?

—He's allowed to do both FM and AM spots?

—Isn't he?

—He's not on our list.

—I got a list today from the Nose, he gave it to me direct. Didn't you get one? Course not. Stupid question, right Lou?

—Name is Brad, and those carts -

—I'll check, Harvey, you probably know more than we do, and stepping away from the window Mare let the slot door close and picked up the telephone. Megan, sitting behind a second desk, her computer's amber screen turning her glasses to surfaces of shifting light, asked what was up. —No one tells us anything, hello? Denice, Mare. Listen, Mitch, is he bi? No, no, now – that's right, sorry, funny, no, I mean can he go on both AM and FM? Listen, stop laughing. Can you hear her? Megan nodded absentmindedly. —He can, since when? Well I'd like to be told that, you know, get a memo like you and Harvey. What? Where? Oh, wait a minute, sorry, yes, it got buried under copy, okay, thanks. You know, a Friday mind. See ya. Well, okay.

—What is it, dearie?

—We can use Mitch for both, they just change it without telling you. I'll make copies of this for you and Hilary, motioning to the momentarily unoccupied desk. —Meg, where's -

—At the feed. Look, we need another computer in here, Mare. You and I got them, why doesn't Hilary, instead of a typewriter? The door swung open. —Where the hell's the, hi Meg, where's the copy? Thanks Mare.

—Do the Formal Wear first, Mitch, then the beer one. Must be a rush on -

—Yeah, but I need the beer one to do the beer one, I mean the tag line for this, this beer thing, yellow paper fluttering at the end of nicotine-stained fingers. —I have to drop it in about 6,000 places, don't have it, what the fuck good is it? You guys got it around here some place, can you find it while I'm here, the formal one's only thirty seconds, I'm not going to sit on my ass doing nothing in that room. What's this, a death notice? A white sheet of paper landed on Megan's desk. —Sorry babe, I don't do death notices, is the tag line in there?, gesturing to a typewriter. Mare saw a sheet of yellow paper with Seamus Distillery and Brewery written on it. —Good eyes, Mitch, removing the paper from the typewriter and handing it to Mitch. —Which one is it? as he shuffled two sheets of paper.

—What? Oh, sorry, forget the backing sheet.

—We have Black Dog Beer: What fresh hell is this?, and Be satisfied. There's two?

—You can see which one, the one that says Seamus.

—What'll they think of next, jerks, trying to sell a beer like this? Desperate, man.

—Got to do what the sponsor says. They know best.

—Sure. This other sheet, throw it away?

—A backing sheet, so the top sheet won't slip.

—Why isn't Hilary on computer?

—No money for it. Mitch mumbled as he left, the second sheet now in Mare's hand. —Like Braille, came out of her to no one, her fingers running over the pockmarks, the brief line of black ink surrounded by the fierce yellow of the paper, as though the sun were raging down on a troop of helpless figures in a desert, wondering —Be satisfied, Megan? What does that mean?, as she replaced the sheet.

—Who knows. You going for a beer after work?

—No, tonight I think I'll just - hi, Tyrone, getting back into it?

—Sweetly and tenderly, Mare. Is Hilary -

—Doing the feed in Production Room 3. Megan regarded him coolly, adding —Don't you remember, Friday is the day for sending out the religious programs, Lutherans, The Living Voice of God, Second Fundamentalist Church. You can hang out there.

—Outreach ministries, God's hand stretching throughout His domain via -

—Something you want? Megan's brown eyes flickered. —Since I got back, Megan, you've been a bit prickly. What's with -

—I tried to help, Tyrone, that's all. Maybe you're the one needs the attitude adjustment. The telephone on Mare's desk rang. —Hello? Oh yes, Mr. Lewis, yes? The Hamilton spot, yes, we did that this morning like Bob wanted, her fingers twisting strands of hair. —The copy, yes, I have it, sure, I'll bring it right - no, we didn't change it at all. No, Mr. Lewis, I'm positive. Well, no, I didn't hear it, but I don't think the announcer, unless he may have read it wrong, yes sir. Harvey didn't - just, yes, Mr. Lewis. Yes. Yes. Yes, I under - yes, I'll hold. Christ! I'm in for it, Megan, where's that copy, did you see it?

—Calm down.

—Yellow paper, did you see it? Where -

—Under your -

—What?

—your -

—Hello, Mr. Lewis? Harvey probably has it. Yes, I'll bring it right over sir, yes, right away. The handset rattled down. —Where'd it go? That's not it, Megan.

—Trouble in the Emerald Forest? Tyrone sat on the third desk. —Lewis' office is done up in red, didn't you know? I guess he hasn't asked you in since you came back. Mare, calm down.

—Calm down, sure, when I find that - Lewis wants me in his office like five minutes ago with that spot, Megan. Where the hell is it? A problem with it, he doesn't want it on air yet.

—Lewis or Hamilton?

—Lewis! Harvey! came Mare's voice through the opened hatch, repeated twice more, but his attention was divided between Mitch and a visitor. —You here for carts again, Uncle Lou? Told you I don't have any, it's Frank you need. Can't go giving carts away, I don't come out to the newsroom looking for anything from you guys, do I?

—Harvey, over here!

—How many more of these bitching drop-ins do I have to do, Harv? I say brought to you by Ukobach Advanced Kitchens again I'll throw up.

—The name's Brad and it's not about -

—One calamity at a time. Stay there, Mitch, we won't be much longer with those.

—Harvey! His face greeted hers from the other side of the slot. —Yes, my child. How long has it been since your last confession?

—Harvey, listen. The Hamilton spot, you got it?

—Hamilton? Which one?

—You did it this morning -

—That's history. Flynn has it, copy too.

—Shit. Thanks.

—In nominae Patri, cut off by the slamming of the hatch. Mare dialled 427. —Come on, Keith, answer.

—Mare, relax.

—You weren't the one talking to him Megan, and Bob and the Nose are there. They're all sitting in the office waiting on, her words interrupted by another telephone. —Megan here. No, she's on another line, Bob. Yes, certainly. He wants you to call him.

—I'm in it now.

—What's so special about this thirty-second miracle? Does it -

—It's just a commercial. Don't you have somewhere else to be?

—I'm getting reacquainted with everyone, Megan. Meg.

—Don't start, Ty.

—Coming back here is like coming back into the arms of -

—Keith, it's Mare, hi, I thought you weren't going to answer. Do you have that Hamilton spot? It's in the control room? The script, you got that? Can you get it down to me, now? I'll explain later. Mr. Lewis wants to see it. No, I don't have a copy, can you get it down to me like pronto? Thanks, bye. Did you hear that? Tyrone, open the door. From the speakers in the corridor ceiling they heard Mare Montgomery being paged to call 401. —This must be some commercial. If you play it backwards does it have a satanic message?

—Hold that door, please! Thank you. A rotund man, fleshy and pale in the face, stood in the doorway. —Ms Montgomery, Mr. Lewis sent me for the Hamilton advertisement.

—Keith's bringing it down now.

—How long?

—Right away.

—Mr. Lewis is most insistent -

—Hi, how are you, I'm Tyrone Vann, and you're -

—What? Oh, yes, I've heard of you. Pleasure. Perry Hornocker. You're back with us again, I understand, but in a slightly different capacity than before.

—Good to meet you. I was telling the - yes, swing shift. Telling the ladies this is like being back in a family, don't you think?

—An interesting perspective. Of course, as it's my first time with CCII -

—How is it going, then, Perry? I thought you were new. You're the -

—Personal assistant to Mr. Lewis. Being a family is probably what makes CCII number one in AM and number two in FM. The team spirit, you know.

—Just like it was three years ago. Good things never stop working. Course, neither do bad things. But I guess business has picked up, Perry, Mr. Lewis never had a dogsbody, I mean PA, before. The telephone on Mare's desk rang once again. —Hello? Yes, Mr. Lewis.

—Speak of the devil, Perry.

—Yes, when Keith Flynn comes - well, no, I didn't. It's not on computer. Hilary, that's right. Keith, yes, and Perry's here -

—And Tyrone, who can leave any time.

—Tell me, Mr. Vann, what did you do for your three years in the wilderness? So to speak. Another radio station, under a different name?

—Under my real name I learned about human nature again. Starving helps you do that. It wasn't so bad. In fact, I shouldn't complain, because down teaches you about up, if you see what I mean. For every adversity -

—Tyrone, leave that stuff alone.

—you get used - Megan, I'm talking to Perry here. Tomato soup every day for weeks on end. I couldn't have been more than a year and a half unemployed. Persistence paid off, and not letting the economic climate and people's grimness get to me. We have to keep our wits about us, right Perry?

—On your own, how very admir -

—Aren't we always on our own, even in a relationship? Seriously.

—I suppose there's . . . something in that.

—Why don't you quit it?

—Megan's unimpressed with my story, Perry.

—But you've come back to a family now. CCII is a good family, I can see why you applied again.

—Applied? No, no, I didn't. I went to see your boss' nephew, not Phil but Otis is the one I mean, and he said -

—A very capable administrator.

—no job for me at all, but I rang Bob, or Mr. Henderson, as you probably call him, a few days later and I was hired. You look surprised.

—No job one day, a job the next? What happened?

—Otis still has his nose out of joint over something I said years ago, if you ask me. His true talent was for wiping the windows of the company cars on wash day, most people think he peaked at fifteen. Ask around. In the silence they heard through the still open door a call for Keith Flynn to contact 401. —What did you say? Perry brought out through splayed yellow teeth. —You came back here, to this family you called it, and you insult Mr. Lewis -

—I was talking about his nephew Otis. Philip's a fine boy, don't you think? Newsroom should be winning awards again in a few years.

—They're both called Mr. Lewis!

—Three of them, Perry. Alfred, the third nephew, he doesn't like commercial radio, thinks it's sleazy. He'd make four Lewises then.

—Yes, he's not in the business. What kind of -

—Told me it was immoral at the only Christmas party he ever came to. Course he was drunk, I disagreed, said amoral -

—You said his uncle, who took those three boys into his bosom, into his family as his own sons, when their father died, leaving nothing -

—His uncle was amoral? No, you misheard, Perry, and you must be getting tired propping the door open, come inside, that's better.

—Tyrone, why don't you take Perry outside so he can listen to your fascinating take on things, leave Mare and me to do our work, okay?

—You said family, Mr. Vann, I swear -

—Thought we finished with that, but since you want to talk about it, yes, a family, the kind, you know, where the father is a drunk or a gambler, hides his pay cheque, beats the wife and kids, only they love him despite all that. A battered child's love's the most consistent, isn't it? The kids and the wife always come back, and that's radio. You see deejays, newsmen, salesmen shuffle out the front door and a year, five, ten years later they're strolling in the back way as if they hadn't suffered a minute at the old man's hands. But a family's a family, and you can't choose them. I'd rather be a favourite of CCII than adopted by some strangers.

—How did you get your job here?

—Like I told you. The contract's good for two years, by the way. So I guess we'll be chatting a lot -

—Don't touch me! The door, pushed open carelessly against Perry's back, moved him further into the room. —Tyrone, you old dick head, how are you?

—Keith!

—Jesus, you son-of-a-bitch. They told me you were coming back, I said that cunt'll never show his ugly face. How's it going?

—Getting acquainted with Perry.

—Keith, have you got it?

—Mare, I always got it. When do you need it, and how often?

—Lay off, Keith, she just wants the copy. We've had everybody in here today and I'm trying to write a spot.

—What the fuck's wrong with Princess Megan today, Mare? And why's everybody been after me? Whose shorts are up their crack?

—Keith, the Hamilton copy.

—Right here -

—Let me take that -

—Hold it, Hornocker. Mare asked for it, okay, not you. Brought the cart too. What's up?

—I don't know. Her eyes raced over the copy. —Looks fine. Mr. Lewis wants it, and Bob and the – Mr. Bennett.

—I was saying, Keith, that must be one hell of an advertisement. I always thought radio was only entertainment, not life-and-death.

—Fuck, you know the score. We do the soliciting, these guys sweat under it, and thirty seconds later we gotta hump again.

—Would you mind, Ms Montgomery, handing that over to me now? Why you didn't have another copy . . . It's very sloppy. You should fix your procedures. Keith's hand kept the door shut. —Listen, Polly, I'll tell you something.

—It's Perry, and please let go of the door.

—Keith, come on.

—You've been bothering the sales assistants, now the copy people, but you didn't call me. Sloppy? You're sloppy, pal. If you were on the ball you'd have gotten in touch with me, and you'd know what this yellow sheet means.

—Keith, come on, let Perry – Christ! Hello, Mare here. Yes, sir, he's on the way with it now. Yes, the script, and – hello? Hello? Christ.

—If you'd excuse me, Mr. Flynn, I have work to do. Perry tried the door again but the salesman blocked it. —Tell me, Perry, what does a yellow sheet mean?

—Let me through, I said.

—Don't push me, you fucking asslick! I'll take this sheet and shove it down your goddamn throat, you try this again! And nobody here heard me say that, right? You don't know what the yellow sheet means, I'll tell you what it means. Hilary typed it. Why? There's only two computers here, in case you didn't know, because they can't afford another one what with hiring a stupid know-nothing ex-civil servant like you, okay? Hilary uses a typewriter and that paper. Now you know a few more things than when you walked in here.

—Let him out, Keith, I think you made your point.

—Just so he knows, Tyrone.

—He knows, he's not dumb.

—Thank you for nothing, Mr. Vann. With the door open Hornocker stepped into the corridor, turning back to the room. — You think you're smart, Mr. Vann. Lipping off about Mr. Lewis and Mr. Lewis. And you, Mr. Flynn, pushing me around, I won't forget that. I'm not going to put up with that treatment. I could have gotten this commercial from Mr. Flynn myself, Ms Montgomery.

—If you'd thought of it, shithead.

—I've heard enough out of you. And Mr. Vann, this . . . talk about families and abuse, let me tell you something. You're lucky to have a contract, you're all very lucky to have jobs at all! Who else would take you in? You should be grateful to be able to come to work in the morning and get a day's wages for it. Be thankful for everything, and don't complain, that's what I say. Hornocker gripped the knob to slam the door but its hydraulics worked against him. He let go and headed away.

—What a scuzzy prick. Lewis is really scraping the barrel to hire a guy like that.

—Would you just stop it? Megan shouted, standing up. —Would you just take this male shit and get out of here?

—Come on, Tyrone, let's grab a coffee.

—Megan, Mare, Perry's nothing. Don't let yourselves get upset by anybody who just happens to come by. Bob knows what goes on. Even the Nose does, or he did. Lewis'll listen to them before anyone.

—Just leave, okay? Now? With the door closed Mare stopped fidgeting. —Megan, what's the matter with you? He was trying to help.

—I hate people I slept with coming back. Don't look like that, it was over a year ago. So I didn't tell you, so what. Tyrone, he so loves being Tyrone. Talks one way and behaves another. But look at you, you're -

—I hate this job, I hate it when - Lewis keeps calling me, there's something wrong with the script or the cart or the announcer or Hilary and you, there was almost a fight. How am I?

—But every Friday's like this.

—You think Perry'll forget what happened?

—Honestly?

—Christ. You still going for that drink?

—All right, Mare! I need you with me anyway, you have to help me pick out a man for tonight.

—Don't you get tired of that?

—Hey, it's only twice a week. The way the men are in this crummy town I might end up sleeping with a dyke just to see if that's any better.

—Don't say that, it makes me – I'm sick enough as it is without thinking of that. I got to go to the bathroom after all this. I'm in such a sweat. Look at me.

—Look, forty-five minutes from now we'll be out of here, away from Perry and Tyrone, bastard, and all the Lewises. We'll have a drink, have a good time.

—We're here for an hour yet. By 5:30 Hilary, Mare and Megan had assured themselves there were no loose ends left to cause trouble on the weekend. Commercials, public service announcements, contest promos and taped programming had been delivered to both AM and FM control rooms, lodged in the Saturday, Sunday and Monday bunks. All the copy for that day had been filed. Along with deejays, salespeople, accountants, newspeople and general staff, the three copywriters gratefully escaped from CCII into the warm evening to start recovering from an ordinary, gruelling week. In another part of Bowmount, Loyola dragged a grimy sweater over his head and deposited it in a chair, feeling muscles ache in his neck and along his left side, sweating as he stepped out of Moscati-Mann. Jammed in a breathless bus he fought to stay awake until his stop near The Great Pan Restaurant, not far from Johnny's Bar on International Street. Somewhere between sleep and wakefulness he wondered why he had not quit after all. Now and then the sun struck his pale features as the bus crawled through traffic. Perspiration soaked his t-shirt and trickled into his eyes and mouth. At least in the bar he would be among others like him, the ones who successfully made it through another day and could not bear speculating about the endless tomorrows.

Primitives and moderns

The bicyclists were flashing by all in gray. —Here're the first ones, from Newtown. Aren't they fast? Vic snorted. —Jack, where're your eyes? Here's the next team, look at 'em, all together, like birds or something, now that's discipline. Like sharks, maybe. Alistair did not want to appear contradictory, especially to Victor, his only black acquaintance, but felt strongly this comparison was not apt. However, he kept silent. —They're good, and the best ones haven't come by yet. Jack? —Paper says 7:15, it's just 7:00 now, practically. Jack folded *The Bowmount Telegram* along the sketch of the bicycle course. —That second team's colours stand out. Purple, Vic? —Didn't seem like it, Jack. We'll ask Sam, he knows that stuff. Alistair would have offered an opinion, but no one asked for it.

The cycling enthusiasts re-entered Johnny's Bar, accompanied by a small clutch of fellow patrons enjoying the warm Saturday night. Resuming their places on stools or at tables, the dozen or so men declared their opinions about the favourites to win the August tournament. One or two viewed the television at the far end of the bar, where a newscast showed footage of the Atlantic. Over it a newscaster declared —sea, and a daring rescue this morning by the Coast Guard. Saving the crew of the *Margaret Beane*, which had been hunting seals in heavy ice, usual conditions for this time of year. Unwelcome at any time. Described by hunters as a state-of-the-art floating abattoir, by animal rights' activists as a ship of slaughter, the *Margaret Beane* was taken over yesterday by the militant Society for the Preservation of Animal Life. Fifteen gun-carrying men and women dropped to the deck from a helicopter, which then landed. The crew, many of whom were asleep at the time, were held prisoner while the contents of the ship's freezers, mainly seal meat and pelts, were dumped overboard or burned. Then the engine was disabled, leaving the *Margaret Beane* powerless in ice. Early this morning, several hours after it all began, the captain was permitted to radio the vessel's owners. The activists fled by the helicopter they came in before the Coast Guard arrived, leaving behind a bomb which detonated fifteen minutes after the last crew member was safely away. One side of the ship split open, and it soon filled with water. Most of it is below ice now, and there is no word on if it can be salvaged. The members of the Society for the Preservation of Animal Life, a new organization, are little known to the police. Authorities say that after today, that will change. It is not known if today's attack on the *Margaret Beane* is linked to the deaths last week of three policemen in another part of the country, the city of Bowmount, when -

—Hey, Johnny! We were watching that.

—What d'ya want to watch that crap for? Nothing but death and higher taxes and – and for God's sake, you got TV at home, don't ya?

—You got cable.

—It's my bar. Now, who's for another drink? One old man, who had not watched either the news or the bicyclists, a rum-and-Coke before him, asked for —Some music please, Jonathan.

—Jonathan? Vic looked around. —Pops, who you talking to?

—Who you call Johnny I've always known as Jonathan. Being friends of his parents, God rest their souls, I -

—Okay, Pops, sure, I'll put in a tape.

—We won't miss the next team, will we?

—Jack?

—We got enough time for a drink. No worry. These guys got it all timed out and monitored, pretty scientifically too, I must say, you know, practically, if you know what I'm saying. Victor, Jack, Alistair and the others, excluding Pops, were keenly interested in the imminent and fleeting appearance of the fabled Carlyle bicycling team, the winner four years running of the Bowmount Three-Day Bicycle Race. The thoughts of every person who dropped a bill or two in Johnny's Hav-A-Tampa Jewels cigar box cannot be known, but it is safe to generalize that the fame of Carlyle's team was a sore point with these Bowmountians. In chorus with the richer merchants, the municipal government harshly criticized the likes of Jack and Victor for not enhancing the prosperity of the City, and it must be said that here a certain ignorance on the part of the City Fathers prevented intelligent coercion of the will and energy these negative-minded taxpayers possessed. That is to say, if the City of Bowmount had been marketed like a sports franchise rather than run like a public corporation, the habitués of Johnny's Bar, representative of many citizens in this respect, would have stationed themselves in the vanguard of community pride. Gladly would they have traded their names on a taxation list, which is nothing more than an infernal ledger of debt with very little credit, for a place on the roster, or a prime seat for the season from which to cheer on the home team. If beer and hot dogs had been provided, that would have been gravy, in a manner of speaking. Perhaps for these once-a-week gamblers, or those interested spectators, their moral nature might have improved. While those who wager and those who speculate are cut from the same cloth, the difference lies in the tailoring, and everyone is hoodwinked by a handsome suit. Gamblers who lose their house, their savings, and their families are outcasts, but businessmen who squander vast sums of money, usually not their own, wind up vice-presidents on the boards of insurance companies or foundations, or turn to shaping public opinion and mores, never forced to bear directly the responsibilities of being charlatans, failures. For the men gathered in Johnny's Bar this late April night, or any night throughout the year, who lived in a poorly lit present and who did not want to think of the dimming future, the City of Bowmount PLC was a jacket which never suited their frames as well as one emblazoned Bowmount All-Stars might have. This entity they would have supported. For them, the sentiment was certainly true that a victory medal outshines all pride of wealth. As things were, these fellows remained aloof from misguided petitions to their civic natures, and resented any changes which benefitted the City over themselves, such as the proposed tax increases.

—Higher taxes for what? For junk, Johnny put it to Sam. —For snot-nosed Mayor Runciman to waste on buildings nobody wants, or re-zoning, or whatever strikes his mind? Used-car salesman, they never should have elected him. And you see that wife of his? A Carlylian. Sage heads nodded at the implications. —No wonder he's getting behind their bicyclists. Bernadette Holloway, who was she? Some two-bit sports star, a figure skater. If you can call that a sport. Running that ritzy members-only club where the rich snuggle up to each other, eat, dance, make deals, who knows what else in those big rooms. Do I get in there? No, I'm not part of the well-to-do, I'm just one of the working poor. I can't even get a permit looked at in decent time at City Hall. Rats, all of them. She's the worst -

—Practically.

—Nothing half-way about that trollop, Jack. Got the Mayor where she wants him. What's today's headline? **MAYOR A NAVY MAN FIRST**. Who's that but Carlyle? This line of talk illustrated the frustration felt by some present over a variety of issues that, in a more energetic or rabid citizenry, would have provoked a meeting. Taxes were too high and always going up, and for what? Yet one could see a kind of logic in the rise of a season ticket's price, and agree that to keep good players one must pay them their worth, for without them you'd be in the bush leagues. To most, though, the City Council, in heavy-handed fashion, rejected all thought of moderate increases, and in the words of Harry Prestwick, one-time union leader, who that minute entered the bar, —You can't tell a Heinz pickle nothin'. The Race, at one time a celebration of Bowmount skill and virility, with the ascension of the Carlyle team had degenerated to an occasion of sin for the senior commentators intimate with its long history, who were upset that the athletic orthodoxy had been challenged by heretics from across the river and over the plains. Without a doubt the course struck many as more challenging than in recent years, skirting or tackling the seven valleys in the north and the four valleys in the west, but the plotting of this route, which apparently favoured Bowmount's team, occasioned mistrust. —They set it up that way to get everyone thinking it's fair. No one argued with Stan, a long-time follower of the noble event, a competitor in it years ago. Some of those who had done miserably in chemistry or Euclidean geometry were fiends at discerning elaborate schemes behind the most legitimate procedures. —You say Grand Design, I say conspiracy theory. People nodded once more at this well-worn saying of Harry, regarded as a thinker in this milieu.

—Look at this. Slapping *The Carlyle-Bowmount Despatch* on the bar to gain attention, Harry continued. —Something else. Paul Sherringham wants – say, where's Frank?

—Not in town, someone replied, and a sigh of relief went through the assembled as though from one set of lungs. —Paul Sherringham, I was saying. He's buying up half the town to give to immigrants, the poor, guys just out of prison, to house them in all sorts of neighbourhoods. See this? Here. No, there. You'll apply, and if he likes you, no, his organization, the Enhancement of People Fund, accepts you, why then you go live in some swanky place. Think you or I'll ever get in there? Some nice big house in Dockside, or on Outerwall? Not me, not you either, or you, but Igor Piddleski and Saddam Saddami and She Who Spits In Your Face could, no problem. Years of shouting over union members had converted Harry's diaphragm to an amphitheatre, and glasses behind the bar chimed in accord with his rumblings. —Look at this guy, where's he from? Ontario? What's he going to do, sell a mansion to beggars from Bangladesh?

—Harry.

—Here I am trying to start a business with my own two hands and some guy wants to give away our land to foreigners -

—Harry!

—Johnny?

—What does it read above you? For the hundredth time Harry read the motto intricately worked in the wood over the bar, only this time aloud. —A man is only happy when he is drunk. S. Johnson.

—Take the hint, and relax. You always come in like this. You'll wind up in hospital again, and you give me a headache. And don't forget, when you're talking about foreigners, I'm Italian.

—But Johnny, I know you. It's newcomers I'm talking about. One of these years when everything – a Manhattan, that'll straighten me up. But brother, let me tell you, Sherringham isn't going to let you buy a three-storey house with a pool and a two-car garage when he can sell it to any joe from anywhere, or rent it as a flop-house to someone named Sabidan-olok. Now, I'm not a racist, Johnny, despite what you might think -

—Did I say anything? I told you where my family's from, that's all.

—but nobody just in here should get something for nothing. When the Manhattan appeared Harry quickly downed it. —Another, Johnny, and get Sam a drink too. Sam! What'll you -

—Would you stop shouting? Pops rapped his blackthorn cane repeatedly on the wooden floor. —Okay, old-timer, sorry. Sylvie, hi, can you bring those drinks over there? Sam, come on, we'll let Pops - what's his problem anyway?

—Listening to the music. Bing Crosby had replaced Anne Shelton, singing about how friendly everyone was in his home town. Victor nabbed Sam as he was steered to a table by Harry. —That first team, St. Cornelius, their uniform. Purple?

—They call it that. I see it as plum myself. Paint-stained hands absently twisted at a loosening overall button. —Ask Fred, he has a good eye.

—He's too weird. I know he paints too, but that's just houses. I mean, you really paint. Jack let Victor know, —It's 7:14, they're due any time. Almost everyone convened outside to observe the Mayor and his wife's favourites, distinguished by their long hair flowing even from under helmets and in crisp navy racing outfits, followed a quarter hour later by Bowmount's bicyclists garbed in jade, a new colour decidedly not as sharp as their chief competitor's. The cheers for this team matched the sullen silence that greeted the Carlyle team. Few people went outside half an hour later to see the yellows of Crescent City and the browns of Ripton go by. —Heck, Jack had muttered on seeing Bowmount's team struggle to maintain formation, —there goes my money again. Practically.

—Betting is a tax on the stupid, Harry whispered to Sam as he led him to a corner table away from the bar. They talked about small matters, but Sam eventually came out with the question that had been bothering him. —That was your book, wasn't it? It's really - what were you thinking?

—Listen. Listen to me. After what happened, those idiots at the hospital giving me a scare years ago, and my GP missing what I had in January, I wanted to get back at them.

—With this? Why not just a lawsuit like – if they find you, and you're not even getting any money for it, so I don't know – it's like a folly, you know?

—You're a good one to talk about money. A painter, an *artist*, lecturing me about money. No, there isn't any in that, none. But there's plenty of satisfaction. Didn't you ever want to get some poison out of your system? Did you see the news? Wasn't it something? A book review, of all things, in the *Courier*. A book review! Hahahaha.

—How could I miss it? Wiping the brushes I saw it, right next to Niles W.K. Gidmery's *Men Who Lope With the Does*.

—You smeared paint all over the *Medic Alert* story? My moment of fame and you just blot it out. I'll remember that when you have your big show.

—Harry, you need a real job, something less aggravating. I don't understand you. You get involved with these . . . if there can be a perverse do-gooder, you're it. A negative image of one. What are you looking for? Wasn't being president of a local enough of a – didn't you always say to George that it was draining? Don't you want some peace in your life? Harry drained his glass and Sylvie appeared with another. —Bless you, you're an angel. Johnny doesn't pay you enough.

—If people left bigger tips . . .

—That's what I like, spunk.

—Don't listen to this guy, Sam. He was your brother's torment too. They waited for Sylvie to serve someone else. —I take exception to what you just said. Everyone asked, Harry, what was it you had going? A non-union, a bunch of professional scabs. I called them Prestwick's Irregulars. Cute, hey? We were a group who knew about thirty trades. Out-sourcing, double-breasting, means lots of money, especially in construction. I had these fellas who were well down on the union lists to get hired for anything, because it's all seniority, right? I stole them right out from under their unions' noses. Whenever scabs were needed I'd have this hand-picked crew go in, do it, and get out, pronto. You think some manager cares how the union's going to feel about it? Not till negotiation time, when they each make trade-offs and you hear them both say, We worked together in a frank spirit of cooperation and mutually resolved the contentious issues. Yeah, right. Now mind you, this business could only have lasted about five years, but that would have been enough to make me a pile, and the workers, they would have gotten money and experience. But what do they go and do?

—You didn't know they'd go co-op on you?

—No! If I did, you think I'd be out of work again? First I get dumped as president, then my own business – anyway. Dumb guys thought: We'll squeeze Prestwick and Harmon and North, they'll have to pay us more. Union Brotherhood of Scabs, Local No. 1, we called them. So they made life miserable for us, wouldn't get to work, threatened to go to the police. Mind you, they were as dirty as us. Sam, let them try to take me to court and I'll damage every one of them. I kept a book on it, a secret history, sort of, and it's safe inside a bank vault. I won't bore you with what it says, you're falling asleep already, look at you.

—Not you, just haven't eaten all day, and the beer . . .

—Heck, is that it? Sylvie! Sylvie! A couple of sandwiches. Ham? Ham, cheese, and some pickles. Make it three sandwiches. You have two, Sam. A painter needs his strength, and if George could ever know I wasn't helping you out -

—Hey, guys, how are you? Phil Horne sat down between the two, and shortly a group comprising Phil, Harry, Sam, Stan Miloz, Camilla Lonegin, Pops, who had removed himself from the vicinity of the bar's doors, and Bartholomew Constantine indulged in hearsay and rampant speculation about business, activists, dead policemen, and from there to yoga, aura massage, herbal remedies, and Sam's painting, once Sam's strength returned. —What's it about, what you're working on? You never talk about it.

—Stan, it's – well, what's there to talk about.

—He's too modest, Stan. You have something in mind. Look at you, greasy clothes, turpentine smell, hands covered in – I was going to say blood, course it's just paint. You didn't eat all day, if it wasn't for me you'd probably never eat. How much money you got on you?

—Five, maybe.

—Dollars? Camilla thought it ridiculous to guess at anything lower, but when Sam answered with —Five cents, she flushed angrily, poverty having this effect on her. —How do you pay for food, light, heat?

—Oh, it's been warmer lately, and if I keep moving then -

—Jeez, Sammy, what's the big secret? What you got to do is trust us more, see? Like, is it something dirty, naked people we know, or boring like, fuck, I don't know, fruit on a table?

—It's a triptych, or at least now it may be, if it works. No one said anything, though Pops nodded. Harry broke the silence with —You'd better explain that, these boys wouldn't know a triptych if they fell over one. Sam vainly tried to straighten his hunched back, avoiding Camilla's narrowed eyes. —Three paintings, one of the Virgin Mary with Child, one of Jesus consoling the sinners, Mary Magdalene's in there, and the third is the Crucifixion, with the Virgin Mary and Mary Magdalene, one or two apostles around him. Can't paint too many apostles, like Goethe said, one apostle's much like another. Trouble is doing it right, the figures, the paints, the style. Even finding the models . . .

Having recollected the one art history course she took as an elective at Bowmount University, Camilla seemed to speak for the whole table. —I guess successful painters have the same problems.

—She's right, Sammy. You go into any Catholic church here, or St. Telesphorus', you see Christs and Marys hanging everywhere. Must be hard doing something different from everybody else.

—Boys, you don't understand. Brother Sam, and I call him that because his brother George was a dear friend of mine, he works with his hands to fashion something immortal.

—Only God creates immortal things, and Pops wondered later at the braveness of his words, since they were practically inviting an attack from any modern man or woman around.

—Another citizen heard from. Look, Sam -

—No, what I said is true, it's in Scripture somewhere, isn't it? Sam? God touches all of us, He's omniscient, which means He can tell what every person is thinking. Not like any of us can do that, is it? God isn't some baby. He's been at this a long time. Immortality, He knows what it is. Pops hurried through the Sign of the Cross. —He gave Michelangelo and Da Vinci their powers, like He's given them to Sam.

—Pops, I respect you, but Sam isn't Da Vinci. Sorry Sam, but -

—No, you're right.

—Never mind this unbeliever, Sam. You'll do fine. Christian painting is always worthwhile, and balms your soul in peace with the Lord Saviour.

—Would you listen to this guy? Pops, jeez, you haven't been to church - when was the last time you found yourself mumbling in St. Adamnan's?

—Those heretics are going against Rome, but the day will come when – if the Pope knew what they were doing he'd excommunicate them! Someone has to tell him what's going on! It took a minute or so for the table to calm Pops down. Regaining the thread of the conversation he turned to Sam. —Your Virgin, she should have red hair.

—What?

—Green eyes, too. There was never any woman so beautiful, she had red hair and green eyes, as green as the sea. Stan could not resist. —Pops, green eyes just means she's horny. The blackthorn cane with its solid ebony handle clattered against the table. —I'm not staying here and listening to such foul - that's the *Mother* of *God* you're talking about! Blasphemer! And in the presence of a lady. Pops hurried away to seek more congenial company. Bart suggested that from what he knew, the description matched Pops' long-dead wife. —Jeez, I didn't mean to upset the old guy. I'll go apologize -

—Maybe wait a few minutes till he cools down.

—Good thinking, Bart. So, Sammy, you can't find a model. Camilla here, she'd be great. I mean, look at -

—Stan!

—Thanks, but I haven't got the figures in my mind, the colouring, the form, the expression. Thought I had. I started with just a Christ, a pale, weak Christ, but that doesn't fit with the Bible, as I understand it. He was strong, so I'm looking at something more virile, humane, dignified, but sorrowful for mankind.

—You're reading the Bible, Sam? News – thanks, Sylvie, keep those drinks coming.

—Anything else for the rest of you? She took their orders, and they resumed the conversation. By now Sam was resentful at having talked so much, but could find no way to stop Harry from resuming the discussion. —As I was about to say, it's a funny thing to be reading, isn't it? And painting the Mother of Christ too. Where's the profit in that? Angels, there's the trick. There's money in that. You could do a bang-up job of angels. Not those little fat boys or girls, but the sort of pear-shaped ones women love. Did I ever tell you guys, I was visiting a – this'll only take a second. I went round with some of my guys one time, the drive was on to get a union into a place, and we were visiting every employee's home, every apartment, every hovel, making sure names on the lists showed up to the meeting. This was five years ago. I went into this one house, a small neat home, six kids peering round doorways, and the lady left me in the living room to wait while her husband got ready. You could tell they didn't have much money, but they kept things up out of self-respect. I see a sticker on the window. Eventually I make out what it says, it said **This House Protected By Angels**. Right, I say to myself, don't start laughing, you need the son-of-a-gun's signature and you need to get him there tonight. To take my mind off that sticker I start looking at the paintings they got hung up, and this might let in a little light, Sam, on a particular aspect of the art world. There was something funny about the things, couldn't quite get a grip on it, but then it hit me. There was this one of a shepherd looking at his bunch of sheep, and a sheepdog there too, blue sky, green grass -

—Morning, Ralph. Right? Anyone -

—Stan!

—remember that cartoon?

—fleecy clouds. Lots of white. The thing was a jigsaw puzzle.

—Harry, come on.

—Seriously, Phil. They'd taken this 1,000-piece jigsaw, matted it, put it behind some plexiglass and in a wood frame, and made a painting out of it!

—It wasn't a painting, though.

—Stan, it was, and why? Because those people hung it up. They thought it looked as pretty as, well, as a picture, and hung it up so they could say, Isn't this a nice painting? They don't mean print, they mean painting.

—I don't believe it.

—It happened! Would I make up something like that? Never would have noticed it if I hadn't had to take my mind off that sticker. A jigsaw painting, and on each wall there's one, four in all, some big, some small. I'm about to bust out and the guy isn't down yet. I notice a birdcage in one corner with two, three canaries in it. Thought it was funny they hadn't cheeped once, but it was 'cause they were stuffed. She figured they were colourful, I suppose. Maybe they'd had a real one and she didn't have the heart to throw out the cage, thinking of the kids. I was almost splitting my sides by this time.

—You saw this here?

—In Bowmount? No, in Scanlon Ridge, Porterville it was, small place, poor as dirt. But this lady, and I guess the guy I'd come to get, though it didn't seem to fit a forklift operator, she made that parlour, as she called it, a showpiece. A showpiece of what? Jigsaw paintings and stuffed birds. There and then I said to myself, good thing there's an angel watching over this place, because it'd be a waste of a good burglar alarm. When that guy got in the union and started earning union wages, out went that junk and in came things worth something. And out went that angel, you can bet on that. But you see, Sam, angels, that's where the money is. God? He's too difficult nowadays, and the Pope's a has-been, with all respect to Pops over there. Everybody relates to angels, 'cause they're like us only better, the good side of us. Presuming you got a good side. Them and the Dalai Lama. But angels and God didn't get that family off a crappy minimum wage and into the middle class so they could afford to send their six kids to school dressed decent. Unionism did.

—But that's not what I want to do, Harry. I'm talking about religion, not superstition.

—Same thing, brother. Now, I'm all for artwork, don't get me wrong, but religion, that's dicey, which is why angels are safe, 'cause that's only, what, what?

—Mysticism?

—Thanks, Phil. No wasting that education of yours. In fact, take Phil here, going out with a good Catholic girl, and he's miserable.

—Not any more. Phil smiled wanly as he regarded Sam, whose palpable fatigue went unnoticed by Harry. —Sandra and I broke up last week. You know, we had different friends, and she kind of liked hanging around with people who believed what she believed. She wasn't multi-cultural. Just had her nose out of joint about anybody who wasn't a Catholic. Most at the table agreed such behaviour in this era of angels, prophecies that inspired seminars, and courses in miracles was a manifestation of medieval thinking. —Typical bigoted Catholic, you ask me.

—Stan!

—So, you seeing anyone now?

—Phil sees more women than Morgenthaler's clinics, hahahaha.

—Funny you mention him. Sandra said he does abortions to get back at white people for the Holocaust. General condemnation of this kind of thinking carried on until Harry, slopping a fresh Manhattan over the sticky table, advised Phil to —Forget her, you'll be with somebody else in no time. You always come up with the winners, though. What was that girl, you know, the one who put on airs, a beauty, an Arab?

—From Yemen. That was a long time -

—There's probably only one of them in the whole country, and he finds her. Not to be funny, but she sure acted like the Queen of Sheba, didn't she?

—The who?

—Stan, try reading history on your lunch breaks, no offence. Get away from the pipefitting world for awhile. I can't remember half the gals you saw. There was Julia, Sandra, Elaine, that cross-eyed Hindu -

—You're exaggerating, she wasn't -

—and that California Buddhist, and didn't you come in smelling like smoky fruit. Incense and crystals, Sam, do a few artsy posters of them you'd be in clover. Unicorns too, and mood rings. That United Stateser was a crackpot, Phil, pardon my saying.

—That what?

—What I'm calling Americans now. After all, they're the United States *of* America, right? Not the United States *is* America. Before her there was that Jewess, now there was a pip, forget her name, strong, just my kind. If only I wasn't married, hahahaha.

—That last one, before Sandra, she was a Zorro-something or other, what was it?

—Stan, she -

—So finally Phil's with a Catholic, we said, someone from this side of the world. What's left, Chinese? Hope you use protection, with these exotic types you never know what you'll catch.

—You make it sound like I saw them all in one week. You're going back six years.

—Six? When are you going to settle down? Here's poor Sam, can't get a model for Mary, and you're out with every woman around. Stan then made the offer of posing as Christ if that would help. —If you want strong, muscles, Adonis-meets-the-Saviour, I'm him, at which point Camilla, threatening in an undisclosed but understood way that Stan would pay for every one of his stupid remarks, led her boyfriend from the table, out of Johnny's Bar, through the streets and back to their apartment, where punishment commenced immediately. —What a couple, Victor observed to Jack. —He can't say a word without her snapping at him.

—Basically, that's the case. Alistair ventured to modify that judgement, but as it was known he held an overly sympathetic view of women no one paid any attention.

—You know, Sam, Sandra said once that religion is for everyone or no one. Do you feel that way? I never heard you talk about painting Christ before, so I just wonder.

—Religion! Heck, Sam's only doing what comes naturally, painting. Last thing he needs to paint well is to be religious. Inspired, that's what he needs, and a good time with a lady wouldn't hurt, hahahaha. Loosen the clogs. Cogs, I mean. How many times do I have to tell you, religion is old-time thinking, caveman days. Sam, you said you're reading the Bible, well that's why you're having trouble, see, it's getting in the way of your eyes. Now, I'm no artist, but when you start mixing the blues and greens with Christianity, you're doomed to fail. It's like a wildcat strike, everything in-side you throws down its tools and walks off, no discipline, management and labour aren't talking, and the union executive and the workers squabble about strategy. In your case it's a riot between your head, your eyes and your heart. Get rid of these anities and isms, clear the junk out of the attic -

—Like syndicalism, Harry?

—Victor, you creeping shadow, how are you? Just kidding. Have a seat and help me convince Sam to forget the Bible and work on painting what he sees.

—When's your show opening, Harry?

—You think every critic painted? Most stopped at finger painting, Sam'll tell you. Where was I? You heard about Phil and that witch he went out with. Good riddance to a woman like her. Now, look at Bart here. He gets into trouble 'cause he jerks off in church and got caught by another harridan. A turmoil erupted and Sam, Phil, and Victor carried Harry away, though his cheerful shouts could be heard from the street. Bartho-lomew Constantine sat abandoned, red-faced, trembling not in anger but in the deepest state of shame imaginable, crudely reminded of his brief period of incarceration for masturbating in one of St. Finnian's confes-sionals. Discovered by an elderly woman, in trying to flee he had tripped near the offertory candles, bringing about a personal scandal, and nearly a conflagration. The result was an overnight stay in jail, publicity, and his being barred from the church for an unspecified time. Such a sudden and brutal reminder of this recent humiliation plunged him into sodden misery. None of his companions returned, and he imagined they were escorting poor, drunken Harry home. Who'll help me? The answer was discouraging. No one, not even Loyola, who promised to meet me earlier tonight, but where is he? At least Camilla left before Harry said that. A woman like her would despise a man who did certain things with his body.

Over at another table, while Bart sank into thought, two bicycle race gamblers, Wes Ferguson and Jimmy Squires, were involved in a conversation so fascinating to Jimmy that he paid no attention to the fuss over Harry, or noticed the grisly footage on the television showing the figure of a murder victim discovered that night in some part of Bowmount, allegedly killed by his son with hot fat while lying in a drug-induced state. Buildings toppled, freak weather shattered homes and lives, but Jimmy and Wes, while in the bar's world, were not of it.

—Role play? Like, you're the chauffeur and she's the -

—No, Jimmy, no, no, past that, that's just sex. We pretend we're like invalids or something.

—Like you get turned on by pretending you lost an arm or what?

—No, no, no. Rebecca pretends – sex ain't got nothing to do with it, I tell you.

—Another beer, Johnny. None for this guy, he's flying. So . . . what? You do . . . what?

—Last week, remember I couldn't lift those packages at work, my arms, I said they were real sore.

—Yeah, nearly sprained myself doing your – thanks, keep the -

—and tender -

—change. I got the point, Wes.

—The real reason is I was lifting Rebecca around the room like she was a cripple or something.

—When'd this happen?

—What?

—She hurt herself?

—No, no, no, she pretended she couldn't walk, a watchamacallit, physically disabled, one of those people with two legs gone, or two arms, not all four.

—Blue parking spots.

—That's them.

—Everywhere you go they're taking up -

—Anyway, Rebecca acts like she couldn't walk and I had to carry her everywhere, 'cause her legs wouldn't work.

—Wes, these guys got electric chairs and everything you can think of, not like us, we gotta walk, and you're lifting her around -

—No, see, if we got the chair it'd cost money, right? And they're way too heavy to lift. This way, it's only us, no money, and what if the chair broke down anyway? I seen guys trying to get into a store only the door wasn't wide enough.

—When? Not -

—Years ago, Jimmy, not now. He was stuck on the sidewalk and screaming at the clerk, saying I'm gonna call the cops.

—No blue parking -

—Came later. So that's how I did it.

—Did what?

—Strained my arms.

—What did she do for you?

—I made out like I lost my leg to frostbite, hobbling around every-where.

—So what's the kinky part?

—The what?

—The sex, Wes, where was the sex? Did you do it like disabled people?

—Jimmy, Jimmy, Jimmy, there ain't no - look, sex ain't part of it.

—Disabled people don't have sex? Then what the hell'd you do it for?

—When one of us gets old, you think we want this sprung on us? At least if we do this now, we get some practice in.

—No shit.

—Yeah. Next weekend I get to be incontinent.

—Which one?

—Just drink up, Jimmy. They sat in silence for a moment, Jimmy glancing over at Bart. —See him over there? Went to jail, you know.

—He can't help it. Heard he got hit pretty bad by his old man when he was young. Or maybe that was some other guy, and he fell out of a tree. Can't remember. What about him?

—Jail must be a scary place.

—Ask Frank, he knows all about it. There's a guy who's sick. Sure glad when he's not around. Jimmy nodded. —Let me ask you something, Wes. You were talking about getting ready for being old. What would you do if you knew you were going to prison? Would you sort of make sure somehow it didn't hurt so much when . . . those guys did what they do?

—I think you've had enough, Jimmy.

—No, listen. If you knew, would you, like . . .

—What?

—I'm thinkin'. Say, get a carrot and -

—What are you, sick?

—Well?

—No.

—Why not? Wes whispered in Jimmy's ear so Johnny could not hear, his hand clenching into a fist and making a rapid motion.

—No, they wouldn't. Wes nodded. —How'd you know about that? You ever been . . .?

—What.

—You know, what you just said.

—I said me and Rebecca were getting ready for when we're old, or in case there's an accident or something. We're not playing sick games!

—I was just asking because you -

—Makes me sick thinking about it.

—Okay, okay. You gonna finish your beer?

—You have it, suddenly I ain't thirsty.

—Thanks. In continent, huh?

—Just finish up so we can get out of here. Johnny's giving us funny looks.

Brood

Duncan Lonegin checked his watch, saw it was noon, and parted the heavy curtains of the top-floor library overlooking the back-yard. Crows and a few gulls tore at the wet grass. —Vermin, driving out honest-to-God birds, yellowhammers, blue tits, jays, even sparrows are too afraid to come round. Beasts, scavengers. Given a chance, Mr. Lonegin would have stated that the era of avian excellence had passed, that the birds were more songful and cheering when he was a young man, compared with these rapacious species and their grasping ways. More garbage now the City's so big. The River stinks, I'm surprised the gulls eat what fish are in it. These reasons for the increasing numbers and escalating boldness of the crows and seagulls were cold comfort when he would step gingerly through the grass in the wake of the marauders. Gulls sitting on people's lawns made for an unnatural sight, obscene from a certain point of view, and a parliament of crows was an unwelcome portent. Wasn't life unseemly enough thanks to newspapers and television without the help of such low and common scavengers? It's as if our world has been left defenseless, set in motion and then forgotten, to be picked apart and then swallowed by these voracious gullets.

—Dunc! Dunc!

—Yes, what, yes, here!

—Are you rapping on the window again? They don't pay any attention. Dunc? Well, see that you're not. Put your hand through today of all days and ruin . . . Mr. Lonegin let the curtains close out the unwelcome fowl and gray skies. Settling in an armchair he wondered when their child would arrive, for it was near dinner. Like her mother, Camilla never arrived on time. In this darkening world she was a brilliant candle, and he waited for her visits more eagerly as time trimmed his own wick. Camilla rarely gave her parents much about which to be concerned. However, in Mr. Lonegin's opinion, her female friends such as Mare Montgomery and Krysta Jordan, whom she'd met while working at CCII, though good people, weren't fine enough examples of rectitude for Camilla. Friends outlined who you were, what you thought of yourself. He regarded some of her female friends as vulnerable women, the kind who, for example, ten years after the fact would accuse someone of sexual misconduct, and wasn't this due to their failure to do something in the beginning, certainly sooner than in ten years' time, therefore bringing down a hundredfold portion of shame and misery on themselves, their families, and the accused? It happened at St. Ita's in Kissling and St. Cassian's in Franklin Plains, where priests and brothers had taken young boys and one or two girls – but this topic Mr. Lonegin refused to dwell on today. Instead of waiting for Camilla impatiently, he would calm himself with the classical radio station while reading his favourite British paper, *The Independent*, a week old but what does that matter when you're sixty and newly retired? He snapped the broadsheet open, stopping to read about a borzoi. —For two weeks it has waited opposite Gower Street Hospital in London. It is presumed the dog is owned by a patient, for it approaches people tentatively, barking as though in greeting, retreating hurriedly when approached to resume its former position. Enquiries within the hospital have so far not identified the owner, who may be very ill or have died. The dog is becoming a familiar sight, and students, pedestrians, and nurses are leaving it food and a few toys. Only some of the food has been eaten, and the rubber bones and coloured balls go ignored as the dog maintains its vigil.

What rarities, loyalty and devotion. Look at my situation. Forced to retire, albeit with a good package, because the government's cutting back, when I've more good years in me. Now I'm home with Marian, I'm a useless thing. We were loyal to something once, our country, our family, something. No trust, no faith, no promises kept by those who swore oaths, and so no better future. Mr. Lonegin tried to find an item that would cheer him up, and from a letter a phrase leaped out containing an unfamiliar word. Niddering? Letting the newspaper slip, he contemplated this strange word. As it spun round in his head the music seemed to rise in greeting, or else niddering sank on a bed made of violins and cellos, such a British word, he concluded lazily, as it changed shape and meaning, dwindling in significance until it vanished.

—Dad? Dad?

—Yes, what, yes? Camilla? The library door opened as Mr. Lonegin stood to embrace his daughter. He could hear Stan's buoyant voice below. —You've been sleeping?

—What time – one o'clock?

—Dunc! Camilla! Dinner's – Stan's putting the plates out. Mr. Lonegin touched his daughter's hand. —You look very pretty in that dress. Reminds me of your mother, in a way. She's not – today, you know, she's thinking about Grandma. Otherwise she wouldn't be how she is. They exchanged diplomatic smiles. Mr. and Mrs. Lonegin, Camilla and Stan, and Ursula Nelson, Marian Lonegin's widowed sister, were soon seated at the dining room table enjoying, or trying to, a meal of roast beef and vegetables, with chocolate cake, apple pie and ice cream for dessert. The nap disrupted Mr. Lonegin's mood entirely, and he responded sharply to his wife's quiet nature, objecting silently to her third glass of red wine. Ursula, a thin, inordinately tall woman of fifty-three, physically like her slightly older sister but temperamentally less vivacious, struck Mr. Lonegin as exceptionally waspish this Sunday. As for Stan, who Camilla liked for obscure reasons, he bumbled through dinner, interrupting entertaining stories just when Mr. Lonegin had the main point in sight, dinging his knife or fork against a glass, saying —Time's up!, with a foolish smirk as if this was the greatest joke he and the ladies could share. Mrs. Lonegin certainly got a kick out of it, Stan offered in his defense when Camilla criticized him, and she couldn't reply as she wanted to, that her mother drank too much and her parents had been silently fighting for years, as once said it would expose the diminished love she felt for them. Ursula would chuckle delightedly sometimes when Stan threw out a faintly titillating conversational item as an impediment to one of Mr. Lonegin's anecdotes, partly because, in recent years, she enjoyed seeing her brother-in-law baited and defeated by a young man with little breeding but some good sense.

After dessert, Mother's Day gifts were opened in the living room, Mrs. Lonegin exclaiming at bathing lotions, hand cream, boxes of chocolate, a pair of miniature vases for her collection from her husband, and from Ursula a bottle of wine. Marian's sister did not drink anything stronger than coffee, favouring soft drinks, and she could, quietly, empty two-litre bottles quite quickly. Mr. Lonegin contemplated this gift of blueberry wine with hidden disgust, wondering what the hell Urs had in mind. As quickly as possible he corralled the gifts on a table against the far wall where they could be seen by anyone entering the room. Conversation about topical matters began, such as the goings-on in Queer Town, a fairly notorious section of Bowmount known for its illegal and seamy practices.
—Without the City doing a blessed thing to stop them, tut-tutted Ursula.
—Plus there's that investigation into the pet store killing of those three policemen whom you know, they say, and a lot do, Marian, that they were part of some . . . brigade! or force within the police force. Makes you wonder.
—Yes, Ursula, it does. Sometimes you don't know who to trust when – Stan, if you're having one, a little sherry would be nice. Sherry for anyone else?
—Way I heard it, guys who'd know the score say the -
—Who, Stan? What guys?
—Harry, Phil, you know.
—Them, and Camilla made it sound as though she rolled her eyes.
—Quidnuncs.
—What's that, Mr. Lonegin?
—Nothing, Stan. Go on.
—Anyway, there's talk the three were gay, or they'd been hazed or something, and pow, lost it when they went in there.
—Is that so? I didn't think gays would be in the police force, you know.

What with so many men with guns around. There was a collective shrug after Ursula's comment. Stan helpfully warded off silence. —They said that about the priests.

—I feel very sorry for them, and Mrs. Lonegin looked regretful between sips.

—One thing about homosexuality, it certainly makes normal conversations hard to come by. It's always . . . there! when you don't want it or expect it. The least people could do is keep it private.

—You know, Ursula – look, he's asleep. Dunc. Dunc.

—Mom, let him rest. I woke him when I got here.

—So you should. He's been sleeping at an alarming rate lately. I'm worn out by it.

—You were saying, Mrs. Lonegin? As much as Stan infuriated Camilla, when he cut off one of her mother's criticism about her father it revealed a side of him she almost wished he would cultivate. But if he was sensitive I couldn't order him around like I want.

—Thank you, yes. Not being Catholic I can't say anything about the priests. But look at Mr. and Mrs. Fanning, they're in their seventies, and how sad they are.

—What do you mean, Marian?

—They talk about the incidents so much. I think, and Camilla, correct me on this, you're practically the only Catholic here as your father hasn't been to church for a while. What was it? They've gone and joined some revitalizing movement, they called it, that's trying to inform the Church and get things ship-shape.

—Sorry, Mrs. Lonegin, inform the Church?

—Reform the Church, yes. There's about twenty-five of them, I gather, and probably -

—What are they called?

—I don't know, Ursula. I don't know! They wouldn't tell me. I tried to see if Dunc might be interested, considering how - but no, he told me they were, what was it, misguided and . . .

—Inauthentic? Having no husband to keep track of any more, Ursula paid particular attention to her brother-in-law.

—Thank you. How he knew what they were I don't know, as he barely heard me out. Unless you knew something about them already. Dunc?

—Mom.

—All right, Camilla. As I was saying, he categorically refused to have anything to do with schismatics, he said. Imagine, calling Bob and Sheila Fanning such a thing, and they in their seventies.

—Marian, it might be said we're not ones to talk. We've enough problems with women ministers and gay ministers and the rest of it. Honestly, some people think the United Church exists solely for their convenience. They come in only because no one else wants them. Like it's a sanctuary! I wish they'd go start their own church, if that's the way they feel.

—But Camilla, could you tell me your father's objections? I was trying – not so much, Stan, I don't want to spill – where was I? Trying to get your father interested in something. If only to give him a way to occupy his time, and have him get outside the house now and then. For his sake, you know.

—I'm not sure I can help. Dad took those incidents pretty hard, and seeing the priests were people he'd known for years, grew up with, it hurt more. You think you know somebody's character . . . But Mr. and Mrs. Fanning, I don't know what they're in. It could be anything from a charis-matic movement to a Bible study group.

—The last thing you'd call Bob Fanning is charismatic. Most colourless man I ever knew. Honestly, Marian, I don't know how he hooked up with such a wonderful girl as Sheila. It always seemed odd, you know.

—The only thing your father said was that despite what some might say, there can be schisms within the Church. I could have told him that, mind you.

—Of course, that's part of history. That's where we come from. The sisters nodded at each other and Mrs. Lonegin continued. —He calls the Fannings and their friends schismatics because, and I hope I have this right, they want the Mass in Latin, and don't like the modern way of doing things generally. Then they talk about Vatican II and it's all I can do to keep my head level with my shoulders when they get into these . . . very technical things! The sherry glass tipped up and back. —Can you explain this to me?

—No. I don't think any of it is important to Dad. It's like he's in shock.

—Doesn't affect his snoozing, ha-*ha*! Stan grinned in approval of Ursula's remark.

—I see. Well no, I don't. A lot of Catholics seem very upset, but nobody will tell me exactly why! It's only the older ones, not even all of them. You never mention it, Camilla. You weren't in shock, were you?

—I grew up in a different time. I went to your Church sometimes, and to St. Finnian's a lot. Dad comes from a Catholic family, it means more to him. When those priests and brothers were arrested he couldn't accept that they were doing what they'd been doing. Now he's acknowledging it, maybe that's what's the matter. And you know he loved his work, and he doesn't have that any more either.

—It's those pederasts who did this, Marian. They're the real ones to blame for Bob and Sheila's turning to something. Charismatics, ha-*ha*! I'd like to see Bob Fanning with the slightest life in him. Why, he wouldn't even dance with you, and we had some of the loveliest girls in school with us. Really classy young women.

—I say pederasts are gays in a hurry.

—Stan! The two aren't even the same, you know that. How can you say that? They're people too, you know, just because you hate them . . . I swear -

—Stan, what do you mean? Ursula was curious about this, as the wedding ceremony of one of her late husband's nephews had been carried out by a gay Episcopalian on a Mississippi riverboat last year, and not a few relatives were concerned that the marriage might not be strictly legal due to the proclivities of the minister.

—Instead of waiting, you know, for the kids to grow up to date them, if that's what they call it, they get them when they're young. I mean, jeez, isn't that the only difference, timing? No wonder your father's sick about it. If one of those guys came up to me - faint fellows, somebody at work calls them, they're not really men. There's worse things they've been called, you can't say them now, got to come up with new words all the time.

—Stan, I don't comprehend you.

—Camilla, it's true. Let me tell you. Apparently asleep, Mr. Lonegin had listened to the whole conversation, tuning out now before the boor unveiled sexual mysteries to the room. He mimicked an unconscious state so perfectly that he enjoyed much of what went on around him without contributing anything. Today's symposium on Duncan's delicate condition, as Marian might have termed it if it didn't suit her more, disturbed him primarily due to the almost cavalier broaching of the topic. As ever, Camilla stood apart from her mother and Ursula's snipes, for she was loyal, at least caring enough to try and understand his dilemma, though groundlessly optimistic concerning his well being. For three years he had grown used to an ever more menacing silence, and regrettably, retirement provided time to dwell on his abrupt loss of religious certainty, tantamount to hearing the infinite reaches being eaten up by voracious termites.

Not long ago, Mr. Lonegin possessed a first-class faith in a worldwide religion, an unshakeable set of beliefs which in fair and foul weather supported him. When murmurs about sexual and physical abuse were first heard, they did not sway him. —Every man, no matter what his office, can err, but more importantly, the Church as a beautiful, living organism, directed by God, cannot err. These were sincere convictions. Trial after trial weakened them, not through the fall of this or that mere mass of weak human flesh, but by the absolute determination of the Vatican to refuse to accept a substantial degree of moral responsibility for the actions of its perverse members. How could this abdication of duty be reconciled within himself, and allow Mr. Lonegin to receive communion from the hands of an unrepentant clergy, his parish priests? These were only the first steps of his retreat from the Church. As the province's diocese allowed morality to be suppressed in favour of legality, he came to regard himself as unworthy of this Church, and this Church unworthy of its founder.

Wasn't he sinning by adhering to the rules of this corrupting body, in a sense – along with many others – helping it cohere from outside, as algae forms on the shattered skin of a sunken ship, knitting its broken hull with their own fragile lives? In short, was it true to God's purpose that the Catholic Church should live on at any cost?

In the minds of some of Mr. Lonegin's acquaintances such questions, if they had occurred at all, would have been seen as the product of needless self-examination. Faith is faith, and you either have it or you don't. Faith in what? would be his response. Faith in a dying thing? Living things are generous, with a warm heart beating inside, while dead things are acquisitive, have no heartbeat, and want your heart to stop beating too. Three years ago while taking up the collection Mr. Lonegin experienced the sensation of his heart struggling to turn over. Sweat made his hands greasy, his skin cooled, and he retreated to a spot in the back of the church to catch his breath. Fr. Jerome Ryan's homily that day on forgiveness had ended with him asking the congregation to remember in its prayers a recently deceased priest, Fr. Michael Doyle, imprisoned for physical abuse. After the service Mr. Lonegin left and never returned. There followed a miserable time when shock would have been an appropriate word.

Trained as an architect, Mr. Lonegin did well at it, and in some of his spare time took the opportunity to become an autodidact, estimating his education deficient in the humanities. He mulled over what he read, and as literature and Catholicism meant much to him, he could often be seen with books by Nobel-winning authors, by historians and by the Church Fathers, as well as current journals and Catholic papers. With his relationship to the Church of his parents, grandparents and great-grandparents sundered, it was inevitable for such a man that education would be reached for to repair the break. Perhaps if he lived long enough he would come to see the irony of how his self-teaching rendered his faith weaker than ever. In his misery St. Cyprian's words reached him, not as a poultice for his wounds but as a summons to be obeyed or disobeyed. Unable to condone the arrogant behaviour and questionable policies of Archbishop Mason – recently brought in from outside to clean the Augean stables of immorality, and equally to purge the local churches of their old-fashioned ways – Mr. Lonegin knew a decision must be made that would in one way or another ruin him forever.

Cyprian's words were that anyone not with the bishop is not in the Church, and furthermore, if the Church is not the believer's Mother, then God cannot be his Father. Believing these words at once upon reading them, unable and unwilling to deny this knowledge, or argue by pitting theologian against theologian, Mr. Lonegin questioned how he could continue as a reverent churchgoer when the Church denied its role as protector of the innocent and sinful alike. Try as he may, through intense reading, discussions with priests, and increasingly in prayer, which took the form of a dialogue with God, if one allowed silence as a response, Mr. Lonegin could see no alternative to a solitary spiritual existence, which meant that in time he would have no belief left at all, for without a community how can faith remain vibrant? Watching your faith die, feeling the fabric of your soul tear, undoubtedly formed the prelude to an existence in hell.

Camilla would never understand this even had her father tried explaining. As for Marian and her suggestion to join with the Fannings, she did not realize her offer of help brought only pain. Try as they did to dress in the uniform of a militant reactionary Catholicism, the Fannings were nothing more than a ragged splinter group agitating for a swift return to the purity of pre-Vatican II. Yet Mr. Lonegin pitied them and their friends as the new order installed thirty years ago increasingly pushed many towards the margin of history and, most definitely, outside the Church, when once they proudly occupied the front pews. Now at an advanced age in a volatile world in which little could be relied on, and where men and women were never as good as they appeared, the longtime faithful wished to be wrapped in the comforting embrace of Mother Church. Instead, years of faithful service were regarded with cold disdain by those now in power.

Unquestionably, the Fannings and others were faintly ridiculous in attempting to overthrow the establishment, but their pariah status warranted some considerate treatment. Where could these ardent followers of Christ gather to voice grievances and insecurities concerning the direction of the Church? No forum existed, though counselling might illuminate for the recalcitrant the shadows of the new Church so they could, with a pacified conscience, do as instructed. Who wanted to listen compassionately to their opinions, and act upon reasonable suggestions? No one, since the Church was wiser than any individual. Edged out, treated contemptuously, or ignored altogether, a small number, uniting in a common aspiration, transformed themselves from compliant men and women to, as Mr. Lonegin saw it, spiritual recidivists. They imagined themselves the custodians of the true spirit of Christ, the rightful practitioners of His teachings, a cleansing force that, given time and energy, aided by the grace of God, would triumph over the derelict hierarchy that for three decades increasingly followed the lead of morally bankrupt radicals who had insinuated themselves in positions of power within Catholicism, using it as their personal podium while allying themselves with those who had no respect for tradition. Such an analysis of the terrible condition of the Church was central to the Fannings' circle, and Mr. Lonegin disagreed with it strongly, wondering if perhaps the Orthodox Church would be the most spiritually acceptable place for these old believers. In any event, did it matter which version of the Church he approved of? His interior collapse set him outside the Church as it existed, and he had no desire to nail a manifesto to its doors. How could he ever make his family see the terror behind these thoughts?

The doorbell rang, jerking Mr. Lonegin from his morbid gloom, and he sprang off the couch blinking and dazed, unwittingly supplying proof his daytime slumbers were deep indeed. The visitors, coincidentally appearing on the doorstep together, were Fr. Jerome Ryan and Dr. Ralph Davies, a boyhood friend of Camilla's. —Drinks for everyone! Stan! Disappointingly, only tea and coffee were requested, but Mrs. Lonegin obliged. Soon the priest cornered his host. —Duncan, you've not been round for a chat in such a while. How are you, are you all right? We miss you at -

—Here's your coffee, Father.

—Thank you, ah . . .

—This is Stan, Camilla's boyfriend, Father Jerome.

—I see. Thank you. Now, Duncan – yes, sugar, please, no milk. Good. Everyone is asking, How is Duncan doing? Bill and Ted have a little joke that the collection isn't as much since – but you look well, fit and rested, doesn't he, Doctor?

—Pardon? Excuse me, Ursula.

—I was saying Duncan looks well. Retirement must be agreeable.

—It's how you feel that determines things, I'd say. Ralph looked steadily at his patient.

—Mood is everything. Camilla noticed Stan always became very quiet whenever her friend was around. Perhaps he's uncomfortable. Serves him right for pouring drinks down Mom's throat. He earns the punishment. Something made her turn her head. —I'm sorry, Father, what was that?

—I said to your father, you two make a lovely couple, you're so attentive to . . . Stan? Yes, one can see a – dare I say it? – a ring in the future. Camilla lowered her head, a blush creeping over her, and from the corner of her eyes she saw a faintly pink Stan. There's a ring in our present, and this arousing thought threatened to bring on laughter. To prevent this, she concentrated on the holes in the tops of the priest's tan socks.

—A wedding? Well, Father Ryan, I believe you've pushed these two a little further down the matrimonial path than they've admitted – at least to us! Camilla? At times Ursula mischievously provided a trap-door disguised as an out. Looking at Camilla's face Ralph introduced a surprising subject, turning to her mother as he spoke. —Mrs. Lonegin, did I ever tell you that in my practice I keep a genealogical chart, of sorts? A chart of diseases. This removed the spotlight from the couple, giving Stan a perverse reason to resent Ralph. —Yes, yes, the doctor replied to sundry questions. —It's habit now, but it started out when I began treating families. Each of them had conditions, and I wanted some visual method to see, at a glance, a patient's history.

—And possibly her future?

—Very sharp, Mrs. Lonegin. As a GP one sees people from the cradle to the grave, and if you know parents or grandparents had heart problems or cancer, allergies, you could keep these things in mind when examining patients.

—Fascinating. Do you mean you have my, what, tree? A disease tree, ooh, how chilling.

—You could say it was blasty, Marian.

—I wouldn't call Mom blasty, Aunt Urs.

—I didn't mean that, I was only saying.

—But what did you mean? Fr. Jerome had lost his place, so abruptly cut in with –Isn't it pleasant we're all together today, diseases or no? Duncan?

—It is Mother's Day, and Camilla stressed the word mother. —Yes, so many of them at church this morning, you would have enjoyed it, Duncan. Everyone in their finery, the young and the seasoned mothers, many of them in dresses despite the weather, most unseasonable isn't it, very pretty ones with their children scrubbed clean. Even the husbands looked like they'd paid extra attention to themselves. I so remember those instances, Marian, when you graced St. Finnian's with your floral garments. You've passed that, ah, predilection down to Camilla here. Your mother's dresses stand out so in the mind.

—Well, thank you, Father. I never knew you noticed.

—Say, Ralph, tell me something. You say you got a tree on everybody. Is that, you know, ethical? I mean, supposing it fell into the wrong hands?

—Stan, good point, and I supposed the same thing, which is why the charts are in locked filing cabinets. As for being ethical, it's no different from keeping a file on you, for instance, or anyone in your acquaintance who's been ill. I mean, your siblings, an aunt. What's good about it is something I worked out about two years ago. It's good to know family illnesses, as things can skip a generation. For instance, thanks to computers it's easy to track conditions in a place like Bowmount, and we can then build a profile -

—I'm proud to say Ryan was one of the founding families, Doctor, of this fair, ah, City.

—Do you have brothers, Father? Camilla already knew the answer.

—No, alas, I was the only son.

—And so, with you the line ends.

—Over the years people from everywhere, continued Ralph, —have moved in, bringing different blood types and inherited genes.

—Yes, and I'm delighted so many of them are good Catholics, but it took getting used to those happy brown and yellow faces among the formerly fleecy flock, if I may strain myself at a metaphor.

—Do you mean TB or something like that, Ralph, cholera, plague, what? Say they're from Romania, or Russia. I read somewhere that in Moscow -

—Where'd you read it?

—Okay, Camilla, Harry told me. That people there were used to this distyeria or whatever they got in the water over there, like we have chloride.

—Interesting point, and it fits what I'm saying. The charts show the people who marry. Individual histories, that's a fairly simple tree, but when families interconnect it starts to become like a forest. My patients' records are printed on single sheets, and each sheet is glued to a piece of cardboard. What emerges is a . . . map, almost, of the health of my patients. It's in sections that could be joined together like a jigsaw puzzle. One week I put all the sheets together, just for myself, and sometimes I sit and look at it, it's so intricate. The information's in code, don't worry, only I can read it. What I want to do, and this is exciting, Ralph said to Stan, Camilla, Mrs. Lonegin and Ursula, as Fr. Jerome had drawn Mr. Lonegin outside the circle, —is get every GP, in time every doctor in Bowmount, to do the same thing, and we could have a genetic chart, for want of a better name, of the whole community, with the provincial medical board using it in a database. That's my goal, and I'm trying hard to get the other doctors in our practice to do the same thing. There were polite noises from his listeners, though one or two were privately dismayed when someone respectable declared they were pursuing what could be termed a Cause. And from so sensible a young man as Ralph, sighed Ursula inwardly, while Stan figured he'd sound out Phil or Harry or Sam about this map. He also wondered if Ralph's name appeared in that underground publication about doctors that was in the news lately, but afraid of what Camilla would do if he asked this of him, decided not to mention it.

While somewhat interested in Ralph's project, Camilla's sympathies were with her father who appeared trapped by the priest, much like Stan looked when lost inside the basilica of one of Mr. Lonegin's ornate stories. Priests have no idea what to do around normal women, they just have these nuns who slave over them. He'll never wish Mom a Happy Mother's Day. Dressed in black with that little white collar, holes in his socks, fat even though he's thin, sharp long nose, he's a magpie. At four o'clock the object of her scorn made motions to leave. —I must be off to St. Geneviève's Home. Mrs. Cranford, do you remember her? Poor lady, she's not been well recently. Ralph also had to leave to pick up Janie, his wife. —She and Alice wanted to be together today, they both miss their mother. It's their way of coping.

—Do you put that sort of thing on those charts too?

—Stan!

—Just asking.

—Well, good-bye Camilla, Stan, Father Ryan..

—Yes, yes, and good luck with your charts of pestilence, dear boy, yes.

—Say hi to Janie for me, Ralph.

—Ralph, thank you so much for coming. The wind had risen, blowing mists from the north, and Mrs. Lonegin wrapped herself in a shawl as they stood in the porch with the front door open. —So sweet of you to remember.

—Mrs. Lonegin, why, this was like a second home to me. Abruptly she seized his hand, catching him off-balance. —Tell Janie I know what she's feeling. You never know when someone will die on you. I know! My mother, it seems like only yesterday even after all this, and I never, ever told her enough how much . . .

—That's all right, Mrs. Lonegin -

—We never talked, do you see? The saddest thing for a child to do, no matter what age, is never to talk to their parents about important things.

With her other hand she reached for Camilla's hair, stroking it, a consoling gesture from years ago. —She bossed everyone, and we resented it. Then when you're older you suddenly understand what you feel isn't hate, not in everyone's case, it's frustrated love. The tender things you wanted to say but couldn't because she wouldn't let you, and you wouldn't force yourself until you were older, and by then she's delirious. Mrs. Lonegin shook, her clear blue eyes firmly gazing at Ralph's face, not one tear evident. —Too late, and you live on cursing yourself, knowing in your heart there's this poison, and this tonic, but the one never drains and the other never gets tasted. Janie didn't have that . . . hardship, but others do, and she and Alice were so lucky to have talked with her mother, to have tended her those last days. Bless her, bless Janie, how I envy her, Ralph! Mr. Lonegin hugged his wife, unexpectedly savouring her as she was at this moment, though he felt the domestic scene was more a blur than reality. One or two people might have wondered if drunkenness triggered this outburst, and if that had been the case they may have been less embarrassed. Some wondered later when Mrs. Lonegin had imbibed such a speech. Unable to leave, the group stood half in and half out of the gray, wet day. Fr. Jerome murmured something to the back of Mr. Lonegin's head, placing his hands carefully on the man's shoulders. With a nod he withdrew quietly. After a moment or two Camilla's mother composed herself, apologizing to everyone for such a tiresome display. Ursula gripped her sister's arm, and Camilla, wiping away tears, for a moment saw them as they were ten years ago when Grandma and Mr. Nelson were alive and her aunt enjoyed life. The two couples had had such fun. At some point Ralph left, though Camilla could not say when. For some days she carried around the sensation of her mother's hand in her hair, cherishing this unexpected tenderness.

The wrinkled homunculus

—Isn't it nice to be in this bright coffeehouse, downing the labour of sweating Jamaican or Brazilian natives, sitting on European-design stools with our elbows on faux Italian marble, the middle class in full view as they contemplate spending their money on artificial flowers, dhurri rugs, vases, crafts, and at the same time cognizant of vices percolating underneath the artificiality of everything, from the exploitation of illiterate farmers, who in turn exploit ignorant, poor slaves, to that woman with the bottle-blond hair whose child, named Terry or Paul, will shatter that dish against the hardwood floor in their renovated old house before three months are up, so she'll have to come back for a replacement, which means a special order as the pattern will have been discontinued? There lurks within this clean-swept café the potential for backroom assignations of the staff when closing time comes, a quick one on a table or more thrilling, with customers waiting to pay. Think about -

—I've only got an hour, Jules.

—But look at that slattern behind the counter, the way she bumps into the brown-haired fellow. He barely sleeps, notice his eyes? That other girl's a tippler, look at her nose, and already she has a double chin. Why, do you suppose? Why is she like that, at her age?

—Boyfriend troubles.

—The fourth one, the other guy. His beard gives it away.

—Meaning what.

—Like Trotsky's. Or a poet manqué, if he smiled. He's too grim, which makes him a commerce student, or political science, working here to pay for next year because his middle-class parents earn too much for him to afford a loan. An intellectual fascist in the making, see that?

—What has gotten into you?

—Loyola, observe the blank spaces in people, the things they don't show. Trotsky there, his face is dead, seized up. His eyes look like . . . like well-handled nickels. Look for the itch that can't be scratched, the black dog inside that whines but doesn't dare bark, or else he or she would be letting go. The suppression. Conjure up his life with your own sensitivities.

—You mean imagine things.

—What an overworked word. It's taken incredible abuse. They ate the chili and garlic bread brought over by Trotsky's look-alike whose badge said he would answer to the name Blair. The reappearance of Jules Deeka after five years both pleased and depressed Loyola, for though it was good to see an old friend, there could be no denying two things: first, Jules Deeka had materially moved ahead in the world while Loyola had not, and second, the Romantic strains sounded by the forty-four year old were no longer the enchanting songs they had once been to Loyola. Had he been able to analyze the difference on that score, Loyola might have declared that the Romantic inadvertently exposed himself as a Sentimentalist. Jules was a few pounds heavier than before, and this enhanced his physical presence. His blue eyes burned with their familiar intensity, his shoulder-length black hair suited his swarthy skin colour, and he wore a brown leather jacket, creased and faded by age and use. As Jules manipulated the spoon and bread, Loyola observed that his friend's stubby fingers now ended in manicured nails. At least there was something new about him. For Loyola, toenail clippers and soap were good enough, and Jules' soft hands said a lot. —You haven't said what you're going to do now that you're back.

—What am I going to do? I'll do . . . things, what does it matter what I do? What I am, that's more important. To be, not to do.

—Saw graffiti in a toilet last week. First line said, To be is to do, Kant. Second, To do is to be, Nietzsche. Third, Do be do be do, Sinatra. Thought it was funny. Loyola chased a spoonful of chili down with a swallow of root beer. —Seriously, what'll you do?

—You never used to ask so many questions, you know that? About practical things, I mean. Look over there, who are they? I think I knew them. Covert glances were cast on a couple at a table. The woman looked to be in her mid-forties, though a permanent scowl wrinkling her face made estimation difficult. Perhaps the loss of her left leg caused the expression. As for the man, his physiognomy featured a scar that, starting under the hairline, went in a ragged diagonal from the brow and across the nose and cheek to the prominent jawbone on the right side of his face. Steel-framed glasses constrained his large head, like a trap set to burst. They ate waffles, bacon, eggs and toast in furious silence. —Remember Xavier Perrigo? Sharie -

—That's them?

—Got married two years ago, after going out all those years. Car accident on their honeymoon, on a deserted piece of road. They were by themselves for hours. When they found them they had to cut her out of it, and she lost the leg. The car lost control in the wind, you know the Scanlon Pass.

—Biggest natural wind tunnel around.

—Harry told me, he keeps up with everybody, he said they started to tell each other things they wouldn't have spilled before, seeing they were dying.

—Aren't they the embodiment of being pissed at the world? I barely recognized them. She was an okay gal, when she wasn't swearing like a soldier. Foulest mouth I ever kissed.

—You . . .

—When you were a chick in the shell. Xavier looks mean, as always. Loyola laughed, not always a nice sound. —Mean? Catch him when he's drunk. Starts bawling and telling everybody about the terrible calamity, that's what he calls it. That's when she loses it. See her cane? Jules looked again. Loyola wiped his mouth. —She taps him on the foot, then the legs if he keeps going, and when he won't shut up she uses it like a baseball bat across his shoulders, till he's crawling around begging for mercy. And she doesn't say a word. Johnny's thrown them out of his place two or three times.

—Not a word?

—Catch him sober and he'd be happy to fight, but when he's drinking? Safe then.

—Why are you hanging around there? Johnny's. I did a lot of drinking there once. The regulars still there? Harry, Sam, Stefan?

—Yeah, but they call him Pops.

—There was a Pops then too.

—Another guy. Did you know Vic, black guy, studying accounting? Phil? Camilla? Frank? You'd remember him.

—Frank, no. Vic doesn't ring a bell either. Phil, Phil Horne? Used to be a student, didn't he? There was something about him I never liked, always rubbed up against it, damned if I know what it was. Too serious about life. Gynolatry, that was something else about him.

—What?

—Too worshipful of women. Made me suspicious. Good choice in women, though.

—He does good with women, the exotic types. Maybe it's this gyno thing you -

—Trouble is, Phil wants the wrong thing out of them. Does he still talk about the imponderables with them?

—Don't know. He's gone out with a lot since you saw him.

—What a waste. All those bodies and he's interested in their minds.

—Sometimes he seems kind of odd.

—You mean gay?

—No. I mean -

Jules drained his coffee. —There's nothing wrong with being gay, Loyola. Lots of good people are homogenic. But I don't agree with the lesbian poet who wrote, Man can only fuck what I love.

—You think it's natural to get your kicks . . . there. Is it?

—Natural? We train kids to put round pegs in round holes. If they didn't we'd worry they weren't going to be intellectually realized or whatever the jargon is these days. Years later we wonder why they're skinhounding for people named Teddy and Antoine. Natural curiosity. Who hasn't put his thing in a place he was told not to?

—But enjoying it? With a man?

—Before AIDS, when things were safer, you went in the back door with a woman, had a bit of anilingus.

—What? Jules explained, finishing with —a pungent meat, like game, make sure you wash before and after. The fundament is one of those places you get a lot of pleasure out of. Slapping, tickling, biting, kissing, enemas if you're into that, so why not anal intercourse? Greatest warriors in the world did that, the army, the navy, you name it. Natural. Not healthy, not now, but natural. You're looking pink. It isn't the chili, is it? Loyola nodded. —You've been eating at the wrong place. What is it you like about The Great Pan? Fried food's a killer, I don't care if they cook it in canola oil. Like AIDS, cholesterol intake is preventable. Every so often, once or twice a year, a bit of fried chicken isn't bad, but from the way you act, it's like you don't cook.

—I do!

—I mean different things, variety. You need to try what's unfamiliar. So, God bless the gays, they opened up the world for the bisexuals, if nothing else, though I don't like them trying to take over the world as they like to think they're doing. You want my opinion? Gay sex acts are a side dish at best, not a main course. A few customers were listening to these remarks, delivered in Jules' characteristically self-assured manner, one Loyola had found in the past, as now, occasionally too public. —They are saying everyone is gay, but that's as easy as saying everyone's straight. You have your masculine side and your feminine side, but for a man, as an example, to indulge the feminine side too much just courts disaster, see what I mean? A little dalliance, okay, but nothing else. Being experimental doesn't mean the same as being a little bit pregnant. It's not you're all one or all the other, all fly or all ointment as my father used to say. And as for setting up a world order on it, that's too stupid for words.

—Do you mean you've done it with a guy?

—I can barely hear you, but – never. The world's trying it now, and that, my friend, is one more reason I won't. You know I've never read *National Geographic*, and why? Because everyone reads it, and I never want to be like everybody. Same thing with things like gay sex, and yoga. Plus I love women's bodies, women's odours, essences, fluids, they're the best in the world. Lesbians are much more aesthetically pleasing than gays, and they're luckier too. You always see a rise in this sort of thing at the end-of-the-century when everything gets raised to the power of ten. Personally, the gay lifestyle strikes me as a matter of style, fashion, not honest-to-God instinctive urges, in nine out of ten situations. It's in vogue, then it's out of vogue, then it's subterranean, then back in vogue, then old hat. I'll give you a potted history.

—It's okay, I -

—The nineties man is a confused guy, he's lost when it comes to how to treat women. It's not just me saying this. Nineties guys grew up when sex roles and gender stereotypes were being smashed, follow me? Consequently, men are trying to find out what to do with women today, except types like you and me who know what they're for. You go into a book store now, you see a wall of books on women's issues. Fine. Then there's this one shelf filled with tall, thin books on men's issues. We're in a pretty sad state as a gender when we need books to remind us who we are. A lot of men, they forgot their membrum virile and started thinking from the head alone. I disagree with a lot that Jerrod Manny Hotchkiss says in *From Toy Boy to Coy Boy: The Feminization of the American Male*, because one thing he doesn't talk about is Mexico where machismo is strong, but that doesn't mean maleness is, and I can come back to that. He does make a good point that in decadent societies – look around us. People don't care about the fact that bean pickers live on top of dung-heaps or in baked mud-and-straw houses, so long as espresso tastes fresh. Where was I? In decadent societies inner dignity – and he doesn't mean that inner child garbage – disappears, from within and partly due to the atmosphere. Most people don't notice it's happening because they're too busy trying to survive. Who has time to worry about the psyche when your neighbour has the stereo on at four in the morning, or your son or daughter needs to be warned about drug dealers at school? Hotchkiss, for all his academic pomposity, makes sense when he talks about the negative results of societal approval about gayness as a norm, which does get under my skin, or at least acceptance of same-sex love -

—But, excuse me, interrupted a woman in her early thirties —if I might, isn't it more to the point - I hope you don't think I'm rude for -

—Pull up your chair, no problem.

—Thanks. More to the point to say that only the male-male ideal of noble love has been recognized by hierarchies, which is where I thought you were headed, whereas Sapphic love has never been so universally tolerated.

—Mmm, that word, tolerated, said her companion, dressed in a plain white blouse under a navy blue jacket, matched with a long navy skirt, and pale stockings. —I've such trouble with it. It's so close to intolerance, you see what I mean? There's no room at all to manoeuvre. Nadeen Sarkissian and Kate Shanahan then introduced themselves as a freelance photographer and a receptionist with a local publisher, respectively. The conversation spiralled among three of the four parties, Loyola admiring anew his friend's mesmeric power over women, despite his creased leathery skin and stocky frame. The tall, well-proportioned photographer who had invited herself to the conversation could only be classed as an exotic beauty, whereas Kate's pale skin and long black hair were more to his taste. —But still, if I may, Hotchkiss misses out on Mexico, as I was saying to Loyola earlier. You see, when the man-man relationship, when it isn't viewed as a degeneracy of health - which psychiatrists only recently treated it as - it's just an - invert's display of machismo! You see? Male homogenics -

—What?

—Sorry, Nadeen, it's a word I picked up, an early alternative to homosexual. Homogenic means same sex, follow me? So this invert machismo is truly an example of pathological masculinity. And you ladies might – forgive me, but I'm old, so I do use that word, no offence intended.

—None taken. You're not old, is he, Kate?, as she smoothed the front of her maroon-and-green silk blouse, matched with a gray skirt that showed off her bare, brown, muscular legs. Kate murmured something. —Compared to the youth and virility of my trim and fit friend I feel only a little short of antique. We're not quite coetaneans, you see.

—What's that? Thanks to Jules' tutelage Loyola could answer Kate. —It means contemporaries.

—Friends? We wondered. Nadeen made an expressive gesture.

—No. And you two are?

—Straight. Kate eyed Loyola's short, thick black hair and gray eyes set in a firm asymmetrical face with less guarded interest. —I was saying, pathological masculinity. I daresay the Amazons would be classified as pathological femininity, but that isn't Hotchkiss' topic. Greece in its halcyon days, the Romans at their strongest under Augustus, Persia during the rules of Cyrus and Darius, the Ottoman Empire, they were all conquerors, all empire-builders. And all flagrant sodomites. Look at the Egyptian pharaohs and, if you want a recent example, the British, with flagellation and buggery part of their education system. Everyone says the British don't have sex, yet they do.

—But too often with little boys and girls.

—Very good, Nadeen! Empire-builders extend themselves as far as possible, geo-politically and sexio-culturally. Those are Hotchkiss' terms, and they're reductionist, ugly-sounding, crossing German word-crafting with Foucault's weakest ideas. Nadeen made a moue, saying —Such a sick man, spreading AIDS to innocent people when he knew he had it. How immoral, and from a philosopher.

—He couldn't hold a candle to any of the Greeks, my favourites, or even later fellows like Descartes, Spinoza. Philosophy isn't what it used to be. Anyway, these rulers, kings or tsars or caesars or princes or autocrats, they forced themselves everywhere. Jules took out a pen and slip of paper on which he wrote:

Empire-building (A) = Pathological masculinity (B)

Pathological masculinity (B) = Sodomy/paederasty (C)

If A=B and B=C, then A=C

—But I think Hotchkiss makes a blunder when he equates pathological masculinity with patriarchy. One is an ongoing condition, the other is a vessel in which the pathology is poured. Subtle, essential distinction.

—Are you, like, a sociology professor or something? Kate twisted the paper absent-mindedly. —Kate, bonny Kate, I'll never curse you for that. Not a professor. I simply had the opportunity during lulls in life to read, more when I was younger than now, but I dabble.

—And you know Shakespeare too, I'm impressed. What about you, Loyola?

—Ah, let's - a man may smile and smile and be a villain. Nadeen smiled. —My friend works at Moscati-Mann, you know them, they dress the news anchors and businessmen and so on. Speaking of which, it's time I got you back to the salt mines. They can't get on without him, ladies. Otherwise we'd tarry. Who else would do the packing and lifting? He's a put-upon workhorse, just look at those arms. Nadeen, and may I say that's a charming way of spelling it, and Kate, plainly spelt Kate, it's been a pleasure to speak to two such charming, if you don't mind an old-fashioned word, women, forthright in their opinions. Always refreshing, Nadeen. Do you need a ride? Nadeen shook her head. —I've a car. I'm driving Kate back to work. I don't keep regular business hours. Her friend tapped her arm. —Tell them. Go on.

—Tell us what? Loyola asked as he checked his watch. —Nadeen, she has a show coming up at the Brogan Civic Arts Centre. You should come.

—A show? Of what?

—Oh Kate, now you have me - photographs. If I tell you what about it'll sound goofy. You have to see it to grasp - if I tried to explain it would take a while and I don't want to make you late, and where it's my first show - installation, to be exact - I'm nervous. I really want to bounce the idea off somebody who can appreciate these things before the set-up's complete. Jules understood perfectly, suggesting the four of them meet some night, the coming Saturday perhaps, for drinks and a discussion. Throughout the conversation Kate's leg bumped Loyola's, and Nadeen had no hesitation about taking Jules' number, so the date seemed assured. The four were about to rise when two arms encircled Loyola's neck. He recognized the watch and bangles as the top of his head was kissed. Introducing Janet Campbell to the table he emphasized she was his cousin, and Kate's smile returned. The newcomer presented her lunch companion. —Everyone, this is Tyrone Vann, Ty for short. He's in broadcasting. I'm with *The Bowmount Courier*, by the way. It's *so* good to *see* you, Loyola, we don't get together nearly enough. You should come by my new apartment, you have the address?

—Yes, it's -

—Listen, have you people tried that new spot over there? It's too late now, of course, you've eaten, but -

—Where?

—Look out the window, to your left. That new restaurant, Waist Not, Want Not. It's good. But we came here for the coffee, right Ty?

—What kind of food?

—Totally diet-conscious, cuz. Don't make a face. Their dishes are broken down into portions, like Weight Watchers but not close enough to be sued, and they have gluten- and lactose-free meals too. It's delicious. You should try it. Of a firmer build than Janet or Nadeen, Kate straightened up at what she took to be a suggestion directed at her. —Not everyone wants to look -

—I don't care what I have if Janet's paying, contributed Tyrone. —She's writing a review of the place for the paper and asked me to come along, otherwise . . . I think Slim Pickins' is a better name for it. But I ate tomato soup for years so food doesn't matter much to me. A great step towards independence is a good-humoured stomach, one willing to endure rough treatment.

—That sounds very like a Stoic to me.

—Huh? Why, yes, Seneca, do you -

—I thought so. It is not the man who has little, but the man who craves more, that is poor. I'm positive you felt that way while eating your soup. Jules and Tyrone eyed each other warily. —How can you *say* such a thing,

Ty? You *loved* it! He's just being contrary. Don't you hate it when men turn on you like that? Always in company. Right, cuz? Loyola smoothed his hair down where she ruffled it.

—Your name brings back memories, Tyrone, and of course, your voice. I remember six, seven years ago you were the host of the afternoon show at that radio station, was it CCII?

—The same. Times change. I'm there again.

—You could look happier about it, Ty. He shrugged. —I'm not complaining, Janet, just looking at the facts square in the face. Bad times, good times, mediocre times, all that's important is keeping your chin up.

—Then admit the meal wasn't *bad*.

—I already said that. It's just food.

—Myself and Loyola, we enjoy a good meal, meat, fowl, vegetables, fruit, from the back to the front of the Horn of Plenty. We're pagans when it comes to our appetites, you could say. But listen, Janet, if I may call you that so soon after meeting you, do you know my friend Nadeen here is having an exhibition at the Brogan? From what she's told me it's going to be something unforgettable. Normally I wouldn't step right up to a stranger and be bold enough to praise a friend, but you're in the media, and Nadeen here could use intelligent exposure prior to the big event. I think you could write a fascinating profile of a new, trend-setting artist, and everyone reads the *Courier* arts section. You two should talk. But Loyola, time to go. Your cousin works for a slave driver, Janet.

—He'll survive. We've heard all about *her*.

—Is she that nasty? She's probably going through something.

—Kate, the stories he tells me - there's the Amazonian principle in action. My friend is the only man I know who works with his hands, and as an almost forgotten writer said, they're the only ones who can have a clear conscience in this bitter world. Jules looked at Tyrone, who had his head turned away, then bent to whisper a few words in Nadeen's ear after she took something from Kate. In the car Jules' first words were —Your cousin, hey? She's attractive, in a brassy way. Wild nail polish. You and her get along, right?

—I guess.

—She hugs you, presses your hand, winks at you. Good thing Kate knew you were related.

—What are you saying?

—Don't you feel it, man? I did. Oh, my quickening humour jelled simply watching you and her. I felt like a voyeur.

—You're disgusting. That's just sick, Jules. She's my cousin.

—How close? Easy, easy, don't get excited. You can't deny the sexual message she was sending out.

—Watch me.

—If you so choose to deny it, well then. The two rode on for a time without saying anything. —That's incest, Jules. And creepy. Besides, she's always like that.

—Then I'd have taken her up sooner on it. No need to get angry, I'll drop it. Sometimes I don't know who I'm talking to, you've changed so much. But Loyola, you have to be more adventurous.

—What I have to be is on time or Starlene'll go berserk, so can you move this thing?

—See you Friday night, right?

—Isn't it Saturday?

—Nadeen told me when we were leaving, she and Kate, Friday night. And look, here's an origami thing Kate made out of my logic, Nadeen said she wanted you to have it but didn't want to give it to you with your cousin there. Sharp eyes on her. Can you tell what it is? Neither can I, note paper isn't made for origami. I said we'd meet them at Johnny's at ten. Look sharp, it'll do me good with Nadeen if she sees you took trouble over your appearance for her friend.

—How come you didn't tell them you had a degree?

—Who cares about degrees? Too many questions then, like you were asking earlier. Why aren't you this, where did all that get you, whatever made you take that?

—A photographer. What type?

—Artist, she said. Probably has a few nude shots of herself and Kate too, maybe uses her as a model sometimes. Puts people together with nature red in tooth and claw, throws in a few industrial scenes, bingo, late 20th century urban aesthetic expression. Hear how she resents painting, and sculpture? Bit narrow-minded there, but what do I care? She's tall, slender, dark Greek, fiery, and – younger than me! I've still got it, haven't I? and lucky you, my charm extends to Kates with dexterous fingers. When you're coupling ferociously with her Friday night send a prayer to your household gods I was there to procure a woman for you. Here we are. It's a pretty dismal building you work in. I have to come up with a way to get you out of there, you've changed because of them, you're a little sour. Keep Friday night in mind, a candle in the window, a torch burning against the dank dungeon walls -

—I'm gonna be late.

—I'll pick you up at nine thirty, your place, Friday. As Jules' car disappeared, Loyola felt a moment of exhilaration followed by one of intense calm. Flowers in the nearby garden exhaled their fragrances. Yes, he would keep the memory of Kate's firm red lips tucked away from harm, taking it out during the week when things were tough. He smelled wild roses as a breeze played with the paper figure of either a bull or cow. Maybe I think it's a cow because of the black ink. No, it's a bull. That's what Kate was thinking about.

A business of ferrets

At the rectangular conference table in Albert Lewis' office suite at 6:30 a.m. the first Monday of June were seated almost all of the ACII network managing board, composed of Bob Henderson, Oswald Bennett, Henry Edmonds, Stewart Mattson, Otis and Philip Lewis, and Perry Hornocker, who were, respectively, the station manager, the sales manager, the program director, the head of public communications, the assistant station manager, the news director, and Lewis' personal assistant. The head of accounting, Stephen Stone, was travelling on business. Waiting for his employer's entrance, Perry nervously flipped through a binder containing notes, bulletins, and drafts of letters. He was not yet accustomed to these once-a-month sunrise meetings. —State-of-the-nation address, Oswald, nicknamed the Nose, described them; —The Dawn-breakers, in the words of Ben Trevelyan, morning talk show host. To Perry, that designation was too ambiguous not to be sarcastic. There lay a trouble-maker, very good with words, subversive. —Gentlemen? The others were talking about new businesses openings in Bowmount. —What are Mr. Trevelyan's latest ratings? Mr. Henderson?

—Untouchable in the quarter-hours between 9 and 10:30 a.m., unstoppable for the last half-hour.

—Fine moneymaker. Salesmen can't charge enough for spots, my way of analyzing it. Remember when he first started? He wasn't a talk show host, just a jock, this is ten years ago. He'd said something, forget what, and Eddie Danforth, he was where you are now, Henry -

—He was program director, Oz?

—For something like three days before Bob fired him. Eddie was steaming about a wisecrack Ben made on air about him. A joke.

—Eddie didn't have a sense of humour.

—So you know Ben isn't the tallest guy around. Eddie went up to him after he came off air and said, You little fucker, don't you ever say anything like that again or I'll smash your head open. Ben points his finger up at Eddie's face and says, calm as anything, Don't call me little! and walks off. After the laughter Bennett continued. —Ben, what a guy. Salesmen love him. Philip added, —The newsroom gets great clips from that show. Perry? Dad's book on the numbers is over on that shelf, third one down, red cover, bound book marked Numbers. Seeing Trevelyan scored very high, Perry slowly drew a line through comments in his notes. Someone mentioned Hilary Miller's impersonation of a hood ornament, then moved on to other illnesses and conditions of the staff. Hilary, now there's an indefinable one, Perry thought. The car was doing two miles an hour, there weren't injuries. Own stupidity, not looking where one's going. I don't see that it could be life-altering. Perry looked around at the red wallpaper, the red chairs, and wondered how his employer could stand working here. It's like living in an open wound. A long, high window faced east, flooding the room with sunlight, making the walls pulse. Didn't anyone else find it hot?

—Jason Shaw's going into hospital to have part of his intestines removed.

—Cripes, no.

—Just what my newsroom needs.

—No kidding, Phil.

—Ruined the vacation schedule. He would pick this time of year.

—I suppose it could be worse.

—Yes, Christmas.

Bennett blew his nose forcefully. —What about hay fever? Wish they'd come up with a cure for that. Edmonds mentioned the fact that some jocks were complaining again about Ruby, who had moved on from asking them what their sign was to offering her body to any of them for free. Otis looked perturbed. —I don't see this in the fault reports. They're supposed to note down everything.

—It isn't the kind of thing you write down, Otis, it's anecdotal.

—Suppose someone takes her up on it? Then it becomes a legal and more to the point, PR issue. It isn't just a story any more. I'm surprised you didn't see that, Stewart. Perry, take this down: All sexual harassment must be duly recorded by announcers and operators to prevent the station from exposure, and so on, signed Otis Lewis. Write that up in the usual way and get it on the boards this morning. Perry's faux-marble fountain pen squirted through sweating fingers, and he scrabbled for it, hoping black ink wouldn't stain the thick, ruby-coloured carpet. —When I worked the board, the best we got was a heavy breather on the line. Now -

—Bob, in your case she was just asthmatic. Oswald's joke went down well. —Let me ask a question, Stewart said after a pause, —who else thinks Shelagh Rogers could give head over the phone? I mean, that voice. Bob and Oswald agreed, though Mr. and Mr. Lewis blushed slightly, Perry noted with satisfaction.

—Speaking of humping, Alice met Tony the other day in the supermarket.

—Tony, Stewart?

—Tony Austin, Otis. DJ at CCCC three years back, left to do consult work at Marshall Press. You know my wife is pregnant. They saw each other, and they go back years, and she asks how things are. He says he has four kids now. Told her, You know, Allie, when the first one was born I told everybody he was fourteen pounds, and they were impressed. He said, Well, What I say is, you get out of something what you put into it! Most were still enjoying this line when the bathroom door opened and Albert Constantine Lewis stepped out. Impeccably dressed, with a full head of black hair and in prime physical health, he commanded a room. His tanned features, weathered from time on his sailboat, lent life to eyes which surveyed the suite as though its furnishings and human materials were inconsequential. The staff at CCII and its sister stations were unnecessarily solicitous about his well-being, for he was merely fifty-seven. A widower for two years, Lewis dedicated his time to philanthropy, business, and the establishment of his pre-eminent ranking in these two fields. A year and a half ago, after a suitable period of mourning, he instituted these early morning meetings, taking a firmer grip on the overall affairs of Olympus Communications, its CCII radio network especially. He was obliged, having two sons of his dead brother to look after as if they were his own. Philip and Otis were well placed in the company but needed seasoning. The third son, Alfred, known to the family as The Unnameable, having chosen his own path in life, could go hang.

—Good morning. Perry, you look flushed. You've all got something? Fine. First things first. I understand one of the staff has been hit by a speeding car. Does this slow anything down?

—When, Albert?

—Bob, I had the name, here it is, Hilary.

—That was in April, and there weren't any injuries.

—I see. Bob, why the hell wasn't I told? People are talking about it as if it happened yesterday.

—Some odd behaviour, nothing affecting Continuity.

—Otis, your opinion?

—I agree with Bob, Dad, a little odd, but -

—Fine. Next, I've discussed with Bob, Otis and Oswald a new program. Ben's doing very well in the morning. We're going to book-end him at night with Dr. Rory Quasten, a syndicated show out of British Columbia. Controversial. Doesn't give medical advice, not that kind of doctor. He's in socio-cultural studies, a hot field. Starting in September we'll run him network-wide from 8 p.m. to 11 p.m. Sunday to Thursday. He'll discuss native issues, sex, left and right, feminism, gays, religion, everything topical. Advertising potential? Enormous. Everyone wants somebody rabid, and we have him.

—If you'd like, Albert -

—Bob, shoot.

—He has three degrees, in cultural studies, law and commerce, so he can market himself as an expert on day-to-day affairs without causing lawsuits.

—How old is he?

—Forty-eight, yuppie heaven.

—I hear he has the legendary third testicle, the women'll love that.

—Right, Henry.

—The what?

—That means great pipes, Perry. We have publicity packages for every-one, I'll just pass these around.

—Meanwhile, Oswald's lined up potential sponsors, and Olympus will welcome him into the province very prominently, give him a big fall push. What this will do is increase our share in the Greater Bowmount area right away in those time slots. He'll be on AM. More when there's more. Henry, Gary Grace's Top 40?

—Signed the contract noon Friday. Grace's contract with CEPJ lapsed, we squeezed in there, and negotiated against the bastards, offering a size-able payload for the program. Done deal.

—But we've already got Tom-Tom Thornhill's show. Two Top 40s on the one day? How will we run this?

—Phil, we bought Grace to make sure CEPJ didn't have him. Thornhill will be on air as usual, the sole national top 40 chart program in Greater Bowmount, Carlyle and Crescent City. Thanks to Henry here we've elimin-ated the competition. Lewis smiled momentarily in appreciation. —All Grace's people get is the money, and the contract – right, Henry? – spe-cifies we purchase the show, with an option to tip into next year. No legal language says we have to play it. Also, when we meet Thornhill in a few months, this is leverage in bargaining with him. It's a win-win deal. Now Bob, you've something else.

—We purchased a show, a really fine quality production about the his-tory of pop and rock and roll. There were some groans. —Hold on. This is up to date, music from the 1980s up to today. We know kids into hip-hop don't care about Styx, or the girls who like Nirvana won't want to hear ZZ Top. But what we've found out of California is a program that's emceed by current pop stars, rock stars, celebrities, you name it.

—Like Brad Pitt?

—People every bit as current. A star of today hosts this two-hour show, and we get a combo demographic of the eighteen to twenty-fives listening to somebody from R.E.M. or Hootie and the Blowfish or the movies taking them through their favourite, I don't know, Grand Funk songs. That's the thirty to fifty-years collared too.

—Schedule?

—Friday nights, 11 p.m. to 1 a.m., AM stations. Repeats on FM Saturday evening from 5 to 7.

—The breaks, drop-in times?

—In an hour you get four breaks, giving us three-minute islands at the top of the clock, :17, :30, and :47, that's 12 minutes of commercial time. The show provides lead-in and lead-out music of about ten seconds at each break to nail the call letters to, plus they send down promos tagged at the end of the show. We have the satellite feed times. I've heard two of the shows, they're fresh, and we start broadcasting in the fall.

—October, Bob? Leave the kids something to look forward to, October 6, say, just into the school year. With Rory positioned Sunday to Thursday on AM, we've a sure-fire week.

—That's thinking, Henry. Bob, I expect you and Oswald and Henry to work out the fine points. You have something -

—Perry, could you hand these out? The show's called *TTMR*, short for *Testify To My Roots*, rousing gospel song on a bed of applause. Blues and soul orientation.

—Bit of a mouthful, isn't it? Sponsors want something snappy.

—That's only what it stands for, Oswald, the show's called *TTMR*. Otis put in, —I like it, high-concept, roots. There's interest in that. From there the executives discussed standard matters such as items on the fault reports, the condition of station equipment and the towers, network visibility in the community, ad revenue, future projects and sales campaigns. Once more CCII, along with CCCI, its Carlyle affiliate, would broadcast updates during the Three-Day Bicycle Race in August, —From handlebar to taillight, as Oswald phrased it. —Got the sponsors for Race cut-ins ready, same ones as last year plus new ones replacing the cunts who dropped out. City's working on the promotional aspect of the Race, so's the Bikers

Club, we're in there, sleeves rolled up, with advice and whatever. Our civic duty, blah blah blah. Stewart's doing a great job liaising. We might even get a big name like Nike in on it.

—A catchy name for it, that's the trouble. Stewart liked to be seen consulting the old farts, as he privately labelled them. —Those new colours screwed the pitch I was working on. No one offered anything, and the situation clearly required a command decision from Lewis. —Navy, jade, what are they to the average man? Call a spade a spade, forget the fancy 1990s colours. Blues versus Greens. The Blue-Green Fight -

—Bikathon, Albert?

—That's obvious, Stewart.

—I'll work on it some more. Lewis indicated he better. As the meeting went on the owner grew impatient, relaxing when they finished addressing the last item under Routine Matters. —New business. We've already had some, I know, but this is big. Bob, Otis, and I have been talking, extensively, wouldn't you say, Bob? Of course you would. The CC stations are behind the times, like our competitors the CATQ network, CEPJ, CEMV, losing ground because we're too gutless to make the right decisions. It stops today. Automation.

—Don't we already have some? The music log -

—Wait, Henry. Bob, how many jocks do we have network-wide? Never mind, the right answer is too many. Radio isn't some game, unless you regard it as a blood sport. Television, cable, satellite, suck the advertising dollars away, which means good money goes out to pay slobs to speak into a microphone and press buttons. It looks impressive when we round up a few volunteers who aren't half-drunk or wired to wear the jackets and everyone in Bowmount or Crescent City sees them, great to fly colours! But operators can do that. The equipment's been ordered to automate a hell of a lot more than music logs. I'm not doing this for any other reason than it's a damn fine target to hit. The machines are there that can do it, so why not do it? It's a goal, an endpoint, and far from saving money, I want CC to make more. Think of it, a station driven by computers and voice tracks. We'll keep the talk shows, the morning drive, the -

—Produced by jocks?

—Hell no, Oswald, I'm trying to get rid of them. Operators cost less. I sit in this room or in my car or at home or on the boat listening to this station and what do I hear? I've done it for thirty-two years, ever since my father Hubert hired me to do what he called character building exercises and I called chores. The music's changed, the formats have changed a bit, the commercials still try and sell things, and the listeners, most importantly, the listeners haven't changed. Thirty-two years later and the main part of radio hasn't moved significantly. You know that study that said the average educational level of a radio listener is grade eight? What do grade eights want in a radio station? Music, sports, a bit of weather to see if they can go out and play, time checks, as little news as possible. They couldn't care less if Casey Kasem or Jack the Ripper was on air as long as they heard songs and lots of them when they wanted. These hot-shot announcers we have like -

—Tyrone Vann, sir?

—Vance Kingfisher King, Perry, our rock show host with the monumental ego and some talent, but take the format away from him, get rid of the sponsors, the ideas for contests Otis comes up with like Rhymes of the Ancient Marinator for the restaurants, with all those jingly rhymes, great, great, and brought in money too, strip that away and the audience would see that King Shit is nothing more than Fart the Messenger Boy. What we're going to do is simple. Keep jocks on from 6 a.m. to 9 a.m., then go into Trevelyan's show, which takes us to 11 a.m. From 11 a.m. to 1 p.m. we use the morning show announcer. The news comes on at 1 p.m., and we're going to expand it. Phil and I've already talked. Phil, explain it.

—Yes, Dad. We're going to marry our local news to a feed from Broadcast News or the BBC, for national and international stuff. That'll be half an hour, or maybe thirty-five minutes, of straight news.

—Straight news?

—With some funny stories at the end, human interest stuff.

—Good.

—Oswald, let him speak.

—We'll have longer local reports, more local content. With the CBC getting stripped every year there's an opportunity to fill that vacuum. They're so used to being fat they don't know how to lose weight, where we can bulk up just a touch, and seem more on top of things.

—Serves the bastards right. Phil, I can see the p.r. potentialities.

—The other half-hour will be sports, weather, health specials, astrological predictions, soft editorials, cooking tips, anything from a whole range of subjects. Sports and weather take us from the thirty to the forty, maximum, leaving twenty minutes to fill with whatever we want. Different things every day, same thing every day, it's our choice.

—I can sell that, Christ, no problem! Who wouldn't want their spots there? When's this happening? Because the present contracts don't expire till February. Can we get CNN for the news, Albert?

—There's a thing about American news, people get it on t.v., and I won't duplicate what's on t.v. I like the BBC, it looks refined. Appearance is everything. Thanks Phil, for the succinct briefing. Now, from 2 p.m. to 6 p.m. we have a second announcer doing the afternoon drive. Let me state this bluntly. We'd pay good dollar for two very capable, personable jocks, no skimping, but no contracts like the few we have now. We'll need a woman, obviously. At 6 p.m. we come on with the news, half an hour, and at 6:30 p.m. the rock show starts, but when we get Dr. Rory it'll only go till 9 p.m., resume at 11 p.m. till midnight. We'll block 6:30 p.m. to 9 p.m. with music and contests, and Stewart has an idea. Go ahead.

—I didn't see where things were going when – Albert's idea is so profound it's simple. Every kid wants to be on radio. We're going to set up a telephone-computer system where somebody phones in and requests a song, and when they call they don't get an announcer. They get a tape saying, and this is rough: Hi! You've reached CCII-AM's You're The Host! feature. Instead of requesting your favourite song, you get to play it. Emphasis added somewhere there. That's right. You get to hear your song on the radio, introduced by you. After the beep, clearly say, I'm, then your name, then say: The next song is whatever by whoever, another hit from the hit machine, CCII-AM. There's this beep, the kid records his message, and the song gets played later.

—Every song, Stu? Henry leaned forward, rubbing his chin. —Impossible.

—Hold on, yes, Henry, but the parameters will be set. The announcer - this is a rough draft, I'm all for feedback - the announcer says, when the - because the computer listens to the call, and checks its memory banks or whatever they're called to see if the song is there, okay?

—Memory banks.

—Or whatever. The automation can handle every song we want. CDs, that's all we use. Each title is in the computer. Somebody asks for, oh, I've Never Been To Me by Charlene, remember that? It won't be in our memory, and the tape will tell the kid: Sorry, we're not able to play that at this time. Call back with another selection, because you mean the most to us. The number they call will be a 1-800 number, and there'll be only one line, two at most. The number of calls between 6:30 p.m. and 9:00 p.m. we figured works out as, where's the - I had the damn count, was it - no, that's -

—Stu, each kid? We could get hundreds of requests for songs we don't have.

—Depends how long the message is, Henry, right? Take, say, one minute to explain, half a minute to record. Then the response is, you know, sorry, or your song can be played, and that's another ten, fifteen seconds. The beauty of the equipment is that the system can be programmed as we want. If it doesn't work out right away, we fine-tune it. And if we get any number of requests for songs we don't have, then hey! you might add it to the playlist. We're talking about a system Albert, Bob and Otis already scoped out.

—Excuse me?

—Perry?

—Pardon me. Mr. Henderson, this equipment, and the music. I'm still not sure how it works.

—The way it goes now, we set out the music log a few days in advance of the play date. A jock comes in and deals with two logs, the commercial one and the music one. He picks out the tunes listed and plays them in order, as many as he can in an hour, for example, leaving maybe one or two songs not played, or one song short, which he fills in using the sense God gave him, or her. With the new computer, from what we've seen so far, I guess it can do the same, only faster. Though we'd have to make sure, Henry, the same songs don't get overplayed.

—The computer can weed the requests out, maybe some message on the tape, Bob.

—Spots, how'd you make sure spots get played? Would the timing get messed up?

—Stewart, thank you. The new system, the LazEx Program Transfer, will take calls on the 1-800 line from 5:30 p.m. to 8:00 p.m. No later. These details will be worked out, but this is good enough for an introduction. The computer will start making a music log at 5:31, 5:35, whenever the first call comes in, so that when the announcer takes over at 6 he or she can pick out the first songs. There'll be a backup log in case there aren't enough calls to fill the hours, and they'll mostly be CanCon, which Henry can arrange. I think a lot of kids want their friends to hear them on the radio.

—It's like a talk show, without a host!

—Oswald, it's a talk show with the rascal multitude as the hosts. Kingfisher, if we want to keep him, looks at the printout from the computer and pulls the songs. He keys the information into the computer, and it matches the taped intro to the song. The order they're accepted, the order they'll be played. Kingfisher might even get to speak once or twice.

—Could we make this a 1-900 number?

—Otis, nice, but that might come across as greedy. Besides, eventually we'll save money by replacing the jock with an operator. That's the next step, having people – we'll call them talent, similar to what we use now for some spots – come in and tape voice tracks. We'll start with the all-night show first on AM and FM, in August, see what the glitches are, then slowly shed the rock show host. I predict this time next year we'll have reduced our need for live announcers to two a day, maybe three. Sunday's full of taped religious programming, so this is a logical next step.

—But the commercials, how will they fit in?

—Details! Oswald, it will all be hammered out, never fear. You and Bob and Otis will see this wonderful LazEx in action before the month is out. But there's something else to talk about now, the sister stations. As you know, for decades Olympus Communications has worked at establishing presence in different parts of the province. CCII-AM and FM is the pivot of the network, while CCCI-AM in Carlyle and CCCC-AM in Crescent City are second and third in stature. CCRR and CCFP lag behind in population and economic demographics, therefore the staff in them are disposable. From September 5 on, which is to say, from the day after Labour Day, Ripton and Franklin Plains will take their feed from CCII-AM, except for the 6 a.m. to 9 a.m. and 2 p.m. to 5 p.m. slots. Trevelyan already covers the net-work, as do the major news broadcasts and the all-night show, but we're adding the rock show and the brief news reports during Trevelyan's show. We'll reduce on-air personnel to two jocks and an operator in each sta-tion, and cut the news teams down. Phil has that plan ready. No part-timers, no summer relief. The ones kept will feel damn glad they're there full-time with benefits, so that'll dilute the hard feelings as they come to terms with the new arrangement. Oswald, there'll be two salesmen for each.

—There are more there now -

—Too many. You tell me they wouldn't cut each other's throats to get the other guy's accounts? If they're not hungry, why are they working for me?

—Seems a fucking shame, Albert, that's all. I worked with some of those guys for years. To tell them they're let go -

—I'll save you the distress, though you're coming close to disappoint-ing me with this negative attitude. Otis, you tell them they're fired.

—Me? But I – all right, if you -

—Reluctance to make tough decisions cripples people. Phil is going to cut how many staff? A fair number. You have to be like that. I've been readying you for responsibilities, and here they come. An embarrassed silence blanketed the table. —Who'll it be? Oswald, Otis? Who's going to rid me of these salesmen? Otis wavered. —Maybe myself and Oswald can talk the approach over first, see what has to – who has to go.

—Get together then. These changes mean CCRR and CCFP can make more money since there'll be less payout. Besides, rural life is dying, people are swarming into the cities like locusts, and I'll be damned if Olympus runs the only operation in ghost towns. Think of it as the Joads leaving Oklahoma, only we're at the front of the line, getting out while it makes fiscal sense, because if we wait it'll be a necessity and that means no profit. Anyone see differently? Good. Besides, in case anyone's forgotten, some bastards are trying to start a union here, and this will cut the numbers down, throw everybody into a panic. People will be too worried about their jobs to think of signing a card. Hell, we'll turn every newsperson into a part-timer if that's the way to stare these ingrates down. Perry!

—Yes, sir!

—Names of those trouble-makers.

—Very hard to get, though I'm working at it. Everyone is rather quiet.

—Not surprising. Bob, do we have some vacated position Perry can fill? Office work, interaction with the employees? Maybe that way he can learn something.

—We haven't had a personnel rep in years. To Perry this seemed an excessively unkind suggestion, and deliberately so. —What about it, Perry? Think you could listen to them yammering all day?

—I'm not entirely comfortable with the idea, Mr. Lewis, as I'm new here. But if -

—Besides, they'd see through it in a minute. Keep thinking, Bob. First out of the stocks doesn't always have to be a winner, though it sure as hell helps. Stewart, keep working on that telephone idea. Find a good name for it, you know, 1-800 something CCII. Get it to me soon.

—1-800-IMA-JOCK?

—Good first try. Punch up the bicycle race too. I hear the mayor and his wife are betting on Carlyle. Phil, see what you can find out. Speaking of news, meant to ask earlier, what's this fuss over some opera?

—Yes, Dad, Karla O'Reilly is covering it. A good little reporter, she has an eye for the right tone.

—Cute girl. Her nose is a bit broad, isn't it? Is she negroid? Reddish-black hair?

—Half-Irish, half Afro-Canadian.

—That's a drunken house party waiting to happen. Phil ignored Henry. —There's a musical going off in October, the Chinese community is upset by it. The name of the group that's putting it off is the Open Conceptualists, they're -

—Them? Oswald snorted. —Linda and myself saw them last year, didn't know any better, taken in by the music critic for, ah, for the paper who -

—What paper?

—I forget, Albert, who can tell? They called it a musical, paintings by a group of seven people set to Aboriginal music, costumes, and trees dancing. Experimental stuff, weird.

—This year it's an opera buffa based on The Long March. Mao, China, communism.

—For it or against it?

—The March?

—Communism.

—I don't know, Dad, but I wouldn't think so.

—Just a minute. I didn't know the Chinese calendar was that different from ours. I know they got the year of the ferret, the lion, the panda. Are their months longer too? They must have one hell of a time keeping -

—What are you saying, Stu?

—The long March. Or is it like saying a long hot summer?

—A march, like soldiers march. Philip looked amused.

—Oh.

—We don't get behind that, communism or calendars, understand? Henry, make sure Ben doesn't touch it with a ten-foot pole. Olympus has too many irons in the fire worldwide to get the damned PRC mad at us. Tell O'Reilly to be slightly negative, but subtle, and bury the story in fifth or sixth place whenever it comes up, unless there's death threats or the theatre burns down. This isn't government sponsored, is it?

—Private backers.

—See if they're Taiwanese. Too bad the government isn't in it, there'd be some juice, but we're better off tiptoeing around it, only make sure it doesn't look like it looks like we are.

—Phil, what's an opera buffa?

—It's like an opera, only funny. Stewart brightened. —That's a switch. Last time we went some kid in the back yelled out, Mommy, why's that man making that woman cry?

—You go to the opera, Stu?

—Henry, with Alice pregnant I'll do anything to keep her happy. She's from Toronto, misses shit like that.

—Back to news, please. Phil, what about these policemen?

—It seems there's some thought they might have been depressed.

—Which one?

—The three of them. They were seeing police-appointed counsellors, or had been, then stopped.

—Stopped, or were stopped?

—Stopped.

—Work on that. If we crack that nut it might win us a prize. Bob, oversee Henry and Stewart, make sure things are in place for Dr. Rory and *TTMR*. Keep Otis up to speed. Henry, your big project is figuring out a way to do without so many announcers, how to do the voice tracks.

—What about commercials, Albert? Who'll do them if nobody's left?

—The talent. Work with Bob on how we pay them, talent fee, a flat rate, or commission and a lower flat rate combination. With the refigurations we've talked about we'll have the pick of voices. Now, I think we're in agreement on the main points. CCII has to advance as the parent company advances, otherwise we're nothing. An empire is only as good as its leaders, its initiatives, and its resources. The subjugation of the people helps too. Gibbon said that somewhere, or Machiavelli. But I don't want you to think, because I know how you think, that the axe is being wielded indiscriminately. We've serious, deliberate moves to make in the next six to eight months. When it's over, the land will be peaceful again. Right, that's it. On the point of showing them out Lewis remembered something. —Perry?

—Sir?

—Perry, I was in AM Control recently, and I picked up a cart.

—A cart.

—Cart! The thing the spots are on.

—Yes, no, I didn't hear you the first time. Yes, commercials, and music too.

—What did I see but – wait. I saw – it was for Ukobach Kitchens, and this is what I copied from the label on the cart. Read it exactly as I copied it.

—Q, colon, best in kitchens full stop.

—Agreed, Albert, not very inspired, Continuity -

—That's not the point, Oswald. Otis, who's our major competitor in the Bowmount market?

—CATQ.

—CATQ. Why in God's name does this label say Q, not C-U-E? Can someone give me a good explanation? Henderson ventured to, but Lewis cut him off, tearing the scrap of paper into particles. —Q. From now on, only C-U-E. Understood? I know what it stands for, Bob, but Q is Q and I don't want any goddamn Qs in this building. Henry, take care of that, tell Continuity. Wait, close the door, Oswald. I don't want our plans about automation or what we're doing with CCFP and CCRR noised about. We'll talk about it between ourselves, but not to anyone else. In the newsroom, are any of your people friendly with the *Courier*?

—They talk back and forth, they're friends I guess with everyone.

—I don't want anything getting out in the press, not that damned rag certainly, unless I give the go-ahead. They say Rumour is the swiftest pest. Well, if there are any rumours, I want them kneecapped. When the time is right for publicity, Stewart will handle it. If I read one whisper of my plans in the papers, heads will roll. There was something else on my mind. Otis?

—Dad?

—Whenever that damned paper gets mentioned, things go blank. Why is that?

The reason was not surprising. Hubert Lewis, father of Albert and his dead brother John, had owned both the young CCII and the *Courier*, then a fledgling paper. On the day his children reached their majority, Hubert, serene in the wealth railroads and banking provided, gave Albert the radio network, and placed complete control of the City paper and its rural cousins in John's hands. While not an empire, the press served as an effective organ for John's conservative opinions, particularly for his relentless assault on unions. When older, John decided, like his father, that money interested him more than newspapers. After Hubert Lewis' death John sold the chain to a richer Bowmount businessman. Albert's fury over the disposal of a valuable inheritance lasted some time, but the brothers reconciled on a personal level shortly before John's unexpected death.

Now, it happened that Albert Lewis' wife miscarried three times when carrying their children, a great sorrow to her husband, who believed frailties like this should be disclosed by God before vows were exchanged. When John's widow left the country, taking a share of his estate but leaving their three children orphaned, Lewis raised them as his own. This caused various rumours to float around Bowmount: that he was in fact their father; that John's Parisian wife, Monique, was utterly uninterested in them; that Lewis feared she would kill them through clumsiness; or that this was a commercial transaction worked out with the sister-in-law. In any event, the children were his property, and while the eldest, Alfred, thwarted his adoptive father's empire-building purposes, Otis and Philip accepted them. They acquired Lewis' drive and bloody-mindedness, regrettably not balancing it with an ounce of sensitivity or adroitness in perceiving how or why people felt and behaved as they did. These defects might have been overlooked if Lewis' business incisiveness or rough charm, admired in the masculine boardrooms of Bowmount, had been passed on as well.

As owner of Olympus Communications, Lewis twice tried acquiring the

Courier for the purpose of bequeathing CCII to Otis and the newspapers to Philip. Once he used to watch Frances' pregnant belly, fascinated that therein resided a prince destined to be a king. Porphyrogenitus was superior to primogeniture. While his wife slept one night, Lewis' finger gently traced a crown on the belly over where he imagined the baby's head to be. Careful not to wake her, he mumbled sentiments about being a kingmaker. Through this coronation of, in his favourite historian's phrase, an invisible and insensible sovereign, Lewis felt such surety about the future as he never felt again. After Frances miscarried the last time some life-affirming attribute, perhaps a poorly nourished one, died in her husband, and the passion behind his plans disappeared. When abruptly handed three potential heirs, half-blood but still blood, he took up the opportunity, but without the same fullness of commitment that had stirred him previously. Schemes to ensure legacies and posterity were set out, but the fulfilment of them appealed more to intellectual vanity than heartfelt desire.

Lewis bid in vain on the *Courier* two years ago. The then-owner, —The Mayor's goddamn shatterbrain brother, can you believe it?, he sold it on to —Some bloody foreigner, name of Stephen Karmiris. This man was the influential owner of the Allecto Corporation, but this did not impress Lewis. From then on any mention of the paper was forbidden in his presence, in newscasts unless a libel action had been won against it, and no one was allowed to quote it on air. Lewis shook his head. —I'll remember it, no worry. But back to the other thing I was saying, no one talks, understood? Everyone agreed. —Perry -

—I won't, sir.

—Not that. Come over here. On a console by Lewis' desk stood a stereo system supplemented by a separate receiver that enabled one to listen to the programs sent out by each station in the system. —Stewart, you too. I'm tired of phoning Stewart when Trevelyan gets on a topic I don't want him getting into, or the listeners more to the point. Someone, who, Phil?, said I could get a computer link to the computer in Production Room 3, which is on while he's talking, but that's too clumsy, and besides, I don't want a guest reading a private message from me. Get me a shotgun mike, that's what it's called, Bob?

—Yes, there's such a thing as -

—Fine. Get me one of those, tuned into Trevelyan's headphones, and have it placed out of the way here, so no one else can see it. Headphones too. I want to be able to turn the mike on and say to him, Stop talking about land claims, and hear him answer Yes.

—We can rule out land claims as a topic, Dad.

—No, the point is I want to stop him, not the land claims, they'll never take away my 3,000 acres up north, it's yours and Phil's when I die, but the thing is that the thing I want to do is be able to stop him. Understood, Perry?

—You want me to do that, sir?

—Get the technorats in Engineering on it. Have it hooked up to Stewart's office, and Phil's and Otis' too. I may want to get them on it.

—They don't have earphones, Albert.

—Right, Bob. Get a flashing light in Stewart's office where he can see it but nobody else can so he'll know I want him on the q.t. I'll call everyone else.

—If you get the bugs worked out, I'd love one of those gizmos, Albert.

—Done, Oswald. Got that, Perry? Have that done by – it's 8:40 now, 2:00 this afternoon. Now I remember. Did you notice something different about the room? No one confessed to doing so. —Look at the curtains.

—Where are they? What are those metal things in the wall?

—Over the weekend I had the curtains replaced with custom-made – wait, better to show you – goddamn it, where's the button? You'll appreciate this. Lewis pressed a black knob. A slight humming could be heard, then from each side of the immense picture window slid a folded metal panel that straightened out halfway across, interlocking with its companion. Set off against the office's incarnadine walls and the ruby carpet, the garish geometric forms rendered the viewers speechless. Finally Perry asked what they were looking at. —*Being There*, by a fellow named Matta. I saw it in a book at Oldford's Art House, and had someone make a copy on metal. It took a while but it's worth it.

—Snazzy purchase, Albert.

—It's not a purchase, it's art, Oswald. Lewis pressed a second knob and the panels retreated, humming. -That's it. Otis, let's take a walk.

—Do you need me for anything, sir?

—Perry, get some air, you look like you're boiling. That's it for now. We'll talk more about what we've discussed as the summer rolls on. This has been the best idea-generating dawn meeting in a while. The door opened and everyone left except Otis. —Dad, is there something you wanted to talk about?

—Not a thing.

—Do you just want to be with -

—Otis, if I walk through the building with Oswald, the staff thinks one thing, and relaxes. If I walk with you, they think another thing, and that thing is what I want them to think. We're not going to talk, there's no business to take care of. The staff will see us and start thinking. See what I mean? Otis shook his head. —You'll soon understand.

Directly after the meeting the station manager and the sales manager sat in Henderson's office. —Can you believe what we heard today? Fire salesmen, with the help of that idiot?

—He's up to something.

—Where'd he get the notion computers can run everything? That's not a radio station, not to me! Is he trying to ruin the business? Henderson looked around, though the office door was closed. —Can you keep something to yourself? Bennett nodded as he blew his nose. —Remember in January these three guys from the Middle East visited, Elect Enterprises.

—Yeah, two Syrians, were they?, and the Iranian. He was a fierce-looking fucker. They were friends of Albert's on vacation.

—It was a buying trip. The whole network, split off from Olympus.

—What? How much did they offer?

—I don't know, but enough. Albert didn't go for it, for two reasons. First, the financing of the deal, but that could have been worked out. The head guy, Manny, the Iranian, told me that privately. But the reason things didn't go through was because there'd be firings.

—They wanted you and me gone? How would they know what I've put into this place? Bastards, they – but Albert stayed by us, good, makes me think differently about him.

—Elect pulled out when Albert said his nephews had to stay. They didn't want to be stuck with them, and said no. So now he's chopping staff, getting more computers, and what have those two guys been studying for three years at company expense? Systems analysis, computer installation, not the day-to-day affairs of CCII. The less staff who know anything about broadcasting, the more valuable the nerds become to another buyer. Visions of aborted futures filled Bennett's head. —Explains a helluva lot, Bob. Because of those two, CCII has to change, and CCFP and CCRR get the shaft.

—That's about it.

—I wouldn't do that for my kids. Nephews. Is it only me, or do you get creeped out when they call him Dad?

—If they called me Dad I'd shoot them. About the deal, I know how you're feeling, I went through it myself in January and February. You're the only one I've told, the only one who'll keep it to himself.

—Now we're working to make sure we save everything for those two pricks. Never worked a sale, never been on air, never did anything, and they're going to take over.

—But you and me, we've only got a few more years to put in, then we can forget it all. Let them do what they want.

—Bad enough with Albert lately, he has a head on him, but those two, Christ. I hate the future and it isn't even here yet.

—You see Perry? Almost passing out in there. I wonder what he knows.

—Rat bastard. But the suckhole doesn't like that office, does he?

—The jocks have a name for it, The Court of the Crimson King.

—That's good! The green looked better. Say! He changed it around in December, didn't he? Just in time for Elect to come bend their knee to him and his princes.

—The Iranian thought he had an in with Albert. Between you and I, they were probably looking for a safe place to dump their money and buy their residence in Canada.

—This makes my day. All I needed was to mention Karmiris in there.

—You almost did.

—Yeah, but when he does, it's all right! Figure that out. There's another strange one. Does anybody know anything for sure about the guy?

—Are you thinking of changing places? Stick with the devil you know. I hear Karmiris is Armenian, or Greek. When he was born depends on who's talking.

—I bet you he doesn't have a painting like, what was it, *Being There*, in his office. Did Albert pay whoever owns it for permission to copy it?

—The Lewises own people who live in the gray zone. The guy must've taken months copying that. You can bet it cost a fair chunk of change. Henderson sighed as he went over to his desk. —We'd better get to work on this shiny new machine.

—Reinventing the wheel.

—Remember we talked about Hilary? Henderson passed over two yellow sheets. —Look at these. Bennett read them. —What the hell?

—They were in with the copy.

—There a message here? Henderson shrugged. —I'm returning them without asking. See the books Hilary reads?

—Screwy. There's something else, Bob. I didn't want to say this with Perry around. Keith Flynn worked late Saturday night after a remote, doing a bit of paperwork. Says he saw the FM jock getting it off with someone.

—What?

—Keith was heading for the Control Room to say hi, and through the glass he sees this woman doing a lap dance on Dennis Hare.

—Dennis' wife, in here doing that?

—Keith doesn't know Dennis' wife. All he saw was someone riding Hare in the chair. She had her back to him. They didn't see him, lot of the lights were off in the corridor, and he said the overheads were off in the Control Room, too. Just a lamp on. Why's that?

—Some all-night jocks like to get a mood established.

—It works. What are you gonna do about it?

—Oz, I'll talk with Henry and let him handle it. Den's an asshole. Anyone could've walked in there on him.

—If I said this in the meeting, you know Albert would have gone berserk, fired Dennis himself. He'd tell Otis to have Maintenance scrape the chair for stains.

—Thanks for mentioning it in private.

—We got enough trouble already. A few minutes later Bob Henderson stood in the middle of the Continuity office, the cryptic papers laid on Hilary's desk, watching through glass a stranger lecture Harvey Cox. —Mare, what's going on in there?

—Mr. Henderson, sorry I'm late, my car, Christ. I don't know what's – do you want me to open the hatch so you can hear?

—I'll go around. Pushing open the door to Production Room 1 Henderson saw Cox backed up against cabinets containing reel-to-reel tapes on which were the jingles of national and provincial advertisers. Tyrone Vann happened to follow the station manager in. A middle-aged man had a finger pointed at Harvey's chest. —Don't you see? Here I am again, and the script is the same, and what does it say? I can recite it backwards! It says that by the time I finish speaking, 400 or 500 children will have died from malaria, typhoid, cholera, plague, scurvy, malnourishment, and whatever else the Worldwide Health Watch Fund says is killing people, and the thing is, Mr. Cox, the thing that has me thinking is, what if I didn't say anything, would they die? You see? I hear my voice in the car radio as I drive by the homeless and the hospitals and I think, will they die if I say anything to my wife and our three-year old, which I do less and less, and that's causing problems, and I've been doing this now for WHWF for four years and it's a little long, don't you think? So when you asked me to do a third take I had to hurry in and simply let you know that what you're asking means 1,500 or 2,000 children could, might, conceivably die, even before the appeal gets aired, and I can't have any more blood than absolutely necessary on my conscience. Do you see what I mean? I'm responsible for so many deaths already, not that I went out and killed them, but when people learn I'm the spokesman they say, Oh, you're the one, and I know what's in their minds. Don't get me wrong, I'm not insane. These deaths just happen while I'm talking, and I don't want to be doing that anymore, but because I'm on contract for another year I'd *appreciate* a little *understanding* from *you*, so don't make me do these things over and over and over and over again and again! Do you understand!? Do you?

Mare, Megan and Hilary were looking through their glass window, and Ben Trevelyan in Production Room 3, ready to go live across the province, watched too. Rick, a young man taping feeds from satellites in Production Room 5, scratched his head at what he saw. In Production Room 2 sheets were thrown on the floor next to a tipped over chair. For most of the spectators, the tirade was in dumb show. Tyrone stepped forward and gripped the weeping man's arms, while Henderson pulled the recording engineer safely away, though what danger there was had passed. —You all right?

—He comes in like he's on speed, starts screaming, jabbing me with his finger. I felt like hitting him but you never know what Lewis' insurance covers. Just get him out of here, would you?

—Tyrone.

—Come with me, Mr . . . Come with me. One step after the other, that's
– Perry! Open the door, will you?

—Oh my, what have you said now?

—Just try and help, would you?

—Not that I care too much right now, but the spots, Bob, who's going to do them? Tyrone's the only one around. Boy, I'm shaking.

—Take a break, Harvey, sit down. Guy just snapped?

—Like a firecracker. The still-open door let in Tyrone and Perry's argument. —What do you do around here? I'm supposed to record some ads, you just told me you were strolling around in the sun, so you could take this poor fellow back to your office and get him a lousy cup of coffee, couldn't you? Exhibit some Christian charity.

—Foist him off on me, why that's -

—Perry! Do as he asks! Perry looked somewhat ugly about it, but obeyed Henderson. Tyrone stepped back inside. —Some people have no compassion. To the various glass surfaces lined with faces Tyrone yelled, —Haven't you seen anyone crack before? Get back to work! Stop looking!

—Tyrone. Ty!

—Yes. Bob, I'm -

—You -

—He reminded me of – it's not the first time I've seen that kind of be-haviour.

—What's new in boxes, huh, Uncle Lou?

—Not much, Papa Smurf. The familiar routines brought out wan smiles. —And this is only Monday, Henderson said, the lunacy of the en-tire morning hitting him. The three men were relieved to find something funny. —Where in my job description does it say I get attacked by voices for relief organizations, Bob? I'm a producer, not a – they pay people to handle nut-cases. Who's going to protect me from every Tom, Dick and Harry with a gripe?

—They're called station managers, Harv. Henderson could not assume Tyrone was joking. Grimly he thought of automation, and the nephews. Who the hell was protecting anybody?

The talent in the bar

I vy Merifield contemplated Camilla's fiancé, thinking again how Camilla continually threatened to divulge some dark secret, undoubtedly seamy, that would reveal the dynamics of their romantic relationship. Stray ends of conversations in the lunchroom of Holdsforth, Tugge & Maw, Image Consultants, could have been joined together if Ivy wanted, but private lives were meant to remain exactly that. Why didn't people expose less sensational matter, sharing their deeper natures instead? Unless, charming thought, people nowadays didn't live rich lives. Did Stan, for instance, possess something unique that touched Cam's heart in a singular way? Glancing at him over her Perrier amidst this crowd of strangers, Ivy decided that Stan acted about the same as every other man around. Did any of them have one exceptional quality? Even the women were undistinguished, with the possible exception of her friend. Ivy knew she was being overly critical, and she corrected herself, as she often did when pessimism dominated her usual nature. Statistically, some of the people here were probably fine enough, but who, seriously, could have met her criteria as a person she'd really want to know? She crunched ice between her teeth, savouring the chill on her tongue. A man, not one man, out of all of them, worth my time. Isn't it amazing? I'd ask Cam about this if I didn't know the response. Her friend would say that Ivy had fashioned herself as some impossible throwback figure who, in the 1990s, came off as faintly ludicrous or pathetic, and in a certain sense this might be seen as true. For Ivy had decided years ago that the only man she would marry would be one who, firstly, respected her enough to wait until wedding night before knowing her carnally, hopefully appreciating his almost-virgin bride; and secondly, would understand her quest for a fulfilling, she was afraid to say spiritual, life. Was there such a man around who would not be jealous of this, who could accept it? Was there one person in this room who might conceivably comprehend her pursuit? Her man, if he existed, would not be among that unpleasant-looking trio at the far end of the bar, for instance.

Camilla and Stan rejoined her, and Ivy caught her reflection in a mirror. A virago, she thought, which could mean something good if I wasn't almost forty and didn't crave male companionship so terribly. No, not terribly, let's not overstate it, Ivy, but someone to be with, because the world is vicious when uninteresting. —You having a good time? Stan laid a second Perrier near her empty glass. —Yes, thanks. She seized the lemon slice and chewed it before the mineral water leached away its bitterness. —It's a nice place, isn't it? Ivy nodded. —Very distinctive music, she got out, depositing lemon seeds in her first glass while a woman sang a song about a fair in an encouraging fashion.

—No rock and roll or pop, right Johnny?

—Right. I don't recognize you, though. You're friends of -

—Camilla, and Stan.

—I'm Johnny, this is my place. Haven't seen you around here.

—Ivy. I'm more a coffee person.

—Nice name, Old-fashioned, in a good way. The neighbourhood's going coffee. I'm selling more wine than I ever did, and orders for coffee? I've been thinking, with me being Italian, setting up a trattoria, convert the place. Yuppies love them, and with -

—That's you, Ivy.

—Stan!

—With my Italian ancestry, I could do this place up special. In Mediterranean colours, no cracked columns, none of that. Tasteful. Come August I'm going to start.

—During the Race, Johnny? You tear the place up and we'll lose prime seats!

—After, after. There was a shout from the rough end of the bar. —Duty calls. Enjoy your drink, Miss. Hope to see you again. Frank, what'll it be?

—Miss? Did he -

—His eyes aren't so good.

—Stan, will you – he shouldn't be taken out, Ivy.

—Just joking. Johnny's like that with most women he sees for the first time. Then he gets their names down pat. The three sipped in silence till the fair closed. —Camilla says you're not dating now.

—You don't mind, do you Ivy? I thought, you never have any luck at your regular places, a new scene might help.

—I go there for the coffee. No, Stan, I'm not seeing anyone currently. Why, do you see anyone who might be interesting? At once she wished she had bitten her tongue in half, for like an earnest retriever Stan gestured at this and that table, physically saying that the world was her oyster. —Jeez, there's plenty of guys here know how to treat a girl right.

—What about women, any of them know -

—I meant to say that. You like painters? There's two over there with Harry. Not hard to pick them out.

—Stan, he doesn't have any money. The one with the glasses is Sam Tynbourn, and he paints Christs. The other one in the matching spattered overalls is Fred Rifkind, a house painter. What a set.

—They don't look very happy.

—Oh no, Sam looked at you, Ivy, I hope – no, it's okay. Fred's in trouble with the City, isn't he? Stan explained that Fred had painted flames coming out of the door and front windows of his house, a lark, and people took it wrongly, calling the fire department so often they called the Council, and jeez, who could fight Mayor Runciman and stupid councillors who couldn't take a joke and wanted to poke their noses into everybody's business? —The third fella's Harry, he's getting into your business.

—What?

—He's partners in this new firm, Virgil-Lawson, they're gonna do third-party advertising, p.r. for local groups, activists, handle their commercials and set up campaigns.

—What about that table? No, the other one.

—Loyola Holden's the young guy, okay enough, but the older guy, what a character. Jules Deeka. No one knows what he does, how he makes money. He has some kind of degree. The black-haired girl, her name's Kate, the one next to her's Nadeen -

—Yes, Cam! I thought she looked familiar. Remember me telling you? She has that installation at the Brogan of black-and-white and colour photographs -

—Celebrities?

—It's a muffler and tailpipe lying in a road, Jackson Close I think it is. It lay there for over a year, and she took a picture almost every day, then later a video of it.

—She put it there? How many pictures?

—Hundreds, and no, she found it there.

—And she didn't move it out of the way? Cars could have run over it.

—Cars did run over it, Stan, that was her point.

—You paid to look at hundreds of things a mechanic sees free every-day? That's art?

—Not hundreds, Stan, about seventy-five, a selection, from different seasons. Sarkissian, that's her name. She says she felt like a witness, to what she didn't know, whether it was indomitable will or a metaphor for oppression, living in a harsh world. I liked it, I think Cam you'd like it too. It makes you think about our place in society. They had an article on it in the *Courier*.

—Seems pretty far out to me, Ivy. Anyway, where was I? The other two women came in when we were getting the drinks, I think I heard the blond one call Loyola her cousin. Don't know the other. Over there is Al Ducey, a telesalesman, he's talking to Bart, who jerked off in a confessional.

—Disgusting person, Ivy. Imagine shaking his hand. They barred him from St. Finnian's.

—I used to go there.

—Everybody used to go there. I went until - you know, with Dad being the way he is, and then the changes. You know they got rid of the side chapels, and that beautiful altar rail?

—I'd heard, but are the priests really as poor as they say?

—Father Jerome is this little dog following Archbishop Mason's lead. Now, there's a fascist, Mason. I go to St. Lawrence's.

—Then there's Jack Morgan, he's missing a couple of teeth, but he hides it by gluing, get this, gluing white cardboard to what he has left. Yeah, I felt the same way. There's some people I don't know, Jimmy and Wes, two losers. That's Phil Horne sitting with the black woman.

—She's an Arab, Stan, Phil told me.

—No, she's African. At the look on Camilla's face Stan said he might be wrong. —He's taken. Not a bad guy. Next to them are Priscilla Hebert and Jochen Garcia.

—Who?

—We call 'em the Spanish Frog, on – ow, Camilla! Jeez, I was just having a little fun. Ivy asked about the men at the end of the bar. —Them? Don't say anything to the guy with his back to us. Stan was whispering, Camilla followed his example, and everything they said was lost under the musical admiration shown an indomitable red, red robin. —I hear he's going out with an Indian. This report surfaced after a blare of horns subsided.

—Native, or Indian?

—Calcutta or Bangladesh, some city like that.

—Who told you that? Harry, I suppose.

—Vic. What do you have against Harry?

—He thinks the sun rises and sets on Harry.

—I respect him, like I respect anybody smart, like your father.

—You respect Dad?

—When he's not boring me with his stories, yeah, sure. This mention of family gave Ivy a chance to ask if Camilla's father was better. —Not really. He sits there looking lost. Do you want to hear something? Her face grew severe, a look her friend recognized, one Stan knew too well. —Next Sunday is Father's Day, so I asked Mom what she was doing for it. Dad was getting groceries, and she and Aunt Urs were playing crib. Mom says, Dear, I hadn't thought of doing anything. I suggest a turkey dinner, Dad's favourite, and Mom said she supposed she could do something like that.

Can you believe it? Then, when I said, I hope you do something, it's Father's Day after all, Aunt Urs lays down her cards and tells me, in my parents' home, sitting in a chair my Father paid for, But Camilla, you have to understand, our Father's dead.

—What did you say?

—That woman can so piss me off. I said, Well, my Father is alive, thank you very much, Aunt Urs, and he's married to my mother. That selfish witch.

—Did she -

—Ivy, she picked up her cards and smiled and said it was a daughter's place to do something for her Father. I could have strangled her. Partly 'cause she's right, I should do more.

—Was your mother -

—She drinks more than she breathes some days. Ivy tried other topics but each brought out splenetic comments from her companions. —Just what I needed tonight, she said in the bathroom mirror at Johnny's. —God give me strength. Returning to her friends she cast an envious eye on the tables where creative people sat, for she knew a painter would have some-thing significant to say, then looked at Sarkissian, being deeply kissed by that man who, for unknown reasons, embodied for Ivy Poe's Imp of the Perverse. A photographer and a painter would have learned about the in-ner aspects of life through what they encountered in the creative realm. They could guide Ivy to a new way of thinking, so that she would envy no more those who lived adventurously, and live peacefully as who she was. In fact, as Ivy took up her third glass of mineral water, Fred and Sam were closing an investigation of the properties and attributes of oils, which the latter decided would fit his triptych. —But I still need a model, and Sam's eyes again caught and threw away Ivy's form, —someone for the Virgin.

—And Jesus?

—Found him at an art school exhibit, one of the spectators. Cheaper, too.

—Tickled fuckin pink I suppose to be asked, he isn't a fruit though, didn't take you for one, you won't get in some kind of trouble?

—No, why I, no, not like – I said he could bring his wife, girlfriend, whatever, if they didn't move around much. I need a Magdalene, too.

—My boy, go out to Church Street, you'll find Mary Magdalenes everywhere you look. Depends what part of the scale you can afford. Now, there's an idea, hire a hooker. No inhibitions about stripping, and if she likes your work you might get a free -

—Harry.

—Trying to help. You look hungry, doesn't he, Fred? Sylvie! Let me get you something. With this new job I feel great. Job? A career! Another chance to put what I know into use. We'll make the establishment notice, you wait. But enough about what I think about my future, what do you think about my future? Hahahaha! Sylvie, four club sandwiches. Come on Fred, you look like a bucket of gall. What are you going to do about your house?

—What fuckin else can I do but change it? Fire department, fuckers, but wait, I'll screw them. Made an eyesore they said in the neighbourhood, I'll give them an eyesore. One big fuckin eyesore. He drained his Black Dog beer. —You betcha. Rifkind behaved strangely enough when happy, but when sullen he had to be handled carefully. Though ebullient over his new occupation, Harry felt bad he couldn't jolly his companions, particularly Sam, out of their funks, so settled to quietly eating supper.

Sam ate the two sandwiches without tasting them, his mind focused on a disturbing problem. When the inspiration for the triptych came last year it seemed a worthy subject that would test all his abilities. He thought that creating a new image of the Holy Family in today's secular milieu, apart from being an expression of faith, would be almost a miraculous achievement, given the history and wealth of their pictorial representation, let alone the pictures people carried around in their own hearts. Harry scoffed at Sam's reading of the Bible; in truth, the impulse for painting the Holy Family undoubtedly had been reinforced by dismissive opinions about God and the role of Christ. This new age yearned for worshipful art, at the same time demanding a scrupulous representation of itself. In the rough sketches made last winter, Sam captured the essence of the projected work, the shape of the bodies, the emotions of the figures, the perspectives, and his soul trembled in jubilant expectation at the imminent release of a flood of energies. It was as though once the brushes and paints were chosen the transference of spiritual craving to paper would result in a mesmerizing and profound display of belief and insight.

Plainly, this had not happened. It did not look likely to happen, for things had come up. By things Sam meant Discord, Scandal. His vision, once tangible, had suffered a brutal death, and lay buried in a deep grave, under a headstone which bore the deceiving words, Aesthetic Problems. I could find a Madonna if I wasn't so picky, and I've a Jesus, so can a Magdalene be far behind? Oil, watercolour, acrylic, gouache – does it matter any more? Sam's fine idea was now a tattered dream, its pieces scattered by the winds of buggery, sadism, hypocrisy, and deception that swept through Christianity. He put it to himself this way. The Holy Family for such a debased religion? What in God's name could it be portrayed as but some postmodern, blasphemous nightmare, where a cuckolded Joseph tattooed Mary with bruises and molested his step-child, creating a father-killer, driving mother and son, already linked by divinity, to incest? Yes, the triptych had changed, the first panel depicting a sickly child held protectively in the blackened arms of a sobbing woman while her husband railed with fists raised. The seduction in the temple would be the second panel, and the third would show the hungry coupling of twin idols over the abusive father's grave while a junkie streetwalker watched. Jesus in the only family possible for one such as him, the family he would never have chosen but to which he always returned, in his special case through the force majeure of a witless, harried Social Worker Supervisor blind to the pain and the suffering.

Was this what that fine burst of inspiration had become, promising flowers but delivering stinking weeds? After saying he would paint such-and-such from passion and commitment, Sam could now only conceive its radical opposite, drawn from impotent rage and disillusionment. How many times had he refrained from outlining a project for precisely the reason that if he didn't do it, people would think he had failed? Sam knew this made him look dimwitted, but rather that than be seen as a talker over a doer. Faced with this impossible project his mind chattered ceaselessly about what he should do. A new gallery expected the work by November for a show on contemporary spiritual art. If he painted what he saw right now, it would further junk the Holy Family, which had never been his aim. In his opinion, Christianity had descended from a vibrant world religion to an artefact from a bygone age, an amusing object in today's world, like primary school textbooks call forth nostalgia in people finished with university. Sam wanted a replacement vision, but he could not find a new vessel for his faith by next week, become a Muslim, say, so what must he do?

Food, ale, and Harry's booster mentality failed to provide consolation. Events, reappraisals, soured everything, and it would take some doing, Sam thought, for any respectable conceptualization of Christianity to occupy his imagination again. Shards of past canvasses by the masters and shreds of bitter thoughts occupied his mind, and he would have been absorbed by them if there hadn't been so much hilarity from where Loyola and his friends were. That party of six were enjoying talking about funerals. —Best one I ever went to, Loyola said, —there was this guy lying in the casket. The room was jammed. People from all over Bowmount there to look at him. The widow, she was standing next to the open coffin, right next to the kneeler, when this -

—A kneeler, I'd forgotten about that. Perhaps due to her successful show Nadeen's voice had gained power, or else she always talked at this volume when she felt comfortable with people. —I gave that up in Cyprus. The Orthodox Church, there's a corrupt group. Roman Catholics have nothing on them.

—Yeah, anyway, this woman came up and said a prayer. When she finished she talked to the widow. She knew her, I think, not the dead guy. I could hear them. She said, How sorry I am for you. Tell me, did he die of anything serious? The table erupted, startling Rifkind, who swore about black eyes and grabbed the neck of a fresh Black Dog bottle. —The widow, she nearly fainted, and the woman turned redder than, than Nadeen's top.

—When I was young I consorted with selected young men solely because of their available sisters. They were procurers without knowing it. Jules smiled at the memory. —One day the father of one of these lads died, a big man, tall, blocky, a miner. This was in Scanlon Ridge. There was only one funeral home. Our black-garbed, insipid-faced recycler of deposited flesh ran a monopoly. I was a friend of the family, and went along the day the body was brought to him. The funeral director measured the father, then said to the three daughters and two sons, who were big-boned like their old man, We don't have a casket in the place that can fit him. I can have one made, but it's going to cost more, I'm afraid. One of the daughters, a sharp wit, said, excuse me, but couldn't you just shave a little off the side? I've never seen an undertaker blanch, he couldn't get a word out. Jules wiped away tears as he led the laughter. —I always liked that girl, too bad she died so young. Kate looked away, not because a sentimental note had been interjected, but because no one important in her family had died. As she turned, she noticed Janet kept a close eye on Loyola, so she touched his hand to remind him he was on her mind.

—Around here there's the phenomenon of the bog-Irish, since their last ancestors to see the Emerald Isle died in 1824 or something. Jules cleared his throat. —At their wakes you look for malcontents, will-squabblers, offspring of incest, autistics, alkies. At one of these affairs in came this rotund gentleman who put his card in the stand by the door before making his way to the coffin. Everyone looked at him, but they all thought someone there was his friend. By the time they realized he didn't know anyone there, he'd knelt to say a prayer. It was a very long prayer. He got up, then for the first time looked at who he'd been interceding for. He stood there for a minute with this peculiar look on his face. People thought something was happening, so they waited. He turned around, made his way through the crowd to the stand, and left, withdrawing his sympathy card as he disappeared around the corner. He'd come into the wrong room, you see.

—Well, *I* have one, let's see. This guy at work told me last week his aunt was in hospital, because she'd been hit by a truck.

—Janet, that was Steve, wasn't it?

—You haven't heard the worst. She went to hospital, nothing serious, just a broken arm and some bruised ribs, they thought. Doctors. That *Medic Alert* book was right. So he's telling me this, that she walked to the store to get some bread, and I don't know *why*, I lost my head, I said, I hope it wasn't a bread truck that hit her. Can you believe it? Glasses rattled on the table, and Janet's laughter drew the attention of single men in the bar. Ivy congratulated herself on not being born a blond. —That's the reporter in you.

—*No*, Jules! But wait, there's more. I sat there and heard myself ask this, and Steve looked at me, he couldn't believe I was saying it, *me* of all people -

—Why's that surprising? Janet's attention was on Jules and Loyola, not on Kate. —But then his aunt went and died on me, after making this re-mark, and I can hardly *look* at him. It's so inconvenient, we work together all the time. Who'd think she'd die from that?

—She probably bled to death.

—Don't get started on blood stories, please. I hate the sight of it. Kate looked around for sympathy. Krysta, Janet's friend, had a bored smile on her face, for she was looking forward to the party the two of them were invited to, which she reminded her friend about.

—And we have to be going too, said Nadeen, —to see this friend whose brother is at a funeral home. Though how we'll keep a straight face -

—Think of the poor man as a car part, offered Janet, winking at Loyola.

—That won't be very nice for the family, and they're good friends of mine, Kate reminded her. —Loyola, I'll call tomorrow. He nodded, perhaps embarrassed because Janet saw how he regretted Kate's leaving. —Sure, around noon? They kissed, and Kate and Nadeen stepped away from the table. Janet rose also and told Loyola she would pick him up for the Camp-bell get-together next week, quickly leaving a maroon imprint on his cheek which registered on Kate as well. As the women went out in pairs, a long-haired young man aged twenty entered with a guitar, the instrument's burnished neck with a gold inlay flashing in the summer sun that streamed through the windows. With him was a tall, swarthy woman eighteen years old.

—Mikey! How are you?

—Hey, Uncle John, great to see you! Do you mind -

—Mind? Everyone, listen up! Johnny stopped the taped music. —This is my nephew, Mike, and his friend, Judith Weinberg. He's trying to get him-self through music school, and I told him he could come in here and roust some of you. Judith's going to pass the hat, so don't go asking for change, and I think, right, Mike?, she's selling needle sets or something for $4 a pop. Be respectful, he's family and she's a deaf-mute. Watch what you say, she can read lips.

—What's he going to play?

—The guitar, Al, what does it look like? What does it matter, he's going to play, you listen, and make a charitable donation. Least you can do for all the times I close up late.

—Jules, you want to cut out before -

—Let's stick around and listen to El Kabong.

—Mike, couldn't you find a nice Italian girl? Where'd you meet her?

—Vic, how are you? She's not my girlfriend, just a friend. She's Israeli, came here two months ago with her parents, they work at the College, I'm showing her around.

—Music teachers? That'd be tragic. Johnny tapped a glass loudly on the bar. —No need to make fun of the girl. Mikey, do your thing.

—Thanks, Uncle John. First, are there any tourists in here? Anybody from . . . Carlyle? His face radiated confidence and serenity, and he took the good-natured catcalls and hissing well. —This song is for anybody like myself who ever wanted to roam the world, like I'm going to do.

—Don't let your mama hear you say that. She'll worry herself sick.

—This is called In Search of Home. He strummed once, adjusted the top string, and began playing chords fast, setting down the rhythm and struc-ture before singing. As he played, Judith went round the room with an old top hat garlanded with a string of orange paper flowers, smiling as she placed it before this or that person.

> *Take me to another land where no one knows my person.*
> *Escort me to a far country where no one's heard my name.*
> *Perhaps there I can bury my past, in a country new and vast,*
> *Or else I'll roam again, take leave and roam again.*

> *Trace a route through the three Romes or cross the Inner Ocean.*
> *Join an Egyptian caravan, it's all the same to me.*
> *An unknown land, a far-off desert, so long as there's no past or present,*
> *Or else I'll roam again, take leave and roam again.*

> *Don't presume that I'm running away,*
> *From a life I'm too cowardly to stand*
> *This is not an odyssey, not a spiritual journey,*
> *It's going where my life begins, so I won't roam away*

> *No heart's been broken forevermore, there's no one crying over me.*
> *No bloody crime of lust or greed will ever be blamed on me.*
> *This is no shadow of deception, instead a deepening depression, which*
> *Makes me roam again, take leave and roam again.*

> *You ask what I'm searching for as if the answer must be novel.*
> *A heart, a home, a friendly land where life will take on meaning.*
> *I expect too much, is that what you say? No such place exists today.*
> *Then damn, I roam again, I'm damned to roam again.*

> *Don't presume that I'm running away*
> *From a life I'm too cowardly to stand*

This is not an odyssey, not a spiritual journey,
It's going where my life begins, so I won't roam away.

Mike finished with a flourish, and the audience clapped enthusiastically, if not so much for the song, then for the performer's spunk. Ivy admired this young man's mobile, sensual face, and even more the blond hair which reached his waist. How much time does he spend on that? If the difference between them wasn't so great – but she'd have to spend so much time training him. The relationship would be tiring, pleasurably so in some ways for the first few months, but still. Think sensibly, Ivy, use your head. There was so much he had to learn before he could be presentable to her friends, her parents. There was no denying he could stir the heart, or something, of girls, with those tresses. She only hoped he wasn't gay, not that it mattered to her, but it would be a shame. She was going to try and forget the sudden flush of spirits brought on by the boy.

Pops rapped his cane on a table. Johnny went over to him. —What's the matter? You're going to split that table, and who'll pay for it? Use the floor if you have to, but what's the fuss?

—He calls that music? He studies that? Get that hat away from me, that's not a song. *Stardust*, that's a song. Handel, Mozart, they're composers. That? What's that? Mike clapped the old man on the shoulder, for the two knew each other well. —We study them too, Pops, but every troubadour has to say his own thing, in his own way. I'll play one more just for you, something sentimental, and you be nice to Judith, don't give her a hard time. He started playing a mid-tempo tune in G-minor.

It started that night with too much to drink,
At a party it advanced to the brink
They continued at home where she suddenly said
A few words which cut him dead
Memories she'd put aside, so he thought,
Soon surfaced once more.
The name escaped her lips while they fought

Of a man he had come to abhor.

The first name on the tip of her tongue
Wasn't his, it never had been.
Her soul and heart were forever won
By a man dead for so many years.

Throughout their marriage she'd imagined the dead
Taking the place of the living some time
Could it truly be as she now said,
"The fault is yours and not mine.
If once you had been kinder to me
Memories of him might have passed
But he stands there like a monument
To the strength and tenderness you've never had.

"What do I do now?" she addresses the room,
"After years of sweetly-spun lies.
I've no more energy for starting again
And no good reason to try."
He hears this and starts to cry.

The first name on the tip of her tongue
Wasn't his, it never had been.
Her soul and heart were forever won
By a man dead for so many years.

This time Pops did not mind donating to Mike's fund, and as for the others, they added a little bit more to the hat. Sam tugged at Harry's arm.
—How much money do you have on you?
—About - wait now, you're not going to give it all to that guy -
—The girl, the girl, she's . . . Sam's eyes could not leave her.
—She's selling needles, so be careful, if she sees how you're looking at

her she'll probably stick one in your eye. Look, here, $20, is that enough? Sam scribbled his address on a piece of paper and waited for Judith to come by. When she did, he folded the bill around the note and gave it to her, making rough gestures with his hands. Red-gold-brown-coloured fingers stumbled as Sam tried to remember sign language. She replied, amused at this attempt, pleased, but at the same time wary of this stranger's eagerness. —You'd be better off telling Mike, or Johnny, Sam. But Sam paid no attention. Years ago, when art instructor at a camp for the hard of hearing, he had learned sign, and though rusty, the vocabulary had not left him entirely. Judith watched him, looked at the note, then beckoned Mike over. —Some trouble here?

—No, I -

—Sam, let me, you're flustered. Mike, is it? Hi, I'm Harry, your uncle knows me, knows the two of us. My friend here, Sam Tynbourn, he's a painter, and -

—He wants a Virgin, contributed Rifkind, barely looking at Judith. Mike tilted his head purposefully, the attempt to look tough defeated by his hair. Harry waved his hands, sloshing his drink. —Don't mind that guy. Sam's looking for a Virgin Mary. Look at his hands, he's a painter. He'd doing a painting of Christ, see, and he's been having a hard time finding a model for the Virgin Mary. I think he wants your friend to pose for him, for it I mean. Strictly on the up-and-up. I think he gave her his address and $20 for you, so you can see he's not a bad painter if he has $20 to toss around.

—Is that right, mister?

—About the modelling, yes, her features are classic, perfect, I've been trying to - if you want you, or her parents, they can see what else I've done. She has - Judith has my address -

—I'll make sure she understands, and that it gets to her parents, and is this nude stuff?

—It's the Virgin Mary, why would I paint her nude? No, this is - she'll be closed, yes. Clothed, I mean.

—He's a bit excited. Rifkind snorted over Harry's explanation. —Relieved, I mean. Rifkind snorted again, and drank half a bottle of beer.

—Your phone number's down here, yeah, all right. Twenty dollars? Thanks, thanks a lot. See ya round. Mike and Judith went up to the bar, a fresh round of applause greeting the musician. —Uncle John, thanks for the chance.

—You come back Wednesday, there's lots of people with pay cheques in then.

—I have something to ask you. Bending over the bar the nephew quizzed the uncle about Sam. When finished, Mike and Judith were ready to leave but Frank stopped them, asking if they would join him in a drink. —Maybe you might get a song out of one of my stories. You types are always looking for material, aren't you? Like Woody Guthrie? Johnny shook his head behind Frank's back but though Judith saw this Mike did not, and to be polite they sat down at the bar.

Often Frank frightened people with his moods, his fits of inexplicable laughter, the things he did and said he did, and no one predicted a good end for him but one of the two people in his company this evening, Buster, who also once said, —He's strange, but he's solid about that, you know? It's like whatever's in him will come out, you always know how he feels, he puts his whole fucking heart on a table for you to see.

—Don't always like seeing it, the other friend there tonight had replied. —He has more guts than you'll ever have, Ivan, best part of you ran down your father's legsky, see?

—Can it, Buster.

—You're jealous 'cause he gets girls. What are you stuck with? Business women think they're getting some down-on-his-luck Russian, when you've never seen Russia, you only speak it 'cause your folks were too stuck-up to learn English. How do you stand those women with their asses hanging low enough to get splinters? I'd be pretty sick of myself going around with them, call yourself an escort, gigolo's more like it.

—Watch your fucking mouth, least I can hold down a job.

—Call that a job? That's just sick, that's what it is.

This night, with money in his wallet and a new audience, Frank felt good. The sun and the bar lights gleamed off his bald, onion-shaped head, animating his heavy-set face with its piercing black eyes and full brown moustache. He drained the last of a rum-and-coke, setting the glass down delicately. Loyola and Jules, positioned close to the bar, were among the few outside Frank's immediate circle who heard his tale. —There was this girl, she was in a store the first time I saw her, with this punk, looked like an imbecile, father and mother were brother and sister if you know what I mean. This was the usual description of anyone standing in Frank's way. —Got a look at her. In this public place, a card shop, where I was buying a card for Mother's Day, she had on a thin blue t-shirt that stopped above her bellybutton, and cut-off jeans for shorts. With rips and tears in them, okay?

—How old was she? Frank considered Buster's question. —Fifteen, no more. She was wandering round looking at birthday cards, well, what else is there to look at. I saw her from back on, didn't get a good look at her face, she had curly brown hair. Those rips were all over her jeans, and she'd cut out a hole in the backside.

—No.

—Yes! There was this hole, not a patch over it, no threads, a hole. You guys are thinking, That's not a lot to get worked up over, except she wasn't wearing underwear. Frank was pleased with the significant muttering. —She was busy talking to her mongoloid friend, and I was sizing up her bare ass.

—I don't believe it! Buster forgot his role in this drama. —I'm telling you what I saw. Anybody else disagree? Sure? Because I can go somewhere else and get a drink, for free, not like some places where they call you a fugging liar to your face. Two or three people signalled Johnny to pour Frank a drink. He raised the fresh rum-and-coke, smiled, and swallowed it quickly. —Where was I? She bent over a little for something, her jeans shifted, and that, gentlemen, is when I saw her anus. Just a glimpse, but I said to myself, That's convenient, and not for shitting out of. I moved closer to get a look front on and saw the geek, not much to him, he was all of fourteen, no muscles. Look at these! Off came the jacket and the shirt-sleeves were rolled up. —Go ahead, boys, feel these muscles. No one did, though Buster's hand ventured close. —How did I get these? Bustin down doors to get money owed, not playin video games like that faggot.

—But what happened next? Ivan normally stayed quiet while his friend talked, but tonight the cocaine-alcohol mix made him perturbed. —Always interruptions. Why can't I just sit here and talk? Where's common courtesy? Resentment crossed the storyteller's face. —What's the difference between a raconteur and a rake?, Jules whispered to Loyola. —A rake's actually done it. He's a magnificent type. A fake, but they're spellbound. Loyola frowned, continuing to sip his drink.

—To get back to it. This girl wasn't bad looking, not great, but hell, I'm no Fabio. So I said to myself, it's too bad, young pussy, we're in a store so I can't do anything. I write her off, and Frank's hand flicked out emphatically. The audience instinctively drew back. —I'm dry, where the hell's my drink, where – thanks, Buster. Jump ahead three days. I'm cutting across this gas station's lot, about 9 p.m., and who's getting air in her bicycle's tires? She's wearing a white t-shirt on this time, but those same cut-offs, and no panties. I say Lord, you're putting temptation in my path. Or opportunity.

—What'd ya do?

—Hold on, I gotta wet my throat. There. She's walking along, taking her time, not on her bike, waiting for a break in the traffic so's she can go up Allen's Path and through the fields. I run a half-circle to get on the path before she does. Pretty soon she comes along, right beside the trees where I'm hid. I knock the bike down, and drag her off the path, pushing her face into the dirt, and she's trying to call out but she's winded. Everyone listening had dry throats except Jules. —She was kneeling head first and I said to her, Here's $40, and I threw it on the ground in front of her. She saw it, and I said, I don't want to do anything but take you, okay, there's your compensation, what do you think of that?

—You thought of a big word like that when you're doing – wow.

—Buster, when you've been around you know how to handle situations. She's staring at the money, these gasps coming out of her, and I knew she was ready to try something. But I say, real gentle, I won't hurt you, and then I do it. I drove my dick right up her anus, right up to my hilt, through that fugging hole in her jeans, that's what I did. No spit, no warning, hehheh. Told the slut how she'd been advertising her asshole, all she needed was a neon sign. I buried her face in the grass and buggered her, let her feel every bit of my dick, and I got eleven inches, had Lala measure it. Anybody wants to call me on that, we'll go in the bathroom. Honest bets only, no faggots.

—How'd you keep her from calling out? If that was me I'd be afraid she'd scream and everybody'd run over, and then there'd be this thing where I'd run and the police'd catch me, and I wouldn't want to go to pris-on. Didn't you think like that about it when you was doing it to her like you said you was or was there something else in there I missed or what?

—Ivan, shut up, rasped Buster, his face hectic.

—Ivan, so much to learn, and so small a head on you. That girl wasn't gonna do anything. She'd have to explain to her mommy why she dresses worse than a whore. Plus she has $40 staring at her, and if anyone saw us I coulda said she solicited me, how'd I know she wasn't eighteen? Think of the parents of a fifteen-year-old dressed like that, what they'd be like. They'd hush it up to cover themselves. Next, what did I do to her? Did I kill her? Did I chop her into pieces? Nobody died, she just got a sore ass, and I bet you it's still sore, hehheh, and she got $40 to boot. That's cheap, you pay $50 for a blow job with a condom. I shoved right in, Ivan, knowing I'd get away with it. She had to take all eleven inches, let me tell you. I didn't hurry myself, had her face down right in the thick grass, she musta ate a mouthful of it. When I came did she jerk, and my other hand squeez-ing her tits. She tried to kick me off but she's nowhere near my weight. And these muscles, right? Keep any fugging bitch in line, let me tell you, they keep my Lala in line. When I finished I got up, wiped my dick off on her shirt, picked up the money and tucked it into her jeans. She stank of shit, she'd pissed her jeans, and passed out. She never saw my face. I rolled her over to check her breathing, covering her face with one hand, in case. Then I picked her bike off the path, using my handkerchief on it, and dumped it near her. There wasn't anyone around so I left, cool as you please. I left the money just to make her feel so goddamn guilty she'd never tell anyone what happened. Tell you, she'll never wear those jeans again, and after that she'll always want a man, not some fag boy, but she'll never find one as good as me. When I take someone, I take 'em forever, right, boys? Frank drank down another rum-and-coke, eyeing Judith. —Is there a song in that for you, Mike?

—Mikey, here's your money, I rounded it off to $100. You and Judith go on and get a good meal. Go on, now. The shaken musician and his friend, who had not read Frank's lips, left the bar, and Sam watched their retreat through a front window. A few minutes later Frank, Buster and Ivan drifted out, to the bar owner's relief. —Sick bastard, Ivy heard him say, though she couldn't make sense of the remark.

—Whenever he talks with his hands I know he's lying, Jules said after Sylvie placed two vodkas on his and Loyola's table. —Erotic stories have to smack of the truth to be erotic. Otherwise it's pornography, and anybody can write that.

—He's not telling a story, he's telling what happened.

—So you're saying he admitted to rape, buggery, sex with a minor, assault, indecent exposure, to people he doesn't really trust? Loyola thought about this. —Maybe he gets away with it by making people think it's just talk. Maybe he's smart.

—You think he's smart? Cunning, maybe, like an animal.

—You always call people who never went to university cunning. And you try and poke holes in their stories to make sure they don't sound as good as yours.

—Come on, that's -

—Like tonight, with that story about the guy choking to death on some Certs. When people hear you they ask, What do I know about this guy? If you didn't act like a mystery man they'd believe you, just like they believe Frank. I've known you six, seven years, and you haven't mentioned your parents a dozen times.

—You know what? I think this has nothing to do with Frank. Nadeen's asked Kate to pump you about me. You're not subtle. Let's get off this topic, it'll only start an argument. We were talking about Frank's stories.

—Even if they're the lies you say they are, people believe Frank's stories. You tell the truth, but people still ask questions. How come?

—The stockroom boy finds romance with the pallid gopher, a melodrama in five acts of copulation, and having found love encourages his friend to settle down. Is that what's behind this interrogation? Asking about my parents, and what I do. You've been on that kick since I came back. I think tonight you're being manipulated by a suddenly tiresome Greek through the apparatus of Kate's cunt. Vaginal ventriloquism. Hold on, you had your say. I don't appreciate friends telling me how to behave. Let Nadeen do her own dirty work, and don't let her screw up our friendship. I'm surprised at you, letting Kate get to your heart. She'll dump you when someone with money sets eyes on her. You're just cunt-struck.

—You aren't listening. You don't know Kate, what she -

—She's no different from any woman, except that she's the one going out with you. Jules threw money down on the table. —That's for the drinks. I've a feeling you won't be seeing myself and Nadeen together again. You should have just been open and said she was using you. That's what a friend does for a friend, but you tried to be sneaky. Which means you take her side. Men are supposed to stick together, but I forgot, no man should count his friends. After that gnomic utterance Jules left and did not call Loyola for several days.

Love, or perhaps a technical exercise

—It's so good to be here with you. I was looking forward to this so much, with my parents out of town I can relax. To be able to stay with you to-night . . . I couldn't wait to come over today.

—Why don't you live on your own? You're old enough.

—Are you saying I'm old?

—No, but you could. Move in with friends.

—Oh.

—I didn't mean . . .

—No, I know, and it's too soon anyway, for us. Maybe in – but not with Nadeen, in case you're wondering. She's been absolutely foul since you talked to him.

—Not surprised.

—He hasn't called?

—No. Well, yeah, left a message. I couldn't understand it.

—Why?

—It wasn't in English, it was in Latin.

—Latin.

—You learn it in a seminary. He studied it for that degree. For what good that kind of learning did him.

—Nadeen likes that stuff. Or liked it. What made him break it off? Don't just sigh, tell me.

—You know, you've a beautiful body.

—None of that till we get this straight. Put your arm under my pillow so we can snuggle.

—Better?

—Umm-hmm. Go ahead.

—I remember Jules telling me about the different cums he had, the different women. I think he's always kept score. He doesn't want to stop. He loves women, but in a way - hell, I'm no good explaining me, let alone him.

—You're doing fine. Let me encourage you.

—If you're going to touch -

—Don't get excited yet, there's talking left to do. Nadeen came out of her shell with him, you may find that hard to believe. She could talk photography, art, sensuality -

—He loves touching things, clothes, the earth, trees even, fabrics, and beautiful women. He used to make it a hobby to brush up against women he'd never meet again, you know that? Just for the contact, he'd say.

—Sick. Nadeen has a new project because of him, she says. Something about the masculine complex regarding the penis, done in collusion with the gay culture in an effort to undermine the natural urge for straight sex and procreation. That's what she said they talked about.

—How do you remember that?

—Don, my boss, says I have a mind for details, figures, dates.

—Can I make a date with your figure? Say, now?

—Not so fast, you have more explaining - look, the shadows, what are they?

—Pigeons on the balcony, the sun -

—Looks like they're dancing. Why is Jules treating Nadeen so badly? What'd she do to him? I know she can be opinionated, but so is he, and she has a good heart.

—I guess that's not what he wants, or more than he wants. I used to know him better back when I didn't know much, but since I know more, I know him less. Jesus, that didn't make sense. Your breasts are throwing me off.

—It did make sense, in a funny sort of way.

—Not what Jules'd call a good presentation.

—Don't compare yourself to him.

—Why does this bother you?

—How would you feel if one of your friends got dumped by one of mine?

—It's not like Jules is the only guy around. Nadeen must know lots of people.

—That's not the point!

—No pinching!

—The point is she was going out with him, and for no reason he calls her and tells her off for trying to change him. She calls me, and lets me have it about you maybe saying something you shouldn't. I know what you said, I know it's not your fault, but she's the one hurting. She figured he had a psychotic fit or something.

—She said that? That's pretty . . .

—What?

—She's no psychologist, is she? To say that because he doesn't want to see her any more?

—That's my friend -

—He's mine, I think -

—She was hurt! She said it right after he called her. You're allowed to say anything when you've just broken up with someone. So long as you calm down again after.

—I must've been stupid to get involved in the first place. She should have just told him herself what -

—He listens to you.

—Not to things he doesn't want to hear. Look, are we going to spend all our time talking about them? Today is supposed to be just us having fun.

—I know, but fun is about talking too. And I wanted to ask about to-morrow.

—Father's Day.

—You sound so happy about it. Makes me wonder if you're a father of somebody somewhere who I don't know about. Don't look surprised, I get told things.

—From me to Jules to Nadeen to you, is that it?

—Fat chance. He's like one of those monks about you. Like he's protecting you.

—Not after last week. I really pissed him off. Maybe it's for the best. I learned a lot from him, but now he treats me like I'm the teenager he knew years ago.

—I thought you didn't want to talk about it.

—Right.

—What are you doing tomorrow? Are you going to see your father?

—Tomorrow afternoon.

—When can I finally see him?

—He's not – look, the old man isn't in the best of moods most days. I never know what he's going to be like. So no, not tomorrow, maybe in a couple of weeks. He and I end up arguing over nothing at all.

—It's that bad?

—How often do I talk about him? Do you know how little he was there for me? Can't see the reason to do much for him.

—He's your father, you don't hate him, I know that.

—More like disappointed. He has this – oh, forget it.

—No, go on. It's all right. Did he, what, ignore you?

—Never taught me stuff, but chose the most bizarre ways to warn me of things. Cryptic stuff that scared the shit out of me. Once he told me, I was eleven or something, Son, if you feel a pain between your legs, don't worry about it, it's normal.

—Go on. What else?

—That's it. Not another word, but later, like, years later, I figured out he meant my testes would drop. We hadn't even been talking about sex, we were just driving along in the car, Mom not there, and then he just said it. What else useful did he say? Oh, yeah. I was fifteen, maybe, and he said, Son – he called me that a lot – Son, one thing, I'm glad you don't have a flat ass.

—He said what? What?

—Those were his exact words. Strange, right? No explanation. Now he can't keep his mouth closed. Mom was a tomb, especially when it came to sex, so what I learned – nothing from them, that's for sure.

—You do all right.

—Not at first, but I learned fast. So, that's enough about my father. What are you going to do on Father's Day?

—With my folks away till tomorrow night, and no date with you, I'll ring Emma. Maybe we'll have lunch or see a movie, or something. Where are you seeing your dad?

—My aunt's house, my mother's sister.

—What's her name again?

—Evangeline. Ugly, isn't it? Everyone calls her Bunny. She's my mother's twin. Her husband's Jacob. They're okay. Probably Uncle Edgar, my mom's brother, and his wife Linda. There'll be Aunt Babs, her real name's Gwendolyn, my mother's other sister, and her husband Roy Stockton, and their son Terry and his wife, Val.

—And your cousin will be there too?

—Her parents' home. I guess she'll be there – ouch! What the hell's -

—See! You never would have told me if I didn't ask, would you?

—You don't have to pinch, and not so close to – I knew you'd get uptight. You always do when she's around, even if I just mention her. You tense up.

—I think she's strange.

—She's not strange, not in my family. We've known each other since we were kids. We went on picnics, played, the usual -

—House? Doctor? Post office?

—That's enough of that, you're talking like Jules.

—He's said that, about her?

—He gets to imagining things, and then thinks what he imagines is real. That makes him no fun to be with, sometimes. Ask Nadeen about it.

—But about Janet -

—Before my mother died the families were close. Well, they still are. The cousins all played with each other, there were six of us. I'm an only kid, remember, so it was good to have everybody around.

—So is she.

—Is there a crime in that? Are you jealous or something?

—I don't know what I am about her. Why isn't she married? No, I'm not jealous.

—Why aren't you?

—Should I be?

—Married, I mean.

—She's older, she's the one who should be married. I'm young. She's twenty-six.

—Three years older.

—That's plenty in her line of work. She meets people every day she could be with, so why isn't she? I've met you and Don, and maybe one or two other nice guys since leaving Sheppardville. But she has so many contacts, she says.

—Can we stop this? First Jules and Nadeen, now Janet. Who else do you want to drag into my bed?

—That's - oh, that's revolting, just the thought of being with those people in that way. Ugh.

—Then forget them. The sun's pouring in, we have some okay wine. No one's going to be looking for you. Forget about tomorrow, about where I'm going. I'm not thinking about it, I'm thinking about you. Right now, I'm thinking about down here.

—Go on, show me what you mean.

. . .

—Are you awake? You passed out.

—They knocked me out, and the heat. You're still hard. How do you hold back?

—Practice. You don't seem to mind. But we're not done.

—No, saving a good thing for - but there must have been half a dozen, and your finger right on my clitoris. Did you always know that?

—Someone showed me.

—I should be jealous, but I'm not.

—You have a raunchy laugh, sometimes. There it is again.

—It's not because of what you do, but I mean, what you do helps. It's because – I love you, Loyola, I love you. Do you love me?

—Yes.

—Good. You wouldn't lie to me, would you?

—No.

—Was I very loud?

—The traffic blocked out the yells.

—You're funny. Oh! My nipple -

—I've never hurt you yet, relax.

—Tell me what you're thinking about.

—Feeling, more like. Flowers, flowers and water. It's like when you're out walking in a park, and you see this flower, its petals open, filled with rainwater. The water in it, and you take it in your hands to smell, get the fragrance and the light smell of the water, feel the softness of the petals against your face.

—Your tongue is so nice there, but your teeth -

—Your beautiful swelling nipple. Water from rain is the purest water, and water in that flower is the sweetest of all. Caught by the flower and scented by the flower, and you take that flower and drink the water, and you smell the rose or the lily, and all you can taste is rosewater, with the soft petals brushing your lips.

—Your mouth, don't stop, do everything to me, keep your finger right -

—The softest part of the flower, and the rest of the water held in those tender, moist, fragile petals, that you suck on and slowly take inside. The scent fills your head and the softness your mouth, and the water tastes like nothing else can. Water in a flower, on a summer day like today, the softest petals, only one or two days like it in a year, and you only find that water when you're by yourself -

—Come inside, please, please. Who taught you to talk like that? Let me feel you, Loyola!

—Kate.

—God, I love you, what you do to me. Never let me go, never.

Beliefs

Bunny Campbell proudly accepted the many compliments from her family, her florid face scrunched in a smile as she shooed people from the dining room. —No need to bring in the plates, Janet and Terence will do that, won't you? Loyola, be a dear, get your father and everyone settled in the Long Room. How many for tea? Coffee? Good. Loyola, I didn't see what you wanted.

—Beer'll do me fine, Aunt Eve. I'm sure, he added in response to her cocked head and inquiring expression. —Dad, come on, let me -

—Help me up, this damned -

—help you up.

—This unmentionable condition, temporary but - ooh! aah! - I wouldn't wish them on anyone. Loyola and John Holden linked arms, following Edgar Gibson and his wife Linda, and Aunt Babs and her husband Roy Stockton, parents of Terence, to the parlour, where Jacob Campbell busied himself readying after-dinner spirits. —Just to give some taste to the hot beverages.

—But not the tea?

—Good God, Kahlua in tea?

—Eastern Europeans do that, I heard, kills the uranium taste. Filthy habit. Any of you tried butter tea? They put dung in it, you know. No one argued with Loyola's father, who possessed the queerest pieces of information, gleaned from television and tabloids, and a few in the room thought if he were more active he wouldn't waste his time gathering such trivia. Babs and Linda just knew that Karen, his dead wife, would never for a moment have let him just read and watch science channels, she'd have kept him active through parties, clubs and sorties. Seeing Bunny, Karen's twin, forcibly reminded them of their loss, particularly on these occasions, with everyone paired off, except for the children, who did not count. Their number would only even out through subtraction at Linda and Babs' expense, since Edgar had a heart condition and Roy was diabetic.

Loyola sat on his aunt and uncle's new sofa, his beer and tomato juice on the coffee table, hoping his father would stick to odd topics and not introduce, as he had tried three times over dinner, the subject of Queer Town. In the last few years the number of foreigners there had increased, primarily from Eastern and Central Europe, with a small number from Africa, but to Mr. Holden these last were the most visible. Whenever the topic of robberies and muggings arose he provided the reason for its increase, which he had tried to bring out during the meal. —What I see is this, that the people from away, those people, they come in, and who can blame them for wanting things they've never seen, when they've no trade and nothing we can use here, don't you see? They immediately try to get the other fellow's goods, easy as pie, no work, no employment record, and meantime the government is paying them as, huh-*huh!* refugees! We're paying the criminals to rob us. Then they get what they want, cars, radios, VCRs, CD players, sell them -

—At fifty-seven my hearing is going. What earthly good is a CD player with its better fidelity?

—But that's not the point! Crime, Jacob, that's the point, and what are we going to do -

—Another cushion, John?

—No, thank you. Well, all right. Crime, though, that's the thing, it's going up, shooting up, and my friends at the police station – you remember Quinty Adams?

—Doris Adams' brother? She and I –

—Not her, Linda, no, her cousin. He visited me the other day and we talked about how things have changed, and we both agreed that nobody was safe any more, and your property? Forget it. The one thing to settle was this African business.

—Dad, just stop that now, come on.

—It's true!

—Uncle John, how many Africans do you know?

—Janet, be a good girl, run into the kitchen -

—Mom, I want to find out -

—Know? You see the news, you work in the press, and you must watch the television. I'd think you'd know even better than me, not as good as Quinty, but still, just what the difficulty was. Don't you?

—Don't I what?

—Do those things.

—Yes, but -

—Well then. When the telephone rang everyone turned their attention to the caller, and Mr. Holden's hobbyhorse was left alone. When he tried to bring the conversation around to it for the last time over pears stuffed with dried fruit and topped with whipped cream, several disparate conversations broke out at once and he could find no way to air his opinions. Now he appeared less cantankerous, perhaps made happy by the meal, though Loyola swore to watch him carefully as the afternoon went on. But everyone was settling in quite comfortably, taking up their accustomed seats by windows, doors, and near the piano played by no one, in the newly refurbished parlour. The French Provincial furniture which dominated this room for longer than he could remember, reupholstered and augmented over the years, had been overthrown by a paisley suite in green, purple and yellow. The new regime fought for attention with the wallpaper design of vines, tendrils, Roman columns and arches, more out of place now than before, a pattern once fascinating to Loyola, who remembered that as a young child he often ran his fingers over the paper in the hopes that somewhere he might feel the softness of grapes, the roughness of vines, the cool marble, the jagged edges of the broken columns. It was as though he had been dropped in the middle of an abandoned city, its life strangled by these exuberant, luxuriant emblems of Bacchus, and here he stayed, oblivious to his parents, his hosts, his cousins, as his eyes sought to trace each tendril's origin, a hopeless, useless, thoroughly enjoyable pastime. Now this world's time had passed, the images faded and, in more than one place, been torn or rubbed away. Soon the room would look completely different, by Friday in fact, Aunt Bunny promised, when the decorators arrived. In that far-off, disappearing world lived his mother, a woman he resembled more as he grew older. How could this brilliant, firmly felt, classical world of childhood be prevented from dissolving to a cold antiquity of mists and shadows? There he would lose her forever. Everything must be done to keep her alive, but what, how?

—Loyola, how's that job of yours? Anything interesting this week? Maybe not.

—No Uncle Roy, it's pretty much the same as -

—I forget exactly what you do. Make boxes? No, that's not it.

—I put clothes in boxes -

—Yes!

—and we ship them to -

—Suits, is it? Jackets, pants, tuxedos. Am I right?

—Trousers, yeah, to stores across -

—Must be interesting.

—Well.

—Figuring out overhead, cost reduction, postal efficiency, order size, volume of business, popularity of each suit, gross number for size scale. Sounds interesting, anyway.

—But that's not my job.

—Then you got lighting, the humidity factor, transportation, not boring at all. Your father told me it was boring. It isn't boring, not at all.

—But -

—Weighing the numbers, I said to him, getting the variables out. That's the challenge, hey? The variables, wouldn't you say, Edgar? Edgar thought before asking, —Do you have anything in my size, 46 short? I think that's what it is. Been so long since I bought a new suit.

—We sell, yeah, up to 50 short, if you, but Uncle Roy -

—Yes?

—That's not my job.

—Tell Edgar, I buy from a store. Loyola can't sell you a suit from the warehouse, Edgar, and besides, he's not a salesman. Are you looking to be one? He works the variables. Coffee and tea arrived, along with cookies, breads, and tea biscuits. Terence had one tray, Janet another, and they started at opposite ends of the room, meeting at Loyola. —I didn't ask for anything.

—Cuz, take the coffee I made you. It's *exactly* how you like it.

—Or this tea. Aunt Bunny wanted you to have something hot. You know she always looks out for you. Don't hurt her feelings, guy, it's a little thing to you, means more to her.

—Terry, you were always a pain. But a good pain. Coffee.

—*Told* you. We had a bet going.

—Children, does everybody have something? Where's your father?

—At the stereo, Mom.

—Jacob? Not too loud, you know my ears. Does anyone else find things deafening nowadays?

—Uncle Roy's ties -

—*Janet!* You - you saucy creature. I'm sorry for my daughter, Roy.

—What was that? What?

—I was saying life was quieter when we were their age, and cleaner too. Would you open that window, Roy, it's so hot. Jacob? Her husband put one arm around her while balancing a tray in the other hand. —Another splendid repast, sweet, and now -

—Oh! exclaimed Babs. —Someone To Watch Over Me! I haven't heard that in years. She settled down with her knitting, drowsy, content to listen while others talked over Affairs and Issues.

—I knew you'd like it. But I must see to -

—Yes, and the napkins! I forgot them. You children, thank you for serving. Get yourselves something. Does everyone have enough? Cups, plates, cookies and voices were raised to assure Bunny, while her husband offered Loyola —A drop of something for that? Circulating around the room Jacob dispensed Kahlua, Drambuie, cognac and, for John, a glass of vermouth. Terence and Janet drank tea.

—What do you do with your time, Terry? Val's still out of town, isn't she?

—Till next week, Aunt Linda. The usual things, visits, catch up on office work. I'm trying to paint some of the house, right now the living room. You know how oils give her a headache. I was doing that this morning, and Aunt Bunny – oh, she's not here. Uncle Jacob, it's really good of you to have us in like this. An impromptu cheer went up, with murmurs of Hear, hear! coming from John, who followed politics and approved thoroughly of this expression. —We would've had Dad and Mom in, but with Val called away suddenly it gave me the chance to do the painting. You go in now, there's paint cans everywhere.

—Must pull that the next time Babs wants her bridge group over. What do you say?

—Now, Uncle Roy -

—Only kidding, Janet.

—Terry is trying to surprise Val. She's such a lucky woman to be married to someone like *Aunt Babs*. This brought out mock scolding and laughter, and Bunny came back in hurriedly. —Is the coffee cold? Is that what -

—Darling, nothing like that. Come in, sit down. You've been running around all day, and yesterday too. I told her she needn't kill herself over this, but as usual, she wouldn't listen to her husband.

—And aren't we the better fed for it?

—Linda!

—What woman should? she added. —If we left it to husbands to organize things on Father's Day, we'd be eating cold cuts in front of a baseball game.

—Now, now, if we're going to get into a battle of the sexes -

—I agree with Linda. Everyone looked at Babs in surprise. Her needles clicked as she continued. —Men aren't the ones who work to make their guests comfortable, it's always the women.

—Thank you, Babs, and are you enjoying my brandy?

—Not as much as I did Bunny's ham, sweet potatoes, parsnips -

—Jacob, Babs, you're both playing, aren't you? Yes, you are! Bunny never knew what her sister would say, except that it was usually provocative.

—Who remembers Mantrap, that old television show?

—John, you're set with your drink. Roy, anything else? Loyola, Terence - I'm sorry, I forgot, you don't drink. Linda, would you accept another glass, as an olive branch, or a grape branch? Jacob's wolfish smile reminded Janet of the corporate lawyer he had been, and she recalled the numerous meetings and late night sessions in his study, how in her bedroom on the third floor she could smell his pipe, and the cigars, cigarettes and, she later came to know, the joints his clients and colleagues enjoyed. It's been years since he smoked, ever since his strep throat, but I always think of him with a pipe, and that look he just gave Aunt Lin, a smile but cold underneath. Thank God I look like Mom. All of us look like the Gibsons. Terry and Loyola and I, and Uncle Edgar's three kids, we could be brothers and sisters. Too bad they moved away, it'd be nice to see them again.

—Janet?

—Yes, Mom?

—Where were you, girl? Pass that plate of cookies to Uncle Roy, he looks parched. Hungry! I mean. Bunny gave her daughter a warm look. She had two miscarriages before Janet, and the doctor warned against their trying again. But the Virgin Mary had seen to everything. How many shingled rosaries had she and poor Karen said while she carried? Maybe that's why she and Loyola, the dear boy left without a mother, and me without more children, maybe that's why they got on so well. Thank God Janet has always been healthy, and if a bit spoiled, who could blame us?

—Did anyone see that thing in yesterday's *Carlyle-Bowmount Despatch*?

—You mean the picture of Premier Burke, smiling like a shark, Gascoigne right beside him, there's a little toad. Wouldn't you say? I would.

—Not Burke, no, the letters' page.

—John, I wouldn't say too loudly you read a Carlyle paper, not in front of Janet. Say, Janet, what's this fellow Karmiris like? A real mystery man, isn't he? You must've had dealings with him. Sounds like an enigma to me. What's the scoop?

—I must say, Janet, Allecto publishes in a very beautiful spot, all those trees around it, and the river. No one's ever had a house up on those hills, a proper house, I mean. There were some shacks, years ago, but I guess they're all gone now. We used to love to walk up there.

—Aunt Babs, the spot is *lovely*, and we have such a view. We can walk in the woods over lunch, or along the stream -

—We always knew it as a river. Did they dam it, or -

—Don't know, Uncle Edgar.

—The White River, wasn't it? Named after the fellow Bowmount had with him, not quite a ghost writer, we'd call it – I forget what.

—Amanuensis.

—John, you didn't get that out of a crossword, did you?

—Handy for Scrabble.

—But an apt spot for a publisher, the historical connotations, hey?

—I mentioned the letter, I wanted to talk about the letter!

—Easy, Dad. Uncle Roy had -

—Just asking about Karmiris. Janet has the inside story.

—Uncle Roy, I don't think I've seen him to talk to him more than five times, by myself. He's *always* in his office, we call it his inner sanctum.

—Are you there, Raymond?, and Bunny smiled as she often did at her husband's small jokes. —I don't know how much truth there is in this, but the story goes that he comes from Georgia via India, made his way out of the Soviet Union during the Second World War, smuggled out by his parents in a *shoe* box. He says he worked around the world, that he saw his first snowfall in Boston in 1947 when he was four, and then that he traded up and down the Red Sea in the 1950s.

—Industrious little fella.

—He says all this? He does, I guess.

—Somebody I work with is tracking down every anecdote he tells, in case there's a book in it later, like on Robert Maxwell. He's *obsessed* with it! They say Karmiris is worth a lot, and the newspaper costs a bit to put out, the Sunday edition especially, so maybe what he says is true. Some of it, anyway.

—Traded in what in the Red Sea? Guns, explosives?

—Supplies for the oil countries. He did tell me, and this is a direct quote, Iran won't change for six generations. He was given a watch he still wears by a BP executive, the man took it off his arm in a moment of generosity. Karmiris says he's had it for nearly forty years, which makes it mid-fifties when he got it, the years he was working in the Red Sea. It's all a mish-mash, no one will ever be able to tell us -

—But it doesn't have anything to do with my letter! John was indignant at finding the monologue he wanted to have turned into a conversation on a different topic. —Another drink, John? Now, tell us about this letter.

—Yes, Jacob, it's a letter! One I can't make sense of. Tell me what you think, you in particular, Janet, since you're in – the letter goes – and it isn't very long. Findley Aylward of Carlyle. He writes, In these terrible times, when the world is plunging into the night without end, to re-awaken at the sound of Gabriel's horn, the Archangel called by God to make mankind understand his vision (Dan. 8:16), there exists in plentiful numbers minions of Satan who seek to fulfil the Bible's injunction to go out conquering and to conquer (Rev. 6:2) for their own sinister purposes. These are the ones who wish the world governed by an overarching super-government, and whose evil aims are set in this direction, and who we ignore at our own peril, who we see among us working to destroy freedoms of assembly, of self-protection, of smoking, when we have licensing and regulations for simple things such as logging, fishing, trapping, camping, and ownership of property, and firearms, to determine our every thought from one central location, the fastness of the wilderness of the so-called Republic of the United States of America (see Luke 4:1-13 for a physical description of where they live). Through their control this world has seen its end-time come, signalled by the graying of our moral natures, where blacks and whites, wrongs and rights, are never decided, where the relativists are in command and people have given up their belief in absolutes, to the detriment of us all! Gray is the first sign of moral incontinence, and this is what the servants of Satan, whose names are legion, want, sapping our moral strength to prepare souls for eternal banishment to Hell. Awake, awake! Before the Last Call of the Final Judgement, harken to our Lord the message of the Bible, turn away, from the corrupters of Christianity, seek first God's kingdom and His righteousness (Mat. 6:33), ignore this world and its seductions. God is merciful, but He will judge you on whether you chose black or white. Repent, or else be damned for all eternity. Our politicians provincially and municipally should be aware of as they give more power to the eager overlords of bureaucracy.

John Holden looked up. —My question is, Janet, do they at the paper, the copy editor or line editor or an assistant, do they when they type this in, or set it up for type, do they edit it to read as bad as that, or - do you see what I mean? Do they -

—Uncle John -

—Wait now, just let me - sorry to interrupt you, Terry, but I'm old, you see, I have to get it out while I think of it. Not like my younger days when I could remember everything.

—It's true, Karen always said he had a mind like a trap.

—Thank you, Bunny. The thing is, do you people or some people just let it fly as is? Let it go in word for word when it's as poorly written as that?

—Yes.

—Oh. I see. No changes.

—To a letter like *that?* No. It's not important enough to spend time on.

—Very well. That was it, just curious. Because when I read this I said, it can't be, some words must have fallen out along its travels. Nobody would have written a letter like that, and then somebody publish it?

—They publish letters like that all the time. John's face indicated he preferred his own suspicious intuition over this explanation of policy. —I know, Linda, but -

—Well then, why do you ask? Linda set her cup down sharply on a table. —Any fool can type. What bothers me is that it's always Christians who write letters like that, the fundamentalist ones, quoting the Bible and giving everyone a bad name.

—Sounds like that fellow is pretty ticked at the world, at everybody. Probably lost his job in the government, most likely. Do you think?

—Isn't it terrible the way they're letting so many people go? Bunny's hands fidgeted in her lap.

—Why don't we ever read letters from, I don't know, Jews or Muslims that sound half-mad? That's all Mr. Aylward is, you know.

—Interesting you mention the Muslims, Linda. Roy felt obliged to keep up his end of any intellectual discussion. —If they wrote in, chances are we wouldn't understand a word of it. We all know the Bible. Isn't that right?

—Janet doesn't, do you? Jacob circled the room refilling glasses. —We kept her away from that religious stuff as much as possible. Nothing but harm comes from it. Look at the Muslims, Northern Ireland, Israel, Egypt, Algeria, Pakistan. Need I say more?

—But we raised her Catholic, Bunny said in her defence.

—The Koran, you talk about an interesting - oww! John had a pained expression on his face. —Damned nuisance, these. There's a book -

—Written by Muhammad, wasn't it?

—No, Linda, as I was going to say, dictated by Muhammad. The book was always in the air, God's words just waiting to be discovered by the Prophet. So the Koran isn't a human document after all.

—I think I could trust those people more if he'd actually written it.

—Moses and Christ didn't write anything down, but you trust them.

—That's very different. Very different. The Church is there for us.

—Sounds like you've been watching a couple of those cable channels, John.

—I should have taken history up earlier.

—What else do you watch, Uncle John?

—The science channels, all those nature shows, the history programs, the parliamentary channel, news, anything but entertainment.

—It's all entertainment, Uncle John.

—I saw a fine program the other night, for instance, on the Shroud of Turin. Ever hear of it? The whole historical she-bang, scientists, theologians, Vaticanologists, lay people, cardinals.

—Did you see the one yet about Veronica's veil?

—No, Jacob.

—The Sack of Rome?

—Not that one either.

—Way I see it, John, Jacob'll back me on this, there's too much religion in the world. Isn't there?

—Roy, Jacob, please. Bunny stopped, indecisive about whether to let the gentlemen carry on with a potentially controversial discussion, or to cause a domestic scene between husband and wife about what was fit conversation. —Surely there's something else we can talk about? Linda and Babs nodded out of sympathy, perhaps, while the three children talked quietly among themselves. —Bunny, we were just following up on John's letter. We're all adults, it's not like it's going to end up in a fist-fight like schoolchildren. I say, Linda, and the heavy crystal decanter swung easily in Jacob's hand, —that the reason it's always Christians writing in is because they're the most confused.

—What about you?

—Edgar, myself included. Think about what we Catholics, John, Roy, myself and Linda, were taught. All you Gibsons, you're lucky to be Anglican.

—Karen was Catholic too.

—Yes, John, sorry, she converted. Anyway, Catholics are asked to accept that God chose one man out of millions, or billions, who knows how many people lived then, two thousand years ago, that he impregnated Mary somehow, that the boy grew up, turned into a preacher in his last years, and wound up nailed to a cross. From which he ascended to heaven, to reappear to the Apostles. I just can't believe it like I once did, like my parents did, can you? Honestly? Without question? A virgin birth? If God was all-powerful, why did he need a son? Then there's Mary, venerated equally with God by many people, and why? Because she doesn't treat us as God does. When a baby dies, or a plane crashes, or a marriage falls through, or somebody goes to jail, and I've seen this, who blames Mary? Bunny dropped her head. How could he forget Janet's being saved through her intercessions? —No one. God is the one, and why? Because people ultimately don't trust him. They go to Mary because she's a heavenly ombudswoman.

—Jacob!

—I exaggerate only for effect, Bunny. People don't believe God is all-powerful because he doesn't do everything we ask, and we all think we deserve the best.

—That's too crude for me, Jake. I mean, people get angry, or sad, and they blame God, doctors, society, whatever. Sounds like they just need to blame someone, something, because they're upset. Not forever, just at that moment. Roy tried to discreetly adjust his trousers. —Isn't that human?

—Dad's right. Terry looked at his father. —But who can figure out God's reasons for doing anything, or letting anything happen? Sometimes, if what people say is true, things are sent to try us, and we're supposed to learn from that.

—When Valerie dies, God forbid it, you just remember what you said. Be so calm then. There was a short, awkward pause after these words from Loyola's father. Before him were two living images of his wife, one as she would look today, in Bunny, and the other as she looked when they first met, in Janet. It was very hard, sometimes, to keep to his resolve not to break down when confronted by her image, even after these many years. —Terry's right, saying things are meant to tax us, Jacob resumed cautiously, —but when we fail these tests, then we see what we truly think. I believe in God, despite the horrible things in this world, but I can't accept Christ's physical resurrection, or the birth story. I mean, if I accept that the Virgin can have a son, a man of flesh and blood, the Child of God, then why can't it have happened more than once? And why can't God have sent down Muhammad, Buddha, Zoroaster, for the same reasons? But anything to do with Mary is hard to swallow. Where is it they think they get her messages? John?

—Medjugorje. There's a lot of literature about it, *Poem of the Man-God*, by Maria Valturta, I was reading it this winter.

—Dad, why would you read a thing like that?

—It passed the time, Loyola. I didn't read every word, just skimmed it. Very interesting. But that book is on the Vatican's banned book list.

—What isn't?

—But the Virgin at Medjugorje -

—It's terrible what they allow to happen there.

—Where?

—The war in Yugoslavia, I mean.

—Oh, that.

—Mary likes it, you see? This causes problems, because people who be-lieve those children and the messages they get, what do they do? They're stuck, and like I saw on some show, they had this panel on discussing – but the topic or issue was a choice. John cleared his throat, and Linda quickly jumped in. —A choice? Between ...?

—Between them.

—Between who? Honestly, John, you have to tell us more if you -

—Between the Pope and Mary! Whatever pope, and the mother of Christ. Jacob nodded. —Another schism in the Church, some would say, but the Church is very catholic, small c. The Church would recognize my beliefs, I'm sure, idiosyncratic as they are.

—Really?

—Well, why not? It's only the theologians who argue about these mat-ters.

—Excuse me, Uncle Jacob, but you know I used to go to Church, still do for funerals and weddings. I find -

—Been to a First Communion lately, Terry? Linda and I were. The priest had the congregation raise their arms in some kind of blessing. The whole church, all these people looking like they were about to say Heil Hitler. Like the children were Nazi youth.

—Edgar, it wasn't as bad as that.

—Sounds pretty bad. What'd you do? You couldn't do anything. Went along with it?

—I didn't do a thing, Roy. But I know what it looked like.

—But this just adds to what I was saying. That fellow Aylward, you can tell he reads the Bible and doesn't understand it. Imagine him buttonholing you on your doorstep. But he's not so different from some Catholics we know. I've done some thinking about this, talked with a few friends, and we've pretty well divided the Catholic Church into three groups, maybe four.

—Jacob, are you sure you should -

—There's the Heterodox, capital H, which I am. Some would call us pick-and-choose Catholics. But we're not, we're pragmatists, the ones who want to keep the enterprise moving into the next century, because on the whole it's not such a bad thing. We can agree abortion and the pill are necessary at times. And we can see there has to be a figurehead, a pope, but he's as much use as the royalty. The cardinals and bishops, they're the ones who control it all. Then there's the Orthodox, the post-Vatican II Catholics who are primarily superstitious. The ones who want to raise their kids in a religion, but don't expect anything to be demanded by that religion. They give the Nazi salute Edgar saw without reflecting on what it means, because they love symbolism, ceremony. They're not out for reform, God help you if you say to one of them, What do you think is wrong with the Church? They'll be offended. They'll admit there's problems, but none that moderation and tolerance can't fix.

—Call it lite Catholicism, say. What do you think?

—Roy, that's them. Then there's the pre-Vatican II people, people our age, mostly, who want the Tridentine mass. They like Opus Dei, Latin, fear and respect for the priest. They're the New Reform Catholics, and thankfully they're old, and too small in number to be more than an obstacle. They're the ones who think Armageddon is around the corner, when it's not, that's just foolishness. The Heterodox are with the times, we understand the Church has to accept small contradictions in order to survive. Lastly, there's the Militant or Radical Catholics, the homosexuals, the feminist Bible scholars, anyone who wants their whims respected and incorporated into the Church. They want a Catholic Church that looks like them, but then it won't be the Catholic Church any more, it'll be nothing at all. They're the ideological children of the New Reform, only, typically, they want revolution instead of evolution. Because they come from half-a-hundred power bases they won't achieve much. They'll have to side with somebody, and the minute they do, they'll taint themselves. No, our biggest challenge is the Orthodox Catholics. Roy had lost track of Jacob's argument. —And they're the what?

—The superstitious ones, the ones who want their kids brought up learning their religion in school but don't want them graded on it, because religion is between them and God.

—Wait now. I'm not Catholic, but I don't agree with most of what you've been saying, to be honest.

—Fair enough, Edgar. These are just ideas, not set in stone.

—Not to cause an argument, I won't get into all that about - but there are superstitious people in every faith, and I think I'd have more respect - I think, now - for an atheist than for a superstitious person. The atheist, at least in my mind, uses his head to arrive where he is, but those others - well, where do you think New Agers come from? That's the real danger to the Catholic Church, from the witches, crystal believers, aromatherapists.

—Would anyone like more tea? Coffee?

—I'll consider that. I think where you and I agree, and it's important to find contact areas rather than gulfs, is that the superstitious, the unthinking -

—The anti-scientific.

—Exactly, those who react only from the gut, where all their quivering emotions are, they're the harmful ones, they keep everyone from progressing.

—What about those people, you hear them everywhere, who believe that if you're about to die and you confess every rotten thing you did to a priest, everything is forgiven? They give people like Roy a black eye, don't they? Babs coloured at issuing what was for her an emphatic declaration.

Janet worried about her health, for her skin colour seemed to be yellowing, though this impression may have been caused by the sunlight in the room.

—I'll get some more tea and coffee. Janet, Terence, help me! Bunny was slightly shocked at how the conversation had gone.

—Yes, Babs, you have those who – sorry, Roy, you -

—Yeah, hold on a minute, I got to get into this. How many of us have heard of some old guy who, well, maybe I shouldn't use that word. We're getting up there, aren't we? How many Father's Days have we seen? Anyway, he gets saved at the last minute. Like nothing lousy he did existed. Like Hell's an idea just to scare people. So, in Heaven a saint and a sinner can talk to each other as equals? Catholic as I am, and I'd say a God-fearing one, I can't believe, can you, some old reprobate who confessed on his deathbed can charge up to St. Peter and talk his ear off. More so than any one of us that've lived good Christian lives. There'd be something unfair about that, wouldn't there? There would.

—Well, a socialization or class-system in heaven, an interesting -

—Talk about unfair? John stirred uneasily in his chair. —What about, let me think, that old fella when we were young, did you go to him? owned the shoe store on top of Minworth Avenue, was it -

—Davidson.

—No, next to him – what, Davidson? He was the one – no, on the other side of the street, near the barber's shop with the busted up pole where Bertie O'Hara cracked into it with his Ford that time and they arrested him and found half a dozen bottles of stolen rum in the back.

—Bertie? asked Roy. —Bertie O'Hara, or Bernie O'Mara you're thinking of? Bertie. Jacob snorted. —Six bottles of rum? That's the trouble -

—Larry, wasn't it? Had a sister with one eye? John looked around the room.

—with this place, even the venality is half-hearted.

—We said she had one eye, she had two, Roy, but she was blind in one, so we said she had one eye. Not that she was a a a a -

—Cyclops.

—Exactly, Jacob.

—But what does this have to do with heaven, John? Isn't that what -

—I was getting to that, Linda. Now this fella Polbury, the one who -

—Who? Where did he come from?

—He was related to that old fella who owned the shoe store and I can't think of his name for the love of me.

—Polbury?

—No, I got his name! The other one, the one who had the -

—But who, what -

—The shoe store, Linda, his wife's name was Kitty, her parents owned the feed store -

—I thought this was all about the man who you said, Polbury.

—Yes!

—We have his name. You thought of it. Linda's legs twitched, and for the thousandth time she felt like smacking John in order to make him talk sensibly.

—Polbury, yes, wait now, the other fella, the old guy -

—Dad, is this story about the old guy?

—No, I just want -

—Then get on with it, would you? Loyola seldom refrained from, as he put it, pressing down on the gas pedal of his father's stories. —All right, you don't want to hear about it, and John, by now half-in and half-out of his chair, shrugged his shoulders.

—This was about heaven, wasn't it?

—Roundabout heaven, I should say. More wine, Roy?

—Don't mind if I do, Jake. I'm staying out of this one.

—Anyway, Mr. Polbury, Sylvester was his name, called after his father John – what a wonderful name! – who used to own the blacksmith shop -

—Wait now, wait now -

—For God's sake, Linda, don't stop him.

—I have to, Jacob. Named after his father?

—Well, he couldn't have been born before him, could he? Ha! So Sylvester, that one, he was a shark, a card shark, a great white shark, a loanshark too I don't doubt it, but at the end he upped and went away for good, and do you mean to say we'll have to talk to him like we talk to St. Bonaventure? No one present knew what John meant, and a barrage of questions followed. —I thought it was clear he died, the fella died. Wasn't it? There was a unanimous no. —Well, he died, but he died with a priest at his side, Father Carmen Melendy, who -

—What, who?

—That's what we called him, because he loved Carmen Miranda so much. Ask anybody.

—What about him? The guy who died, I mean.

—Sylvester died in his arms, almost, converting to Catholicism right at the end, and does this crook get to talk to me in Heaven as well as anybody who went through all the sacraments not because they had to, but because they liked them, not just someone scared itless with an S-H before it? There's the issue.

—What issue?

—You talked about fair! Is that fair? You were talking about fair, weren't you?

—I can't remember.

—Oh. I thought you were. You'll have to excuse me, and my repeating myself, Loyola's father said, bending over to Janet, Cinzano scenting his breath, —but I'm old. The conversation drifted towards politics and the intercity war between Bowmount and Carlyle as to which was the better place to live, which bored Loyola, who also saw Janet fidgeting. When Terence left to finish his painting they brought the used glasses, cups, and plates to the kitchen for Janet's mother. —Want to go for a drive? It's a *beautiful* afternoon.

—Top down?

—What's a convertible for? The Stocktons promised to drive John Holden home, and soon the two young people were racing through the valleys around Bowmount in Janet's Mazda, the warm, grass-scented air in their faces. One thing Loyola admired about his cousin was her taste in music, which he considered masculine, though she was anything but masculine, as her khaki shorts, olive t-shirt and thin black vest showed. He noticed her legs and arms, as well as her throat and the top of her chest, were brown. —Don't you work? he shouted above the music. She gave him a familiar sideways grin. —What kind of crack is that? How do you think I afford this car?

—I meant your sunburn. Your tan. Lots of time for -

—Poor guy, stuck indoors all day, or in that bar.

—I can't hear you. Her hand stopped the music. —What do you say we swing by your place, you get some trunks, and we'll go to Daye's Pond for a swim? I have a bag in the trunk ready to go. Unless you're meeting Kate. Loyola was not expecting to see her until tomorrow night. He had not heard of this place. —It's pretty much my secret splash spot. Where I got this tan. What say? As she waited for him in the car outside his apartment building Janet looked around at the seedy bargain stores and eateries. Cuz, this is a rotten neighbourhood. She felt the same protective instinct towards him she always had, though lately it carried an indescribable sensation. Like I know something might happen to him? She spied someone familiar seated at a restaurant window and got out of the car. There sat Kate with a man a good deal older than Loyola. From the way she acted she seemed flattered by his attention. A woman joined them briefly, then left, coming out and disappearing around a corner. That could be Emma, Kate's friend, but the man? She's probably just having coffee here so she can meet Loyola later. I wonder who that is. Not some old friend, she's acting too shy, and she's too interested for it to be an old boyfriend. Someone she works with? Just met? She backed away cautiously, making sure she was not seen by those inside. Loyola came out a minute later with a bottle of wine and a couple of towels wrapped around his trunks, dressed in sunglasses, a red t-shirt, and black shorts which emphasized the pallid colour of his legs. Janet noticed for maybe the first time his muscular figure. —So, how serious are you and Kate?

—We're not getting married next Saturday, if that's what you mean. It's all right.

—She have a key to your apartment?

—Too early for that. She stayed over this weekend. I left before she went with Emma.

—What's Emma like?

—Never met her. Why're you asking about marriage?

—You never know who's going to get hitched.

—You're a lousy liar, but Loyola was himself startled when he saw her face turn red. What had been a joke in an effort to uncover what Janet was thinking only confused them both. —Talk about getting married, what about you?

—What about me.

—Every girl – woman thinks about it.

—Thanks for the correction, you dog. She gave him a light jab with her fist. —Because I'm older than you I should be getting married?

—Older? Give me a break. It's that you must have a boyfriend. Since Rudy, I mean.

—That bastard sort of turned me off guys for a while. I know a few, slept with some, but nothing serious. I'm not attached like you are. What's the matter? You don't like me saying I slept with a lot of guys?

—It's nothing.

—Women talk about it with each other, not like men do, but we do talk. I bet you don't know how many men Kate slept with.

—She doesn't need to know about me, either.

—Like Krysta, for example. Boy, did you look pissed off when we saw you at Johnny's. She knew we were going to see you, and she was fine about it, wasn't she? but men never are.

—Did I forget to thank you for that?

—Loyola, you're so funny. I remember, but Janet broke off to concentrate on traffic. When they had passed some cars she resumed with —Your face when she walked in. In truth, she recalled Krysta telling her about a guy she'd known who gave —Excellent fucks, with his hands, his tongue, his dick, I had orgasm after orgasm, honest, every time, but then he drops me, tells me I'm not who he's searching for. I hated him, but I have to give him credit, he was good. Jesus Christ, he drove me wild, I couldn't get enough. Krysta eventually told Janet the man's name, and from then on she regarded her cousin differently.

—Memories are meant to be forgotten.

—I think we forget too much.

—Jules once said -

—Him.

—Why does everyone say that?

—I didn't say anything.

—It was the tone of voice.

—What does he do? Anything? Nothing? Speculates, maybe rents ghetto housing, what?

—Don't get into that, it reminds me of Queer Town and Dad. I'd like to know what the hell's happening. He's been getting more like that with every year since Mom died. It's not hard on him alone. He's forgotten everyone but himself. Drinks more too. Last month he said to me, Loyola, I'm going to the *drugstore* to get some *medicine*, I feel a flu coming on. I asked him if it was one of those twenty-four ouncer ones. He laughed. First time he paid attention to me in weeks. But he has gotten funny. You know. Almost cold.

—I feel sorry for him, all the same. For cold, you should see my Dad. He never did the things with me fathers are supposed to do. Never, not once. And I still don't like him for it, after all these years. I mean, I love him, but I don't like that about him.

—Dad read this book by somebody Fast or Fort or Fart last year. He figured he'd do what that guy did, put pluses and minuses down on the calendar for each day, see if it was good or bad, and figure out how his life was going. After about three months he threw the calendar out and doesn't want another. Sad. But I was telling you that Jules thinks our memories are like a starry night sky.

—Sounds like a pick up line. Loyola ignored this. —He says what we remember is like the stars. Everything in between, all the black, that's the life we don't remember. The way Mom cooked eggs every day, or made jam, or playing catch with Dad. The weather. Knocking around with you and Terry, Patrick, Susan, Liam.

—It's too bad they're all in Ontario. Aunt Linda misses them. Watch it, you asshole! Sunday drivers, old men with hats, worst -

—He says scientists can put electrical charges on your brain and re-activate the areas where those memories are, like lighting up that black sky. Say you forgot your first kiss.

—You and me playing post office.

—But don't you think Jules -

—It's a nice thought. Too bad it's from *him*, I can't trust it.

—Back to you getting married, then.

—*Loyola!*

—If I tell you something, can you keep it to yourself? You know Camilla and Stan? You met them at Johnny's. He told me in Johnny's bathroom last week she makes him wear a penis ring. Janet turned her head sharply. —Seriously. She makes him do it as a punishment, or obedience thing. And they're getting married in the fall. But get this, he likes it. Not all the time, but sometimes it turns him on. She keeps the key around her neck, on a chain, right next to her St. Christopher's medal.

—What fun is there in that?

—Sometimes, he said, she tucks it into her bra and tells him it's there, and that if he's really good she'll unlock it. This gets him excited, right, and his penis – the ring starts to hurt him. He was so plastered when he told me this I don't think he knows what he said.

—You have sick friends. Submissives, ex-union people working for peace groups, masturbators. There's the guy who painted his house with flames. In next week's Sunday supplement there's going to be a picture of his car -

—Fred's not a friend -

—a Malibu with fluorescent-orange Stucco on the outside. Aren't there any normal people around?

—You tell me how you judge normal. Everyone has a different stand-ard. Are our parents normal for going on about religion? Nobody else does.

—That's Dad, he gets them worked up with his pet peeves.

—But he's considered normal, right? They all are. Take Starlene. She has a good job, she's single, in her thirties, and she won't speak to me, not even about the weather. She does crossword puzzles and can't spare one word for me. Is that normal?

—She doesn't like you, that's all. I hear New Zealand women are sluts. They'll sleep with you for a meal. So a friend of mine says. Sounds like your type of place.

—I didn't call you a slut when you told me you'd slept with a lot of guys, did I?

—*Some* guys. You didn't feel comfortable, admit it. I can't imagine you listening to me tell you about what Joe or Bill was like in bed.

—Because we're cousins!

—If Kate started telling you about some guy from her past, you'd be okay with it?

—Depends on how past, doesn't it? Wouldn't it be the same for you? Janet thought about this and had to agree. One thing bothering her was when to tell Loyola she had seen Kate with another man who, come to think of it, she *had* flirted with. For now, —Why don't we forget about every serious topic, about our jobs, and only think about sun and water?

—Where's this pond?

—Not far away, ten minutes after that turn-off.

—Okay, nothing but jokes. It was evening before they left the pond, tired and in good spirits. They had a quick supper at a place on the highway, and as Janet drove Loyola home she told him about Kate's lunch companions.

Manipulation by fear and desire

—You picked a funny place to get together.

—It's peaceful, that's the important thing. Alistair sat next to Bart in St. Mark's Presbyterian Church, examining the spare wooden pews, the simple altar, noting the battered song books in the rack before them, imagining he could hear water dripping from a tap somewhere. —It's like this warehouse I worked in, high ceilings, nothing but crates and lights. Utilitarian. Bart rubbed his eyes. —I have to be careful. Too much visual stimulation and, his hands completing the sentence. —But they don't have confessionals. Alistair regretted this remark immediately, but Bart did not take it wrongly. —It was because it was dark, private. Some old woman told Father Sullivan I'd gone into an empty one. If I'd seen her - but it's those bodies hanging everywhere in St. Finnian's, in the chapels, when you could get to the chapels, on the walls, they're so lifelike. I got to looking at Mary Magdalene and the Virgin, their tears, and Christ half-clothed, blood pouring from his side and his head, then there's this tightening sensation, and before I can stop myself I have to do it.

—Why go to any church?

—You can laugh when I tell you I believe in God and all the rest, despite everything, but I do, so I need to come to church. But here it's safe, that way, I mean.

—And . . . ?

—Nothing.

—You could pray anywhere, couldn't you?

—I need the right place to do it, Alistair, to feel God is there. I guess this is close enough. I hope. I hope he hears me. Nobody bothers me. One time I was asked who I was, I said I'd been away for years, no wonder they didn't recognize me.

—You come here and pray? Or what?

—Or what? What's that mean?

—I'm just saying, you come in here and sit all day, and pray?

—To pray, or sit and think, or feel. It's the only place outside my apartment I can relax. Oh, there's the movies, sometimes. If I went to Johnny's I'd see Loyola, but he ignores me when he has a girl.

—He looks like an okay guy, though things are a little tough for him now. You didn't hear? He and that girl Kate had a fight over some guy she was with, her boss they say, some old boyfriend maybe. That was about two weeks back, but they're trying to patch it up. And you know Camilla and Stan are getting married.

—Why would he do that?

—Why does any guy get married, hey, she probably talked him into it.

—No, Loyola. He always picks a fight with the girl when he has to work at it with them. The conversation lapsed. After counting the rows of pews in each of the three sections of St. Mark's, that faint dripping sound in the background, Alistair presumed enough time had passed. —Loyola's your friend, he's busy, like all guys with a woman. And you're upset. But I never got the feeling you were that close.

—For a while, till Kate. No, before, when he started going out with some -

—I guess he sees women different from you and me. I like them, but they're messy. A wing down, always, my mother used to say. Now you, you'd probably go out with someone with a good personality, but Loyola goes for the easy lay, so I hear.

—Me? Who'd look at me? I don't talk smart, or think quick, I'm a loner, always have been, with a reputation for, well.

—So you're happy like that? Bart sighed. —Happy like everyone else is happy.

—Meaning?

—As close as you can get to not being miserable. Alistair considered this. —So you and Loyola aren't -

—He knows I have this problem, he accepted that, but he stopped talking to me so much when I told him he was sleeping with sluts. Kate isn't one, but he'll blame whatever happened on her.

—Loyola was okay with you and your, ah, what have you?

—Surprised?

—He struck me pretty much as a guy's guy. Maybe a little too much, like he's over-compensating.

—He was fine with it.

—For a while.

—No, always. I told you, it was something else, what I said to him. Let me tell you a story.

—Okay.

—What do you mean, okay?

—I'm listening.

—It's a true story, all right? You're not supposed to listen like I was telling you a joke.

—All right, all right, relax.

—Sorry, it's this not sleeping, I don't rest. I worry about not getting another job, and my family, they send a cheque now and then to make sure I don't come home. The arrest did it for them. But what was I saying? So hard to keep things straight. One time there was me and another kid, we were in grade four, and one afternoon we were in one of those small plastic pools with the built-in slide. It was May, and hot, and this older kid, probably two grades ahead, passes by my backyard where we're playing. He says, Ooh, look at the two of you playing with each other in your pool, isn't that cute? We looked at each other. This guy's already out of sight, to him it didn't mean anything, what he said. When I see my friend in school the next day he makes fun of me, and we're not friends any more. We weren't doing anything wrong, but this bigmouth comes along and - I see him around town today, you know, the older guy I mean, and I just get sick, angry. I know what happened with my friend, I know he got self-conscious, because of our age. Maybe it was too small a pool. But if it had been Loyola he wouldn't have stopped being my friend. It's his cheap taste in women, he only wants to sleep with them, that's what I don't like.

—You saying he's embarrassed? Or that you're envious, maybe.

—Envious? Over those women? You haven't talked to them. Foul-mouthed, that's what they are. No, he doesn't like me, or anyone, not liking who he's with. He and that guy Jules make a perfect pair.

—I guess you know him best. Some time passed. —Ever wonder about bums? Alistair's concentration on the dripping water broke, and he was unsure whether Bart added something else. —You see them everywhere, they're fascinating. But Alistair, they frighten me.

—Bums. You mean -

—Homeless people, right, that sounds better. When you're young, the age I was in that pool, you see people as adults and kids, you don't categorize them. Your parents warn you about some of them, and then you see them give money to this one or that one who's missing a leg or an eye.

—I'm not sure where this is going. A moment ago -

—I'm not explaining things well, I'm tired. I wish I could sleep, but I just lie there.

—What goes on in your head while you're in bed?

—Mostly has to do with getting up the next minute, and how I don't want to. Smashing things. But I was saying, all of a sudden you see six or seven types of adults. Not just good and bad ones, but the ones who could go either way, the ones who failed. Maybe you find out later Uncle Ed embezzled money, or fondled your sister when she was young, and it's only when he's dead you get told. Or Aunt Sophie pointed a knife at your mother when doped up on medication and booze. Seeing a bum is different. This is someone you never knew, a total washout, stumbling over a curb and breaking his nose on the sidewalk.

—Well -

—Wait. How does somebody become a bum? You hear about social programs helping people. Maybe it's guys who didn't finish school, or lost their job, their family. But look at all the people who get ahead in business, or anywhere, and didn't have too much education. Mental illness? There's a lot of drugs that can help people. Right? There's family and friends, but a person becomes a bum anyway, despite everything. How?

Alistair could not take his eyes off Bart's weary face, and unconsciously rested one hand on Bart's thigh. He's really upset. That kid in the pool, thinking about it after all these years.

—What'd you say, Alistair?

—Did I say – was I talking?

—Your lips were moving, there wasn't any sound. Bart moved his leg away from under his friend's hand. —Nothing much. What were you saying?

—I see this one guy, he keeps his stuff in a shopping cart. Saw him yesterday in Sinclair Park, he had blue and green garbage bags in the cart, a heavy coat, some other things. He'd rolled his sweater sleeves up. His clothes must have been maggoty, but the way he shoved that cart, you'd think he was king of the road. You know he's alive with lice, stinks, but what he did next, I can't get it out of my mind. He stopped in the middle of the park, near the round pond, took out a comb and a mirror, and combed his hair, then his long yellow-white beard. When he finished he put the comb in his back pocket, put away the mirror, and shoved off again with his cart, yelling God save all here, God save all here! at the top of his lungs. Think about it. His clothes nothing but rags, but he stops and makes a point of -

—Grooms himself.

—Yes! What kind of man was he before? That's what I've been asking myself. He had a life, friends, a home, like you and me. Dignity. What did he do wrong?

—A bunch of things.

—Or maybe just one thing, one fatal thing.

—It has to be everything he did -

—No, it can be one thing! The *right* one thing that changes everything, like getting hit by a car, arrested, and nothing in your past life connects to it. Don't you see what I'm saying?

—I hear what you're saying.

—Is that a yes?

—Jesus, sure it is, Bart, but just because a guy does one wrong thing, I mean, there's checks and balances and safety nets for everyone, support groups -

—Where are they, where? Does that guy know about them? If he did, why is he a bum? Friends? Look at Loyola, there for a long time then – gone. Where's anyone when you need them? All you have is yourself, right? Bart quivered, anger and fear replacing the fatigue in his face. His voice acquired a shrillness Alistair found deeply unattractive as well as unsettling, and it drew glances from a handful of people at the front of the church. —Even bums had friends once, they had to be babies, they played hockey, they were regular kids.

—Calm down, you're just exhausted. What's all this about, anyway? Loyola? Jesus, I should've kept my mouth shut. Hey, are you crying? Here, I got a – take this handkerchief. Absurdly, Alistair thought, he wanted to hold Bart's shaking frame, let his head rest, only for a minute or so, on his shoulder. With the handkerchief Bart wiped his eyes, mopped a pale face made rosy from anxiety, patted the neck above a mis-buttoned shirt. Glimpsing Bart's exposed condition provoked in Alistair a type of giddiness, as if he had taken the first sip of that one drink too many before driving home. He transferred his attention to the stained glass windows on their side of the church depicting significant events in the Holy Family's life. Pure July sunlight splintered into rays of blue, purple, red, gold and white, with a disquieting regularity in number. Excluding the clear panes, there were the same number of coloured ones in each window, each colour represented equally. Alistair assumed the same percentages would be found in the windows on the opposite side. That something intended to aid reverence should be so mechanically composed disturbed Alistair, but it merely confirmed his opinion that even in little things religion would be found wanting. Who could feel something inspiring in these modern, manufactured poses set out in rigid proportions? It would take a very naive believer to appreciate these things. But perhaps their sole function was to serve as welcome distractions during dry homilies. Besides, finding the Almighty anywhere in this dull environment would upset everyone's equilibrium, as ridiculous as seeing Jesus' face staring up from your bowl of porridge and raisins, or at you from a display of jujubes. As a consequence of his upbringing, Alistair knew that if Jesus manifested Himself in the church of any sect of Protestantism the congregation would never recover, judging it a terribly tactless thing for His Father to have done to the faithful. They cheerfully worshipped a God securely stationed in Heaven, but if His Son descended to Earth the only foreseeable result would be hysteria, mass panic, bloodletting, self-examination. It would go against all good taste and sense, and later people would feel extremely foolish over their behaviour.

More bothersome than the unimaginative panes, to Alistair, was his lifelong habit of conscientiously dismantling things, atomizing the most humdrum objects and actions. It was not enough to notice Bart's shirt, he had to notice its condition, and then the appearance of what lay under it. Alistair had determined how many lamps hung in the church, how many pews there were, and could conceivably estimate, using the racks in view, the number of song books displayed. Now the soothing use of coloured glass had been reduced by a cold-blooded inventory to a comment on the sensibilities of Presbyterians. Was it any wonder he felt confused in a world of myriad objects and people, and split within himself as to -

—Alistair, you can let go of my neck, Alistair. Alistair!

—What? Sorry, I - you're okay now, you're -

—Are you?

—You're the one who was . . . you keep the handkerchief, I have lots.

—I'll get it back to you.

—No rush.

—Thanks, thanks for it. I'm sorry, I don't know what came over me. Lately I've felt so disgusted, afraid.

—Yeah.

—I've pissed you off.

—Look, it's nothing like that. I was off somewhere, it has nothing to do with you.

—Because I'd understand, what kind of guy wants another guy crying around him. Alistair shifted in the uncomfortable pew. —You know,

Europeans are better at this, emotions. Italians, Greeks, I mean, not Norwegians. They get upset, the men, they yell, and cry, then play music and drink as much as they want and nobody feels bad. They don't get uptight. I remember going into St. Telesphorus with this Greek friend. You'd never last there, Bart, all the icons. And feeling so much emotion, but I don't know why. The service went on for hours, I was only there for my friend, I thought it'd never end. But they handled it.

—Handled what?

—What they were feeling. It was some special service, Good Friday or something, feast of a saint, Virgin Mary, that's not important. You could tell everyone was ready to let go, in a good way, and even I got into it. Powerful, it was really . . . and it's been awhile since I felt anything as strongly as that.

—You never went back.

—Me and my friend, we went separate ways. He got married, and I don't care what they say, when a guy gets married he never treats his friends the same. You know that. Loyola.

—Loyola.

—Exactly. Tell you something, you said where are friends when you need them? It's funny, at work I'm getting less and less caring.

—But you're doing well. You always have money.

—Yeah, 'cause I don't give a shit about the guy at the other end of the line, what I'm focused on is the pitch. Telesales is a bastard of a business. You can make fifty to eighty calls a day selling advertising in books that don't exist yet, to people you'll never see. They get you on the line and you're just this pain in the ass. I remember working in England at the same type of job, and we worked only on commission. You'd put in a forty-hour week and whatever you sold you got paid for the next Monday. So if you didn't sell anything one week, and sold something the next Monday morning, you'd go two weeks without any dough. Don't get me wrong, I knew what it was about when I got involved, but Jesus it was hard.

—Why'd you keep at it?

—Money, it was the only job I could get, and I did real good after awhile. I had this hunch who'd buy and who wouldn't. When I came back here, it seemed the right thing to work at. I don't know people in important positions, no school friends offering me jobs, and then the recession comes along and nobody anywhere's hiring. But telesales is a burnout business, they always need someone. I could brag about talking to air-conditioning people in Inverness, architects in Hungerford, pipe-fitters in Eire or Cork, lighting installation people in Cardiff, everywhere. Lots of experience, and I'm good at it. Why? Because I'm desensitized. See these windows? In England – London – I called up a woman who did this sort of thing, told her we were putting together a book for a builder's guild. All the banks and building societies and construction firms will see your name, you'll be the only stained-glass maker from Northumberland or Cleveland in the book. She worried over it, said Those are the people I want seeing me, but I only have a little set aside for advertising. She spent it with us, about $300 on a half-page ad, spot colour for her logo, in a book that only gets printed, I figure, in a limited edition. Not the 15,000 copies we quoted, but for however many people advertise in it, plus the association members, and some promo copies. The company didn't belong to an auditing board, see? No one could check how many copies of any of its books were printed. What did I care? I got to eat the next week, and the woman spent her whole year's budget on an ad in a book no one in their right mind would look at.

—How did that -

—Make me feel? Then, I wanted to call her back the next day, if you can believe it, tell her to cancel the ad. I didn't. That was the start. Right now I don't care about how much or how little they have, I want it all, so I do well. Especially for charities that hire us to collect money for them. I know all the sob stories, the approaches. But it comes out, you know, that feeling.

—What feeling? Of -

—That I'm robbing them, so I'm a shit. You'd think the more I earn the more generous I'd get. Well, I don't care about the poor, the sick, farmers and their rotting crops, but sometimes - back when I went to St. Telesphorus, there was this prayer I learned, do you want to hear it?

—Sure.

—Are you sure?

—Why not?

—Because I'm - Bart, this isn't easy, but I got to tell someone something about what goes on. Since that last time I was in church with my friend, I haven't been in one, not even for a wedding or funeral.

—Not one?

—It was too much. And Jesus, you would want to meet me here, of all places. You know I was raised as an Anglican, but my parents never really believed. When I went to St. Telesphorus it was like eating this huge meal after not touching any food for, fuck, years. Tell you the truth, I felt bad after it.

—Why would -

—Let me get my breath. See? What do they call this in those damned self-help books, a recognition? The prayer, that's what I was going to say. It's simple, goes like this. Lord Jesus Christ, Son of God, have mercy on me as a sinner. Short and sweet. Like we'd say at work, it sells the sizzle, not the steak. I think about it now and then, not so much lately. Now I have other things on my mind, and to tell you the truth I'm worried about what that means, not saying it any more. It used to be like some kind of mantra that used to be a help to me.

—You say you don't care about anyone you're talking to, but you sit and listen to me.

—You're not anyone I'm selling anything to. Alistair knew he looked worried. —I can't explain it, but work is making me this bastard, I'm not making any friends, but I'm doing great. They want me to be sales head, not just of a team, but the whole works. That's a fixed salary, no more phone calls, and get a slice of whatever each team makes. This oughta make me happy. Jesus, who wouldn't want to be successful? But the stress of it . . . Bart did not look squarely at his new friend as he replied, —I can't imagine it. Alistair found himself possessed by the need to count the pa-

rishioners, whose number had quietly increased. He did, then checked the numbers three times more. The dripping water made him wonder if in his apartment he had turned off all the taps, removed the plugs from the sinks and bathtub, turned down the electric heat, switched off the lights and oven, and locked the door. Quickly he retraced his movements, satisfying himself that before leaving home this morning everything there was
—As safe as safe can be.
—What was that?
—What? Oh, my apartment. I was thinking about it.
—You moving out?
—No, no, just – the building I'm in, a man next to me, he has Alzheimer's and drinks a lot, and lives by himself. Sometimes the smoke detector goes off and he doesn't even notice, mainly because he's passed out on the couch. The super has to get in there and turn the stove off, wake the guy up. I keep thinking I'll go back some time and find the whole building in flames.
—How many storeys?
—Four, about eighty apartments. Most of them got two people in them.
—What made you think of it?
—You know how your mind works.
—I wish I did, things'd be a lot better.
—You'll be fine, Bart.
—Yeah, all I need to do is get aholt of myself. And you, what about you and your job?
—Me? I have to figure some things out. I'm not worried, except about my neighbour. If they had not been in church, Alistair would have laughed to show he was relaxed. Instead, the silence drew attention to Alistair's unease. —Say, you want grab some lunch, Bart? I have my car, we could drive to The Highwayman's, enjoy the sunshine.
—Are you sure? I'm not good company. But I don't get out of Bowmount enough.
—I can't stand the fucking place.
Bart thought of adding how he now enjoyed Alistair's company, be-

cause talking with someone who was experiencing difficulties made him feel less isolated. As well, Alistair emanated a peculiar attractiveness, not revealed until today, most likely stemming from his unhappiness – which at the very least was a change of subject – and showed a surprising degree of sympathetic understanding, which previously had not been in evidence. Bart contemplated this, and other feelings provoked by their conversation, but they are inaccessible. As for Alistair, once in the car and speeding away from the church, he noticed that discussing the promotion with someone outside Radcliffe Publications had relaxed him, for the right-left, left-right, left-right, right-left counting affliction had stopped, temporarily, and he now knew for sure that nothing had been left on in his apartment. Unexpectedly, today he had touched someone, and been affected himself, and the evidence of this new person coming towards him made this summer's day beautiful. Beautiful, now there's a word I haven't used in a long time. The two men discussed the scenery while subterranean evaluations continued.

The priests

Every room in Eminent House let in drafts and smelt faintly of mould, the olive paint on every wall depressed him, and he knew that the coffee, biscuits, and cakes served as treats at meetings such as the one to be held this afternoon would be tasteless and dry. The Archbishop had descended from the refined heights of Toronto and Montreal, and regarded the priests and laymen of the Catholic Church in this province as boobs. Oh yes, intelligent decisions were made now and then, but less than the law of averages allowed; and of course, good works of a highly Christian nature were performed almost every other week. But to his mind the capillaries of the local Church were clogged by the lacklustre efforts of poor priests recruited from the local population, and by the vapouring of laymen and church committees. There's a critical lack of verve, ability, initiative, wit – and here am I! A servant with an unblemished record shunted to this place, a career derailed. Staring out a narrow window at a bland Saturday sky, the Archbishop anathematized the men above and below him, and for good measure to his left and right, for posting him here, or failing to support vigorously enough his fight to remain where he had happily been seven months previously. In the private sector, unfair lateral promotion could be litigated, and there was much to commend opening the Church to that recourse. —Does my past experience amount to nothing? he had asked, and the response was —Percival, you're just the one to clean up the mess they're in. See it from the Church's point of view, a new face, after the scandals, to win the people's trust and love once more, and to push through reforms the last Archbishop blocked. It's as if they said don't look for rest, you're born to work. In this spot. *Bowmount.* Such an ugly name. Apart from Scarborough and Truro. Carlyle, Crescent City? They were called Bowmount's sister cities, and what an unattractive brood they formed, not a Cinderella among them.

In resigned moods, the Archbishop admitted that every dog needs its home, and in a world rushing to embrace new faiths emanating from the East, and New Age so-called beliefs shooting up like mushrooms, a world, in short, increasingly cold to the authorities within the Roman Catholic, Protestant, and the Orthodox Churches, a dog of his years and disposition could not just turn a nose up at any haven offered. Abide my soul in patience. Only last week word arrived that if he lasted out this situation, redeemed the local church, pressed on with advancements, an elevation in stature might occur. What a splendid return from this Cimmerian world that would be, to be posted to somewhere in the United States. All I have to do is survive. The court cases are almost behind us, things are settling down. This duty may yet offer a source of salvation. He chewed on a hard biscuit and turned to reconsider letters disapproving of the removal of altar rails and the closing of small chapels throughout the province's churches. These things should have been conducted more subtly; had he been in charge from the beginning the requisite evolution would have proceeded in quiet submission to God's word. Fr. Jerome had done his best, but now there were petitions and appeals from the toothless and mindless members of the Women's League, exciting the previously uncaring churchgoers about what were, in the scheme of things, very small adjustments to worship. Those tacky, ill-lit chapels commanded undue veneration and altar rails were outmoded relics from a bygone era. Everything had to be renewed so that the Church could regain its vital role in the community. Strenuous efforts proved essential to encourage people to sit in the front of the church, not sprawl everywhere as if they were at a union meeting or football game. This required removing pews, or positioning them differently, so that no one could skulk around the back doors. Didn't these fools see that unity was a good thing? That, as Ignatius said, our bishops represent the mind of the Lord? No! They wrote philippics to editors of papers he refused to read, formed committees with whom he refused to meet, called talk shows he could not stomach, in an effort to pressure him, and through him the Church, to swerve from the carrying out of God's word! Incredible. As if they were in charge, as if the Vatican had lost its mind. Every parishioner acted as if he were in sole possession of The Way The Church Must Be. The minute anything changed someone brought up buggery at St. Ita's or St. Cassian's as a general rebuke to those in black, meaning they weren't trusted. Such unbridled insolence, such know-it-allness, infuriated the Archbishop terribly. —It'll be like living inside a boil, one well-meaning friend sadly commented.

So it was. Parishioners of all classes came up to him, at social and church-sponsored functions, their mouths working ten seconds in advance, lips trembling and twitching over —My nephew's first cousin, he was molested by Father So-and-So, got no money, not even an apology, whatcha gonna do about it? People were close to each other here, the sweat from one trickled down another's back, they knew each other biblically and in every other way. Marriages between cousins weren't uncommon, as were incestuous relationships, and from the sordid annals of local Catholic history emerged an acknowledged case of adelphic polyandry. The sole offspring from that corrupt family – father unidentified – lived in Bowmount, Frank something or other, dealt in finance, at a bank perhaps. When an old priest related this case to the Archbishop over some terrible wine, the latter did not know whether to be aghast at the existence of such a person, or impressed by the familiar use of such an obscure term. This was the boil in which he must live for two and a half more years.

The Archbishop's teeth whittled another biscuit, but his face had been for so long trained to not register emotion, this small culinary disappointment could not manifest itself. Surely the labourer deserves his food? Service for the Church at high levels for so many years had damped his formerly kind nature, which only those who knew him as a child and very young man recalled. A severe life demanded the suppression of the quick retort, the joke, the familiar remark, the casual smile or inquiry, as at any stage in his career these things could have harmed his prospects. Now, no wretched posting, no immoral, whining population, no dry cookies or instant coffee, would affect his dignified exterior, unless the momentary display of an emotion proved strategically useful.

Viewed from the outside by Marcella Dubois, secretary to Fr. Jerome Ryan, Archbishop Mason had the appearance of a man lost in contemplation, a touch haughty, okay?, but when a man gazed at God continuously and laboured for the Mother Church every single minute of every single day, decade after decade, travelled, met the Pope and Cardinals, you had to agree the normal rules of sociability don't apply. He was an odd one, with a sweet tooth, and Marcella, who now bought treats in bulk for the new man, reflected on the difference between him and ex-Archbishop Connors, a diabetic who never drank anything stronger than tap water. But this minor difference was nothing compared to what some people – not many, a few here and a few there – called the Archbishop's coldness, when in actual fact, to Marcella, it was really, okay? one of his aspects, the Intellect. Look at the man's life, she said to others, the publications, the never-ending pow-wows with government leaders, the heads of other churches (must be flattered by his paying attention to them), the movers and shakers in the business world, what a breadth and depth of learning he had, to be able to talk to them, okay? let alone get the Catholic view across. Would any of these people listen to him if he wasn't what he was? His learning was bestowed as a gift from God, so his Intellect accounted for the unapproachable nature. He's always thinking of this topic or that topic, okay? and that means you don't go up to him like you would Betty or Joe and bother him about something he'd have to think kinda inconsequential, okay? like the new car you bought, why the children didn't take to school, who was moving away because there weren't any jobs, what relative was dying because of an operation a butcher would be ashamed of, shame that *Medic Alert* book didn't come out sooner, isn't it?

No, that type of interruption was inexcusable. Marcella might want to break in on his thoughts, but she restrained herself. There he sat with world affairs on his shoulders, the fate of the faith in his hands, and hands just like his all over this wide world, mustn't forget, as his overwhelming international correspondence testified, letters forever coming out of his office, according to his secretary Rayelle. Small talk? Please! Often he gave the impression no one else existed in the room. Marcella sighed. She supposed that if she suddenly stripped to her frillies or threw herself out the window the Archbishop might notice her. At the thought of being almost naked in front of His Grace she stifled a giggle, blushing faintly. What would he do? But imagining along those lines wasn't proper, was it? What had made her think like that? She must compose herself. Yes, there was a very cold air about the Intellect, but those two went hand-in-hand, didn't they?

Some staff, especially Stephen of *The Catholic Trumpet*, now there was a louse, okay? the organ of the diocese, as Father Liam calls it, but still it's good to have it right in here with the rest of us, keeps us up to date and on edge. *The* edge, not – what was I – right, he isn't too charitable about personalities. —After Archbishop Connors' gentle guidance, Archbishop Mason's rigid civility is downright rudeness, he'd said, imagine. But you couldn't go comparing one of God's Chosen with another, it was harmful, led to backbiting. Marcella paused to wonder why that was not a sin set out from the others, like Greed and Pride and Sloth, and followed this thread into some unknowable region, emerging once again to reconsider the man lit up now by a bar of light, his gold chain and jewellery gleaming. Here they were waiting, he sipping coffee, the right hand taking up a cookie now and then as his impassive face stared out the window, while she sat in a soft muddy brown chair with large armrests on the far side of the room, pad and pens waiting for Frs. Jerome and Liam, the room's silence unbroken for ten minutes. Occasionally the Archbishop cleared his throat. If he held an opinion about that sun or those clouds, Marcella would not hear it. Far more likely, she felt, within himself he kneeled before God's altar in worshipful prayer. An Intellect such as his would do no less, okay? that's another reason why he couldn't make the small change of conversation. If we all had lofty thoughts and half as high aspirations for the Catholic Church's earthly success, the world would be very well off. In these days it's hard to emulate Our Lord, but if we fail at that we can use a priest or this Archbishop as a model of behaviour. It's not so important that he's a bit stand-offish, he's a man of God, and we could all restrain ourselves from time to time. Having reached the end of these thoughts, Marcella jotted down on the last page in her pad certain items to be picked up for supper. Pork chops were always nice.

Fr. Jerome Ryan entered and greeted the Archbishop, nodding to Marcella with a friendly smile. He's pretty happy, considering Father Henry died last night, but then, no, like the Archbishop he was in contact with God too. Marcella never tried to convince herself Father J was an Intellect. He was more a Doer, tirelessly organizing picnics, socials, events aimed at pulling the congregation together at a stressful time in our history. For instance, this summer he'd once again, six straight years, how does he manage, he and Father Ambrose, take some of the lads on a long weekend retreat to a cabin in the Seven Islands area, where they'd fish, hike, talk about religion, these things. Father J, as Marcella privately called him, under the former Archbishop, and in the hiatus between their departed leader's resignation and Archbishop Mason's instalment, had involved many churches in school breakfast programs, in Teens For a Sober Tomorrow, and the admittedly less popular Catechism Club. Engaging, popular, he was a contrast to – but there I go again! A knock on the door preceded the entrance of Fr. Liam Robinson, followed by Darlene and Siobhan bearing more trays of tea, coffee, cookies and a lemon loaf which Marcella, at their prompting, confessed she made yesterday. She was surprised and flattered that Archbishop Mason expressed an interest in trying it, even with so many cookies in him that by all rights he should be full to bursting. Marcella made a note on the pad under pork chops that lemon biscuits should be bought next time she went out. Fr. Liam praised her sincerely, swearing that his mother, a dab hand at pastry, could not beat her talent at breads. His mischievous eyes were those of a perpetually young man, and since he kept in shape by coaching boys and girls in soccer and baseball, his physical magnetism and charm appealed to the three women in Fr. Jerome's office. It was discreetly whispered how a former member of the staff had unwittingly entered the boys' locker room of St. Finnian's School and seen Fr. Liam naked, exiting with a shriek. She soon left for some other job, not before describing the priest's form to two or three female office mates. That happened three years ago. Fr. Liam heard the tales but ignored them, and in time everyone's embarrassment vanished while his standing as a pure specimen of manhood grew, as myths do. Marcella knew one or two girls found him attractive, and sometimes their banter behind his back bordered on lustful, that's the way to put it, but give the man credit, he has a way about him of keeping things in place. He breathes life into the place okay?, but no, never a breath of scandal.

Built in the 1870s next to The Church of St. Finnian, and St. Finnian's School, Eminent House had been remodelled and enlarged over the years, at the expense of its original lines. Traditionally it was the Archbishop's residence, as well as the home to a number of priests, *The Catholic Trumpet*, and the main body of the Church administration, with a portion of space set aside for visiting ecclesiastical and other distinguished visitors. Archbishop Mason hated it, and itched to move to the new rectory attached to St. Adamnan Church, which was warmer, of a modern design with up-to-date conveniences, and where the kitchen turned out more appetizing meals. Why suffer tradition when it meant chills and dankness, rats in the basement, silverfish, and pigeon droppings encrusting the window ledges? Coming up with a diplomatic argument persuading everyone it was in his best interest to move so far proved difficult. They're such damn touchy people, these Bowmountians, infected with a ridiculous pride about this rundown pile. If they found a spot Neville Bowmount had said he'd like to visit but never did, they'd erect a public fountain within a week. The Archbishop thought about changing residence often, and his mind had been on it when Fr. Jerome arrived.

That priest had, under the former Archbishop, grown used to instigating projects and, with his superior's consent, playing a larger role in provincial affairs than expected. The new man was not so laissez-faire, and his personality exceedingly bothered Fr. Jerome. It perturbed this native Bowmountian why he had not been elevated to the rank of Archbishop, considering what he had done on behalf of the local Church for fifteen years.

Being a parish priest was a fine thing, yet forever being one when you could be so much more . . . what a waste of talent. What a change, my assuming the post after poor old Connors, broken down man he became at the end. My God, this bread is tart! Where was I? Yes, delicate . . . headed that way by inclination and constitution. Nothing extra, nothing rich in his diet, he was happy as a pig in shit when you gave him milk, porridge, boiled vegetables and ham, bread with, oh dearie I, molasses. Filthy habit, but his only sweet. A tad too ascetic, and when people knew that . . . they got uneasy, you could hear them saying, Who's he to be so snotty, above us all! Try running one of the biggest entities on earth and looking like you haven't eaten in a week . . . see where it gets you. Connors' face was the face of the past. Today you need flexibility to get bums on the pews. The Church isn't any more a place for . . . abnegation, paring away . . . fine back when, but we're right now. We have to be in the world doing things, look at life straight in the face . . . appeal to what people want while you tell them what they need. Connors couldn't understand that . . . didn't see the old order had rolled up like a carpet and a new dispensation came in with Vatican II, thank the Saviour. Mind, the old fart didn't expect anyone to follow his ways, it was personal, but Mason . . . strictness personified, thinks he's an epitome when he's only an epigone. Can tell from his eyes he doesn't like Eminent House, and I can do without him hanging around. St. Adamnan's or St. Lawrence's, they'd be to his taste . . . if I can get him there, but how?

—Father Jerome, I think we should begin. Archbishop Mason tapped his watch with its blood-red face and skinny ebony hands. Before leaving, Darlene and Siobhan replenished the coffee and tea, and Marcella entered the time the meeting commenced. The first item was Fr. Henry's funeral, which Fr. Jerome introduced. —Archbishop, it's a shame you didn't know him in his prime. A good man, well respected.

—Who'll give the eulogy? I presume -

—I will, yes. We shared many . . . experiences, travelled quite a bit together. I'll miss his humour. I don't know where he came up with things, he had the oddest mind . . . and the songs he knew. There was one about some shaving cream, from the Second World War, I believe. Fr. Liam, you know the one, this fellow always . . .

—Yes! Shaving cream, makes you feel something, shave every day and you'll always look clean. The lines always ended with a rhyme for – well, Marcella's here or I'd say it!

—Something excretory.

—Exactly!

—I trust the choir won't be singing it, Father Jerome?

—No, why no, that's -

—There'll be enough sniping from the malcontents over Fr. Henry getting a eulogy without us introducing scatological songs. I'd have thought by now people would have understood this policy.

—It's hard for people to remember every new lesson, Archbishop, especially so many at once.

—At once? It's been years. It's very simple, Father Liam. We're all equal in the eyes of the Lord, of the Church, thus no member of the congregation should be singled out as special. Naturally, when a priest dies, one whose life's work has been communicating God's message, we must acknowledge it to some degree.

—I remember . . . before your time, Your Grace, May of last year . . . Professor Stapleton died, and his family, you've met his -

—His widow, yes.

—family? Sneaky. When they couldn't get a eulogy, they chose readings that suited exactly what they wanted a eulogy to say.

—Biblical readings? Or from poets? Fr. Jerome shook his head. —Very specific passages from the Bible. Archbishop Connors didn't know what was happening, though he was there. Other matters on his mind.

—Hmm. Just make sure you don't go on for too long. But there's nothing disallowing a few people to get up and say what they feel about the man. The important thing is to make sure parishioners don't think we're above them.

—I take your words as good advice, Archbishop, and add them to my years of experience.

—Then between us we have quite a reserve to draw from.

—You've said that better than I could, Your Grace.

—Now, you've been – what's that noise? For a few minutes Frs. Jerome and Liam, along with Marcella, swatted at a wasp, until it was crushed by one of Fr. Jerome's many books. Unseen by his colleagues, Fr. Liam quickly blessed the tissue-shrouded body, and Marcella covered her smile with her pad. Fr. Liam's action was sweet and silly, just like him.

—Damn bugs. Not a window open, but it got in. How? Turning from the garbage bucket Fr. Liam reminded the Archbishop there were several nests in the eaves of Eminent House, but that exterminators were coming Monday. —I hope they get them all. Now, the church is being cleaned, an expensive procedure. Father Jerome, the media keeps reporting on the stone work, how what the contractor is doing is weakening St. Finnian's.

—They're blasting and hosing the pigeon guano, dust, mould, pollution, away. The gulls and crows have increased in numbers over the years . . . left their mark on the building. Extremely thick in places. When they started using this – I don't think it's called a sander, not the precise name is it, Father Liam?

—I don't remember exactly.

—Anyway, the method means the vibrations shake the tower they're working on, and . . . yes, stones fall inside the church. The Archbishop tapped his pen on his knee and rubbed his face. He detested wasps. They reminded him of Italy where, in Pistoia, as a child on vacation with his parents, he had been terrorized by one. It had entered his room through a window of the stone villa they rented, waking him with its buzzing. Turning on the light he witnessed the wasp inspect the walls, then veer towards him, and with a whoop he threw the bed covers over his head, fearful that at any moment the stinger, surely a foot long, would pierce the thin sheets and impale him on the mattress where his body would lie undiscovered until morning. The wasp retreated, allowing him to cautiously observe whether it had left. It had not. From its resting place on a chair it attacked a wall and then, compounding the horror, a millipede raced over the same surface. For a moment the young Percival hoped the two would clash in an epic struggle, but they did not. He slipped from bed and ran to his parents' room, quivering in his mother's freckled arms until his father scotched the beasts. No wonder I've never wanted a post in Africa or Asia, so many bugs. The flies up north were bad enough.

—Archbishop, are you all right? You look -

—Perfectly. Carry on, Father Jerome.

—Well . . . there's nothing more to say about this cleaning process.

—Has anyone thought about a lawsuit? If one of those stones fell into someone's eye, say.

—My sister broke a crown on a stone in a pizza once!

—Father Liam.

—Yes, Archbishop.

—I see Your Grace's point. The workmen say they can string nets up that'll catch anything that falls. If we . . . cancel morning masses for the summer, the work can go on without risk.

—How big are these stones? Fr. Jerome picked up a large pill bottle, a former possession of the previous Archbishop, and shook out some of its contents. —Stones? Pebbles, more like it. You say they have netting as small as this? Fr. Jerome conceded canvas might be more suitable, but something had to be tried. —Very well. The nets of the workmen, get them up as soon as possible. Also, we'll adopt your suggestion about the masses right away. A peculiar expression came and went across Fr. Jerome's face so quickly it was unreadable. —Your suite is on the same side the men work on, isn't it, Your Grace?

—Yes, but you know I'm up well before they start.

—Still, the noise . . . it'll go on all summer, and into fall.

—I hadn't wanted to complain. It's such a small thing when everything is considered. Fr. Jerome would not accept such an answer. —No, Archbishop, it's intolerable. That work will go on for months, and then there's the cleaning of Eminent House to consider. No one can live like that.

—But you're not suggesting - no, I couldn't take over anyone else's room and force an unfortunate to sleep there.

—*The Catholic Trumpet* and others have long wanted the library renovated, and your predecessor thought to set up a fund for that idea . . . but we could never spare the room. Your suite would be perfect -

—But that would dispossess priests here.

—Archbishop, please, consider your station. You must entertain . . . and while we don't have another set of rooms like that here . . . why, the St. Admanan's rectory does. Close by, very modern, convenient.

—Wouldn't that mean someone moving from there? So you see -

—But, pardon me, but in this case it's only a room they'll need, and we have them here and there. It's the adjoining rooms we're short of. I think . . . Father Alex and Father Don, who's becoming frail now, would happily give up their living quarters at St. Adamnan's. No please, I insist. Marcella watched how Archbishop Mason acquiesced in the end, and thought how kind it was of Father J to make his superior as comfy as possible. She also felt surprised that Eminent House had charmed Archbishop Mason so quickly that he had to be argued out of it. It would be the first time an Archbishop had not lived under these roofs, but it was the stone cleaning that forced this break with custom, and as he repeatedly said, it was a temporary arrangement. The two men had every right to look pleased at doing the best for the other.

With the discussion about the new living arrangements concluded, Fr. Liam handed around a copy of today's *Bowmount Courier*, featuring a cover story by Janet Campbell. Over her copy was a photo of one of St. Finnian's towers wrapped in garish yellow tarpaulin. —It looks like a contraceptive device! And read the caption! Fr. Jerome did. —Protective Sects: Finnian's Erections Safely Swaddled.

—Typical Bowmountian journalism, from what I've seen.

—That fellow Karmiris is behind this, Archbishop! That's his paper. If St. Telesphorus had a tower, and if it looked like ours, you'd never see such a photo. But you can't trust the Orthodox.

—That's been the historical position.

—Since it's come up, the Orthodox numbers are rising, with all the Eastern Europeans we have now. They're raising funds for a Ukrainian

Church in Carlyle.

—But what do we do about this slur?

—Nothing, Father Liam. Silence is the best response. I'm sure some good Catholics will write in in protest about this Campbell piece, but the Church has been too much in the news for the wrong things, don't you think?

—Yes, but -

—Pardon?

—Yes, Archbishop.

—Father Jerome, make a note that there is to be a casual report in the parish bulletin two weeks from now about how the cleaning is progressing. If these articles by that chit of a girl persist - and I know, Father Liam, how exasperated you are with her, but we'll reply as we see fit, not in a knee-jerk fashion.

—And look at her first sentence. The younger priest, not wishing another rebuke, sought to change the Archbishop's mind by showing him the ugly and malicious lies the reporter had written. —St. Finnian's inward collapse serves, some say, as a reflection of the state of the church in this turbulent decade -

—Enough, Father. Your distaste is shared, but we will not be making a statement. We've more important things to spend time on. The next item dealt with Heaven, a topic the Archbishop felt cropped up too often in Fr. Liam's homilies. —Appropriate for the deathbed and the graveyard, but mentioning it in a church full of the healthy isn't seemly. Marcella agreed, but would have used the word frightening, for although she missed her husband Norman, and desired nothing more than to join him, when Father Liam spoke of Heaven he did it so beautifully she almost felt impelled to end her existence, and that was wrong, wrong, wrong. Not his fault, not really, okay? but I get queasy sometimes in the pew, like my soul was going to pass out through my stomach. Yet taking sides in the lively debate that followed upset her, for when two priests disputed how could she guess who was right? To think, theologians did this all the time, they must have thick skins, and how do they sleep? My head would be ringing.

She wished there was a rule that made it clear which priest was right when arguments like this started, like the one she had learned in school during spelling class. Yes, if there was something like when two vowels go a-walking, but I know that's not the way things are, okay?, or maybe if there was a law against this kind of argument at all things'd be more peaceful, but that's silly. Priests know more, it's just where I don't even know as much as Father Liam, not as much as Father J, and nowhere near what the Intellect knows, that's why I get bothered when they're like this. To calm herself, Marcella concentrated on her penmanship.

Partly to balm Fr. Liam's hurt pride, the Archbishop offered suggestions for homilies appealing to everyone. Privately, he viewed Heaven as a bothersome thing to explain. Banal remarks worked best and these should only be uttered when one felt pressed. The Archbishop may very well have agreed, with de Montherlant, that —The soul's longing for infinity, as that writer describes the ache of the transitory for the everlasting, —is a sign that any soul in such a cringing posture is completely unworthy of rest from the travails of this world. Often, when consoling mourners who clutched at his robes with impertinent fingers, a simple weariness, frustration, or aggravation over a recurrent bowel condition, made the Archbishop think along peculiar lines, and for brief periods he felt at odds with Church doctrine. Instead of being alarmed at this tendency, he cultivated it, for out of this orderly ferment emerged the articles that won him notice for his willingness to take on complex subjects, always returning to faith as the sole support in life. While he had definite ideas about Heaven, certainly a contentious topic, he refrained from discussing them with uncultured minds, such as Fr. Liam's. —Here, I've brought some photocopies of articles to illustrate my point. He beckoned Fr. Liam over with his usual gesture, second and middle finger stiffly joined, a gesture Fr. Jerome inwardly despised. —Read the titles, you'll see what I mean.

—From Whose Womb Did The Ice Come Forth? Recalling the Lord's Prayer: The Authorial Audience and Matthew's -

—What? No -

—A book review of *Public Religions in the Modern World?*

—I told the girl to sort them. No, they're too advanced. What I -

—Oh! Marriage!

—Yes, from *The Catholic World*, as we're in the season of marriages. I believe there are three tomorrow in St. Finnian's alone. Let me point out a few things. While the Archbishop did so, Fr. Jerome appraised the sun, the sky, the altar boys, Tim and William, and wondered if today he would reach his goal, the celebration of the Perfect Mass. Wintertime meant colds, dampness, hoarse or nasal lay readers, a restless congregation. In summer, these things to a great extent disappeared. Also in his favour, something Fr. Jerome took a keen, secret pleasure from, was the absence of that annoying Mrs. Hanrahan, a snotty bitch . . . praise be to God, she's freshly buried on Elephant Hill. It had been her exasperating practice to start each prayer, chant, song or greeting one beat before any priest could get the first syllable out. Once while giving the blessing Fr. Jerome heard this woman reach the Ghost before the echo of his Father died. Glaring at where she sat in the front pew in the centre of St. Finnian's, he wanted to pitch everything on the altar at her, and damn the sacrilege. Loudly, his voice distorting terribly through the portable microphone, he began the blessing once more, slowly, his eyes fixed on that dreadful woman who either had the presumption to usurp a priest's place, or else was ignorant of a parishioner's subservient role. While giving her the last rites on Tuesday past, as she suffered convulsions in her home, for the first time Fr. Jerome could say everything without interruption. Mrs. Hanrahan's eyes showed her awareness of this. She wilted under his quietly triumphant gaze, ceased moving her gray lips, and sank into a profound coma which lasted till her death Thursday morning. Upon her removal, Fr. Jerome resurrected the ideal of the Perfect Mass, and today, before the 5:00 service, he planned on revealing his desire to the altar boys so that there would be no mistakes. In his opinion, William in particular must be prepared . . . where he was so inexperienced. Yes, he and I will . . . bow our heads together prior to mass. For a boy to experience the complete arc of a Perfect Mass, from opening hymn to the final Amen . . . it's like seeing God stride across this world, and do his soul a world of good. Anticipating his dream's success, Fr. Jerome forgot himself and his hands jerked involuntarily, knocking papers and books off his desk. —Sorry! Marcella, would you – bless you. I was reaching for, but his voice trailed off. In getting back late to the office he did not have time to put away a book his secretary held and whose spine the Archbishop read. —*Teleny, or the Reverse of the Medal?*

—Ah yes, yes, Fr. Jerome muttered, taking the book from Marcella and placing it on a table to his side, —heraldry. You see, Archbishop, my family, the Ryans, we're . . . tracing our roots back to, and you know, there may be . . . a shield, a crest, something.

—But there's only you living, I always thought, isn't it? Answering Fr. Liam's question, the older priest had the feeling this point had been raised not long ago. —I have great-uncles, and aunts. Very old! No brothers and sisters or parents, so if I don't do it, who will? Ha ha *ha*!

—And the reason for doing it is why?

—Posterity. You laugh, Archbishop, but I know a doctor, Ralph Davies, who's made it his mission to come up with a disease chart of Bowmount families. That inspired me -

—To finds arms for yourself.

—Against a sea of . . . troubles? no, ha ha *ha*, but yes, as a . . . hobby.

—What's that other book? *The Course.* Not anything to do with miracles, I trust.

—My God, no! It's written by a local fellow, Everett Brinston, Father Liam's book. Did you know, the waters of the Mediterranean take . . . seven years to circle around there . . . from going in by Spain to leaving again along the coast of Africa? Think of all the shores it touches on. This book uses the water as a . . . device to follow what certain characters do over seven years, and what happens in the countries. It's like history and fiction at the same time, but the Holy Lands section is the most interesting. Brinston was a member of St. Lawrence's, years ago.

—Do you know him, Archbishop?

—No. But in his eagerness to erase *Teleny* from the Archbishop's magpie mind, Fr. Jerome, with help from Fr. Liam, regaled His Grace with stories of the author's life. Everett Brinston was a man in his sixties who, from an early age, sought out the public's attention via a series of incarnations, first as a sandwich board man sporting Biblical prophecies in a non-apocalyptic vein, followed by his roles as a wit on Bowmount College's newspaper, a French sailor complete with striped shirt, pipe, and cap, then as a jazz bassoon player specializing in street corner and pick-up-band bebop. A short dabble as a radical candidate running for municipal office was viewed by his growing audience as a comedown, and this persona had the shortest life. Picking himself up, he became a pitchman for local car dealers, breweries, shipping firms, and charities, eventually re-establishing his image as a character by costuming himself as a safari hunter, complete with beard and machismo distilled from hunting and military magazines. Brinston earned his living through tireless self-propagandizing, wine tasting, interviewing obscure figures, and sentimental history and travel writing. In 1985 he opened a nightclub to much fanfare, at this point favouring black shirts and suits with orange accessories, living the last years of a debouched life, as Fr. Liam put it. —And then last year, he stopped! Just like that! Married a young girl, eighteen, from a quiet Pentecost family, and we don't see him any more.

—None of his wives have been Catholic, and he's had a fair number. Four, five.

—Since then he and this Donna Louisa Montaigne, I think that's her name, have sold the club, for a pretty penny, he's sworn off drinking, and now, with this book, he's become -

—The Bard of Bowmount.

—Exactly!

—All that to tell me how he came to write a book? The Archbishop almost barked this out, for the loquacity Bowmountians mistook for eloquence infected priests and *hoi polloi* in equal measure, and he was no more interested in posers and one-day wonders like Brinston, who as a novelist could be classed as a self-employed liar and nothing more, than he was in heraldry or porcelain design. His question communicated this forcefully. Fr. Liam nodded meekly. Minor matters were then addressed, leaving one item left. Marcella knew this last was a very sensitive matter, and was more curious than usual as to how it would be handled. The Archbishop began. —Fr. Liam, I'd asked you to prepare a report, which you did, and thank you. We've both read it. Has anything happened since?

—Yes. We know Michael Plumb, the businessman, announced September what he called a plan for a spiritual reawakening through penitential acts. The report you have covers what happened from the fall till late June. Since then, this so-called spiritual reawakening, handled by a firm he set up called Pilgrim's Way, has had a massive success among the – the people, I suppose you'd call them.

—The masses, murmured Fr. Jerome, or at least that is what it sounded like. Fr. Liam nodded. —This new pathway to salvation, this is what the July 3 press release says, is – where was I? – is for those seeking to enrich their beliefs through immersion in the glorious deeds of the saints. Walk with them in their blood-stained footsteps, rekindle your faith in God, the Lord Jesus Christ, the Holy Spirit and Heaven, embrace the faith of old, the one true faith, for the sake of your soul. Join the Pilgrim's Progress, simply by -

—He's kept that name?

—Yes, he has! There's details on how to get involved. It ends by saying what communities are involved, how to join the faith processions. Then, from a July 11 press release, more of the same, but listing this time the events in full. But it has these – disgraceful sentences. Listen. Christianity needs dusting off, for the old faith is no longer adhered to. Everything must be born again, just as the original faith was born of blood, and everyone must be born again in the symbolic blood of the truest followers of Christ! Redeem your soul, quench your spiritual thirst, forsake today's false beliefs, follow the shining, noble, blessed and holy examples of, and then there's the saints' names.

—How many town councils are going along with this . . . lunatic scheme now?

—The final number is twelve, Father Jerome. This – circus! starts July 23, and ends on August 20.

—Father Liam, for the record, read the communities, please, and the dates.

—Yes, Your Grace. The procession begins in St. Cornelius, as I said, on the 23rd. Then to St. Peter's, July 26, Odilian Springs, July 29, Gabriel, Aug 2, Lawrencetown, Aug. 4. The next day it's in Lucy's Brook, then Aug. 7 in Donnanville, Aug. 9 in St. Katherine, then St. Oliver's Aug. 11. The last three places are Aug. 13, Adrian's Glory, Marysvale on August 15, and lastly Sheppardville on Aug. 20. According to Plumb's pamphlet, you can buy a ticket to join the whole procession for $800, or buy tickets for three communities -

—Any three?

—No, the first three, the second three, and so on, four stages. The last one is the most expensive, $350. They're all selling, Archbishop, every one of them!

—Madness. Fr. Jerome seemed surprised at his own description. — Who would have thought it would . . . take off?

—Father Liam, what about the media coverage?

—CCII will have a vehicle in the procession, reports every day. So will the other radio stations, and the television stations. Nightly reports on the days of the, what, celebrations? The papers are sending reporters and photographers. Probably that Janet Campbell type. And, and, the councils have offered to help set up tent cities for the actors who'll act out the saints' lives, and give permits for food concessions. Plumb's making a fortune on this, and the cities are cashing in!

—We've seen this coming. I've been in touch with our superiors, and the orders do not allow any ambiguity. There is a package prepared for every parish, and particularly those in the communities that blasphemous exhibition is visiting. Every priest, in every sermon, from now till August 20, and then the weekend after, is to attack this insult to the Catholic Church. Not one priest, not one, is to be anywhere near those processions unless he's trying to stop people from taking part in it.

—Do you mean like a picket line?

—Nothing like that. They're to ask people, around the sites in the towns, to turn around, to remember who those saints died for, the Mother Church, not Plumb, and beg them to stop.

—But they'll have already paid. This seemed a sensible remark, but the Archbishop brushed it aside. —They'll be asked to come to their senses, Father Jerome. Marshall every priest, the sisters too, lay people, and make those foolish pilgrims realize Michael Plumb has no right to our saints. They belong wholly to our history. They're not there to make money on for some entrepreneur. Immerse yourself, go back to the old faith. Don't you hear the sacrilege?

—We're not going, Your Grace. It's the people in the cars . . . the question is how to stop them.

—We can't, damn it! Except by force of moral persuasion. When I look around I don't hold out much hope of that happening, but we must denounce this. I want those packages, which are due to arrive tomorrow by courier, sent out Monday morning. If we can get enough talk about this in the pulpit and the papers we might have some affect. You asked about those in their cars. As far as they go, we'll do everything we can to make them reconsider. Most won't listen, I know, you don't have to tell me. But we must be seen to be doing everything possible, not with threats, we don't want to alienate anyone, but through pleading. Make them feel ashamed, guilty, understood? Get every priest out there worrying loudly over the souls of those who want to turn some backwater town into Lourdes or, God forbid, Medjugorje.

—There will be . . . objections, people will cite Jerusalem, and say if people can portray Our Lord there on the Via -

—Don't you think that's been taken into account? In Jerusalem, that sort of thing is seen as part of Christianity, but here, or anywhere in Canada? No, this vile sensationalizing can't be condoned or overlooked.

—There won't be much sympathy for us, but Fr. Liam's speech was cut off by the Archbishop's chopping motion. Marcella could not help but notice how emotional The Pilgrim's Progress made him. While the revelation that he could be so troubled spiritually should have made her sympathetic, since she had purchased a ticket for the last stage of the procession

Marcella felt aggrieved that no one thought of asking people who were going to explain their reasons. Not that she would suggest they should, or even hint she would be joining her fellow penitents at Adrian's Glory. Some very harsh things were being said now, and, not one to expose herself to abuse, she would keep her business private, particularly from that snoop Stephen, he has it in for me, because I'm a widow and he wants his friend to have my job, okay?, but I'll just take a few days off and tell people I've gone to see my sister in Crescent City.

—Don't think I don't know what we're up against, Father Jerome. The other night I was at an anniversary dinner for the Women's Centre, seated at the same table as the Mayor, Albert Lewis, doctors and lawyers, accountants, and their wives. Let me tell you, barring the Jews who were there, who were to their credit non-commital, everyone was bullish on the commercial prospects of this abomination Plumb's come up with. It's quite a blow having your opinions confirmed about the low moral bearing of civic leaders.

—Everyone was -

—Everyone, though one or two people condescended to try and make light of it. Not Runciman. His complaint was that too bad Neville Bowmount couldn't have died a martyr to Indian savagery as well as an explorer, think of the business the shops would do.

—It must be said, what with the numbers of . . . different peoples here, particularly in the rural parts, and then the native people, there's always been an . . . audience for evangelists, Archbishop. I remember a Lutheran minister, a mild man, in Ripton, who shot up a travelling evangelist's van. But that fellow came back. Father Liam comes from there.

—Let me tell you something, Archbishop. Adrian's Glory is just a hamlet, named after a botanist who could draw! The first fellow to come along and see the fields of flowers there, really pretty, still are, and that's how it got its name. Some of these places weren't named after saints! Lawrencetown was named after a prospector who didn't find anything. As for Lucy's Brook and Gabriel, they -

—Michael Plumb's failed at more businesses than he has fingers. An opportunist . . . I had a word with him in September, as I think I told you, and -

—Yes, and it didn't do any good. The Mayor's wife, that apostate, practically gloated, while Lewis sighed and said it's too bad there weren't shares in it so he could buy up the company. Was I invisible? No, I was there, among those false Catholics who grace Bowmount's churches every Sunday they happen to be in town, and what are they doing? Wondering how rich Plumb will be after this summer. To think that man is going to re-enact the beheadings, roastings, dismemberments of revered figures, all for Mammon, and prominent Catholics sit around admiring him. Envying his acumen.

—There'll be hundreds of people by the time he reaches Marysvale.

—Try thousands.

—And Sheppardville! Putting someone up on a cross like that. Fr. Liam repeated the rumour that a volunteer might be asked to come forward from the audience at the crucial moment, instead of having an actor portray the last agonies of Christ. Marcella's pen scribbled away, noting down the points they wanted looked into, ignoring swear words and colourful phrasing. —And so we're to make sure every sermon, every social occasion, every baptism, marriage and death, is used as an occasion to condemn this thing in the strongest possible language. The parishioners must be stopped from going to see St. Lucy, whose life story isn't known anyway, an actress portraying her, exposed naked in a brothel, verbally abused, set on fire for preserving her virginity, and then run through the neck with a sword.

—They wouldn't use real fire, would they? Later, Fr. Liam chastised himself for contributing to the Archbishop's controlled fury. —I wish they would, burn up every actor and witness and Michael Plumb!

—Archbishop, I'm afraid it gets worse.

—How? How? Not looking at his superior, Fr. Liam sketched how the lives of Ss. Adrian and Natalia, so the latest press release went, were to be dramatized in an operetta, with original songs and music by local musicians, and some choreography. This news excited Marcella, who knew that combining music and faith ensured a lively night's entertainment. After all, what had the masses of her childhood done but mix music with a foreign tongue and elaborate sets, providing stage directions for the audience? She listened closely to the description, titillated by what she considered a sneak preview, or as much of it as Fr. Liam could get out, of a guard in a prison who is converted to Christianity by certain inmates, and consequently jailed with them for sharing their beliefs. His wife smuggles herself in among the prisoners disguised as a boy – but there seemed to be, from Fr. Liam's account, a bit of smut there, as if some hanky-panky went on before her identity was discovered. Well, men, even Christians, in prison did things, okay? and the guard hadn't been a Christian long, and it was his wife after all. Probably things would be a tiny bit different from what really happened, but that was part and parcel of getting across a Tragic Death Redeemed By Faith, okay? The finale sounded fantastic, as the prisoners, the guard too, were burned en masse in a field, with only Natalia surviving, undetected, creeping in amongst the charred bodies to retrieve the only part of her lover not burnt, his hand. When she died, it was buried with her. How thrilling a story, how cathartic! —With songs! Fr. Liam finished. Oh, they'd have to be love songs! And there'll have to be a song at the cremation site, okay? and then one over Natalia's grave, sung by an angelic choir, about the never-ending love these two felt for each other as they heard God's Voice, and the re-united couple would hear this while enjoying each other in Heaven. How could any man understand that? If she wasn't busy taking notes, she might allow herself a little cry.

—Disgusting. Are we clear on this, then?

—The information arrives tomorrow?

—Yes, and I want it sent to each church Monday morning, with instructions to start preaching against this thing right away. We want extensive media coverage, so you and I will prepare something for the *Trumpet*. But these rustic priests, can they be relied on not to be in favour of this procession?

—Definitely. Well, almost. There are always a few . . . misguided souls, but they won't cause any . . . I'll see to that. The media will be contacting us. We'd do well to have Father Liam be the one person responding.

—Good idea, If, Father Liam, you can keep your emotions in check. A firmly held anger is more effective than a rashly released one. I see it's late. We'll end with a prayer, then let Father Jerome get ready for mass. We'll meet again Monday morning at 10 to take a look at the material before it goes out.

Within minutes the Archbishop and Fr. Liam left and Marcella started typing the first pages of the minutes. Alone in his office, Fr. Jerome calmed his mind simply by re-adjusting the room, which always looked disarranged after the Archbishop's visits. Cookie and cake crumbs were everywhere, and a raisin had been squashed into a crack in the hardwood floor. But soon he'd be gone, in two weeks. Cleaning eased his mind in a number of ways, and after all, he had to start preparations for the Perfect Mass. The sun still shone brightly in the unblemished sky, and the conviction grew that today would be the day. Fr. Jerome returned a portable vacuum to its place, rearranged his books, locking *Teleny* in a separate drawer of his desk, and used the toilet. Checking his watch, he saw that if William had followed instructions he would be in St. Finnian's back rooms in a few minutes, followed later by Tim, whose Saturday soccer practice meant he always arrived about twenty minutes before the service. I must be there to let William in . . . can't have him hanging around the doors . . . parents get annoyed when you . . . Fr. Jerome relied on both boys, who were of such perfect character. They loved doing things for him, you could tell . . . and Tim appreciated his gifts. Today the younger lad would be brought in and told about the Perfect Mass. Locking his office door, Fr. Jerome bid Marcella a good weekend, telling her not to work late, then made his way the short distance to the church, where the intense tête-á-tête went off splendidly.

During the mass later, William trembled slightly in the aftermath of bewildering and frenzied explorations. The thirteen-year-old's white and red vestments would have accentuated his ghostly face under ordinary illumination, but with the sun pouring in through the glass dome no one noticed except Tim. The boy kept his head bent during prayers, one slender hand chiming the bells at the correct times while Fr. Jerome guided everyone through the Eucharistic prayer. Kneeling, William saw how worn the priest's shoes were, and that his pant legs were slightly frayed, tiny threads clinging to mismatched socks, one black, one navy blue.

While the priest invoked God's name over the vessels, William noticed the red wine, which immediately turned black. This transformation plainly was impossible. He had participated in this exact same ceremony over six weeks and that had never occurred. But the liquid was the colour and density of the motor oil his father used in their car. Rubbing his lids to make purple streaks radiate across his eyes, William pretended to forget everything he had experienced within the last two hours, then cautiously lowered his sight from the priest's stained cuffs, feeling momentary relief upon seeing that the water and wine had re-assumed its familiar appearance.

Red is better, it's like blood, not pink like Father Jerome's – I hate pink. William's throat constricted, blood from wine no longer miraculous proof of God's existence but a sinister conjuring trick of man's devising. Right next to that cup brimming with a man's vital juices rested the ciborium in which was packed the meat of a man, both vessels set out for the congregation's swallowing. The sun shone steadily on the figures around the altar, but only William sweated. In his nostrils were the doughy fragrance of carrion, the high sweet scent, once again, of a viscous fluid, and from the votary and perpetual candles a burning stench. His slightly swollen mouth tasted like sour milk and he stared intently at the oval, crisp remains of Christ, and alongside that the Saviour's blood. Fr. Jerome continued chanting, his high forehead knit in concentration and thankfulness, for he saw that today, at last, in view of the people and, especially, of the Maker, he would finally commit the Perfect Mass. Not one parishioner had spoiled the ceremony by letting their brats run up and down the aisles screeching . . . not one note had been sung incorrectly by the cantor . . . the reader had not mispronounced any of the words in the readings. Lastly, the altar boys had been alert, especially William, whose . . . alabaster face looks so beautiful in God's natural light. Content, the priest raised the chalice, the smell of water and wine penetrating his very soul, and over the slight sound of his sipping he heard William collapse, sending the bells flying.

Push

I vy slowly drank her coffee, pretending to read *The Bowmount Telegram*, but more often she gazed out Winterton's picture window at a large field and baseball pitch where a handful of children were playing. As it was 9:30 in the morning, the sun had not yet hardened its light on the road and sidewalks, nor made the angles of houses protrude sharply, and the green of Bowmount East Park, fringed with myriad flowers, seemed as welcome a bed as she could imagine. The softness, this gentleness, in a part of town undisturbed by tourists, helped Ivy relax, and, slowly, recover from the hospital procedure. Breakfast helped too, after a twelve-hour fast. Winterton's poached eggs, wholewheat toast with jam and marmalade, bacon, and hash browns made for a meal she would never cook herself. Invariably Ivy had either hot or cold cereal, one orange, and one cup of coffee. This spread, to use her word, had restorative qualities, giving her energy while at the same time partial consolation for what she had been through only forty-five minutes ago. Ivy's stomach gurgled, and when her bowels shivered she sat upright. The paper lay by the emptied plate, its headlines – **Teen Murdered By Hot Fat: Drunken Father Jailed For Copy Cat Crime, Hail King Ernst?, Incest Okay Says Nova Scotia Family** – disregarded. Her body recalled the rubber, greasy penetration of the flexible sigmoidoscope, its camera transmitting pictures of pink flesh, white flesh, red veins in chain lightning patterns, the camera bungling around the nooks and crannies of her intestines during its serpentine intrusion. She had felt a precise discomfort from the beginning which, as air inflated her, became pain, making her mind frantic. At these moments the nurse's gloved hand patted Ivy's, and it felt surprisingly welcome, bringing a human note into this exploratory business. How embarrassing to lie curled up, rump to the world, writhing now and then, moaning two or three times. Her doctor, a woman, outlined in advance what would happen, yet no one could describe anything other than the mechanics. When the scope was removed there was a blotting of the picture, a soft sigh as her rectum closed, a wet sensation on Ivy's left buttock and leg. She cleaned up in a bathroom, experiencing the first of many rippling gas pains, and wondered resentfully if her nice doctor had ever undergone such an examination. Not because she needed to, but to know what the patients went through. Maybe she should have checked Camilla's copy of *Medic Alert* to see Dr. Laura McAuliffe's ranking.

Another woman Ivy knew who had a scoping said, —I've had half what any gay guy'd envy, but as she slipped on her skirt Ivy disagreed, for no one, whatever their sexual inclination, could find anything arousing in what she had gone through. All her body wanted to do was expel the intruder. Thankfully, as the doctor pointed out again when Ivy came out of the bathroom, everything looked perfectly healthy. The presence of blood in her mucus had been caused by burst nodes which foam enemas had resolved. Two weeks ago Dr. McAuliffe prescribed their use. A few days after the last home treatment, because of Ivy's age and family history, the doctor would —Take a peek inside, you know, kind of a precaution, what with you nearly forty. But don't worry, one look and I'll be out of there, you'll probably never have another. Shouldn't have too many anyway, they're not, well. How pleasant, this dangling sentence, what did it signify? Such thoughts filled her mind as her car left the hospital parking lot. Last night at 6:00 sharp I drank that purgative, what a mess. Topped off by this morning, a great way to start my vacation. To say she felt betrayed by her body would be an understatement. —I don't drink, she pointed out to the rear-view mirror, —do drugs, smoke, and Christ this. I don't even have sex more than once in ten years. She concentrated on driving to Winterton's, and just underneath the navigating lay the treachery of her body.

People get sick every day, live with it, but I'm not sick, or am I? It's a mild condition, it's not the c word, what a scare I got when I saw the blood. Her g.p., an old friend of Camilla's named Ralph Davies, calmed her down, saying cancer would be unlikely, but recommended her to a specialist —To be sure. He must have seen the expression on her face, that with every movement Ivy's fear increased. Certainly it was irrational, but the body isn't your mind, it isn't logical and capable of reasoning, not that reasoning's given me much happiness, the body's random, wild. Dr. McAuliffe proved sympathetic, but doctors only do so much. No one's explained why my body's suddenly turned against me, and I've lived a virtuous life. Well, not spotless, but very healthy. Ivy gave blood and plasma without fear of transmitting infectious or venereal diseases. She took pride, not an inordinate amount, in how she tended herself, —I rarely wear heels, I take vitamins and eat lots of vegetables, exercise, and I only ever use safe oils and gels and creams, so why doesn't any man notice me? But wait, where the hell did that – I was thinking about something else, isn't it funny what tricks your mind plays on you? See, there I am, thinking about my body and how it attacked me, and my mind just carried on with this dialogue – to who? for what? – about men. Men, men. And being under-appreciated. It's always the same thing, you're thinking about one thing *with your mind* and your *other* mind is busy undercutting you. But this all started with my body, how I hate it that people who lead dissolute lives weren't on that table this morning getting a tube rammed up their anus by someone who essentially didn't care you'd lost faith in your physical self, who would never, would she, comprehend why you were shaken by crimson toilet tissue. How alarmist! you could see that in her face, his too, though less so, maybe. You do everything by the book and where does it get you? You watch the cholesterol, the fluids, the potassium level, the sugar, yet something sneaky and dirty comes along and rips everything away, tramples on your confidence, undermines it, as if a disease had intelligence, forcing you to question yourself intensively. And what's my self? Which mind, and I have to stop saying that, it's the same mind, inquisitor and tortured, is my self? But the self, it's really mind and body and heart and soul, and if I feel my self threatened, or sick, or unreliable, what then? A struggle, and isn't life struggle enough without fighting how you are, what you are? Do you have to fight to slip rather than fall into death? A graceful exit, Ivy murmured as she pulled into a parking space. She looked in her rear-view mirror. Pale and tired, God, what could I expect? Gynaecological exams never made her feel poorly, half the world went through them, but this morning had been too personal.

There was no consolation in philosophy. Sitting in the hospital waiting room, in a shift both excessively utilitarian and verging on immodest, surrounded by identically dressed men and women, the majority senior in years, Ivy tried to concentrate on James Redfield's book, but found the glimpses of flesh too startling, the television too loud, the paging system too insistent. "As we gave him energy, Dobson became even more eloquent and inspired with his description of the new human culture." She searched for something cheerful in this, but found herself questioning how you could have a new human culture with the humans around her, at work, in a shop or spa, at Johnny's Bar. There were either too many human cultures, or they were all one, and how many culture-philosophies did this century need? A new human culture meant getting rid of who? Mine, yours, your friend's? Because most people had trouble with change, wouldn't change, couldn't change, so you weren't just tossing out cultures, you were tossing out people, and such discriminating power required a steeliness of nerve, a dead heart. Was there a type of spiritual eugenics at work here? Where did Dobson's energy come from, and could he separate the wheat from the chaff? How many of these people, all of us trying to walk in these ridiculous slippers, forget about positive energy, they're experiencing the insurrection of a deceitful body. You injected yourself with a cool foam that burns, you took inside a barbarous tube that felt, and I have to be crude, these gas pains don't help, like you were having the longest shit you'd ever had, a shit without end, and no amen to that? Why was she – and Ivy posited another Ivy inside herself, or more accurately, alongside herself – letting herself down? Oh, I could call it it, but it's me, and now I'm fighting myself for my self, aren't I? Is that what mad people do?

She reached for the car door handle but her hand kept falling back, resisting escape until the question ran its course. A provisional answer would be all she could invent. Where was it? Where was any relief from a good life with no rewards? Where was the value of it now, on this earth? Forget heaven, I'm talking about while I can enjoy things. When was the last time I enjoyed anything without knowing the end of it beforehand, second-guessing the inevitable disappointment? No man, no love, no adventure, even mild ones, no brighter tomorrow – a horn blared somewhere, and Ivy pushed down on her own horn. Reflex, she thought, and a silly grin crossed her face as she waved on a passer-by who thought she was signalling. I must look foolish, sitting here and debating myself about myself. Either a good laugh or a long cry would come soon. Right now, her smile was replaced by a grimace as gas swelled her intestines. Ivy realized how hungry she was. These upsetting speculations and self-doubts were brought out by the scoping. Wiser to forget them for now, concentrate on making myself feel better, starting with using the toilet in Winterton's, then eating. This time she could leave the car.

Now, thankful for friendly service, grateful for the replenishing food, Ivy tried to relax. Nothing had been solved, but the flurry of questions had stopped. They were always the same questions wrapped in disguise. Something would set her off agonizing over how unfair life truly was, and how much she hoped for a deux ex machina to resolve the major problems, to help her resist an inertia growing in strength as the years passed. How much time had she spent waiting, eating vegetables and dip at home through movie after movie, talking to the screen to hear a voice in her apartment? It's big, much bigger than I need, this place, I hardly use the furniture, and sure, occasionally a friend stays in the guest room, but I could live cheaper elsewhere. But it's a nice apartment, and the view of the hills and the four valleys is so restful, and can you put a price on that? In the public relations world she and Camilla occupied there was never time for peace, because each day a new project presented itself. The future collapsed backwards, filling today with commissioned campaigns, elaborate unfoldings of vendettas and propaganda, though she felt the increasing similarity between those two things.

On Camilla's desk, located in the same office as Ivy's, stood a calendar that offered supposedly cute or insightful comments on life in business, which meant, for most in the company, Life itself, so consumed were they by mercenary interests. You'd never see them debating Dobson's choice, would you? Not likely, it's just me, and look at them, they're not troubled. The **One Golden Day At A Time** calendar, devised for business and media people who at odd moments wanted to indulge in lofty thinking, presented inspirational sayings or verses in —Splendorous, Beautiful Words, as the box enthused, aimed to help one smile through March 21 or April 28 or July 13. One calendar leaf Ivy kept in her purse, coming across it today as she counted out money for breakfast. It was next to the drugstore's receipt for the cortifoam enemas. The ragged slip of paper, the author's name lost to time, read:

> The world in which Advertisement dwells is a one-day world . . . The average man is invited to slice his life into a series of one-day lives, regulated by the clock of fashion.

A one-day world indeed, but it wasn't just advertising. Everything lived the briefest of hours, and you know love's in there too, dying the moment after it's born. Prophecies went unfulfilled because there weren't enough hours for them. The future? Simply theory. Confidence vanished in a world like that, self-possession fled on seeing blood in a bowl, and everyone waited for that time after the word until. Until the weather improves, until my ship comes in. A vast amount of waiting interrupted by moments of intensity like this morning, and dreariness again. No pushing forward, but lots of lasting situations out. The Fabian approach to life. How to live in the void after "until," there was the secret to happiness, and no Zen Buddhist had the answer to that, no New Age book reconciled you to an earthly encampment outside the doors of desire when your intestines fouled you. Where was the strength to hold on, let alone push? Where did it come from? Not the energy Redfield spoke of, I know that, everyone's as empty as me. Almost everyone.

Ivy recalled a conversation overheard last week in Johnny's Bar, which she had taken to visiting since no one hassled women there. Depending on her mood, she did not know whether to be relieved about that or not. At times she wished that boy with the golden hair and sensuous voice would return, with or without his guitar, and he did two or three times, usually to meet the mute girl who would be sitting next to the painter. Two women who Ivy recognized though she never spoke to them were talking, and one said —This is more than I can bear, but I have to, because who else will, right? The other nodded. —It's just you, us. We gotta be strong. —Deb, I don't know 'bout you, but I hate being strong. It's easier to be weak, right, to let it all go, stop struggling. —But we can't, can we? 'Cause there's no one who'll help, is there? Mute consensus, then —Christ, but if this goes on. Ivy agreed with the hidden words behind these sentiments, an exchange carried on at a much deeper level. At that level resided a fatalism that blackened the blackest life, a nihilistic force capable of blighting the strongest pleasures. If that's where the strong were headed, make me weak, Lord, like that Indian lady, Lala Sastri, the girlfriend of that man Frank. His woman, he calls her. She doesn't look like he beats her, that'd be too easy, she's terrorized by him, grateful at the same time. Would I want to be wretched like her, or strong like people think I am? The answer that night was neither yes or no, but what kind of miserable choice is that? What about Nadeen, standing and pointing at Sam, not angry, emphatic, —I take photographs instead of painting because it's faster art. Someone else who knew the futures market was an abstract, that photographs gave you the fresh past, and didn't stretch time out to the chaotic distance. Strong like that? Well, she's an artist, she's achieved something. Me, I've -

—Ivy? Ivy Merifield, isn't it? Hello! It's Don, Don Coleman. D'you remember me? A man of average height and regular looks, with wavy blond hair and pale blue eyes, sat in the chair opposite. There were one or two other diners who heard this introduction, and Ivy felt slightly embarrassed at being singled out. —D'you mind me sitting down? You looked -

—Why no, hi -

—lost in space, sort of, and if -

—No! It's been so long, don't be foolish, yes -

—I'm not bothering – are you sure?

—Yes, my. It's been years, hasn't it? It has. She knew him from high school and their first two years at Carlyle University. He had been a nice memory.

—Gee, it's good to see you. What a surprise.

—Well, and you. You're looking sharp, well dressed, and that tie. How nice to see a solid tie with no pattern, and not too wide either. Although the suit's a bit warm for today, isn't it?

—There -

—Listen to me, I'm here talking about your clothes, when it's not even important, well, they are important. Obviously. A gas pain shot through her and she straightened up. —But you, how are you? You must be doing well. Seeing how you're dressed!

—Yes, well. And the tie, old, isn't it, the style I mean? I was never stylish, like Derek was, and you and Sharon. I've been at this memorial service. Oh, it wasn't anybody we knew in school, no, Chris Greenland, I met him after we, ah, took different paths, I guess. You went away, didn't you?

—Journalism school. But he was a good friend?

—We hung out together, only not so much these last couple of years. Got together once in a while, you know.

—You say I don't know him. I wonder why his name sounds familiar.

—Right in that paper you're reading, probably. Don's finger indicated a story tucked below an advertisement for a hair restorative. —He was one of the cops who – the pet store?

—Oh, for the hostages! Yes, there was something in here. It was awkward to speak about, and after not seeing Don for so many years, starting things on a morbid note did not make catching up easier.

—If we'd known he had troubles we could of been able to help.

—To think, all of them -

—Their inspector's being investigated for sending unstable people into that situation. Couple of 'em volunteered, though, like Chris.

—The papers said – they always say something. About a death wish, death pact, was it? Do you know something?

—Hey, you're the reporter, aren't you?

—Me? No, no, I'm in p.r., took that degree and did a few jobs, but I came back here after a while -

—Hard to stay away.

—and found a job.

—You know, I don't see anybody from University round. Don paused while cautiously evaluating the changes nearly twenty years had wrought in Ivy. She bent down, picking up her purse, to hide her physical discomfort. —This friend -

—Like I said, he had troubles. Susan, his wife, left, took the two kids, 'cause Chris was depressed. That got him more depressed, but yeah, it made sense to her. He was getting counselling, on a desk job for a while, but still. A lot of cops here, did ya know this, were pretty angry after those riots in Queer Town a while back, and then some of them had to work on those sexual assault cases with the priests and brothers. So Chris and his partner burned out I guess. But they were sent out by their inspector, he figured they were cured, walked right into that shop with another cop who was off duty but recognized them, and bam, the place goes up. Department did everything to keep their mental condition under wraps, but somebody blabbed to CCII.

—I'm really sorry to hear about your friend.

—So that's why I'm dressed up.

—I'm so sorry. What about you, what have you been doing?

—That's going back pretty far, 1978, isn't it? Heckuva long time. I'm a consultant for insurance companies. Not a lot of giggles there, but it pays the bills, and it's secure. Don't worry, I'm not gonna sell you a policy. How are your folks, Ivy?

—They moved to Ontario to be with Tod. You remember my brother? He and his wife have four kids, a big house, and the weather is nicer.

—So you're on your own here. No family, I mean.

—No, none. As they exchanged each other's discreetly edited stories, Ivy recalled how she once felt attracted to Don. He was kind, polite, more articulate than others his age, and she liked his plain honest looks. In high school, when he had dressed himself up as a cowboy for a Hallowe'en party, complete with a little make-up to darken his features, she had commented on how handsome he looked with a tan. Another time they had encountered some female friends of hers, and she had left to chat briefly with them. On her return, he had commented on her smile. She told him her friends said she looked very happy. A week later she asked him, when they were alone in his parents' house, if she could wash her hair in the bathroom sink. She was nearly nineteen, he seventeen, and he remained oblivious to her signals. At a bar some weeks later, she suddenly stood and loudly declared, to him and to the room, —I'm going to see if there's some *men* around. Their friendship cooled and they saw each other intermittently over the next two years. She considered, as he spoke of Julie, his wife, and their plans to have children, that they had always walked separate paths. Perhaps the slight age difference had accounted for his lack of interest in her, combined with Don's naivety regarding women. Whatever the reasons, he never recognized the hints she dropped. How it hurt her to be ignored in such a way by a boy she felt would become a decent man.

—Enough about me, I've been going on, what about you, doing well?

—Yes, I guess I am. There's always something happening that needs handling.

—What's it you do, exactly? Set up press conferences? You probably hobnob every day with the rich and powerful, I can see that, easy. You'd be a hit with them.

As she explained her work, another part of her wondered if beneath his friendliness things were happening that required observation. After the initial awkwardness, their conversation had gone smoothly, and Ivy found herself again enjoying his company, despite gas flare-ups and a developing headache, the latter a result of relief from this morning's stress. I should say, enjoying the company of a pleasant man, that's more specific. Undoubtedly he has memories of us, we were so young, another life.

On Don's part, he had hoped that a quiet cup of coffee would relax him after the memorial service. Since he never came to Winterton's he had assumed the chances of meeting acquaintances were low. If the person opposite had been a man he would have nodded, bought his coffee, and returned to his car, but he never shied from women, and it had been twenty years since they had seen each other. Since Chris' death Don's thoughts often turned to friends past and present, Ivy particularly, and now, as if summoned, here she sat. One friend buried, another resurrected. Good-looking, better looking than in high school. But I don't want her thinking I think that! I need to change the channel. —Speaking of that, we vacationed in Hawaii in June. We'd been saving up for a couple years, working overtime, Julie's idea. Don described that state's natural beauty and Ivy listened with half a mind, the other half divided unequally between the headache and curiosity over Julie's rising prominence in Don's story. Don't tell me he lives through her. He keeps dropping his wife's name, making up for that compliment, he feels guilty. Thrown off by seeing me. He'd come here to cry the way most men do, that is, brood. Or sulk.

—Say, you all right?

—A headache, it's been coming on all morning. Not enough rest. Don looked at his watch. —Sorry to hear that. I gotta say, it's been great seeing you, but I gotta go. Took part of the morning off, but I need to get back to the office. Can I do anything?

—Thanks, Don, no, I'm going to sit for a couple of minutes, let it pass.

—If you're sure. All right. Here's my card, maybe we can get together. I'll write my home - our home number on the back. Ivy watched him leave, wondering who would be the first to give up the pretence of calling the other. Resting her head against the back of the booth she closed her eyes for a few moments, not noticing anyone take the seat opposite. A quiver in her intestines intensified the pressure in her spinning head. A rest in bed, that's what I want. No talking, nothing but quiet, he's as nice as ever. How would he feel about fatherhood, changing diapers at his age? He never said. Were children Julie's wish alone? No more travel to Hawaii, that was the last hurrah. Selfish, if she's the one behind it. Or pushing them into it, telling him about biological urges, they can be resisted. Look at me, hit on by husbands and skinhounds - why the hell can't I meet someone like Don, a good man, a *single* man? Ivy opened her eyes, startled to see a familiar but momentarily unnameable figure on the other side of the booth table.

—Are you feeling well? You looked so wan with care.

—Who are you, what – how long were you sitting there?

—It seemed you were ill. The vapours, on such a hot day? The company, perhaps? We're co-patrons of Johnny's Bar. You're Ivy. Now she remembered, —Deeka, Jules Deeka, though she had not seen him there for some time.

—Good, good. He slid a black and yellow hardcover to one side, setting his mineral water down. —More coffee?

—How long -

—At the most a minute, a diamond minute set in one golden hour, as the sermon goes.

—Christ.

—He was in there somewhere. You looked as if you were saying a rosary, but I couldn't hear a thing, don't worry. Then I thought, epileptic? You're positive you're -

—Just a headache. Ivy tried to rise, but a gas pain bent her over. —Here, that's not good. Waitress. Waitress! Water here, now.

—There's no need for all that shouting.

—Who's shouting? That slattern's been chewing her nails for the last hour, yawning when she wasn't masticating. She'd do both together if she could. Here we are, no, leave the pitcher. And take these plates away. Go on. *Thank you.*

—I thought . . . the lady . . .

—Thank you again, she's in good hands. You're nosy, that's all. Call one of your boyfriends, that's why they put the telephone in here. I've some Aspirin, Tylenol, Advil, Gravol. In a fog, Ivy, despising both her condition and requiring a stranger's help, took two tablets of something and drained her glass. —Don't be so hard on that poor girl.

—She and that bearded boy feel each other up passing between two tables. Two planes, if you will, joined through geometry by cone and rod. She rides horses, I heard her, stimulated -

—Please.

—More water, of course, stimulated when she comes in, horsehair and all. Last Saturday at noon she complained, Won't that door ever stop opening?, because she didn't want customers interfering with her fondling Trotsky or working on a Bowmount 1-900 number. Not since her drinking days had Ivy experienced such nausea, intestinal disruption, and a spinning head while someone kept talking, uncaring, despite his watery concern, about her discomfort. Not like Don, she thought, and no wonder I gave up drinking, this isn't funny. Had she trusted her legs and bowels, Ivy would have left Winterton's immediately, but here she must sit, stranded with this strange man, his bad manners, his citrus aftershave. —You go out with Nadeen Sarkissian, don't you? This was one of the few things Ivy knew about Jules, and hopefully it would draw him away from the staff's sexual habits.

—That's how you know me, through her? Or by her?

—Saw you at the bar.

—I don't go there now. Nadeen, a creature of instinct, and intelligence, just an aggressive kind. I gave her some pointers on the ideas behind her art, but her attitude about us disappointed me. Shit, thought Ivy, why didn't I remember they'd split up? —She's a good photographer, yes, very loud too, but not when we first met. Here, in fact, myself and a young friend of mine, Loyola, you've seen him. He met Nadeen's friend Kate here, Kate the curst, broke that youth's heart cruelly, an affair with her boss. Someone spied them together when she said she'd be with a female friend. This is an unpropitious place for meeting a woman. But things can change, can't they? To prevent Jules from pursuing that topic Ivy desperately said, —Nadeen, too loud? That's what broke you up?

—She talked about us too freely, it reached other ears, and I can't abide that. As for her loudness, it suited our passions perfectly. She enjoyed to the fullest what could be called the ecstasy of the unbounded, and set my ears ringing with her unfettered, lusty cries. I'd swear the glasses in the kitchen sang merrily along. But everything in its place. Loud? The wrong word. Shouting. You could hear her whisper a mile away. Except, and this is curious, when speaking to her mother. You know Nadeen's Greek Cypri-ot? Her mother won't learn English. Often Nadeen would hang up the tele-phone after hectoring an art dealer or exhibitor, at what she considered a perfectly modest volume, then call her mother. It was as though you'd gone from a revivalist meeting to a Quaker house. Speaking to her mother she possessed the most beautiful voice, musical, mysterious, enchanting, arousing. I can see why Odysseus had himself tied to the mast, for fear he'd plunge into a sea of passion. That's what Homer's sea stands for, you know. And Odysseus chose to have himself tied to a mast, a substitute penis, and stay with his men. Try taking a photograph of that voice, I said to her. I did, with her consent, take two shots to compare, and you can see the face muscles straining against the bones, or at least I can. Sadly, Nadeen hates Greek, she only uses it for her mother.

—You left her because she talks loudly in English, not softly in Greek?

—No, talked to others about us. In English. Talked loudly, snored loudly, farted loudly, you asked, I'll be candid, banged doors -

—Honesty, and able to gossip at the same time -

—How could I love a woman who despises her mother's tongue, thus her mother?

—You smiled when you said love, it's -

—When I say love, I define it as -

—Love? You only slept with her. People talk about relationships all the time. Loudness is nothing to break up over, it's no crime.

—Not to be immodest, Ivy, but just sleeping with me isn't a small thing. Minor miracles have been wrought by the sexual act, if the partners are compatible. Can't you imagine that? By the way, isn't it amazing what a restorative water is? Moments ago you were near collapse, now you're quite bullish. Beware the lean and hungry looks -

—Don't try and get around me with poetry. They're only lines, like, what was it, ecstasy of the unbounded, like whether my bark went down at sea, no more influential than remember my name, you'll be screaming it later.

—Do you know, Every word she said, the lively malice of the hazel eye?

—From what I overheard Nadeen say, the word love doesn't mean anything to you.

—She said that? Ivy took sudden pleasure in reminding Jules his philosophies and attitudes were common knowledge. —Here, as elsewhere, she and I disagreed. Love, a word cheapened by overuse, we sign cards love, we love pistachios. Women like Nadeen, maybe like you, I'm only getting to know you -

—I'm at a disadvantage, the minute I can get up -

—or Don's Julie, who sounds a bit shrewish -

—How the hell do you know about him, them?

—I was sitting behind those plants. I heard an interesting but strange conversation. It's very quiet, there's no one around -

—That was a private -

—You carried on like this was your home. I'd brought my book to enjoy with a coffee in peace, and what did I hear? The two of you chattering about children, vacations, Don's exciting career as an insurance consultant, your job ad nauseam -

—You sat and listened.

—Who listened in on Nadeen when she told Kate what -

—Told the whole bar.

—happened between - speaking of people talking, why did Don keep saying he loved Julie? You have to start suspecting a husband who goes on about loving his wife when talking with a beautiful woman. All I had to go on were the pauses between words, but they were pregnant.

—You don't stop, do you?

—You're free to leave. Or are you too weak? For a moment Ivy wanted to say —My bowels are on fire, my stomach's in agony, and this migraine, but the word weak stung her. Fuck him and the horse he rode in on, I won't fold. —Tired, tired of men who think like you.

—There can't be many of them. I'd say some feel as strongly, no question, but think? For instance, this morning I was pondering the question of the plotless existence.

—The what? The -

—It comes up from time to time. We each have these black dogs howling around us. Don't you have one? Don't you worry about where you're going?

—No.

—In the seminary, the thought that everything could be chaos diminished whatever Christian beliefs I possessed. Today it put me in a February mood, so to say, and by chance, design, who knows, I opened my book, before the two of you started catching up, and came across this passage. Jules read:

> This month of Caesar Augustus is a hot, good-natured, casual month. During its thirty-one days the foison of many a broad acre grows ready for the harvest; indeed, the countryside, far and near, lies basking under its hedges, like some swart, amorous dairy-wench, in sultry contentment, her vagrant longings at last completely satisfied. In the month of August the power of the Priest is at its nadir. Let him raise pale, vestmented hands before never so many ornate altars, let him thunder in the garb of an evil crow from never so many Puritan pulpits, it will profit him little.

—Fine sentiments, a different perspective that improved my spirits. Just like Redfield does yours, I expect. The book's peeking out of your bag. The plotless existence poses such a horrible puzzle, doesn't it? The choice is whether there's a God, or whether nothing can be predicted. You see people every day professing their belief in God at mass, but they hedge their bets and look elsewhere too, on the off chance he's up and left. God isn't enough, don't you see, or He's too much. It comes to the same thing. People say, and I'll take it from personal experience, show you I've a sense of humour about things, I'll never sit next to that maniac with his views and theories again. But they do, they sit or stand at a bar and ask what I'm doing here, what my job is, as if it's any of their business, and we're off.

Too late they realize what they've let themselves in for. I'm not unconscious of myself. They go away and say, In hindsight I see that was a mistake, or, I knew he'd bend my ear. They look backward and say, There is a pattern after all but it can't be counted on, because I may have changed, he may have changed, a chandelier might fall from the ceiling and crush one or both of us, or we might actually, a faint hope, interest each other. It's silently comforting not knowing what's going to happen, because you don't go around getting excited for no good reason. The details of life, that's the other side.

—The other side of what? I can barely see -

—Close your eyes, drink some water. The other side is there is a God, but if that's so, then how come He won't help me find my favourite tie, or help me pick out the winning lottery numbers, or why didn't He save my father from dying of a heart attack? No, if God's in the details, what a morbid life you'd lead. But belief in a plotless existence ensures a minimum of crushed dreams. If things happen randomly, you stand a faint hope of good things coming your way. But to install God there? We say the Devil's in the details, but that character's as dead as the Doges, there's no room for him in this century, what with Stalin and Hitler and Mao Zedong and Pol Pot. Who needs mythical bogeymen when you've seen the real thing? What we're left with is a choice between a haphazard life, or a piss-poor Dad. As a female friend of mine said, not Nadeen, this is beyond her, Vatican II enshrined in the Catholic Church the post-Freudian view of the father figure. No one wants a mean father, do they? So shame, guilt, don't exist. The Old Testament God? Replaced with Sylvia Plath's father. Or for those who haven't gone that far, there's the image of a hopeless old man bumbling around upstairs, slamming doors in rooms closed for eons that we'll never see and muttering about his war buddies who've been dead for ages. Ivy, this age is fouled and black, and your New Age prophecy, and my dusty pantheism, and someone else's Zen Buddhism, are diversions keeping people's mind off the rot, or they keep the black dogs at bay. To remind us of the beauties of this present world, this August, so we can get by and not throw ourselves off a cliff.

—Is that why you can't define love? Living from hand to mouth every day.

—Not every day, but surely you've had those days. Haven't you? To their mutual surprise Ivy answered the question. —Yes, but to set the standard of how you'll live by the worst days?

—We've each got something unique that beats against our windowpanes at night. I have chaos, what do you have?

—You didn't answer me, about defining love.

—It's a rare thing, love. Everyone says they knew it once, but I don't know. I remember my first love, one truly intimate night alone with each other is all we had. Not intercourse, there was some sex, but more importantly something closer. We were very tender about each other's feelings, I can still feel it. I was sixteen, she was eighteen, and I would have surrendered my life for her. Melodramatic, but true. One night, that one night, we were lovers, two days later she told me her friends thought it too soon for her to be going out with me after breaking up with someone else. Incomprehensible. Three weeks later she was with another boy, then with another fellow a few weeks after that, and another, then another. Years later I found out she had a problem with self-image.

—Maybe you couldn't satisfy her.

—That won't get a rise out of me, Ivy. True, I couldn't have been what those older kids were, but I loved her, and it would have increased, I can feel it today. After that, no girls for two years, until I decided the priesthood at least gave my virginity a respectable cloak, and all I've ever needed was a cloak, a stick, and bread. She finished the idea of pure, romantic love for me. One glimpse of heaven followed by misery. This isn't said to get you to sympathize with me, I doubt you would. We're not making friends with each other here, clearly, but you do have a mind, and that's admirable. No, I'm simply stating my whole way of thinking changed at seventeen. If you ask me what my definition is of modern love, for men, I'd say it's the pain a man's imagination experiences when someone he might have been able to sleep with gets away.

—Revenge on the whole species.

—You mean gender.

—Denying lovemaking, a normal life, for everyone, because you don't have it.

—And you do?

—We're not talking about me.

—No, we're not, are we? Hardly a fair exchange, but this isn't your sparkling self. A normal life, what's that?

—Ruling out love because of what happened when you were a teenager. Think of all you're leaving untouched.

—It comes to making a choice. It's better to not be with someone and grieve over a potential life lost, rather than be with someone and grieve over a potential life lost. Do you see?

—But the young girl? You don't grieve over that? Jules frowned, and too late Ivy sensed she had pressed hard on a sore point. —That was only once, it never happens a second time, never.

—Back to love again.

—Love, and husbands.

—You would know this from personal experience? Not according to Nadeen -

—I don't know who that Greek is consorting with, but not you, you're simply using her – any weapon that comes to hand, is that it? You have gall accusing me of gossiping when you keep quoting Nadeen, who doesn't know you from Adam. Ivy tried to stand, but collapsed again into the booth. Bright coloured balls flew across her vision and she felt herself shaking. Later she recognized this as a fear response, her body's way of telling her to escape, but her bowels and the headache prevented this. What she had undergone at the hospital, the miserable strain of thought following the procedure, Don's unsettling appearance, and Jules' twisted ideas, were causing a revulsion towards the world of the senses, to the world of thought and feeling, but she was trapped in this booth turned infernal echo chamber, forced to wait Jules out until she felt better. I can't let him intimidate me, let him see me like this, he'll pounce, I have to keep going. What was that, he'd gone back to —these gender notions of love, you see? As in sex, you women bring that shared love into yourselves, no trick to it, elementary psychobiology, or ingestion of that love. Which means the -

—Look, this, my head -

—love, that ideal, is more important than the husband. Because the love is shared. If the husband's off hunting and gathering, if he beats her or ignores her or sleeps with other women, it doesn't matter, as long as that love is left unhurt. It's almost more sacred than a child. Jules spread his hands apologetically. —Sorry, but a man puts his love in one woman, while women love the idea of love, you're in love with love itself. There's the unfair, ugly fact of life. A man attaches love to a woman, and God help her if she starts to bore him. The woman views their discrete loves as something that unites to be shared, it's the centre of the relationship. I've been in what the herd call love a hundred times, but a woman is faithful to Love, capital L, while man is faithful to one woman in one place for a limited time.

—That may be true for you, but not for every man.

—How many times do women say men are always like this or that, or are pigs? Out of politeness, if a fellow's around, they may say present company excepted.

—That boy Loyola may believe you, but what you're saying is wrong. What would you know about a woman's condition?

—You can't refute what I've said, only disagree. Too bad, but then you're unwell, although the flush seems to be fading, and your eyes are a little clearer. If I'm wrong about women loving love more than a man, prove it. Where are these good men? I've not seen any, and I've been on this spinning globe for almost half a century. These true-hearted men, like Don, why haven't they burst on to the scene, made the paper you have there, been filmed by CNN? Where are these fine, unmarried men who love love like women do? Why don't you have one, if they're so common?

—I'm not getting into my personal life with you.

—But you'll ask about Nadeen, and not think twice about repeating her words to me, and that's personal. Hypocrite. When all I did was come over and ask if you were all right.

—You eavesdropped, then you were a Peeping Tom -

—Of all the -

—If I wasn't this way -

—Your friend Don, and Jules' voice grew quite loud, threatening to bring back the buzzing which had almost tapered off, —is almost as bad as the goddamn castrati.

—Castrati? What -

—You don't have a boyfriend, but you want one, and why don't you have one? Your personality? Your looks? Your brains? Yes, the last would frighten the average man. So who do you know? Mostly gay guys, married men hemmed in by rules, and then there's the coterie of boy-men who cluster around women like you, they're smart, rude or shy, but feeble. To them you're not a woman with a vagina, with sexual desires, you're the mother-lover, the one who cuddles them but poses no threat, who won't unmask their unmanliness. Your body's free to fantasize about, though. By now Ivy could stand. Though she staggered towards the exit her vision and control were returning. —Some nervous kid, continued Jules, following her, —who forges pictures of you riding him on his bed. They think that's satisfaction, they don't know the climax of masturbation versus sex with a woman is like a volcano with no towns to bury. Degeneration, the best a castrati has to offer! Remember that! he shouted while Ivy fumbled with the keys to her Mazda. He stayed where he was, half in and half out of the café, the upper part of his body visible. —Goddamn it, I don't know, but the slamming of the car door cut off his, what, apology? after that? more words, useless words? and she started the engine. —Get me home, dear God, please, before I throw up or shit myself. By the time Jules left Winterton's with his book, having paid their bills, her car had disappeared. Settling in his Jetstar 88 he wondered why he had pushed her, but that thought receded as he considered what she might have meant with that crack about Loyola. —What the fuck's going on there, and with him?

This sunlit chapel

Turning onto Prospect Avenue from Kinsworth Street, Janet saw Loyola standing in a green square contemplating a beech tree. As she was about to blow the horn, a side door of the Moscati-Mann building opened and out stepped a blonde woman. —Loyola! It's not 5:30, there's two suits hanging in the packing room for Pierre, he's picking them up at six sharp on his way to the airport, so get in and do your job and leave on time, understood? The door slammed. What a voice. It's 5:35, what's her problem? And what's with her face? Loyola crossed the street, barely acknowledging Janet, paused, and entered the building. I could've done without seeing that. Janet parked near the warehouse doors. As the minutes passed she felt drowsy in the August heat. Had her air-conditioning worked she would have been happier, because through the rolled down window came the smell of burned food sprinkled with urine, and a peculiar odour reminding her of wet plastic wrapped around decaying candy. She loosened a button of her top, fingers brushing perspiration at her throat. —I thought this'd be cool. Glad I didn't wear a bra. God, the stink. And those birds. Gotta be a story there, folklore, dying gull as metaphor. Maybe Gilbert'll let me write on *that*, since the fuck – stop. Janet hummed along with the radio until the irritation passed. Bowmount's crowded with gulls, owls, crows, hawks. A lot of dead ones, like the black swan in West Valley Park. Carlyle has them too. What did Runciman say? Hide your garbage, throw ammonia over it. Great for the environment. He should smell this place. With his wife by his side, the Lord Mayoress the jerk calls her, and how many people know Bernadette Holloway's clit's pierced? Would that stimulate you? With Runciman she needs it, got a whiff of his breath once, terrible. Fillings must be leaking. The friction, there'd be chafing, at first, wouldn't you be going around all day rubbing yourself? Nice, maybe, I could use some of that these days, with a guy who'd treat me right, and this weather doesn't help. Her eyes snapped open and her hands flew to the wheel from somewhere as her cousin got into the car.

For several minutes Loyola stayed on one topic, Starlene. —You saw her. What was it, 5:28? Two minutes early. She called me back to do two suits she just put out. She could have done them, but she knew I was getting picked up, the -

—Hey!

—the, the cunion. What was it she said? Loyola, if you'd stayed till quitting time they'd be done, and your girlfriend wouldn't be waiting.

—She what?

—Bet you he's not coming. He'll call from his car, tell her to send them out in the mail tomorrow, there's no rush. But she'll be seen working late by the customers who tell the salesmen who tell Toronto. She's always there, she has no life, talking to her shithead friends. They come in and take over the goddamn place. I'm on the phone to some drag-ass customer who can't find the suit number or doesn't know blue from navy, and they're laughing away. I can't hear myself. If those guys had work to do, why don't they do it? They look at me like I'm the one who doesn't belong. Buying up damaged returned clothing at 20%, 30%, 40% off wholesale -

—That's cheap.

—Goddamn steal. You know she has a list of their sizes and what their wardrobe's missing? This is how one of them put it, I need a cashmere overcoat, my wardrobe isn't complete. Houndstooth and Prince of Wales check suits, double-breasted white dinner jackets. These guys got taste. They won't take any old rag. Anthony knows, he -

—Who?

—The boss, Coish, the accountant. A born liar. Get this. Made him coffee today, first time, he looked busy, I wasn't for a change. He'd put on the kettle, then his phone rang. His cup has coffee in it, so I pour in water, the milk, no sugar, and he comes and asks how I made it. First words! Not, Thanks, Loyola. How did you make it? I tell him. No, no, no!, and he throws it in the sink, The milk, then the hot water! Didn't I know that completely changed the taste? No thanks from the -

—Aunt Karen used to say, not a hello, good-bye, kiss my ass, or nothin'. Loyola's face changed from re-enacted fury to a more troubled expression at hearing a close imitation of his mother's voice. —Who cleaned the mess up? They're pissed off at each other, but you know they can't fight out in the open. They take it out on me. That's my real job. Sorry, Janet, I've been going on. Sorry for cursing.

—Just I get it all day, I'm trying to stop.

—Her friends get me. Looking down at the poor stockboy, like I'm a half-wit.

—She know you went to university?

—Like I'd put that down, so she could make fun of it. Janet hadn't taken as Gospel Loyola's version of life at Moscati-Mann, but today what were once been regarded as tall tales had gained a degree of credibility from the style of the building and the palpable atmosphere of the street. If his own dad doesn't get along with him, why would Starlene? How does he provoke her, what are the dynamics? But it can't be one-sided. She looks and acts like he described her. Janet looked at him. —Cuz, it's warm enough without seeing you bundled up in that sweater.

—Usually I leave it at work. He had certainly changed shape in a year. Janet felt the sweat at her throat trickle through her cleavage. —Starlene's face . . .

—Like someone whacked her nose with a club.

—She dresses well, and her figure's not bad. How old?

—Thirty-four. Her figure? Never noticed.

—Come on.

—I never noticed the way you'd think. She pissed me off early. But add that voice to her nose and you get ugly.

—She isn't ugly, you just don't like her so you'll say anything. Didn't you say all these guys came around?

—Not for that.

—Not just for a suit, you know that. They - hey, twerphead! Watch where you're going! Christ in a - no, Jiminy Cricket.

—You couldn't help that one.

—Where were we?

—On that guy's back end if you -

—You think because she runs you ragged she doesn't see someone? You're telling me how she treats you means no man would touch her? Some solidarity of brotherhood?

—When the candles are out, all women are fair.

—That's not you! That's Deeka. You still hang around with him.

—We go back. He's been acting kind of weird -

—You finally -

—for about two weeks.

—Starlene, so she has a funny nose, and she's bossy. Outside of work, in the right company, she could be nice.

—I'll never know, will I?

—So?

—So why even think about what you can't prove?

—You think she's a shrew.

—Not my word.

—She probably thinks you're a kid without much ambition. Is she right? Loyola looked out the window. Janet realized she had gone too far. —Sorry. You okay?

—Sure. Mind if I change the channel? Your boyfriend's okay, but CCII's not -

—Where'd you get the idea Ty's my *boyfriend*?

—It's a joke.

—*Ty*? Not funny. We slept together years ago, but go out with him? He's too old, too negative, always finds the worst in a situation, just so he can say he's tough.

—Seems like he's being cautious.

—Everyone's afraid of doing anything, nobody cuts loose - hey! What the fr- frig, is that swearing? Loyola shook his head. Janet blared the air-horns and a van venturing across her lane swung away. —What the frig was he doing? He's a whiner, you know. You ever meet my father's brother, Ben? He's sixty-four. Everything today is garbage, he says. Clothes, music, food, people, the clouds, trees. *People!* They grew them taller and wider back when, you know? That's Ty. CCII's doing great, top in the ratings, and Otis Lewis, son of the head man, wants to put his hands in there and change it all. If he does they'll lose their audience.

—So he -

—That's what Ty doesn't need, a *real* thing to complain about. It'll only encourage his stupid attitude. There's no place like CCII. CEPJ there has nothing on them. But he loves to get in trouble, making out like he's standing up for people. It's just the whiner coming out in him. I keep saying cool it, but - did you see that?

—You could slow down.

—I tell him what Dad drummed into me when I was in school, give your life direction or it'll take its own. No one wants that. I don't recognize what's playing.

—Me neither, but it's okay. They play different stuff.

—No wonder CCII - Ty got a promotion, that's why you're hearing him in the afternoon.

—What happened?

—They fired this FM guy for making love to his wife in the control room, right in the middle of -

—The control room?

—Layla, the long version I hope. She was riding him in the chair when the chief engineer walked in, right at the end from the sounds of it. Out he goes, there's a shuffle, and Ty gets afternoon drive. He's a personality again, more spots, more remotes -

—Spots?

—Radio jargon, they call advertisements spots. A group of them are an island, or a cluster. They intro, they extro, they do everything in this language outside of dictionaries.

—It's too bad your air-conditioning's shot.

—Now people think there's cameras in the emergency lighting. On top of the microphones they know are already there. He's paranoid. What was that?

—About your air-conditioning. Buses should have it. I catch myself falling asleep. Figure people think I'm drunk. Janet wondered why a lasting picture of friends was impossible to maintain. No choice but to suppose a guy acted pretty much the same no matter what. His face when Starlene yelled to him, his hand on the door handle. I know, every woman knows, what he meant when he said he isn't looked at like a person, it's like he's this nobody for eight and a half hours. To go through that every day for so-so wages, staying a year or forever? Now Janet imagined Loyola in a crowded bus at 5:45, struggling to stay awake. What else would people see him as but a grubby young man wearing an idiot's expression? Janet wrenched the car around a corner to dispel this vision. But that's not the whole story, there's more, to do with me, not him.

Loyola asked what was going on at the paper, and Janet replied that the assignment editor, Gilbert, had bumped her off the Pilgrim's Progress story without good reason. They speculated it was because she refused to sleep with him, or that it was the old boys' network seizing the best stories in a town having few truly juicy ones. —Maybe they figured I'd editorialize. Frig, you don't need to do that on a story like this, it's all out in the open. I'd rather be Wicca than Christian right now.

—Wicker?

—Wicca, a witch. Not that I'm one. Their belief is, Hurt no one. We could live by that. Editorialize. *Me.* Do you know Jim Gordon?

—Whispering Jim? Who doesn't? The newscaster. He's on this station in a couple of minutes.

—Remember in January there was talk of a nurses' strike? His wife's one, she didn't want to go out, he didn't want them losing the money. What did he do? In the newscast he'd shove the story down four places, read it in a boring voice, whatever, so it barely registered. It wasn't a strike so the papers didn't have it on the front page. He's burying it, the public doesn't listen past the first three stories, management and the union can't get their side out. I bet you he wasn't the only one who did that.

—Ben Trevelyan, CCII's talk show host, isn't his wife -

—Doctor at some hospital, and there wasn't one day about it on his show. Course maybe that's Lewis' doing, he hates unions.

—There's a doctor coming in there, another talk show.

—Rory Quasten. Ty's voicing the pre-promos now, sounds like it's going to cause a stink. But that's off the topic, the thing is I'm tired of Gilbert, and Karmiris. I took these days off to cool down. I wanted to talk about this over supper. Between you and me, I'm thinking of leaving for B.C.

—Leave? You can't – leave to do what?

—There's other newspapers. I have a good rep, and I'm twenty-six, Loyola. There's lots nicer places too. Everyone's gaga over this summer, forgetting how freaky it is, and that the winters are rotten. This isn't the kind of place for people like us. Leave it to the Gilberts and Starlenes. Whatever Loyola said was covered by car horns as Janet turned left on a red light. She thought she heard him mention her parents. —Dad's a pusher, always asking me how I'm doing, like he did when I was in school. Only then it was, And how did Alice Mary do? Always competition. What he thrives on. He'd love to see me win awards for some important paper. And he'd like to see me break my neck trying. There's a puzzle. You find that funny?

—No, I -

—Because he thinks that way, all parents do. Succeed, but if you can be humiliated, that's a good second best, as long as it's only yourself. Proves to them you'll never be a parent. Frig that for a game of jacks. I'll do what I want, I'll get ahead, and no thanks to him.

—So you'd leave -

—In a minute.

—But people like us, you said.

—Yeah. Hey!

—Us?

—It's a green, stop hitting the brake! People.

—I don't get it.

—Loyola, people like us, young people! Want me to reinvent the English language and all the words in it? Look *around* you, for Christ's sake, there's nothing. Oh frig. Frig, frig, frig, I was doing so well! They drove in silence, Loyola numbly recording trivial sights while imagining this city, his world, without his cousin. He saw a sign at a gas station that read Interac + Subs, and underneath that, Worms Lumberjacks Soft Drinks. She said us. What's that mean? Two people came into view, one obviously a man, the other wearing a hat with a brim and a sports jacket. —Look at that, fags kissing in front of everybody. Gives me the creeps.

—Know what you mean. Only the guy with the hat's a woman.

—What?

—I can see it in the rear view mirror. Loyola turned around. —You're right. But for a minute -

—Say, you never mention that guy Bart any more, I don't see him at the bar. You and him were friends, weren't you?

—Me and Bart?

—You and Bart. What's the matter?

—That's why we're not friends.

—What?

—Because of that me and Bart thing. With what he's known for.

—I saw him and another guy at a movie. Tall, red-haired.

—Al.

—But you were friends.

—But not friends as in me and Bart. You can say that if you mean, I guess, Bart and Al.

—I don't -

—It's the two of us put together that way, that's what's wrong. There was me, and there was Bart, or the two of us talking, but not me and Bart. You know what I mean.

—Touchy. Okay, where do we eat? It was The Great Pan versus Waist Not, Want Not, with The Olde English Inne, the alternative, winning. After dinner they drove around the city as twilight became night before decid-ing on a nightcap at Loyola's. While he took two bottle of Black Dog beer from the fridge, remembering in time that Janet liked a glass, his mes-sages played. —You mind me hearing these? Janet shook her head. His father had called to see how he was, and maybe they could see each other this Sunday. Jules Deeka drawled out, —Meet the John the Baptist of the senses Saturday, Ferber's Gallery, noon. The third message was from Kate. —Loyola, it's Kate. It's seven o'clock, I'm coming over to pick up the box, the few things I – all right? Oh, at 8:30. I left a message Monday, I hope you're there. I just want the box, that's all.

—A whole box. You and she were serious.

—It's a shoe box. There, on the chair. Make-up, that's all.

—What's she use?

—How should I know?

—Mind if I look? Loyola hesitated, the bottle's neck scraping Janet's empty glass. She lifted the lid and the intercom buzzed. —Jesus! The bottle jerked, sending a trickle of beer onto the counter. —He- hello? Yes?

—It's me, I'm late. Can I -

—Sure, give me a sec. You shouldn't be around, it might set her off.

—You didn't tell her I said anything -

—No, but she doesn't like you.

—Where -

—The bedroom.

—Give me my beer.

—This'll take five minutes. Janet closed the door and crossed to the window, setting the glass on a small table. Black curtains were tied back to provide light to an African violet on the ledge. Kate gave him that, I bet. What a view. Look at that sky. She listened, but Kate had not yet knocked. This is what his room looks like. A set of large weights rested in one corner, a guitar case in another, a bureau, a hamper, a closet, two low tables, two lamps, and a few other things completed the neatly laid-out furnishings. He's not a hopeless bachelor, Janet thought, eyeing the duvet cover patterned with a Greek green and gold fret. Or did someone give him that? On the bureau lay coins, photographs, a watch, and a pen container, a souvenir from New Orleans, given him by her mother years ago. From outside she heard a tapping, her cousin answering, and Kate's soft voice with its nervous edge. She wanted to check the box to make sure everything was there. Why did I want to know what was in it? I have nothing against her, I'm not nosy. Janet crept to the bureau to examine the photographs. One was of Loyola dressed in a white buttoned shirt, white shorts, and white sneakers, wearing a school tie. In the black-and-white photograph it was impossible to pick out the tie's colours, but Janet knew they were the red and gold of James the Less Elementary. A hand-written date indicated the picture had been taken in May 1980, two months before Aunt Karen's death. Loyola, eight years old and proud of his school day uniform, stood against a flowering bush. Uncle John had taken this picture, for it included a great deal of sky and cut off the tips of his son's sneakers. Even then her uncle had worked to be different, favouring black-and-white film over colour. No one knew why.

The second photograph showed a Loyola closer to the one listening to Kate as she apologized for spilling the box's contents on the kitchen floor. Taken in 1990, the picture showed a young man with sideburns holding a guitar, and behind him in someone's living room stood Deeka. Loyola's smile changed when Aunt Karen died. It used to be in the middle of his face, around 1980, and in 1990 it goes halfway up his right cheek. He's still like that. Nicer when he doesn't smile, really. She caught herself in the bureau mirror mimicking him and snorted, just when Loyola and Kate momentarily stopped talking.

—What was that? There was a noise in your bedroom.

—I didn't hear anything.

—Who's there?

—No one's there.

—You're lying.

—Lying? Who was screwing you behind my back? This guy you work for, Don, wasn't it?

—I told you, he's my boss! That's all! It was a coincidence, Loyola, and you never let me explain. Who said I'd met anyone?

—Coincidence. Fuck, sure.

—I told you about him -

—And he's waiting downstairs, is he? That's some boss.

—There isn't anything going on with my boss! What do I have to -

—Someone else.

—What?

—Someone else's waiting for you. How many were you fucking when you were with me?

—No one! You bastard, I loved you, don't you remember me telling you that? I told you it again and again, from the start. Did you ever love me?

—Not when I found out -

—You never did! You made love to me, went through the motions, but you didn't love me. Who were you in love with when you were with me? There was always somebody there in our way, like right now -

—I'm not the one with the boyfriend downstairs. You're crazy, and a whore. Three guys at one time. Janet heard a hard slap. —Don't ever call me that! You want a whore, you know how to find one! Nadeen's right, you and Jules, you're twins. You don't care about anyone.

—That's not true! Get out of here. Go back to your twosome, your boss and whoever it is. Why don't you just take 'em both to bed at the same time? It'd save running around.

—Maybe you'd like to watch. Isn't that what you said, you'd like to be two people so you could take me front and rear at the same time? Whoever's in there, maybe she'd like that!

—There's no girl, not there or anywhere.

—Deeka, then. In the unwelcome silence that followed, Janet focused on the remaining photograph, that of Loyola's mother at a young age, a trim woman with a tender smile, perched on a bicycle near one of the trails in the valleys to the north or west of Bowmount, a hat set jauntily on her head. The face was undeniably Loyola's, and Janet fancied that by bobbing her hair she would look like her, or her mother, even more than she now did. The hair style set off her aunt's cheekbones, which explained why Loyola regularly had his hair cropped, though Janet preferred it when, at a certain length, his natural wave reasserted itself. The photograph dated to the 1970s, Janet thought, her hands shaping her hair as she emulated her aunt. For once Uncle John had taken a decent shot.

Something disturbed her. Quietly she examined her surroundings. The room was vacuumed, dusted, orderly, spare, and at its focal point stood the bureau. Outwardly, nothing distinguished this room from the others in the small apartment. But no swimsuit calendar. Loyola had little money, but poor college students, such as she had been, often put up posters to relieve monotonous walls. The plant on the ledge held no secrets. The bureau was not peculiar, and if she looked through the drawers she would find usual articles of clothing. On going to bed Loyola would probably place his wallet, keys, and the pocketful of objects one picks up during a day next to the coins and the watch. No flaking paint marred the walls and ceiling. Whatever touched her existed outside the mundane world. The bed, on which Kate had lain, that bed which she didn't want to leave, so she's telling him, is it sending out *vibes*? Don't tell me I'm a bed psychic. It's not the bed, or Kate and the bed, Krysta too, for that matter, and her story. No, the bed's got no part in what's spooking me.

Janet had been looking at the photographs, thinking nothing in particular, until she saw the young Aunt Karen. No, the room isn't different, what I'm getting is from *this* picture, on *this* bureau, there's an aura about it. No, a suggestion. Pictures of him and his family, I've seen the two albums he keeps in the living room, the change, the watch. All normal. But it's like this spot's independent of everything. Like a museum display? No, that'd be history, dead. Concentrate, despite Kate out there being a pill. Janet rested her palms on the bare surface of the bureau and took a deep breath. Everything about the room remained placed in her mind, from the smallest detail in the far corner to the amount of money in pennies and dimes near her right hand. She felt suffocated by the room, made so by the sun shining on this side of the building for hours and which, in its last minutes, spread thin gold shafts through the heavens. Of course he'd sleep here, it's the brightest room. The fading light made her reflection in the mirror lurid. Rough-edged, swollen purple clouds converged on the dying sun, smothering it, while under this combat lay a fragile pink sky. Janet did not recognize herself in such hues. Swiftly and convincingly, as though her invocation of the sun had been all that was necessary to dispel the umbra in which her intuition hid, the one word came forth to describe this place out of time. She blinked upon hearing it, barely breathed it aloud as she stared at herself and the photograph of her aunt magically in her left hand, and jumped as the bedroom door swung open, one hand jerking to her heart.

—I told you to be quiet. Didn't you hear her?

—Kate, is she gone?

—You didn't hear her go?

—No, I . . . No.

—You had to hear what went on. Loyola cocked his head, saw the photograph in her hand, and stepped forward, breaking the spell, as Janet termed it later. —What's the matter? She placed the photograph carefully on the shrine disguised as a bureau. —It's goddamn hot in here. And I was trying *not* to hear the argument. Her cousin opened a window. A slight breeze came in and Janet felt her thin top clinging to her back and stomach. —I need to go to the bathroom, I've been standing here for hours, it feels like.

—Ten minutes. They weren't fun out there, either. She slapped me twice. In the dim light Janet saw hectic spots on his right cheek. —Kate's left-handed, and Janet started to laugh. —It's not funny. You hear what she accused me of? Sick bitch. Sorry, I didn't mean that.

—I know. I know you try. She leaned on those words, hearing them groan under an unexpected and unusual weight. Janet feared if they broke she would be forced irrevocably down a strange path. She excused herself, taking her beer from the table, and emerged from the bathroom a few minutes later outwardly composed.

They stayed together an hour. Janet tried to guess Loyola's reaction to the scene in the bedroom. Her cousin, though angered by Kate, nevertheless had taken in Janet's face, a patchwork of colours, and that she held his mother to her breast. Singular though this sight was, too much came before it for him to reflect on the matter. Kate's hitting him, and her crude, foul insults about his sexual interests, had shaken him. The idea that Janet could leave Bowmount forever, which he dwelled on as the days passed, upset him terribly. They spoke little, the occasional remark about Kate drawing a dutiful reply from Janet, for both had sunk in torpor. Once it became obvious they each had too much to digest, Janet left. Driving home she marvelled at how an apparently average day could suddenly contain so much mystery.

Emerging vision

—Harry?

—Sam, told you I'd drop by, see how -

—Did you?

—the splish-splash was going. Course I would. Can't miss the painting of the century. Heard the noise, figured someone was in here. Like a lecture in here, is that -

—Who's that in the – is that a car?

—Rifkind. You seen it? It was in the paper.

—No, no, it looks . . .

—Don't tell him, he thinks it's a statement. 'Tween you and I, he has some vendetta against City Hall, taking it out on them with the car, and his house painted like some gigantic bruise. Don't go near it drunk, let me tell you, blue and purple and yellow, veins everywhere. The front door alone's enough to make you chuck. Nice place this used to be, Duffy Machinery, Supplier for Bowmount, Carlyle and Beyond. Affiliated with G. Wells & Sons, Ltd., of Toronto and Montreal.

—That's a pretty impressive memory.

—It's painted right overhead. Yeah, nice place from the outside, inside, talk about ball-breakers. Sent a gang of men with clubs to beat up the picketers in '57. The clubs had nails in them. My uncle lost the sight in one eye. Duffy, there was a rat.

—Is he coming in?

—Rifkind! Come on.

—I'm parking the car!

—He's parking the car. Is that a trash can burning? With all this paint?

—It's for the models.

—They're here? Oh yeah, I see the Virgin Mary. Hello!

—She's deaf, remember.

—Say hi anyway. Manners. Harry approached Judith Weinberg who sat wrapped in a heavy shawl on a gray, armless chair. Behind her stood a screen spray-painted blue and white, to her left an abandoned wooden cross. Farther over was a large papier mâché stone. —My name's -

—Harry, she's deaf. She reads lips.

—Right. Loudly and slowly he introduced himself. —Hello! I'm Harry! A friend of Sam's! We met once before, at Johnny's! I hope he's treating you right! Do you like this? She smiled. —Good, good. Listen! I have to talk to Sam. Okay!? So my back'll be towards you! My mother taught me that was rude, so I thought I'd let you know I wasn't being rude! Okay? Good!

—What the hell's he doing? You can hear him for miles. Union voice, big union boss voice.

—Has he been drinking?

—I can't hear you with that noise.

—Go out and see his car. Go on. When the two men were outside Sam walked around the stuccoed Malibu painted a lurid orange. —You did this yourself? I mean, came up with it.

—Yeah. No trouble finding it in a parking lot.

—Umm. What's up with Harry?

—He's been drinking.

—I know that, that's what I mean. Why?

—Who knows. But we're sitting in Johnny's and he says, I gotta see the Master and his Margarita. Funny thing to call you and Mary there, but she has more titles than the Pope. We'll shoot the shit for five, then I'm taking him back to his car.

—You'll let him drive home?

—Man, give me a break. His house keys are in his car. Too plastered to remember taking them, thought about it when we pulled in here. Rifkind surveyed the three-storey building with the word Duffy fading out, at its barred and intact windows, its crumbling masonry and fading paint, surrounded by buildings of the same vintage showing the same signs of age.

—Quiet, I bet.

—Yes, what I needed, the -

—Addicts?

—They bang on the door, but it's solid, made -

—Cops bother you?

—No, only once or twice.

—Quiet.

—Yes. He shouldn't be drinking.

—Why not?

—His heart, he had that incident in February.

—He'll outlive us all. My old man didn't kick off till last week, he was ninety-nine.

—Gee, I'm sorry -

—If I'd had the guts I'd of smothered the fuckin son-of-a-bitch in his sleep years ago. Know what he left me?

—No.

—A tuba. He won it years ago in a card game. Never learned how to play it. What the hell use is a tuba? You seen enough?

—Oh, yes. The car, doing it this way, your idea, I knew. Did you paint it yourself?

—You think you could hire just anyone to do this? They stepped back inside where Harry was in the middle of the room singing, —Someone's in the grotto with Mary, someone's in the grotto I know-oh-oh, someone's in the - Sam, give us a peek.

—Not yet, I -

—You got to show it some day. What's with the backdrop? You couldn't come up with clouds and a blue sky on your own?

—It keeps the draft off the models, there's a vent in the wall and some-times -

—Where's the others? Jesus, Joseph, Mary Magdalene -

—You ain't painting the manger scene?

—No, this is - there's three paintings, a triptych, and I do one of them when the models are free.

—Surprisingly economical and practical for an artist, wouldn't you say, Fred?

—I wouldn't know. I'm not a Rembrandt, I'm a house painter.

—So, where's Jesus?

—Practising his Mozart.

—The other Mary?

—There isn't one. There is, in my head, but she's based on a real person. That woman Sarkissian. After that argument we had, her saying photography is better than painting, I had to put her in.

—As is?

—Changed, but her complexion, and her eyes, the perfect colours.

—But it's mighty flattering, don't you think? For someone you don't like?

—I don't think she'll think being in a painting, a painting by me, is anything special.

—You know best, Sam, I -

—Seen enough?

—Fred, we just got here. Haven't even seen the painting yet. How about a view? Critics get 'em, why not friends?

—Not the one of Judith, with her here – no, I can't.

—Jesus, then. Sam went over to a far wall against which rested a very large canvas shrouded by cloth. —How do you keep the paint from sticking to that?

—Wooden braces, on the board, they keep it off. The canvas is smaller than the board. Sam used a small ladder to reach the top of the painting and began unfastening the cloth from the braces. Seeing the activity, Judith came over. —Now, remember, this isn't complete, it's only one-third of the whole thing. I have to finish the other two, and join them up, paint where the connections are. Then there's the last step. This is the middle panel. Mary will be on its right, Mary Magdalene on the left.

—The last step?

—What I have in mind – don't ask, Harry! I shouldn't even be showing you this, I'll regret it tomorrow. Sam gently removed the cloth, slowly bringing it away from the painting as he stepped down, his gaze alternating between his creation and the audience. Both men were noticeably affected, in unique ways, by Sam's depiction of Christ and the Agony on the Cross. The most arresting aspect of the portrait was its sheer physical presence. Apart from patches of gray-blue sky above and to the sides of the cross, and the brown-gray mound of earth where the cross had been rooted, the painting was mainly of an oversized figure, painted in a subtle and vibrant blend of colours, a figure capable, it seemed, of life outside the canvas if it desired. The head, torso, arms, and legs filled the viewer's eye, the precise, scrupulous rendering of the unadorned male body saved from scientific coolness by the intensity of the brush strokes which presented a living, tactile passion, an ardour for God's purpose, transcending earthly torment. Harry and Rifkind were silent for a minute and Sam watched their faces eagerly.

—Well, it's . . . It's a – Sam, I don't know what to say. Jesus. Never seen one like that before. Fred?

—Your Lord, he doesn't mind being shown like that? Is that his face?

—No, yes, it is, he doesn't mind. He's vain about, well, it, Sam replied, pointing. —But is that all -

—Hard to say, Sam. What I think, I mean. It's not the meek Christ I thought it'd be.

—No, I wanted something virile. It makes what happens more devastating.

—A spear in the side. To a guy like that. To a guy in his prime.

—Something like that, Fred. In a way.

—Huh. If this is – and Mary here – there I go, talking about her and she not hearing me. Listen, did you paint her without clothes too? Because if I recall, her parents were -

—No, she and Mary Magdalene both have their clothes on. This isn't pornography, Harry, it's art. I'm not finished with this yet.

—Maybe some cloth thrown over the -

—It won't look like that when it's done. What you see will be altered by the time it's ready to show.

—Good. Trying to save you from scandal. Not trying to interfere with your vision, but folks, Christian or not, might see red if they see . . . that.

—Your model, he looks like this?

—Yes, Fred. Harry, relax. What you're thinking of won't happen.

—Sam, this could end up in private hands, or the Vatican's forbidden art collection. But all right, you're changing it. I guess you have to paint what you see to get rid of what could start a fuss. It's a helluva job. Fred?

—Yeah. No, don't cover it yet.

—Give us another second, Sam. We won't tell anyone, right Fred? Rifkind stared at the face of the model. Judith moved away from him to stand beside Sam, who told her in sign that he believed his friends liked what they saw. She asked him if the sullen man was a friend and he signed no. She nodded her head. —Enough of that whispering, you guys. Sam, a drink to your masterpiece. Harry pulled out a flask from his jacket. Only Judith refused. —You shoulda told me about this. You could've been on the Pilgrim's Progress, getting a good fee for -

—Me?

—showing the faithful – yes, you, why not you? The teeming multitudes. I'm waiting for the miracles to start.

—Why would I have gone on that? It's ridiculous, a travesty of faith. There's enough of that going on. The painting, that's my focus.

—You could've brought it along. Go on the road with it.

—Harry, you don't take a painting and models on the road. You need a studio. Peace, quiet, light.

—Then what's this fuckin racket you got on? Rifkind gestured to the two boom boxes on a table. —Somebody from somewhere jabbering talking about the Koran, and that music.

—I need – don't turn them down!

—I think the – Fred, leave it. Your model, she thinks you're talking to her.

—She can't tell he ain't just waving his arms around?

—Look, I like that. It's a way into the painting, those holy texts. The music, it's Arabic. Helps me get my -

—If he talks about his soul I'm leaving you here.

—No, not that. Not exactly that. The Qu'ran and the Bible, both mention Mary and Jesus, and Joseph, and I thought if I had those places, passages, read while I painted, and over some music, things would click for me. And they have. There's something about all of it, the way Muhammad -

—It's noisy, is what it is.

—Taints your Christianity, doesn't it? I mean, you're not painting Muhammad. Add the Hebrew faith in there. You saying you need three religions to paint a Christ? Not that I'm pro or contra anything, understand. If it sells, fine, but it's odd. Like Phil, who's seeing this Muslim woman now, from Montreal, where's that going to go?

—Harry, it helps me, and it's too hard to explain. Maybe when you're -

—Not drinking, that what you mean?

—Yes.

—Never trust you not to say what's on your mind, Sam, give you that. Just like your brother. But I'm not drunk, you know. Do I sound drunk?

—I know, I know.

—Right? So long as you know. We'll get into the meat of it later.

—Yes, when it's done. It's inspirational, Harry. To remember what the golden rule is, to listen to the words and not the arguments any more, to hear the connections between Moses and Christ and Muhammad -

—We going?

—Soon, soon. Listen, you eaten today?

—You think I'm talking like this because I'm hungry?

—Could be, but no, maybe not. Seriously, you need something?

—We'll get an early supper soon.

—It's ten o'clock already, in case you didn't notice. Here's a twenty, no, a fifty. Take it, take it, you showed us the painting. Look at it as a viewing fee, if you won't accept it any other way. Have something to eat and get cleaned up. Her nose still works, doesn't it? Take a shower, people'll start thinking you're English.

—Thanks, but -

—Don't mention it. You both look starved. Never saw till just now how good-looking she is, it's her face. Had to say it while she was looking away. Seriously, speaking of money, you could've let the faithful saps see it. It'd be perfect.

—No, no, it wouldn't, it's not done.

—Yes, yes, but look, it's how you bill it. Poets, writers, they take their stuff out to bars, book stores, just to hear the sound of their own voice. Swear sometimes they write passages just to be read on radio, like The sun setting on Lapland's rough hills made the milk of Helga's cows sweeter than and all that crap. Even when it's something they haven't finished, they read it. They publish drafts of stuff in magazines to publicize a book, and when you read the book it's different. Works in progress, that's what I'm thinking about. Rifkind muttered something Sam did not quite catch, though he thought the words juicy and thick were in there. —You take this, see, and you show a bit at a time, a little more in each town. Progressive revelation, we'll call it! Lead them on one bit at a time, so they don't get confused. It's like getting a guy into a union. First a chat in the coffee room, then a meeting or two, then his card, voting rights, and before you know it he's running to take over from you. But it's too late now. We could've bandwagonned it. Get everyone agitated, show more crucifixion, a halo, cleavages, in every town. She has it to show, you can see that, and I'm not telling you to paint porno, no. Only that dress is too modest. Hey, Fred?

—Hadn't thought about it.

—You mean drag it, them, around -

—Whetting people's appetite, that's all. You get them talking, the press clambers on board, pretty soon everyone's wondering about it. Gallery owners'll buy it to sell quick to someone named Edo Kamikaze who has money and taste. What the hell do they care about Christianity, it's the object they want.

—But you don't throw your - that's insane, it's never been done!

—How many things have never been done? We're doing them all the time. We're not talking about a cave painting here. It's some canvas, paint pots, brushes, and a couple of models. What more do you need?

—A van.

—Thanks Fred, a van. You'd have plenty of room left.

—That's mad. What you're suggesting -

—Naysayers, naysayers. You say no one takes their stuff out on the road? What about this guy Crisco? Wrapping islands and hotels and -

—Cristo, Cristo. He's nothing like me.

—I'm not saying he is, I'm just talking. Get back to those cave painters. You think the first guy to paint a stag or a mastodon - it had to begin somewhere with one guy doodling on his wall. And there's his mate carping in the background, You mess up the place and I'll kill you. The first guy. If he hadn't done it, where would you be? There's always a first for things.

—They -

—Art's what those stupid pilgrims want, beatific smiles and Aryan Israelites, not a hint of exotic blood in them. A weak, puny Christ so they can identify, some blonde Jewess with nice tits, and a bloody cross. Angels flying around their heads like doves, or vice versa, and an unhappy hooker. Because that's them, that's us, whoring six days a week and asking forgiveness on Sunday.

—Speak for yourself.

—Fred excluded. He uses all seven days. That's a joke. You show them that, artistically of course, and you make money, get your name out there.

—But I paint, when I paint -

—Inspiration, I know about that.

—Yes, and to do that, when I do it it's all of me. I need this place, this quiet, to recover. Draw myself together. I'm completely in the paint, in the brush, in the canvas, in the models, I'm everywhere when I paint. To do that on the road? There's nothing left of me after a day's painting, just me.

—That's fuckin romantic crap. It's just a job. C'mon, Harry.

—Let's hear this out.

—Someone said an artist isn't anything but the dregs of his work.

There's nothing good left of me outside this painting.

—Fred's right. Suppose you cut yourself, and you need a tetanus shot. You go to the doctor. Is it your arm getting the needle or these dregs? It's your arm, yes!

—You don't understand.

—No, I don't agree. That's just bunkum. You think all I am is a strike, a protest, a negotiation? I'm a union man in everything, brother, let me tell you that. Or I try to be. You're saying, Art is everything and I'm nothing. Whoever said that led a miserable life. Art? It's great, but it's not the be-all and end-all. You do it, then you go home.

—Paint the walls, do the trim, tidy up, walk away.

—Fred has a different take on it.

—I've done some fuckin good jobs. You try that, Mr. Dregs.

—Sam has the point. You make it sound like anyone who's a bus driver or an electrical engineer isn't worth the same as a painter. Who put the roof over your head? You squat here, don't you?

—I cleared it -

—Be thankful the bricklayers weren't dreaming of iambic pentameter while this place went up. Smacks of elitism, and you know how that rubs me. Maybe because I'm tired, maybe a little drunk. The dregs? You know what that tells me? I'll tell you. It tells me, first, that you think art is the highest thing in the land, and secondly, what kind of father or husband or boyfriend you'd be. Sam, Sam, Sam. Art's fine, but it doesn't replace being a family man, getting involved with the community, helping your brothers and sisters mount industrial action against multi-nationals that -

—Harry.

—Okay, off the topic. You have to be part of something bigger than you, that's what I'm saying. It keeps you humble. Are you telling me it's better to paint a good picture, heck, a Mona Lisa, than to raise a son or daughter to be honest, hard-working, socially involved? You're not saying that.

—No, no, I just said -

—He said he isn't anything but paint.

—No, that's not -

—The fumes have got to your brain. Okay, you're excited, it's a damn good painting, but remember, there was something bigger than Jesus. God. That's not what I believe, but you do. There's things bigger than art.

—I didn't - what I meant was -

—I'm a little wound up. Didn't mean to hector you, Sam. But I could've packaged you right. Had you and your easel on top of a flatbed, at dusk, say, with the crowds gathered around, and news cameras broadcasting the painting in progress. You say it's never been done. Someone'll do it. Then you'll say, Harry was a visionary.

—You wanted to put a Tim Horton's on the Confederation Bridge.

—If I had partners with guts - but it's too late, I needed to be in there when the plans were drawn up. A nice hub on the bridge, people looking out at -

—Nothing.

—People like that. They like saying, I drank tea on the Concorde. They'd buy shirts that said, I ate a Timbit over the Atlantic. I'm ahead of my time. Rifkind tapped his watch. —Let's get going.

—Right. You two want a lift back?

—Thanks, but Judith's parents pick her up at eleven.

—Go on back with them, get washed up. Eat something, will you? Have they seen her painting yet?

—No. I'm not showing anything again till it's done.

—Okay. Listen, Fred, give us a minute. Fred? I know, Jesus' eyes stay with you, don't they?

—I'll start the car. A minute. See you round, Sam.

—Is he getting worse?

—That City Hall business and he hasn't been working much lately. Yeah, he's getting worse.

—Judith doesn't like him.

—Can't say many do. You know his father died? It broke his heart.

—It what?

—He asked me to go the funeral with him. Not asked me, not directly, but he needed someone. Terrible service there. The minister, forget her name, just came in from New Brunswick. Didn't know the Rifkind family at all. What the hell consolation can a stranger give?

—Well, I . . .

—Listen, I know I'm slightly drunk, but I hope giving you money in front of him didn't bother you.

—You've always been there -

—And talk to you like a dumb big brother. Things are good in this new job, my kids are working themselves through university, and the mortgage's almost paid off. When I got a few extra bucks to kick in to your thing, well, why not? Plus, I won a bundle in the bike race. You didn't see it, did you? Cooped up in here with the Holy Family. Who'd think the Carlyle team would be using drugs? Tell me something, you're not really squatting, are you?

—I talked to the people who own this place. They knew George, they seemed happy to help out. They know I'll be gone in October.

—Your brother knew the Duffys? He never told me that.

—No, the Wolfe family, they bought it from the Duffys.

—That's a break, and you deserve it. Poor George, he'd love to see you working away. He always carried that pencil drawing you did of his hands just to show us guys. A car horn blew. —That's Fred. I gotta go.

—Harry, you should watch your drinking. After that scare -

—It's the job. Great pay, but we're putting together this campaign, it's brutal, a lot of work. It's hush-hush, but you'll see it in October, if the government doesn't back down. That Burke is a real bastard. Knew him years ago, he spoke for the other side. This thing we're doing, it's different. You won't miss it, trust me. But desperate times call for radicals.

—I don't follow politics. But you don't look happy.

—You're better off away from it. And I'm consulting with some people at CCII who want a union. This young woman, Krysta, she – Fred again. Keep the faith, Brother Sam. Did I tell you that's a beautiful painting? You got a title for it?

—It's a secret until all three are done.

—Fair enough. Say goodnight to the Madonna for me. Are you and her together, in, you know, a -

—Just friends.

—That's a good beginning. Even drunk I can see her eyes are on you all the time. You need someone, Sam, so does she. Keep painting. You haven't looked this happy in a long, long time.

—It's coming out right, I'm saying something. Not what I thought I'd say, but what I feel. You'll see what I mean in November. The two friends said goodbye. An hour later Sam stood outside his apartment building watching the taillights of the Weinbergs' car disappear around a corner. Happy? I don't even notice the days passing. Time stands still when I paint, when I'm with her.

Long division

On the second Sunday of September, warm winds carried the penetrating smells of rich farmland from the valleys and the sun shone as though autumn lay months ahead. Alistair sat near a window listening to street sounds. Since the age of eleven, Sundays had affected him terribly, and though lulls had occurred, he could no longer dispute with himself that what produced anxiety in his boyhood self now, at the age of twenty-nine, accumulated more malignancy with each passing year. Perhaps the accumulated mass of Sundays had lately paralysed his will and body, rendering him more anti-social and irritable than usual.

Alistair's dislike of Sunday stemmed from primary school, for the next day had meant returning to a hated environment. Shy, inarticulate, disinclined to participate in sports or join clubs, he had had few friends, a regrettable state in an all-boys school, a state that worsened in the elementary grades. Once the other pupils had gathered around his desk beside the library shelves, and as it was a reading period this had looked natural. As Alistair recalled, the minute the teacher stepped outside he became the target of feet, knees, fists, palms, rolled up scribblers, books, and pencil points. It was an unexpected attack, provoked by a note from his well-meaning mother who wanted him excused from showering after gym, on the grounds that plunging into cool air after sweating and a hasty wash would bring on flu, pleurisy, bronchitis, pneumonia. The physical education instructor, Mr. Warton, looked up from this appeal and viewed the pale, slightly overweight, and gangling eleven-year-old with renewed contempt. Alistair's peers, then in the midst of discovering their gonads, if sketchy on the exact details of their use, giggled and shrieked, and whipped towels at each other, hurling —Fag! and —Pansy! around freely. The defection of a student from this fraternal roughhousing unified a class of thirty-one disparate souls as few things could. —Ducey's not showering. —C'mon, Ducey! —I heard his mommy wrote the principal, said he ain't got no balls! —Is that right, Duce? Your mother checks ya every night, do she? Ya fag. And don't go looking at me. Alistair had never told his parents of these ritualistic, and simultaneously casual, slanders. One note had done enough damage.

Mr. Riggs, the grade seven homeroom teacher, a thin, wispy-haired man with an expressionless face, had done nothing to alter his students' behaviour. He regularly cracked off three-foot yardsticks on desks, walls, the chalkboard, and sometimes snapped them in half with his bare hands. Sundays quickly deteriorated to waking nightmares, and Alistair prayed to God, whom he increasingly believed had no time for him, that the next year would bring him salvation. It was not until grade ten that his old enemies were scattered throughout Bowmount's vaunted education system.

The badgering and infrequent shoving matches from grades four through nine had been replaced in high school by crude psychological pressure bolstered by unchecked hormones. Groups became gangs, a metamorphosis, the principal admitted to parents, impossible to control without recourse to corporal punishment, a method proven to be plainly damaging to the children's self-esteem. Alistair perceived this erratically regulated world as the adult world in the making.

At times he would bump into a fellow alumnus in a drugstore or supermarket, and he waited for them to say hello. When that happened, he wanted to unleash years of pent-up fear and rage. Due to the lesson his parents drummed into him, that the only response to derision was a snub, the closest he could come to showing anger in his comments to a grown-up Paul or Greg was to be abrupt. Inside he wanted to corner a Ray or Chris and say, Now you're being friendly? Too late, you dumb fuck. I remember how you treated me, you think I'd forget that? Jesus, I hated you, and still do. What are you going to do about it? In his daydreams Alistair threw Bill or Sean through a store window so he could watch them bleed on the sidewalk.

Sometimes Alistair wanted them dead. In grade twelve a teacher had broken the news that Dennis, one of his more sophisticated tormentors, was suffering in the grip of cancer. —Your thoughts should be with him, Mr. Flanagan had urged the class. These many years later Alistair recalled the acute pleasure it had given him then, and still gave him now, to realize that God was going to inflict on Dennis a miserable death that would drag on for months, wrecking the whole family in the bargain. If selected others had suffered identically, he would have had a truly contented childhood. Whatever sparks of freedom, happiness, or tenderness resided in his life were impotent against the leaden grayness of daily existence, especially on a Sunday night when his uneasiness sharpened and he asked himself, Why do they hate me? What did I do?

The intense dislike of that particular day receded when he had studied commerce in university, but those same questions revisited him when he entered his first full-time job after he had received his degree. They had gained interest, as he put it, an inheritance or trust fund established for his future by parents, teachers, and fellow pupils, and administered by him. In an office setting Alistair's personality had struck others as snotty. The personnel director said, —You need to be a team player, Al, y'see? We're all players here, we play to win, and sure, sometimes one of our teammates lets us down, but we pick up for him, if we see he's trying, just like he'll do for us. Am I getting that across? Don't think you see what I mean. In an effort to make a fresh start, Alistair had gone away from Bowmount and travelled in Europe for three years, working at whatever came to hand for money under the table. In London he had found his vocation. Employed as a telesalesman, he originally found the job unrewarding, but it became apparent he had the coldness necessary to work past rejections to persevere and close a sale. He had stayed with Quine Media ten months, living frugally and saving the earnings from his commissions. His career had unexpectedly flourished, but he had made few friends, though there had been scattered dates with secretaries who, by answering his sales calls, blocked his pitch to the advertising manager. His accent proved a novelty to some of these bored women, and on weekends, having talked to a girl at most twice, he would take a train to Tunbridge Wells, St. Albans, Gravesend, or, on a Bank Holiday weekend, Cardiff or Edinburgh.

Those interludes had been valued more for the travel than for the generally mediocre sex. Alistair had found it relaxing to sit in a comfortable car, a *Time Out* or Saturday *Independent* on his lap, while watching London recede as the train pulled out from Paddington, King's Cross-St. Pancras, or Victoria, to be replaced by the industrial scar pattern similar to all railway lines, even Monaco's. Scrubby landscape merged into grassland, and ploughed fields would take over, very quickly one community replacing another, for the distances, to a Canadian, were laughable. Often another salesman, Winston, would ask Alistair, not entirely in jest, when Canada planned to leave the Iron Age, to which he as often replied, —This from a place that advertises showers on television? And we get itemized phone bills. Being a Canadian in England was an advantage over being a United Stateser, as that guy Harry Prestwick had taken to calling Americans, because you usually weren't sneered at as much.

Fatigue, and a desire to show to his hometown that he had become a cosmopolitan citizen who had thrived abroad, worked on Alistair enough so that, some years ago, he had decided to return to Bowmount, where he quickly found a similar position for better pay. That opportunity seemed a good one, then, but the months became years, and the old sensations around Sundays had revived. As sales manager for Bowmount Books, he held the responsibility of ensuring continued financial prosperity, and would help oversee a diversification to call centres. What had once been a challenging task in a lively foreign country had become, without his noticing, a career that supported a car, insurance, rent, groceries. He was entrenched in selling useless things to gullible people.

These blue thoughts invariably presented themselves on Sunday. Not in the morning, when he treated himself to breakfast out, nor at noon, but around 4:00 p.m., when the rest of the day held insufficient time to do anything that could neatly obliterate the dreary feelings. Today he had gone to a matinée of an art house movie, thinking to expand his mind and be free of himself. Instead, he had left the cinema with a headache, asking why he subjected himself to wan, dull Canadian movies. Even the most light-hearted stank of fear and disillusionment. When you felt rotten, Alistair thought, the last thing you needed was a movie telling you you have good reason. He knew *This Age of Light* would win dramatic and cinematography awards in Canada, maybe because it sought to deliberately confuse the audience. First, a cast of unknowns, whose voices nevertheless sounded as though he had heard them in beer commercials during a hockey game. What most confused Alistair was that, in an English-language film, two sets of subtitles appeared on screen, one at the bottom in English – why not French? – the other on the left side in Chinese. What the actors said in perfectly comprehensible Central Canadian tones rarely matched the English written on the screen. Obviously, either set of words – perhaps the Chinese said something else again – could go with the dramatic situation, the interconnections between characters. What one character did could be interpreted two, maybe three, ways, Alistair concluded, but that didn't make sense. Did it? A guy lies to his girl, really elaborately, and the subtitle just reads No. And for the soundtrack, it has a trombone. It might as well be a banjo! Am I supposed to laugh or cry? Alistair's head throbbed; sitting in the silent living room he wondered if a flu was coming on, anticipated the stress of lasting out this day, and worried over his relationship with Bart. —Relationship? He meant to say friendship.

He set his drink on a side table, looking out at the clear blue sky, and said aloud, as he did while devising sales strategies, —I can't be homosexual. Jesus, I hope not. Images returned of his intermittently satisfying times with women. He especially liked oral sex, but it had been the case that while a Rosalind or Sherry took his penis inside her mouth he wondered what it would feel like if a man did it. Would the pleasure be the same? —If I kept my eyes closed, what difference? Just coming, that's the thing. From this unsurprising, to him, fantasy his mind moved to penetration. This he knew began with one girl in Somerset who, admittedly while they were drunk, played around his anus with her tongue before thrusting it inside, while one hand caressed his scrotum. Later that night, or the next, he sodomized her, to her delight, or so he recalled. On pulling out he saw his shit-covered penis and abruptly sobered. While she slept he showered, panicked that he might catch AIDS, yet aroused despite himself.

Since returning to Bowmount, he maintained a form of chastity. Which is to say, when he wanted a woman he almost always left town to pursue one. Even this desire had disappeared and it had been months since he had had sex. His last engagement, with a woman named Leah in Crescent City, advanced him along a strange road. Alone in her apartment he went through her underwear, specifically her panties, wondering how the velvet would feel on his skin, or if a thong might softly caress his anus. While he could not fit her clothes, he posed naked in front of a closet mirror, holding the various garments to his body. What a feeling, he concluded, better than y-fronts and bikinis. The thinness of the material appealed greatly, and he thought he would feel quietly strong in such underwear. Leah's bras were of no interest, unlike the stretchy, see-through panties with lace trim, or the simple, sporty kind with a lined crotch. Hearing a noise he came out of his reverie, but she had not come back. Alistair replaced her panties and collapsed on the bed as March rain beat against the window. He knew he had not done this unconsciously. He had commented about how things looked and felt, admired himself modelling Leah's things, speculated about buying one or two pairs. He went and threw up in the toilet. By the time Leah returned he had showered, shaved and dressed. Their faces showed how much they had drunk the night before, and she said that sniffing amyl nitrate, though a blast, was a habit she so wanted not to start. They parted as strangers.

Repercussions from that day were felt at once. No purchases of women's cloths, nor of sexual toys for self use, were made. He did not eye pre-pubescent boys, nor did he buy skin magazines or surf the web to view naked males. He refused to think of visiting gay bars and refrained from passing opinions on homosexual issues. Patterns developed. Even on the coldest winter nights he slept without clothes, the sheets rolled down to the small of his back, the curtains open. Bored by the arrangement of his apartment, he moved the furniture, tossing out some pieces and placing the foot of the bed in line with the window. From it he could look across the square and observe the slightly taller condominium opposite. It did not bother him that he could be visible to a voyeur. As well, after the episode in Leah's apartment, while falling asleep he would imagine a man, usually black, at times Asian, knocking on the apartment door for an unspecified reason. Seeing Alistair's partially clad body, the stranger would come inside, kiss him fervently, and take him with rough or gentle regard. Inevitably Alistair stiffened, yet it was more enjoyable to feel the impulse fade as his waking mind gave way to sleep.

For a short time, Victor at Johnny's Bar, to put it in Alistair's words, was the steak and the sizzle. However, the quest for a perfect relationship moved on. AIDS was prevalent enough in the straight population, but in the local homosexual community, particularly the *demi-monde* of Queer Town, its incidence ranked higher than the provincial average, a statistic the City Fathers vociferously campaigned against. Alistair congratulated himself on rarely dating women from or living in Bowmount and not once did he entertain the idea of approaching a Bowmountian man. Since late spring, his most frequent dream lover was himself, an exact duplicate, who knew precisely what to do, a guy name Al, disease-free, unattached, who played the dominant sexual role but in every respect was a slave. Joining with Al, his braver self, Alistair would feel everything the two of them did. He could be there at the beginning and end of lust, and of caring, for he deserved to come home at the end of a hard day to a home-cooked meal and a blow job.

When the idea of possessing his double seized his imagination, Alistair's mood briefly changed, for he found what eluded him these years. Not another man, thank you Jesus, but me, me. This explained why during intercourse his mind substituted a Dick for a Jane. He loved sucking off women, and most of them admired his willingness and technique. Would taking a penis in his mouth be so peculiar? Certain conclusions were the result of much thinking, or brooding. The creation, or summoning up, of the double solved every problem, clarifying once and for always, as his father used to say, that he must bond with himself, and not a version of his maleness. Why settle for a man? I want to meet me. I wonder where he's been hiding?

Just as the possibilities of this theoretical solution appeared, restoring his equilibrium, he began talking with Bart, possibly because Victor, Jack and the others ignored Alistair. In St. Mark's that July day he found himself examining his friend from a previously forbidden angle, going so far as to touch him. Their day together was not exceptional. Bart worried about a life with no hope and Alistair found himself under attack by his usual fears: had he turned off the lights, the heat, made sure the taps were tightly closed, turned the CD player and television off, unplugged the coffee maker, made sure the oven and stove were switched off, and locked the door? Before leaving the apartment and immediately after closing the door, he ran through a checklist to see if he had forgotten anything. He never did, but remained unsure if that were the case because, in fact, he had turned everything off the first time, or because he went through the apartment three or four times before leaving. Staring at the oven he would look at the knobs from right to left, left to right, left to right, right to left. Alistair recognized this behaviour as neurotic, and knew its roots quite well. His parents regularly burned pans and kettles, and his dorm mates had been unable to distinguish Off from 1 on the oven. Girlfriends left taps running in their own places. Now entrusted with the keys to lock up Bowmount Books when he worked late, this meant turning off lights, making a sweep of the staff kitchen, and locking the main door within thirty seconds after setting the burglar alarm. Constant vigilance did not allow rest. Thanks to his neighbour suffering from Alzheimer's, Alistair worried about his apartment when away. Sometimes he rang his answering machine from work, reasoning that if it functioned then the building had not been burned down through Mr. Beresford's carelessness. These fears first appeared in April, he remembered, swelling in size and potential ludicrousness just after receiving his promotion, which was near the time he first met Bart. He figured that when he was used to being a sales manager, a position he had not so much wanted but felt he deserved, matters would improve.

Alistair never considered himself a thinker, except in business matters. In other realms he believed intuitions, or suspicions, led to the truth just as surely as systematic analysis. Since that day in the church, with its dull stained-glass windows, his grip on his temperament had slipped. Occasionally the mere idea of Bart made his esophagus spasm. Alistair permitted the use of the word friends, balking at anything suggestive of closer intimacy, such as good friends. They told each other their troubles, Bart because he rarely kept his worries inside, Alistair because he had restrained himself too long. For the former, confession was a well-worn conversational path, for the latter a trail hesitantly blazed. Alistair spoke about work, his parents, or his tics. When it came to revealing one's most private concerns, he shared his father's view that misery shared is misery doubled. —There's no point talking to Bart about sex, that isn't the problem. I know what I want so why bother? He moved back from the window and stopped himself from reaching for the drink on the table. —Too much of that lately, and I need a clear head.

Two days ago he and Bart, after seeing a movie and visiting a couple of bars, had returned to this apartment, where they talked for a few minutes, Alistair in his chair, his friend on the couch. Within half an hour Bart had passed out, and his host had lifted his legs onto the couch, taken off his sneakers, and covered him with a blanket. Alistair had knelt at his head, studying the wrinkled brow and the tightly shut eyes. —You're like that when you're awake. No wonder you don't rest. His friend's breath, scented with popcorn and gin, had sounded regular and deep through the slightly open mouth. This may have been what encouraged Alistair to kiss his lips lightly. Surprised at this action, but neither excited nor repulsed, he had waited, but Bart had slept on. The second kiss had lasted longer, yet without a jolt of emotion. Rising from this peculiar experiment, Alistair had walked unsteadily to his bedroom, undressed, and fallen asleep instantly. The next morning he believed a test had been passed successfully, establishing that though he regarded Bart affectionately, no deeper attraction existed. Part of him, however, doubted the reality of this osculatory act, saying it may have been an hallucination caused by over-drinking, grafting his nightly dreams about his double on the uncommon presence of a male friend in the next room.

Today he had no patience with such wishful thinking, as sober reflection made moot questions about Friday night. —If I did it, I did it, and if I didn't, did I want to? But I did it. Alistair listed disturbing facts. He did not miss women as women, nor, to complicate matters, desire men as men, but craved sexual experimentation with one safe, silent partner whom, in a secondary role, could take care of the apartment when he was not here, relieving him of an increasing burden. Mostly what he wanted was sensual gratification. Did it matter what sex sucked his penis, or whether he entered a man or a woman? Not particularly. Did it matter whether he was ridden by a Janet or mounted by a Victor? He answered no, but less certainly. What did it mean that over the years he had gone from idolizing the sixteen-year-old girl next door when he was fourteen to fantasizing about young black or Asian men, leaving that behind for a willing double who was male because Alistair was male? —That has to be past homosexuality, I flew right through it into . . . Finally, what did the other night mean? Alistair speculated that there should have been a reaction to kissing Bart other than a delayed atomization of texture, taste, shape, and a pointless comparison with women's mouths. Had drinking numbed him to that extent? Was it so insignificant, or did that act contain too much for him to deal with?

Much of Alistair's thought, on this Sunday as on most days, remained out of reach, even to himself. He recalled how, as a child, he was amazed to learn the water that flooded his cousin's basement, until his uncle installed a pump, came from an underground river. Alistair pressed his ear to the earth, yet was unable to hear it, which frustrated him immensely. In the same way, he knew within him, inaccessible and influential, ran fears, hatreds, and memories. A week ago he visited a book store in Carlyle and purchased two best-sellers, *Men Who Lope With the Does* and *From Toy Boy to Coy Boy*, along with a manual on gay sex. The authors of the two acclaimed and controversial books struck him as sympathetic and authoritative while he stood at the rack, but at home they revealed their finger-wagging, prescriptive natures. He admitted to skimming the contents, put off by dense language and what he sensed as opportunism under their ideas. Aside from those objectionable traits, the two authors did not share the indisputable condition of their new reader: they were not Alistair Ducey, had never been, and, for all their theorizing and reliance on advances in cultural studies, despite their in-depth examinations of the Western world, they could not know what he went through. For its part, the manual furnished his imagination with depictions of men enjoying each other, but its wearying detail of the risk of infection and the complicated procedures to ensure safe sex confirmed Alistair's belief that cloning was more preferable than male same-sex dating.

Two items from the sociological studies leaped out. In a chapter from the Hotchkiss book on derogatory names for homosexuals, the term *suffix* was entirely new. Alistair recognized its humour and what the author called its —linguistic invention, while exhibiting deliberate denigration and crashing insensitivity to those who, like the fascist who had coined this term in a 'literary' work (with poor sales and often out of print), threatened to overturn the traditional power structure in England in the 1920s and 1930s, in a diametrically radical and liberating way. The other book by Gidmery offered a description applied to the manifestation of desire: —In the words of one neglected Englishman, a nerve or worm of unbridled, frequently obscene desire, what we would classify as normal longing – the classic paradigm of the late Victorian confusion over ego, id, sensuality and the sex act generally.

Alistair instantly identified with the words nerve and worm. —It's like there's a thing living in my gut, growing down to my balls, saying Do this, Do that. Where was it Friday night? I always know why I sleep around, so why can't I figure this out? Because I was drunk? I've been that before. Wait. Never been drunk and did *that*. If I'd been sober . . . I knew the next day I wasn't myself. Can't have that.

It flashed through Alistair's mind that since late July he had avoided seeing people he once knew, such as the patrons of Johnny's Bar, and put off a few of the girls at Bowmount Books who would not mind, in his expression, a loose night. They simply did not appeal to him, nor did the offer by a wild girl from CCII named Megan, a brunette, who he met in May. She hinted that she could go for getting together with Alistair and a second female, but he had no real interest in this. One woman was difficult enough to please. Then he met Bart, a man Jack called —A self-milking cow, if you know what I mean. Practically. The two loners saw in each other's personality the antithesis to their own nature, and wished to incorporate in themselves a small amount of the other's self-possession or unselfconsciousness. They were fire and ice, Bart said, exact opposites, and physical attraction was irrelevant. Bart was five ten, heavy-boned, round-shouldered, pale, with red-rimmed eyes, and a frame worn down by insomnia and constant worry. In contrast, Alistair, long past the gawky stage, stood at six-two, kept himself tanned, and worked out at a gym where, as a matter of course, he assessed men in the showers. While not handsome, he knew women found him interesting to look at, which he accepted as a good and longer-lasting alternative to beauty. He dressed well, if conservatively, and used unguents and gels to enhance his skin and hair. Bart, who neglected his health, regularly wore corduroy pants, a t-shirt, and a secondhand brown leather jacket frayed at the cuffs. Would the worm come alive if his friend looked better and was more confident?

That bald question hid a dreadful wish or an ugly truth. Considering he had moved from sleeping with women to a desire for himself, Alistair pondered on whether this turmoil could be anything but imagination seizing upon Bart as an avenue for experiencing new sexual adventures. Had his dreams put on flesh, the most unlikely flesh, a wan, sad, Anglo-Saxon masturbator who had not expressed any interest at all in sex? If what I want to do is dabble, that's better than being a homo, but Jesus in the garden, with him? He's not what I think of. But he's real. That kiss. Kisses. Do I have to do it while I'm sober to know? Get him drunk, then see? That's low. Alistair's speculations sank within his chthonic self; when he emerged he found himself in the kitchen looking at the stove. The burners were off, as was the oven, but his eyes noted each knob, verifying the black line pointed to Off. He tried not to blink. It often happened that in checking the stove he would think about any number of things, ruining his concentration, and this Sunday evening proved no different. Soon he realized he had been standing there for three or four minutes. He closed his eyes, took a deep breath, and calmly scrutinized each knob again, right to left, left to right, left to right, right to left. Satisfied, he wondered why his left hand hurt, and raising it saw the mark of his nails in the palm. —I need to do something about this. Even a wrong step. Maybe that's what I need. Smash this life once and for all, find what I'm missing. Easy to say now, but when the time comes . . . Lord Jesus Christ, Son of God, have mercy on me as a sinner. On a Sunday night, this ejaculation from a time long past might not help him.

Smooth times

—Oz, close the door, we have a few minutes, there's something I want to show you.

—Seen the fault reports, the log's stuffed, okay, okay, Bob. If the CRTC loosened up we could play more spots on AM, wouldn't -

—Relax, it isn't business. You'll get a laugh out of this.

—Need it. Albert's gonna squeeze our balls like he always does before pissing off to Hawaii. Glad to see him go.

—Leaving Otis in charge?

—A change -

—The Little Prince's sat there for years and doesn't -

—Not even how to get along, Bob. Bennett sighed. Henderson tipped his chair back, looking at the shuttered windows of his office. —I don't understand how he can work here, knowing people think he's an idiot. If he wasn't related to Albert no one would have anything to do with him.

—One day Otis'll let it out. Payback time, that's what he's waiting for.

—The way the network's going he'll only have five employees to scream at.

—Can't even argue about proposals because he's never worked on air, in advertising, any grunt work, so doesn't have one fucking idea what actually happens. Stares at you like you're out of your mind to suggest something contrary. At least Phil, you can talk to Phil, but him?

—You remember when we hired Stewart. We thought, Here's a communications guy, respected in the community.

—His contacts. Henderson nodded. —Turned out he didn't have one clue about radio. But he has those contacts, and his two talents are golfing and drinking. He hangs with the right crowd, the young -

—Guys who'll get their fathers' businesses handed to 'em. Next in line.

—So he has his uses. Not what we had in mind, but we adapt. I thought he'd help keep Otis in line, they're about the same age, but – anyway, we have the meeting in a few minutes, and I wanted to show you this. Take our minds off things. Henderson passed a thin rectangular cardboard package over to Oswald Bennett. —New promo stuff? A what? A calendar for 1996. Where's the logo?

—Flip it open. The wall calendar featured a colour photograph for every month, each photograph showing the same man, sometimes with a moustache, or beard, or both, or neither, against a backdrop of different settings: an office party, in the corridors of CCII, in Engineering, or on the parking lot. The thematic element linking the twelve photographs was the presence of either a cast or large bandage. Ken Greer, the assistant engineer, often injured himself, breaking his collarbone, an arm, an ankle, or tearing off skin on ragged edges of machinery. Most remarkable about this chain of accidents was not that he had survived, but that none had occurred on company premises or on company time. His car had been rear-ended moments after leaving CCII. A nail had grazed an eye in his home workshop and while entering his doctor's office for a last check of that injury, he had slipped on the clinic's steps and fractured a leg. He had returned from vacation with a face swollen by mosquito stings, and often came to work with a blackened eye from either sneezing violently or squeezing his eyelids too tightly during some performance or another. These injuries were documented over the years by his brother-in-law Stephen Stone, head of accounting, who through a friend had this pictorial history printed. —Ken see this? I gotta have a copy. This is priceless. They were enjoying the memories each month evoked when the telephone rang. —Bob Henderson. Yes Tracy, we'll be along in – what? Yes, he's with me. Just a sec, I'll ask. Albert says to make sure you bring the stats on CCRR and CCFP sales. Yes, he has them, Tra – yes. Yes. No. We'll be there in two minutes, thanks. She's never going to change.

—Remember when she was the receptionist? First day I was here, that's twenty-two years ago, she cut off a long-distance call to me and I bawled her out. What does she do but storm into my office and ask me if I'm on the rag that day or what, she'll circle my periods on her calendar for future use. What a mouth on her. How do people like that stay on, hey? Why can't they get computers for them?

—They don't have her vocabulary. People think radio's glamorous, like Perry did.

—He's had his eyes opened.

—Now this meeting . . .

—Albert said yesterday he wanted to move on the salesmen in Ripton and Franklin Plains, or me and Otis to tell him what to do. Should have worn black. Perfect timing. We get to fire people and the next day he takes off.

—I'm there for more computer stuff. A system like the LazEx.

—Anybody else be there? Henderson sighed. —Perry, I'm not sure about Henry, and Stewart. It shouldn't take long. Speaking of which -

—Short but intense. I hate these good-bye meetings. I'm gonna grab a coffee -

—Tracy has it waiting.

—Designer coffee. Give me instant any time. Seated in the red environment of Albert Lewis' office minutes later, a Sumatra blend in their hands, Bennett and Henderson joined Otis, Phil, Perry, Stewart, and their employer at the conference table. They discussed the unqualified success of Dr. Rory Quasten's sensationalistic program, now in its second week, and the upcoming implementation of the 1-800 number for what Henry, the program director, termed the audience-hosted rock show. —Fine. Everything's up and running, I expect progress reports on my desk when I get back. Too bad Henry had that doctor's appointment, but Stewart, where are we with the all-night show tracks?

—Yeah, I taped a few myself last week, see how it would go, ran a simulation. We can use one reel-to-reel for a time check, another for bits. Four bits an hour, four time checks, max, and the weather.

—All the same announcer, Stewart? How would you handle the forecast?

—Not the weather, no, sorry. Whoever does the midnight news puts the weather on cart. We can have the temperature on a reel, saying It's 12 degrees, it's -1, say from -30 to +25.

—So, three reel-to-reels.

—The guy who's on, does he read the news?

—Phil?

—Yes, Dad. Oswald, the newsroom gets the Broadcast News feed on the hour, which we tape. The operator gets the tape, brings it out, puts it on the machine, and plays it. Stewart put in, —Followed by the carted weather, to which Phil added, —Then the reel-to-reel current temperature.

—That's a lot of tape. We could have engineering patch the BN feed to the board, tie it to a pot, and have the operator fade out the music into the news.

—That's optimistic, Bob. There's the promos, the news stinger, then the feed.

—Or four tapes, yes.

—Bob has a point, and so do you. There's too much tape. Which brings me to the LazEx. It has a sister system whole networks are using, Simul-Cast Model 2, where everything is on computer. We're going to get into it. The talent will be recorded on computer, and the advertisements, music and news too. A complete six-hour program. We've all been aware of it, it's just been this nostalgia for a warm body at the microphone that's kept us from progressing.

—But Albert -

—Yes, Oswald, the listeners will need to get used to it. Use this four-tape approach for now until January or February. We'll let the audience get used to one voice, and it'll give you two boys a chance to see the new system in action. When it's installed, we'll just need someone in to record personality bits. We won't even need an operator for the all-night show, just someone to throw a switch at the end of the 6:00 p.m. to midnight shift.

—Dad, we'll need a computer programmer.

—One person for many? A deal, no matter how much they charge. Bob, you want that connection between the newsroom and the control room, but hell, in four months things will change again. Maybe we don't even need news at night. People get that from TV now anyway. No one wants anything from commercial radio but the music. Yes, Phil, keep that in mind, a review of the all-night newscasts, AM and FM. By the way, that expanded 1:00 PM news sounds great. It's getting attention, people come up to me and say, We should have got rid of the CBC a long time ago.

—Albert, the spots -

—Otis, check that out, you and Henry. Liaise with Oswald when you come up with the answers. More on the SimulCast next month. Now, gentlemen, Perry has something serious to tell us. Well, go ahead. Regretting the rich coffee which never failed to give him indigestion, Perry Hornocker, after clearing his throat, explained, in stops and starts, how he had come upon a disturbing find. Telephone calls going out of the station were logged, and in light of the subterranean union activism it seemed vital to determine who at CCII repeatedly rang suspicious numbers. Obviously, Perry regarded management as above investigation. The news department proved the most time-consuming to check, as there were many numbers that were not listed anywhere. Thankfully, the computer could spot repeated numbers and -

—Jesus, Perry, get to the fucking point. Who's doing it? Bennett pulled at his nose, a customary habit, and looked directly in the other man's eyes, seeing there, not for the first time, distrust and malice. In that instant the sales manager knew Lewis' personal assistant had in fact checked the management's phone records too. That's all right, I can wait the fucker out, it's not like he has friends. If that cunt tries anything on me, he'll know it.

—Well, yes, the point. I've isolated a series of numbers, but they come from different telephones. Two outside numbers in particular.

—Perry, why didn't you tell me this?

—Sir, I got the results just before this meeting, otherwise -

—Fine. What are they? Who's calling them?

—One's a bakery. We can rule that out. I'm sure. The other is a consulting firm, Virgil-Lawson. Lewis stood abruptly, not noticing his body hitting the edge of the table, slopping coffee from the Russian cups. —Who? Who?

—Vir-Virgil Lawson -

—Those bastards! I was there yesterday, they handle Olympus Overseas Trading, we just gave them our account! Who's been calling them? Who have they been talking to in here? Names! Hesitantly, Perry explained that calls had issued from various offices, precipitating accusations and confusion around the table as each executive charged the others for slipshod handling of their departments. This infighting ended as quickly as it began, for it was silently agreed, almost simultaneously, as is the way of such things, that the staff were to blame for this short-lived, understandable, painful lapse of trust, and if the staff could have been called forth, merged as one body, management's anger would have found the right target. As this could not happen, Hornocker served as a substitute, a not-altogether poor one, since Bennett's insight had been everyone's insight. Who's this miserable pile of crap to spy on my people, snoop in my records? would have been, in all likelihood, the question of the collective, if they had not assumed it was only the sales team agitators or the newsroom leftists who were under suspicion. But that healthy expulsion of steam, though it was unfair on Hornocker, had to be put aside, for the investigation would need to focus on uncovering the subversives. Either every staff member rang Virgil-Lawson, or else it was the work of members of a cell who could walk freely in and out of every office in the building. —Which is it?

—Jocks. Fuckers mooch here, mooch there, stand around in Copy and Recording all day. Lots of phones, they -

—Or it's the salesmen, Oswald, they do the same, and they're out driving around meeting people. If you want to get like that.

—Stewart, none of my -

—What about the newsroom? They're either in the feed room or whispering down telephone lines, who knows who they're interviewing? Lewis stopped the fracas by pounding on the table with both fists, continuing well past the point where silence prevailed. It may have been an expression of rage, or a trick to take people's minds off their disagreements and focus solely on the sight of a well-built, expensively tailored man repeating a violent, loud action, or something else entirely. —Quiet. Perry, show me the number. Hornocker slid a piece of paper to Lewis. —This doesn't look familiar. Whose is it?

—I didn't have time to check, sir, not on the name. I just know the number is listed to the company, from a friend of mine in the phone company. Not one of their public lines.

—Didn't know you had a friend . . . in the phone company.

—Stewart, enough. We all want to find out who this is. Oswald, you've a cellular. Get it out. Do you realize all of Olympus' overseas information could be open to this union? Am I the only one who sees the ramifications of this? This could jeopardize the entire corporation -

—No one from my -

—Anybody! When we find out who owns that number, we'll work backwards. Each of you check your department. Perry, draft a note on this for Henry, make sure he's kept up to speed. No, no note, keep this verbal. Nobody write anything down. Understood? Have Henry check the announcers and operators, the traffic people. Ben Trevelyan too.

—Ben?

—Everyone, Phil.

—Sir?

—What?

—The calls, if you'll look here, they occur from 9:00 a.m. to 5:00 p.m. Mr. Trevelyan, he isn't here past 11:30 in the morning.

—Neither are a lot of the jocks, Albert.

—We've gone around on that topic. Rule out Trevelyan. Rule out anyone who isn't normally here in the daytime. Oswald, good, hand it over. On second thought, Phil, call this number, pretend you're looking for someone named Smith. The rest of you keep quiet. Philip dialled and everyone watched. An answering machine responded, and he wrote something down on a piece of paper, disconnecting at the beep. —I hope he doesn't have call display.

—You could be calling anyone.

—Who was it? Henderson looked at Lewis, who held the paper in his hands. His face changed several times before he passed it around so that everyone saw the name. —At least it isn't Ambrose Lawson. I'd have strangled him personally.

—I recognize this name. Why?

—Union leader turned consultant, Stu. He was in the news a few times, this and that strike. Henderson shook his head.

—Phil, here's what I want you to do. Call -

—The detectives, Dad?

—I'll do that. You get me the archival stuff on him, every news story. Who's interviewed him most.

—If the person, and I say if, who spoke to him is from the newsroom they'll wonder why I'm doing that. It'll tip our hand.

—Then do it after hours. We'll catch them if the detectives don't.

—You're gonna have this guy -

—Watched like a hawk, Oswald. No one interferes with my business and gets away with it. And I'll talk to Lawson, make sure Olympus' business stays quiet with him.

—Why not just give it to someone else?

—Because they'll know we found out, and I want to catch everyone in this thing. Perry, good work. I'm sure it's appreciated by everyone. There were sulky sounds of commendation. —We have to nip this soon. Unionism is like a weed, you need to burn the earth, then salt it. I'll want heads rolling because of this. Lewis slapped the desk, his face shifting. —It makes me sick to think about what some trusted employee who I've fed and clothed is up to. Anyway, we'll fix him, permanently. The next bit of business. Oswald, you and Otis are going to tell me who gets fired from CCFP and CCRR.

—Albert, after a lot of-

—Let me say we -

—One at a time. Oswald.

—Just to say we looked at the track records. In Franklin Plains we got Lundberg, Kelly and Wilding. One has to go. Lundberg's had bad sales lately, his wife's been sick, but it's a hard choice to -

—Who is it? Who goes?

—Ah, Lundberg. Lundberg.

—Fine. And Ripton?

—There's MacKenzie, Taylor, Young and Wagner. Young's the worst.

—But she's a woman, Dad.

—I know what she is. Nice ass on her too. Who's next?

—Taylor.

—The only black man in the network. Otis?

—Yes, he is.

—No, I mean -

—Oh, his sales figures are terrible -

—Worse than Young's?

—Client-wise, Albert -

—Otis, worse than Young's?

—I'd say as bad.

—What do the stats say?

—Only marginally better, yes.

—MacKenzie and Wagner, how do they stand? Never mind, I know. Well-liked, Mackenzie's older, near retirement.

—A year and a half away, so you're right, letting him finish out would save us all a decision.

—Otis?

—Oswald and I worked on -

—Who's going?

—Tough to call. If we fire Taylor and Young, I see two more cases before the Human Rights Commission or the Labour Relations Board, which would make five complaints this year.

—Otis, who goes? That's all I'm asking. A simple question.

—MacKenzie and Wagner.

—You're letting the best go.

—Less exposure to bad publicity. Stewart can tell you the backlash -

—I don't need anyone to tell me that. Oswald?

—I'd give MacKenzie early retirement, and keep Taylor. Fire Young, keep Wagner.

—That leaves CCRR with two salesmen. Otis?

—We disagree, on a cost-cutting basis, and on the lawsuit front.

—So no consensus. I see. Let me say that you're both disappointing me in not coming up with one plan. What's the point of making a decision if you don't agree?

—Albert, pardon my saying so, but I made a decision. So did Otis.

—You did, true, a wise one. Otis, you'd let us keep rotten salesmen because you're afraid of a lawsuit? Publicity? I know, I know, it's the cautious approach, but I don't want rotten apples in my barrel. Taylor goes, Young stays, Wagner stays, and MacKenzie gets pensioned off. We can afford that. He's a good man, brought in the dollars.

—He'll hate not working, Albert.

—Don't push it, Oswald. You'd keep him on, but that's your sentimental heart. As for Taylor, who cares about a lawsuit? We can say we're letting him go because of general incompetence. That's grounds enough. We don't need to impress farmers and miners with how enlightened we are by helping a lousy salesmen because he's black. Young'll do. Otis, you could learn some things from Oswald, like keeping an eye on the future, not on the next day's headlines. Henderson did not miss the quick smile of triumph on Philip Lewis' face, nor did Otis. —While I think about it, Phil, I heard Brad Dombrowski an hour ago reporting a policeman hanged himself. Was this auto-eroticism?

—Gerry McNamara, he was in charge of those three cops who substituted themselves for the hostages in April. You remember they were on desk jobs. But the reports said McNamara deliberately sent them out, or they volunteered, one final brave act. He couldn't take the pressure, I guess.

—Or he was guilty. Look into that. Dig, dig. They don't train cops well anymore, not like I brought up you boys. Speaking of which, when I come back the hunting season will be open. We'll go up north and get some moose.

—Did you want me to go into the sex angle?

—Was he into kinky things? What else was he hiding? But be discreet. Who's on it?

—Karla O'Reilly.

—The police must love her. Black and Irish. I'll bet they don't know whether to arrest her or ask her to join up. I read something yesterday, where the hell is it, tore it out of some damn magazine. Listen: The glorious new world order sweeping everyone up is the Internet revolution, linking villages in Africa to New York, London, Paris and Toronto in a virtual second. This Information Age is in perfect synergy with what I call the Business Age, when exporters, multi-nationals, and small businesses can sell or advertise in Cairo or Singapore through a web page cheaper than in their very own local newspapers. You see what this means?

—Who wrote that, Albert? Sounds like a salesman.

—Naturally it's a salesman, Bill Childs. I think he's national.

—Upper Canada's newspaper? One or two people appreciated Henderson's joke, appropriated from a provincial politician. —No, not that thing. It means -

—That we have to get CCII on the Internet, Dad, asap.

—Yes, Otis, Olympus is working on that. Thank you for the reminder. Do you know how easy it is to merge countries now? North America and free trade, the EU ready to get bigger, Asian nations with their act together. Go to Vancouver and you'll see China, Hong Kong, Vietnam, Japan. Who's a Canadian any more? Do you see where this is headed? Oswald?

—We position ourselves to serve a world community, the network of the future, programming through satellite. Linking up with different small networks we can sell spots anywhere. Massive exposure for our tourism, mining, forestry -

—It means, and am I the only one in the room who sees it, the white race is disappearing. No wonder you're surprised. It's happening without us knowing it. People coming in from shithole countries, and what do you end up with when they start mingling with Canadians? Someone like Karla O'Reilly, some Afro-Gaelic-Canadian, or whatever she calls herself. Or Dombrowski, where's that from? Eastern Europe? Or this stinking Greek, Karmiris.

—I don't know as we have much to worry about here -

—Open your eyes, Bob. I'll bet you the Jews in Germany said that before everything went to hell. Bowmount's full of Turks, Lebanese, Ghanians, Rumanians, and even a handful of East Timorese, they were on the radio this morning, saying the West should disinvest -

—We didn't cover their protest, Dad, I -

—Appreciated it, son, and that you did it without even being asked. Olympus is working on a deal there now, and if it gets caught up in human rights, six years of negotiations with corrupt politicians goes out the window. Bob, I'm talking about the extermination of the white race. Who profits from it? Then you come across a piece like this one by Childs, where he says, what did he say, talking about the glory of the global nation, the death of nationalism, the rise of a world government. He's talking from a technological base, but we know goddamn well technology seduces people, people follow business, and business leads nations. Governments tag along. It's bad enough our beloved premier had to put Drewnicki and Amaral in his cabinet, it's like asking the Goths and Vandals to manage Rome. We might as well move the government to a reservation. We're witnessing the death of a nation, and no one wants to acknowledge it. Too damned scared to raise it in bald, practical terms. If businessmen don't lead the way, who will? Politicians? Activists? Academics? No, it's people like me and you who see what a Karmiris is doing.

No one felt he could contribute to this topic. Although sad to see his employer upset, Hornocker could not quite agree yet with Lewis' tirade, however calmly delivered, which he believed flowed from the union issue, and was most probably only an outburst. He wished something profound might come to him to ease the tension. It took Henderson's casual —Anyway, Albert, to loosen this knot of people. Lewis stood, tucking his tie behind the jacket of his Odërmark suit. —Fine, okay. All of you, see who knows this Prestwick. I don't want this hanging over us. Stewart, get these voice tracks on by – this is Wednesday, the 26th.

—The 27th.

—Have them in place for midnight Friday. Put it on FM only, like we discussed. Leave the news out. Just the music and the ads and the weather.

—Leave the news out?

—That should make things easier. Bob, who the hell's reading Archie comics in the FM control room? Damn disgrace.

—The weekend relief, I'll -

—Get a memo up, Perry, jocks and operators aren't allowed to read on shift. Bob, is the feed to the stations going on now? Lewis had a look on his face Henderson knew as a signal he wished to play a malicious joke on someone. —Hilary's doing it now, or should be.

—Otis, Oswald, Bob, come with me. Phil, bring me what you get right away. Perry, clean up that mess. Replace whatever's chipped. The four men walked down the twisting corridors, and at their approach people broke off conversations and resumed working. Once again Lewis congratulated himself on insuring the doors to the offices contained so much glass. It was far more essential for him to see in, not that they should see out. You had to learn to think like a zoo keeper when dealing with radio people. He would teach Phil and Otis this, especially Otis, who had distressed him by misjudging what to do about CCFP. I'm leaving him in charge, so today he might as well start making a name for himself.

—Let me see if Hilary's there. Henderson looked through the small window of Production Room #5 and saw an LP on the turntable. This was the Copy and Continuity department's first notice for the CCCC, CCCI, CCFP and CCRR recording studios to stand by for an incoming transmission. —Bob, we'll go in, you tell Hilary to wait a few minutes. Stepping inside Harvey Cox's studio Henderson heard the new jingle for Tophet Green Disposal Company, sponsors of the 1:00 PM newscast. —Hello, Uncle Lou. It's a real party in there, isn't it? Who'd you bring? Otis, Mr. L himself, the Nose. What are you doing cramming all the heavy jackets in one

room? Sure hope nothing blows up, know what I mean? one of those electronic charges, the board in there's a bit wonky, and zap!

—I thought Hilary was here.

—Just missed each other. Somewhere between here and Copy, or back
again, but is it about the feed? Anything you want I should -

—Yes, we don't want -

—Because this stuff here has to go. Hilary'll be back for them in a split-
cart second.

—Say that the feed has to wait a few minutes. I'll explain later. A tapping on the glass separating the two rooms interrupted Henderson, who
left —Something new in boxes, Uncle Lou? for —Bob, the music stopped.
Henderson pressed a button which sent an electronic signal down the line
that activated the reel-to-reel machines in the other stations. —Now
what?

—We have to send something, Otis. Henderson turned on a microphone and adjusted a level indicator. —Stations, good morning, Bob
Henderson here. We'll have Hilary in with the, ah, spots, and jingles, and
whatever else you need, but first there's a message for you. Hold on. Keep
recording. He turned the microphone off. —They're ready.

—Otis, sit in front of the microphone.

—Me? What . . .?

—Sit there, that's all. You remember we decided to fire people today.
Well, tell them.

—Tell them?

—Say MacKenzie is being pensioned off, and Taylor and Lundberg are
gone. Got it?

—Albert, Jesus, on tape? Not a phone call -

—Oswald, they're being fired. Do you know a good way to say that?
Why is that phone ringing?

—Bob Henderson. Yes, Mary, we're sending something down any
minute. Right, then Hilary. Yes. Yes. The contest is coming too, I see it
here. I'm not Hilary, I don't - yes. Yes, no. No.

—Give me that. Lewis here. Who's this, Mary? Get off the phone, you're screwing things up. Understand? Hello? She hung up on me.

—You -

—I know. Bob, turn that pot on. Otis, do it.

—Dad, do I -

—Otis.

—You want me to -

—Start acting like an executive and stop behaving like a child! Do it! Henderson tried avoiding Otis' panicked glance, concentrating on listening to the young man come up with inadequate phrases conveying management's distress at having to make tough decisions needed in these, ahem, rough economic times for the betterment of the operations of the CCII family. This needlessly cruel ordeal, for Otis and the salesmen learning their fate, caused Henderson to feel a small amount of pity for anyone Lewis loved. It was better to be ignored than to be the object of such a man's ambition. Oz seems dead, keeps his head turned while his staff are cut, like he can't look. Who'll they blame? Me, Oz, Lewis, but Otis bears this public humiliation for all of us. Henderson knew that right now, in Carlyle, Crescent City, Ripton, and Franklin Plains, Otis' edgy voice, a slight hiss behind it, was issuing from the speakers in large rooms, where people heard the fates of their colleagues, or maybe even themselves. The tape, when played later for those absent when the news was fresh, would stretch his voice a little, muffle it slightly, and he would come across as a mouse training to be a rat. From now on Otis would no longer be the Little Prince, and some harsher nickname would circulate, reaching his ears soon enough.

When the announcement ended, Lewis clapped his hands on his nephew's shoulders wordlessly and drew him out of the room. Henderson sat behind the microphone, one hand cuing Hilary's record at the beginning. —Stations, Hilary will be along in a few minutes. Don't call here, nobody'll answer. At the same time he started the turntable, Henderson jabbed the microphone button with a finger, sending its plastic casing rattling across the console. —Cheap piece of crap. He snapped the Off casing back over the exposed bulb.

—Jesus, Bob, can you - is that off? I don't hear anything. Henderson turned the monitor back up. —That he just did that, no warning. Is he crazy?

—He does what he wants. He doesn't give warnings. I don't believe it happened either.

—Otis looked like he was gonna stroke. I almost felt sorry for the dumb fuck. But he did it.

—Lewis made him, Oz.

—He could've said no.

—Would you? We've both been in situations when Lewis -

—Okay, okay. We'd better get out of here. Let things go on as normal.

—Like that was normal. Like Lewis is normal, or Otis, or Phil.

—They're all fucking nuts. You know that bastard Perry checked us, *us.* And Hilary's commercials, you read them?

—What? Why would I -

—I've seen them, Bob, there's something funny going on.

—You just said that about Otis -

—Albert wanted to break his cherry. Now he's a man. Jesus. What a morning. But I know, I know, we're not in it much longer. We keep telling ourselves that, but the days don't get any shorter, do they, Bob? We'll pretend everything's smooth. No problems. No unions, no snooping on the salesmen. Why shouldn't they trust us, be loyal, after this? MacKenzie's - wait, open the door. Henderson did, and they heard over the internal speakers —Mr. Bennett, line 315, please.

—MacKenzie's calling. Or Taylor, or Lundberg. Jesus, Jesus, Jesus. Shut the door, shut it.

—Listen, Oz, you know Lewis' friend Charlie Jones is buying the CATQ network.

—Yeah, but that's hush-hush. Only you, me, Albert and those two cunts know that.

—They have stations out near Franklin Plains and Ripton. Get them to apply there. You know Jones is going to want to run those places as if he wasn't Albert's man.

—He has to, otherwise the CRTC -

—Right. You know Jones. Pass along Lundberg, MacKenzie, to him. Forget Taylor, he's not worth going to bat for. Maybe they'll get a second chance.

—Maybe.

—Let's clear out, Hilary needs the room.

—Damn phone's ringing again, didn't they listen to you? What a bitch of a day. Harry Prestwick, I knew him in school.

—Think you should let Albert know -

—Before that slimy cunt Perry digs out yearbooks. I'll tell Phil, make him look like he has something to report. Won't look bad for me either. I have a feeling we'll need all the good deeds we can do to get out of here when we want.

—The road to hell, Oz.

—Seems to me we're already there. Maybe I can turn around and get off it.

—By talking to Phil? Bennett made a resigned gesture and the two men left the feed room, its ringing phone, and the record playing its last minute.

The fortress

During the wedding service many people allowed themselves, or were compelled, to transfer their attention from the bride to her father who, in the wake of Fr. Jerome Ryan's arrest on the Lonegins' doorstep Sunday last, had become newsworthy. Seated in a back pew of Tupholme Street United Church among nattering seniors – who, beneath the deliberate delivery of Rev. Agatha Batalus, whispered forth and back clichéd remarks about how poor Duncan looked and how disgraceful priests were – a stranger to Bowmount would have pieced together a version of what happened seven days ago. The minister solemnly assisted at the joining of Camilla and Stan in sacred matrimony as they built, in her words, a fortress against the blows of ill fortune. Many considered that an oblique reference to the scandal and a portent of much future hardship for the couple. Not a few predicted that Mr. Lonegin, abruptly feeble, would be lucky to last out the year. These people considered what were to them unquestionable facts: Father Jerome had been Duncan's confessor, hadn't he, and a friend too, sort of, if that type had friends like you and me, and you could count on him dropping into their house a couple of Sundays a month, couldn't you, regular as clockwork. And he'd been set to perform the ceremony today at St. Finnian's, hadn't he? All the guests knew of Archbishop Mason's offer to take up the tasks his gentle brother necessarily, regretfully, unavoidably, and temporarily, was obliged to set down until the unwarranted allegations from a confused child, influenced unduly by the media, were dismissed. However, appalled at having entertained a paederast, and in the absence of an apology from the Church, the Lonegins knocked on the U.C.'s door. Further, wagged that same tongue, you know that's Marian's doing, he wanted his daughter's wedding legitimized and blessed by God's only Church, not in this second-rate version. A nattily dressed businessman, a friend of Duncan Lonegin's, approached the matter differently. That's the U.C. for you, open to everyone. You could come in here a Communist and they wouldn't say boo. No need for anyone getting married under their roof to take some stupid marriage preparation course the Church calls essential. Just one phone call and there they are. Efficient. No one's beliefs go against their own, you can be a homo, tie cats to tracks, be married clergy, whatever, only not noisy, and they'd do anything to help. The Switzerland of denominations, where you deposit what you want, withdraw what you need, no questions asked. Now that's religious tolerance.

It should be said that the bride and groom did receive some attention, though, as at most weddings, the groom was a negligible figure except to his friends, for whom his predicament and outfit were the topics of sniggering jokes, and his parents, who regarded him as the handsomest man in sight. Camilla, in a simple auburn dress that reached her ankles, with a spread of lace extending from the throat down to the top of her pale bosom, captured much more notice. Most women agreed that with such rich material and clean lines the dress, with a minimum of alteration, could be worn at many functions. The bouquet of lilies and carnations, with purple roses intermingled, was considered odd, but in keeping with the bride's personality. Men paid no attention to the flowers, but admired the dress for the figure it hugged, and there was a touch of resentment mixed with good cheer in their joking with Stan after the ceremony. The maid of honour, Emma Mendoza – there were no bridesmaids – wore a dress identical in design to the bride's except it ended below the knee. The style and colour accentuated her brown skin, firing the best man's imagination as he contemplated the close dancing only a few hours away. Lastly, the flower girl, Ilene Miloz, amused everyone with her unconscious and innocent expressions, for she frowned, yawned, filled her cheeks with air, squinted at people and decorations, scratched one leg with the other, reflecting, people later made clear, their feelings about Rev. Batalus' lengthy, considered address. —Built to last, her defenders said. —Made to bore, rejoined her detractors. —All right for crocks, but young people? —What'd you want, that old buggerer instead? Damn sight more honest, seeing she's married. Among the invited guests this debate erupted at the reception, while in the back pews, among those who attended every christening, confirmation, wedding, and funeral announced in the church bulletin, it was carried on *sotto voce*, accompanied by commentary conveying endorsement of or disagreement over the minister's sentiments.

In the front pews, significant glances and shrugs followed Duncan Lonegin's gestures, from the walk down the aisle with his daughter to the processional after she and Stan had been announced as wife and husband. Situated two rows behind her friend's parents and aunt, with Dr. Ralph Davies and his wife Janie next to her, Ivy could not refrain from thinking about Mr. Lonegin even as she watched Camilla's movements. He looks ten years older, everyone's seen his house in the paper, on television. Look at him, gray, his face lined so much since last week. It's not like he's sick, he walks like always, holds himself well, but his face, there's no expression. Those CCII people staring at him, Mare Montgomery, Krysta Jordan, friends of Cam's, plus their dates, they're waiting for him to break down or stroke out. Looking at him like he's an exhibit. At least Mrs. Lonegin stopped drinking. Cam said she hasn't been like that in years. Let him go to bed for two days, a near collapse, when the police charged Ryan with molesting that boy William, and she took over. Insisted they get married now, not wait. And Stan offered to, now, that's a surprise. He was thinking of them, or was it cold feet? Is he really as bad as I think? Lowbrow, and anyone who'd let himself be a slave – but then, he sticks close to the family, does what he can, never tries to – what am I saying? He's the same bossed-around passive guy I met a year ago, same guy he was two weeks ago, he's not changing because he's marrying Cam. He's no different in a tux than in a boiler suit, and he has a ring no reverend's going to see. Good God, is that what a wedding does to me, I start to see a guy like him as acceptable? Next I'll say Deeka's not really a bastard when you get to know him. Should go by the bar, he probably thinks he frightened me. Without Cam, she'll be on her honeymoon, and I won't rush out the door this time. Two months ago that was. He must think I'm chicken. All because that morning I was stirred up, seeing Don for the first time in so many years, my guard down. Barely remember what Don said, how he said it, but why did he have to pop up? Then? To be dealt with, I guess, happy holidays. And then Deeka.

Next time I'll know what to say. No man's going to mess up my thinking, no matter how shitty I feel. Or even when I'm okay and get disturbed by a guitar player. Everyone gets to me, everyone upsets the delicate balance, and if marriage is a fortress I'm in a pup tent. Imagine being with Stan forever, or any of them? Cam looks ready, though she's young. Him too. Why does he let her do things to him? Why does she want to? So much happens that's never explained, we never picture people doing, well, perverse things, like, say, that conversation with Deeka. Suppose even part of what he said was right, that doesn't mean he's anyone to talk. So much of us is unseen. A fortress, you see the outside of it, not the cells and passageways, escape routes, but it's not hard imagining them. Not the same for people. Take that bastard priest who's ruined everything for so many people. How many times did he have tea and Mrs. Lonegin's pineapple squares? Was it on the same day he buggered a thirteen-year-old in his office? Rumour says he'll spill stuff about other priests, police chiefs, social workers, politicians, even the Sisters of Eternal Redemption, how they used to feel up the girls at school, punish disobedient students, girls in skirts with bare knees, by making them kneel on cracks in the tiles and saying the rosary over and over.

Unbidden, a dream from last night emerged. Although the action and circumstances of the dream were irretrievable, one sequence stood out. On entering, or exiting, a white-bricked institution whose facade hid its purpose, through a side door – and Ivy may have paused to consider whether that small detail held significance – she noticed a motto written in Latin, which she first translated as I am the voice of the many, but which on later reflection – and she hesitated when this later occurred – she decided read The multitude may cause trouble, but it always starts in one place. Both phrases sounded vaguely familiar, but not until the dream re-introduced itself did she have time to think about them. It struck her how close, and yet distant, the interpretations were, and she inferred her mood in the dream must have changed for her to devise two distinct renderings of the Latin.

Why can't I remember what the motto looks like? My dreams never make sense, like the one last week where my teeth fell out and I woke up convinced it was true. I'm still having my periods, now my body says I'm falling apart. Great. But Ivy, don't start thinking like that. There I go, my mind's two ways about itself again, about everything, constantly second-guessing. Although that's not strictly true, it's only now and then, less as years go by. I wish I had a friend to talk with about dreams. Cam's too young, she hasn't lived enough. I don't know if that'll change once she's married for a while. If the minister ever shuts up so they can exchange vows. Does marriage change you, deepen you? Make you lead a richer, more philosophical life? Not that people think about it but you know what I mean. That's what I need, a man who understands that impulse. The voice of the many, versus the troublesome multitude, what does it say about my life? Did I read them somewhere?

A sigh drew Ivy's attention to Duncan Lonegin. He stopped going to church when Father Ryan asked the congregation of St. Finnian's to forgive the guilty priests as Christ instructed. What'll he do now? Everything of value for him, his faith, what it says it stands for, it's gone. Most people wouldn't understand, wouldn't care. People talk more about spirituality than religion, as if they're interchangeable. Cam's father believed in God and the Church equally, and now, how could be believe in one without the other when he had said more than once that he belonged to both? Even this wedding, the Church ruined it. Letting men like Father Ryan behave that way, without punishment, for years. Belief in God, ever since he could spell or say prayers at bedtime, it's supposed to last, like he thought it would, till his death, and to have that mocked and paraded on the evening news? It's momentous. I can't be the only one here who thinks that, but if I look around I don't see anyone else who isn't just nodding along. Doesn't anyone here take that in, other than his family and a few friends?

Stan? Try telling Deeka, he'd laugh and call him deluded, or those CCII people, or Janet what's-her-name, typical reporter's attitude about religion. Paid sceptics, and conservatives call the press liberal? Ridiculous! Tell me what's liberal about a sceptic. It's conservatism in disguise, it's reactionary. They'll snipe at New Age stuff, and some of it's ridiculous, or harmless, sure, because there's no demand for sacrifice to anything outside your own happiness. You're always praying to yourself, call it what you want. That's what today's New Spirituality is. But the press is afraid of religion, because that means there's an organization and a set of firm beliefs everyone's expected to follow, or try to. They let Buddhism by, it has no real dogma, and they say nothing about Judaism in case they're accused of anti-Semitism. Everything else's fair game. If you stick to generalities you can spread whatever lies you like about religion, especially if you're thought a liberal. Camped outside his home, cameras and microphones, Do you have a statement for us? Those lousy – Ivy, calm down. You're upset for him, and for that miserably unhappy, underfed boy, William. Relax. And work upsets me as well, we do public relations stuff for rats just like Mason, or worse, every day to make them look good.

The subject of Ivy's sympathy struggled to keep his daughter at the forefront of his thoughts, and despite that intent kept slipping away from the ceremony to a remote place within himself. It might be supposed by members of the congregation that he re-visited last Sunday's events, and while that day would never be forgotten, it became increasingly overshadowed by a sickness of the soul. He could not reveal this to his wife, thanks to the sheer unspeakableness of his misery, and partly due to rage. No one would have been surprised Duncan Lonegin was angry, since it was not a common occurrence to have a priest seized by the authorities in one's home, yet the true source of Mr. Lonegin's anger was his wife. In this week Marian had given up alcohol altogether, cancelled St. Finnian's and arranged Tupholme United, sheltered her husband from callers, encouraged her daughter to stick with the wedding date, while exhibiting a composure not seen in some time. Though consumed by personal affairs, Mr. Lonegin and Camilla, in separate ways, acknowledged that Marian now acted like the wife and mother of old. If Camilla had not had the wedding to prepare and her father's despondency worrying her, she would have quizzed her mother about this sudden resurfacing of self-possession. Where had it been the last six, seven years? Why were you such a weak woman, you gave me nothing, nothing to admire. When she had a chance to think about it, the word resurrection came to mind. Her good strong mother was no more, her father complained privately, hasn't been around since her mother's death. In her teens and early twenties Camilla asked What could Dad have seen in her? I love my mother, I know he loves her, but what is she? She taught me to read, sew, and cook, get stains out, but where's the role model? Okay, her mother died, I know that it was ugly, and I came along late in their life. Did she run out of energy, waste it all on that old woman and save nothing for me? Old eggs and tired sperm, is that what I am? No, it's not, I won't let it. Dad's always there, quiet, he holds us together. I hope I can be like him as I get older.

Generally, Camilla followed her father's example until two years ago when Mr. Lonegin's self-imposed exile from Bowmount's Catholic community began, and he turned to her for support which she resisted. It's Mom's job, I'm not his wife, but look at her. Aunt Urs doesn't help, needling him, that snotty bitch, I don't care if she is a widow. I'm not Dad's wife! Neither of them's strong, and they'll suck me dry. No way. Her resolution to be tough was carried through, and with Stan she determined always to be in control. He considered her scrappiness, so he called it, seductive, and one weakness in him led to another. Weak? He's a man, isn't he? Most women are tougher, except my mother. Ivy isn't weak, but look at her, not laid in years, and she thinks Mr. Right's out there waiting for her. You take what you get and shape it into what you want. Stan I can handle, and he fits in. He can't do without me now, but he's not my father. On the eve of Camilla starting a new life, Marian's re-emergence as the woman she had once been confused her daughter. Sure, like, it's wonderful, but maybe it's like Ivy said, a final flowering. Trust Ivy to quote poetry. But why the hell did it happen this week when I have so much to do? If she stays this way I'll have to change, again. Why don't people act like they're supposed to instead of making trouble for me by changing?

Mr. Lonegin asked a similar question, along with others, during the ceremony, just as he asked them last Sunday night, and on Monday, and on each day since, having nothing to do but think as he moved from bed to the study's couch. He reflected that it was a good thing a father's primary role at this time in his daughter's life is to write cheques and tie ribbons to the car. He listened to the telephone ring, the door open and close, as his wife and daughter, with Ursula's help, arranged everything, and imagined Camilla and Marian were closer than they had been in years. Lying in bed, he could hear the newspaper people and television reporters asking his family for comments on Fr. Ryan's behaviour, and was relieved when another sex scandal broke out, not only because it left the Lonegins in peace, but it had nothing to do with the Church. Several men had been filmed, over the course of five months, having sex with each other in a public washroom of Bowmount's East End Mall, and the media were off in pursuit of names and details. The police assured the general public that only criminal activities would be presented as evidence, with the rest of the footage destroyed. For the moment, Mr. Lonegin was thankful the gulls had moved on. In truth, he could not have added one more example of sexual perversity to the many he had. The image of William, so formal a name for so small a boy, gripped by Fr. Jerome Ryan's hands, filled his imagination and he tried to attach his mind to the activities downstairs. Stan's doing his share without fuss, in good humour, the endless running around to see the caterer, going for flowers and decorations, he's pleasant to me . . .

Camilla's father could not continue in that spuriously positive vein, neither at home nor while listening, now, to the well-meant encouragement of Rev. Agatha Batalus for the young bride and groom to treat their imminent union as a fortress. He heard the word tolerant muttered nearby, in what context he did not catch, and applied it to the minister. Yes. This is the place of last resort for people in my situation. Our situation. They're doing us a favour, but – tolerant? No, no, no – the United Church is so flexible it can be bent into anything, like metal without integrity. And we need that . . . laxness, now, damn it. The reverend's doing her best. Once I might have agreed that marriage is a fortress. Mr. Lonegin passed a handkerchief across his face, not because he felt warm, but a small gesture such as this prevented him from shouting. I live in an aerie, and around me is desert! He swallowed, almost choked, and swallowed again. Marian's hand pressed lightly on his arm. His thoughts could not be shut off by a touch. I brought my child to that man to baptize, allowed him to give her the body of Jesus, all in His name and the name of all His Church.

If this is the junction of the paths of wickedness and good, the attractive path and the frightening path, I'll stop and sit forever. Who was I to blame the Church for not recognizing its own sinning members when those same men heard my confessions, rubbed chrism on my daughter's forehead? I'm no smarter. In one hour my last belief was ripped out. I used to think I had witnessed God's hand in my affairs once or twice. Ever since I was a young man, an altar boy like that William, I presumed everyone, since we were made in His image, mirrored an aspect of God. Even the worst people carried on a constant dialogue with Him. Now that's all over, everything's . . . quiet. Maybe this is peace. Since Sunday? No, since Marian's mother died, that's when my wife began to disappear. No one knows what I suffered watching her lie there, she'd say. If you'd been there the moment her spirit left her eyes! her spirit! dead! and her body still going! Oh Dunc! Why did this happen to me? How do you live with a martyr? If it had just been me – but Camilla missed you. Instead I did double-duty, and that's when the dialogue became muffled.

Duncan tried to drag himself from the morass in which he now sank regularly and back to his current physical surroundings. Had he missed a cue in the service? People were smiling or nodding while he had been occupied in thought. If I can call misery thought. Blaming it solely on her, that's not fair. Though it did weaken me, I insist on that. And here she is back to what she was seven years ago, and I'm supposed to be grateful. After watching her sit in that chair, drink in hand, eyes half-closed, saying Stay home tonight, why are you always out, the shopping can wait, your friends must, that meeting . . . So I could share your tragedy, witness you relishing your sorrow? Seven years! I won't have it. Stupid woman! That's what you are! Or were. If you'd stayed that way it'd be something to ignore, but if you're strong? Because the minute I rely on you, you'll fold. People think you've taken charge, and you have, and I hate this, it's come at the wrong time. We don't talk any more, how could we, you drunk or sullen, your sister not helping, and it's dragged me down to this. How many times did I want you back to normal, how many prayers did I say? What was the answer? I never heard one.

In that remote place in Duncan Lonegin's mind it seemed he could see the many versions of Fr. Jerome Ryan, taken from all the years of acquaintance, superimposed on each other. I prayed to God and the answer wasn't silence, the answer came through that man.

He chided himself for being so egotistical as to expect the world to stop revolving at that moment. Rev. Batalus continued speaking, Marian kept looking anxiously from him to their daughter, the rustling of clothes and hymnals, the squeaking of shoes, the faint scent of candles, perfume and dampness did not cease or diminish or grow. Absolutely nothing changed. Nothing outside manifested this illuminating solution, and had he taken it for granted anything would have? Later he denied it, but in that moment he desperately wanted an external confirmation or denial of what he heard. The answer to his one question, Am I abandoned?, had been brought to him by one who did God's work. Now he understood. That answer occupied his mind while at the doors of the church he shook hands mutely, for how could he speak while God talked? The uninterrupted answer lasted while he stepped over **AFTER GRISLY DEATH WOMAN ARRESTED: DEAD LOVER FOUND IN BED**, which lay trampled on the sidewalk next to **MALL TAPES REVEAL SEX OFFENDERS' EXPLICIT ACTS**, and echoed throughout the endless photo session, the reception, and the dance that followed, fading out once he accepted it fully. Past midnight Duncan Lonegin collapsed in bed and immediately in a long sleep from which his wife could not wake him. When he did open his eyes the next day, he felt that in the rubbing and wearing of these last eight days a worn-out shape had been discarded, and he lay there quivering like a newborn left to die on a bare hill.

So, beyond redemption then

—When you look at life, it's messy at the edges. You find?

—The centre's not so neat, Henry. Precisely in the middle of Alistair's mind sat, or rested, or squatted, Bart, increasingly less a friend to explore than a dilemma to be confronted. It's been months, I'm going, not mad, no. Jesus. —It's Harry, not Henry. Johnny! He can't hear me. You look miserable, Al, can't have both of us like that. What's it, the little woman waiting up for you? Hey, relax, it's a joke, give me a napkin, I'll – goddamn things come to pieces in your hands. Johnny!

—Yeah!

—Another round of Manhattans for me and my new drinking partner. And bring a cloth. My wife keeps one eye on the clock and the other on my liver. Or my heart. Don't know what'll explode first. You? A ridiculous image of Bart anxiously peering through an apartment window waiting for him to return came to Alistair. Did I say something just then? —I don't know you well enough to bet on that.

—No, do you got a wife? Girlfriend?

—Not just now. Johnny removed the glasses. —You guys aren't driving, are you? Because I got enough problems with those pricks at City Hall. Three months I'm waiting to change this place into a coffee and wine bar, and they keep throwing paperwork at me. I got to pay for this licence, that licence, a permit, wait for a citizens' petition against me to get knocked down. Think Runciman cares about the small businessman? I'd like to yank his balls off and shove them up his ass, the staff he has. Now with that slut wife of his head of City promotions we're all fucked -

—Johnny, those drinks. And a couple ham sandwiches.

—Don't go driving home, Harry. Last thing I need's the cops on me be-

cause you failed the breathalyser. Both men shook their heads carefully.
—Taxis, I promise on my union card. But your concern, comrade -

—Knock that crap off. Someone has to watch over you, and if it isn't me, who? Here're your drinks. And this is that tape you wanted. Things've been crazy, though, so I didn't get a chance to tape over the other side. It's pure crap, relaxation stuff.

—Zamfir?

—No, worse. Whales, and harps, water sounds, some woman talking. You can tell by the colour of the plastic, see, pink, little fruity designs over it. But the songs you wanted are on it.

—I'll stop it when side one ends. It'll beat what's on the radio.

—I'll get Sylvie moving on the food. You don't look so great. Anything wrong?

—I came in here for a belated celebration, and he asks me what's the matter. No, not a celebration, what's there to - a commemoration. Johnny looked at Alistair. —You too? Alistair shrugged. —I guess.

—A Finnegan's Wake. For Frank. I was out of town when he died -

—I knew you weren't serious. Miserable rat, at least his two sick friends don't poke their noses in here any more. People are more relaxed. She couldn't have done me a better turn.

— A toast to Frank. Harry and Alistair took long sips from their drinks. —I'm not toasting that. Even an Italian knows that song, and that Tim Finnegan came back.

—Point taken. All right, it was an excuse.

—Johnny!

—Gotta go. Yes, Vic?

—He's a good egg. Where were we, Al? Life.

—Life. Cheers.

—Hold on. The end isn't pretty either, all that sickness and wasting away, dying with the big C, or some kind of paralysing stroke that leaves you a vegetable. Give me a gun, I'd shoot myself instead of living like this.

—This what?

—This retarded guy on a ventilator, can't even change himself. Once your dignity goes, what's life worth? Hey? What's life worth. He took a sip this time. — And at the beginning we're a blob of flesh squeezed into this jam-packed world. I got a feeling if we saw how we looked when we were born we'd abort ourselves. Don't you? Not just because of how we look, but because of the mess we know we'll make later on.

—Women are different.

—You can say that again.

—They look at a baby and start cooing, he's adorable, she's sweet, innocent.

—It's true, we don't know any better then. See that guy talking to Vic? You know Vic, Al?

—Who's the other guy? I've seen him but don't know his name.

—Phil. Thinks a lot about women, too much of them. And he figures there's answers to everything. Not that we know them yet, but they're waiting to be discovered.

—Wouldn't it be great if there was? Then . . . Then, thought Alistair, I wouldn't have done that thing, wouldn't be wondering what to do about Bart. Me and Bart. —Answers? I'm afraid to ask the questions. Phil there, he's young still. He says someone told him a thing they read saying babies are born with pure souls.

—He's into religion, then.

—Hard to say, Al, the way he talks.

—Science, DNA? Where does he think the answers are he knows are there? Harry raised his hands and gazed upward, not seeing the inscription above him, A man is only happy when he is drunk. —Up there, beyond the senses, beyond this world. Out of step. He's a bit like Sam, you know, the painter. The real painter. Alistair nodded, and they did not discuss the arrest of Fred Rifkind for sexual misconduct in what had been nicknamed Molester's Mall. —Gave me this spiel yesterday on purity, came up because of Frank, you see.

—What did?

—What I just said. Phil said he was told by someone when we're babies we're like these clean plates, or like a -

—Plates?

—Shit, that's not right, it's the skyline talking. My -

—Here's your sandwiches.

—Johnny, are we innocent as babies? Johnny moved a towel from one shoulder to the other as he considered this. —At our age? Harry waved his hand. —Not now, I know the answer to that. When we're babies, are we innocent? The bartender's face cleared. —Sure, why not? What have we done wrong? Nothing. Original sin, maybe, if you believe that stuff, but I don't, and I'm as good a Catholic as the next guy. Why? Your conscience bothering you?

—Should it?

—You tell me. Al, what do you say? Should Harry feel guilty for what he's gone and done? Alistair emerged from the fog enveloping him, a fog not only muffling outside sounds, but making him wonder if he had said or done anything incriminating. It was not a condition dependent on alcohol, for in the middle of the day, perhaps during a bowel movement, he would suddenly start and worry if he had dropped his pants. For an unknown reason, contact with the toilet seat failed to register. —About what?

—Those ads. Harry, I don't like the government any more than you do, but agitating people to get after those pathetic slobs -

—Henry, what's - Harry, what's he talking about?

—He has to have seen them. Those ads on television about cuts in social spending, health care, what the Burke government's - hello?

—People's faces staring out at me.

—All these saps who -

—All right, Johnny, I'll tell him. You'll get it all wrong. The provincial government's chopping everything. Burke and his Cabinet are wrecking this province, closing hospitals, schools, not giving pay increases to unions, or people on social assistance, making students pay more tuition.

—Get to it before he passes out. How many -

—So the firm -

—has he had, anyway?

—I'm with, we were hired by medical people, activists, the school boards, a bunch of third parties, to publicize what the government was doing. So we sat down and worked out a -

—Don't lie to him, it was your idea. He came up with this on his lonesome, to go after the bureaucrats. Not the politicians, mind. Why? Because they're not protected, like that bastard Drewnicki, or Gascoigne. Harry figured -

—Politicians have hides like elephants, Johnny! You want your next hospital bed to be in a corridor? Maybe you don't see the poor mothers waiting for their cheques, not able to pay for food and heat, going to food banks. Does that make you happy? Any of you? Harry's voice assumed union meeting pitch. —You people, you people who want things changed, and never doing anything about it. Yeah, Al, we targeted the guys and girls who wrote up government policy, splashed their pictures in the press, on TV.

—Yeah! Now I know it!

—He knows, Harry, you're famous.

—Silent protests too?

—That's right, we picketed their streets, walked right past their homes, so everyone'd know who was doing what to them. No more anonymity! Everyone's responsible, and they don't like it, but tough! Make the grunts sweat, so they'll take it out on the ministers and deputy ministers, make the management structure crack, a living hell to work in. And why not? If it improves things, why the hell not? Johnny here'll want his nephew, that retro-hippie, to have social assistance there if, God forbid, he doesn't become a singing sensation and gets fired from every fast-food job he stoops to take, and -

—Hey!

—Am I wrong? What are you doing to make sure social assistance is there for him? Direct action, I told you that was the only way.

—So those people's kids at school, they're getting picked on, teased. If I had kids at school, and if one of them came home bawling because I worked -

—Make you think twice about blindly carrying out orders, wouldn't it? It's for their future good, and the good of the cause. Real action takes time, it means being unpopular otherwise nothing'll change! Sure it's hard on kids, I have them too. They're grown up, but I know what it'd do to me if their friends in grade six gave them a hard time. How else do you think I knew it'd work! At some point Harry knocked over his drink, which Johnny mopped up now that his friend had run out of breath. —You see, Al? I thought it was a wake, then I didn't. Now I'm not so sure.

—You hate City Hall, brother, you said Runciman -

—But I won't put their faces on television for everybody to spit at.

—And that's why society stays the same!

—You keep telling yourself that as you get loaded. Me, I have a clean conscience. You asked about babies? They're innocent 'cause they haven't stopped and asked themselves a million times if what they're doing was right. It's not 'cause they're strong. They're not, they're new. But us guys gotta fight to be good, Harry, and who wins that? How many saints do you know? Look at the bar you're leaning on. Brand new, fifteen years ago, and since then you've spilled how many drinks in that same spot? I wipe up the mess, but the beer and vodka sinks right into the grain. Use whatever polish I want, I'll never get this looking like it did the day it came in here.

—You're saying those ads made me -

—This isn't about you, me, Al or Frank. We do things that dirty us forever, and there's no going back. Not even the last rites, you want the truth about it, in my opinion, though I gotta hope I'm wrong on that one. Alistair thought Johnny meant every wrong act blackened one forever, and he felt compelled to counter it. —Okay, then, sure, but if we do some-thing good, isn't that, like, cleaning up? Enough good things -

—Unless I put in a new bar, those drinks'll be there, always. Fancy ma-chines could find the chemicals, or whatever. So you don't get all the stains out, is what I'm saying. Thing is not to get yourself dirtier than you have to. Harry understands about avoiding the near occasion of sin.

—But it's impossible, brother. Harry's voice no longer had a defensive tone. A great wave inside Alistair threatened to overwhelm him. Looking down at the unfinished Manhattan he knew he would vomit, and made it to the bathroom in time. —That was more than I expected. I guess I wanted to forget what I'd done.

—This campaign's low. That's why you're drinking like there's no tomorrow.

—I'll be here tomorrow too. I'm not proud, you understand that.

—But you did it, Harry.

—It'd never been done. They liked it.

—Doctors, teachers, what do they care as long as they get what's theirs. I could tell you stories about the psychiatrists in this town that'd make you take an axe to them. More than you'd get out of that book, *Medic Alert*. Lawyers too. You see this? Johnny rummaged in a drawer and came up with a cheaply printed paperback, *Legal Briefs: Who's Bad and Who's Worse*. —Found it in the bathroom last night when I was closing. Just like that first one.

—Let me see. I'll be damned. Cheaper, though, the print isn't -

—Bifocals, that's what us crocks need. Look at this, and he laid a copy of *The Bowmount Telegram* beside the anonymous book. Johnny read the headline out,—**TERMINAL ESSAY FROM LAST CENTURY USED AS HAZING MANUAL.** They're coming out of the woodwork, it's this computer generation. Right there's a story about Lala. You know what they're saying now?

—Johnny! Two Black Dogs!

—Coming right up, Wes! You keep it. I'm getting Sylvie to bring you guys a pot of black coffee. Waiting for Alistair, Harry read an editorial which read:

```
A  sensational  new  angle  on  Lala  Sastri's
motive  for  the  murder  of  Frank  Joy,  in  early
October,  has  been  proposed  by  noted  local
psychiatrist  and  alternative  health  care
giver,  Christina  Nolan.  In  an  interview,  Dr.
Nolan  com- mented  on  the  defence  the  accused
```

killer is using.

She says that for a woman to claim she misheard her lover's command, during hypnosis, to perform a certain sexual act, as to "fillet him" in the middle of the night, is ludicrous. The only way such a statement could be believed by Sastri, a woman of Calcutta origins, whose reputation, as this paper first pointed out, is tainted by minor theft and drug charges, is, says Nolan, if the planets had made her do it.

"We know the moon, the sun, the planets, and other bodies, exert a gravitational pull on the earth's oceans. That's why we have tides. Women see this happening during their periods."

The noted physician, from her stylish practice in Carlyle, went on to say that "medical science has proven that the glands excrete fluids, and that the endocrine glands release hormones that contain chemicals that influence our physical selves."

"Further," adds Dr. Nolan, "character shapes attitude, and that on the night Sastri killed Joy, which she confessed to, and which no one can dismiss, the heavens were in a potentially body-influencing, character-shaping alignment . . . I think an astrological chart on the accused would show significant motion in specific houses, and of course, her menstrual cycle and hormonal activity must be taken into account. But the police never look for those things, and it's probably too late to help her case. They can't be re-created."

Is this, we ask, what New Age medicine is about?

Alongside this was a picture of the murderess, accompanied by her lawyer and two policemen. In her arms lay a bouquet of flowers which were clearly meant to be laid on Frank Joy's grave. Above the photograph the caption read **It's A Long Way To The Ganges, Lala**! Anything to sell this yellow rag. Harry knew the *Telegram*'s owner, and recalled the unending parade of editorials raging against unionism. Arthur Morgan had been a mediocre businessman, but a series of lucky breaks and some deliberate manoeuvring gave him control of the paper. Telling the average guy from his pulpit what to think, as if that bastard ever did anything for anyone. Turning from Lala and Frank, he read the closing paragraph of an item on how Richard Burton's essay had been appropriated by a degenerate frat house at Carlyle University as a textbook for perverse rites, skipped over the rest of **HISTORICAL EVENTS ON THIS DAY** when it reached back to the birth of someone or other in 1819, quickly flipping past a full-page ad showing the faces of certain bureaucrats and advising people to let their neighbours know what they thought of government cutbacks, recovering momentarily with the **ARTS REPORT**, where Jonas Allan gleefully announced the closure of the Open Conceptualists' new opera in what passed for a review, bannered **LONG MARCH GETS HALTED**. From there Harry flipped to the sports page, draining his Manhattan as his eye caught an ad featuring Santa Claus standing in a car dealership's lot in October. He drank his coffee, unaware Alistair lay unconscious in the washroom undiscovered until —Hey, Johnny, Al's passed out in there. A small commotion followed this announcement, to which Loyola paid no attention, as he was meeting Janet soon. Jimmy tapped his shoulder. —Loyola, hi. That friend of yours was in the other night looking for you.

—Who? Not Bart, he prayed, no more to do with him. —Deeka. Said he'd like to see you but always got your machine. Funny, he didn't mention your name. Called you our mutual, what, friend of Hibernian extraction. Something. He was here with a woman. Made me repeat it three times, you know that?

—Nadeen? That Greek photographer -

—No, Nadeen was a looker. This one, she had an accent'd scrape paint off a barn, and her nose, ugh. You know her? Anyway, he said he'd run into you – what's today?

—Friday. Shit.

—Yeah, no, they're going to the country this weekend. Maybe next week, he said. Got time for a drink? Waiting on your cousin?

—She's at her hairdresser's. She has some big thing coming up and -

—Wedding?

—wants to change her look for – no, won't say what it is.

—Publicity shot, maybe. Ain't seen her in the paper lately. Coulda missed her. At this moment Loyola imagined the worst. Vinnie and her? No, there's lots of bashed up women, and if you come from Crescent City or Dunderdale, they got this way of talking. Bad as anywhere else. No, it really wasn't possible.

—Stay for a drink?

—Sorry, Jimmy, Thanks for the message, but I can't stay. I'll be late for Janet if I don't catch the bus.

—Runciman has their schedules all fucked up.

—Did she have – what colour hair?

—Blonde. Or was it red? Red? Hard to say. These lights, and, well. Jimmy pointed to the empty glasses in front of him. —Thanks anyway. Wes came up just as Loyola left the bar. —That guy.

—He's a regular guy, like you and me.

—Seen his cousin? Great tits, not too big, not mosquito bites either. I got a look at 'em once when she bent over. Gold bra, yes sir, never forget it. Deep tan too. Like him, come to think of it. It didn't end at her cups, you ask me. Right, Pops?

—Keep your filthy thoughts to yourself, and stay away from me! Wes and Jimmy pretended to be afraid of the blackthorn cane waved at them, while over at a table Xavier and Sharie Perrigo took a mean look around. —Speaking of tits, did I -

—Wes, Deeka said something about Loyola. Want to hear it? Okay. He said he's waiting for them to have congress. Get that? Wes nodded. —So I want to know, what the hell's that?

—Sex.

—Sex?

—Sex. Jimmy shook his head. —He don't even speak English. But his girlfriend liked it. Deeka, what kind of name is that? Where's he from?

—I don't know, here, I guess. Look, I was -

—But she's Loyola's -

—Cousin, yeah.

—So isn't that . . .?

—Illegal? Immoral? Jimmy nodded.

—Who gives a damn, they're free, white and twenty-one, as my ma says. Now look, Jimmy, take milk.

—What about it, Wes? What kind?

—Cow's milk, what'd you -

—Could be goat's. My cousin had a farm in Ripton. Killed himself last year sometime.

—Cow's milk, all right? And don't go asking about percentages. So it's supposed to be good for you.

Jimmy snorted. —Tell that to my cousin's widow. Know something? She wasn't bad looking. I could go up and take a poke -

—Jimmy, Jimmy, Jimmy, pay attention. Milk, it's supposed to be good for you.

—All those ads -

—Exactly my point. Babies get breast milk. Why? 'Cause it's a human's milk, understand? Gives 'em hormones and vitamins.

—Sure. I guess.

—So then they get off it, and onto cow's milk.

—Growing up, they need the -

—But if human milk has so much in it, why stop drinking it? Taking milk from a cow? They don't even eat like we eat. I saw this program -

—Wes, wait now, you're saying . . . What're you saying? Johnny! A White Russian. You got me thirsty.

—If breast milk's so healthy, why stop drinking it? Ever?

—Just use -

—Right, right, right. Forget cows, they're pumped full of stuff, it's a whole other ball of wax. Bottled breast milk. Mothers do it for their kids when they go out. They express milk.

—They what did you call it? Hello, Jack. Jack sat down on the other side of Wes and ordered a lager. —How's things, boys? Didn't mean to interrupt. Go on, unless it's, you know, private. Wes continued. —Squeeze it, use a pump, to fill a -

—Like attached to their tits?

—You think it runs out of their pussy?

—Watch your language!

—Pops, you ain't even supposed to be listening. So if we were to go into some place and order a milk shake - thanks, Johnny.

—Your beer's coming up, Jack.

—Yeah, thanks, thanks. What're you guys -

—We order a shake, and -

—Now you're catching on. It's human, right? Not some gorilla milk, or petroleum based product. And a gorilla's closer to us than some cow, evolution-wise.

—Don't know about that evolution stuff, Wes. Dad said -

—Jack, you hear that? They watched Alistair being carried out of the bar by Harry and Victor. Johnny rang for a cab while a man sang about a breeze that stole his love away. Jack's eyes widened. —What, what, what happened to him? It was explained.

—Jimmy says he doesn't believe in evolution. You get this guy?

—No, not me, either. Thanks, Johnny.

—See, Wes?

—I mean, I can't believe it practically either, or not believe it, if you understand what I'm saying.

—You don't? Is that what you're saying?

Jimmy suddenly realized something. —So I'd have milk from, say, Rebecca's tits in this glass and drink it -

—What'd you say?

—Nothing, Wes, I - nothing.

—Better not let me hear you talk about my wife like that again.

—You look at the Sphinx, at Petra, see the pyramids along the Nile, you know that one Johnny? Ha heh, he's not - you know what I'm saying. They cut these tons of stones with - lasers couldn't do it! Could you? Me? No. See, I'd like to go on an archaeological dig, or see those spiders and what-not in South America practically drawn on the ground for these space-ships to see. I mean, what good were they to those people? Back when Antarctica was green. And all these sightings of UFOs, I can go along with that.

—But where do we come from if it wasn't apes?

—It's an experiment. Aliens came here and dropped us off, built the Sphinx, invented the alphabet -

—You gotta be kidding.

—It could happen. And it could not. I'm just saying. Just like evolution could. Or God could've made everything, dated it this year and that year. Wes asked Jack to repeat this. —He could've just invented fossils. Make us think there's such a thing as evolution. Why not? He's God, isn't he? And it's working, ha heh heh!

—Aliens. An experiment. So when's it over?

—Not yet. Maybe never, who can say?

—Where do they come from?

—Probably Alpha Centauri, it's anybody's guess.

—So how'd they evolve? Jack smiled. —Who knows? It's all just guesses, everything. We'll never know. Or we might.

—But someday.

—Sure, when the aliens come back, ha heh heh ha heh!

Wes shook his head. —Cripes, here I'm trying to pitch breast milk, and you got us visiting from outer space.

—Breast milk? What, what, what, is Rebecca pregnant or -

—No. Jack, look at all the women in Bowmount with no husband, unem-ployed. We could make a fortune.

—Off breast milk?

—Yeah. Why not? But not so loud, I don't want anyone stealing my idea.

Jimmy asked what would be done with the babies.

—Good point. Give 'em to yuppies that can't make their own. Kind of a sideline in adoption. But I figure after a couple of years you hire these scientists to come up with synthetic mother's milk. It'd be a speciality. Boutique milk, see? His two friends agreed. —You're always thinking, Wes.

—He's wasted in that car plant, Jack. Wes held up his hands. —Easy, I've only been there five weeks, give me a little more time to own the place. The shattering of a glass, followed by Sharie Perrigo's voice, came just as Louis Jordan began warning his brother about women. —Why the hell do you keep looking at your watch? Am I boring you or something? Victor muttered a few words Ivy did not catch, but she heard Johnny reply, —I thought they'd changed. Xavier Perrigo's pink shirt had come undone from his trousers, which were one size too large, revealing the top of a pair of white underwear, the elastic waistband separating from the cotton in a few places. —Now, Sharie, I was only remarking on the time.

—You limey bastard, that's what I said.

—I'm Italian!

—You were born in fucking Croydon, how does that make you Italian? Looking at the time for what?

—It was two years and four months ago tonight, at precisely this hour, that we – stop that, stop tapping my foot with your cane, I'm not drunk. I was looking, yes I was looking, intently, do you hear me, at my watch to see the time! He removed his steel-framed glasses and thrust them into his shirt pocket. —What are you looking at, my scar? The one inflicted on me when I hit the windscreen?

—Well, knock it off. It bothers me. Windshield, you idiot.

—You gave me this watch. Before! Before it happened, before the car wreck that began this bloody mess we call a mar – stop that, stop tapping my knees!

—I didn't give it to you for you to go looking at it when I'm around. Isn't he rude, Pops?

—Keep me out of it, you hear?

—The hell we've endured, Pops, we – will you stop that? I mean it, Sharie! You don't know what she's done. If you'd heard the filthy things she – aah! Keep away from me, you whore! *Sharie raised the cane and hit Xavier across the chest.* —My glasses, bitch, sow, if you've broken them -

—Johnny?

—I'm dialling. *Without saying a word, Sharie began to indiscriminately aim at her husband's head, neck, shoulders, until he took refuge under the table, which she calmly tipped over.* —No, Sharie, no – oww! I'm sorry, you miserable cunt, please forgive me – ow, my hand! Stop it, help, forgive me. *No one interfered, feeling it was better this thing play itself out as it had many times. By Johnny's accounting, a chipped table and a few broken glasses were nothing compared to an eye, because once Sharie started swinging she would attack anyone. Xavier had reached the door on his hands and knees, his trousers sliding down, giving Wes, Jimmy and Jack a good view of the marks from previous beatings on his pale legs and back. The only sounds heard over the music were the crunching of glass, a whistling as the cane flew back and down, and Xavier begging for his wife to stop. They reached the sidewalk by the time the police arrived. Two of Bowmount's Constabulary questioned witnesses. They knew the Perrigos, and that the husband never pressed charges. Johnny was content to toss them out of the bar for good.* —We'll let them sleep in the drunk tank. Guys like him could do with a break. *As Johnny began clearing up Ivy asked, seemingly to everyone,* —What was that all about? Why didn't anyone do something?

—I'm sorry, Ivy, you had to see that. They get like that. I've run them out of here a few times, and they won't be getting back in again.

—Yes, but why? And no one stepped in.

—It's not safe, *interjected Phil. Johnny nodded.* —That's the truth. Usually she only hits him, but once she damn near broke Sylvie's jaw. They're supposed to be in counselling.

—But you just let -

—What am I gonna do, get hospitalized myself? I called the cops, didn't I? I know, it's pretty upsetting when you haven't seen it a hundred times.

Like when Frank broke that rose seller's nose, poor kid. Look, I gotta get where you are, if you don't mind, there's glass under your feet. Maybe I could – Sylvie? She can't hear me. If I sent you down a couple of cappuccinos, we got the machine in yesterday, what about that? I know you drink Perrier, but maybe this'll be a nice change. On the house. An apology from me, for the disruption.

—It's just -

—Don't worry. You tell me who you're waiting for, I'll point you out.

—No, that doesn't matter any more, it was nobody important, just – I didn't mean to give you a hard time. The police, that was the best way.

—Listen, you go to that booth down in back. Phil, listen, can you explain about the Perrigos to her?

—Sure, yes. Why not?

—It'll just be a few minutes. On the house, like I said. Johnny finished sweeping, then worked his way through the customers, coaxing those alarmed by what happened to relax, joking with Victor about blissful marriages, smiling through Jack's repetitious descriptions of Xavier's body, until everyone felt easier. He put on a tape for Pops and watched the old man's face lose its childlike fear of violence as Ella sang one Porter song after another, the blackthorn cane resting by his side. New people came in, greeted with a smile from the bartender, or by friends with a great story about what they had missed. Johnny looked down at Ivy and Phil some time later, still talking in the booth, and thought how one good thing had happened that night. In his private washroom off the back office he washed his face and hands, eyeing a black and white picture, stuck in the corner of the mirror, of the woman who too briefly had been his wife. —Why'd you go ink your face out like that? I can still see you, I know you see me. I'm trying. At his desk he toyed with the coffee bar paperwork he would wrestle with again tomorrow. A poem he had been forced to learn, either in school or by his parents, came to mind, and aloud he recited the only part he recalled, —Or what's a heaven for. Heaven, he repeated, oblivious to the rising din from the bar, —I don't know about that. But where else would you be?

—Johnny?
—Coming, Sylvie!

Endings

—It's been hectic lately, hasn't it? Mare Montgomery saw yellow pages on Bob Henderson's desk, now under his hands, and knew without being told they were Hilary's ads. Instead of making immediate sense of their presence her flustered mind replayed this morning's conversation with her colleagues. —It's five to nine, already they want this big important meeting at 9:45.

—What does he want?

—That's just it!

—Bob's not a bad egg, Mare. It's not like going to see the Crimson King.

—Well, what is it? A call, Megan, from the station manager to meet him and Bennett.

—The Nose is going too?

—That's what I've been saying!

—You just hung up.

—Hilary! That's not the point! This is serious, Christ, they probably found out I applied for – they must have seen me at lunch when I met them.

—Where?

—Glorious Hannah's.

—Not their kind of place. But like they tell the all-night jocks, somebody's always listening. Could have been a salesman there, fucking weasels. That'd explain why Bennett's going to be there.

—What I needed to hear. I'm going to throw up. They're going to fire me, shit, shit, and I'm not gonna get that other job. I'm going to lose it right in Henderson's office.

—Do it in the Nose's lap. If he touches me once more -

—They *used* to tell the all-night people, Meg. Now there's -

—Yeah, right. Tell it to the machines.

—This is serious!

—Mare, you always get like this. They want to talk about ads. You're the head of Copy. What else is there?

—Not after today, you watch.

Now in Henderson's office, Oswald Bennett sitting beside her, the door closed, Mare could only nod at everything she heard. —Lots of changes, and we've more due up. This is between us, you understand. There'll be almost no announcers by March, only talent. You'll have to work at getting voices in the first part of the year, in the changeover, until the new system is set up. We need to - are you all right?

—I thought this was about something else.

—The fault reports? They can wait.

—Changes, firings. Me. Henderson almost laughed. —No, we'll need you more than ever in the next few months. As I said, and Oswald knows, he'll have to explain it to his salespeople, things will be difficult when we put everybody in this new . . .

—Locate them in their revitalized vocation sectors.

—Thanks, Oswald.

—How Otis put it. Otis, Mare.

—Yes, Mr. Bennett.

—Without full-time announcers you won't have much luck getting spots done. There'll have to be schedules, bookings, we'll get rid of this AM only stuff. Never liked it.

—Otis, again.

—The ads can't stop, and we have to figure out how to avoid that problem the best we can. Though the idea of a radio station without deejays struck her as silly, and unsettling, Mare's emotional state gradually calmed down as they discussed the new CCII and the computer system that would record and play commercials. —Mare, remember Will Donaldson?

—Yes, sir, he left about a month after I was hired. He used to just sit and look out his office window. At nothing.

—Left? I kicked his ass out of here, Bennett put in.

—I was in Production one day talking to Harvey, and Will comes in. He says to Harv, I want a copy of that demo spot for somebody or other. No problem, says Harv. Then Will says, Only I don't want it in one of those cardboard boxes, I want it in a plastic one. That's what Will called reel-to-reel tapes and carts. What would he make of computers?

—All these changes, the talent taking over. Mr. Henderson, what about Harvey? If they do their own spots, like you said, what's his new job? Bennett responded. —We think, and I mean the executive board, Harv's a great guy. Was here before I came, and that's twenty years or more. But as Bob said, we'll get in talent, talented talent, who know boards. All the sound effects, the beds of music, locked into another computer or on CD, all they got to do is open the mike -

—You're going to fire Harvey? You'd do that?

—Fire?

—Oz.

—That makes it sound like he did something wrong, say, help guys do up demo tapes to send to rival stations. We'll give him a package, then he's free to look elsewhere. A guy with his abilities could get anything. Right, Bob?

—You mean – sorry, Mr. Henderson, to stop you – at his age? He's, what, fifty? Someone's going to snap him up? Because you get computers and hire people to work one day and not the next? Whose bright idea was that? I'm sorry, I didn't mean that. We're going to need a head of production. We have satellite feeds, and -

—Young Rick's doing that now. As for who came up with it, the board looked at suggestions from the executive. Some things we approved.

—Mare, you know Harvey's been doing 30s and 60s since Moses was a child. Jocks can do what he does, easy.

—Jocks won't remember what he knows. And the national spots? Christ, he's – sorry – he's human, isn't he? How many times did you and your salesmen beg him to put a demo ahead of a paying customer? Or do a

30-seconder in twenty-five seconds?

—Oswald's stated things a bit bluntly, and it's difficult -

—Bob, let me answer that. Harv's a nice guy, did I say he wasn't, but we don't want a loser who moans all the time. He's from some bygone era, you know, before CDs, before computers, before cassettes. Who do you think's kicking our asses on this? He could stay till he rots, far as I'm concerned, but they don't like him, and you know why? They don't have anything to do with him, don't have the slightest idea what the job's like. Okay?

—A loser?

—Jesus fucking Christ, listen to me when I'm talking, you pick out one thing and ignore the rest. They don't like him, *they*. They'll keep Perry. Harv's number's come up before and Bob and I stood by him and -

—Is that true?

—You don't believe me?

—I don't think, Mare – and Oz, calm down. Getting into past history doesn't do any good.

—Worry about your own people.

—What?

—Oz!

—Bob, you were going to tell her. I lost people just because someone wanted to make a man out of his -

—Hold on. Hold on! Henderson leaned forward, the yellow papers in his hand. —He's talking about Hilary. You know that position was an experiment. You and Megan have seniority, you produce great copy.

—Hilary's isn't good? Why didn't someone say -

—It's fine, fine.

—Well . . .

—Oz. It's fine. Offbeat sometimes, but that's good too.

—Odd, all right, the way -

—Just wait now. Mare, this isn't easy for us, letting people go. You think I'm going to enjoy telling Harvey? The new way of doing things is going to take getting used to. But Hilary can't be afforded. Mr. Lewis is going through the budgets -

—Excuse me, sir, which one? Henderson and Bennett glanced at each other. —Do you mean Otis?

—He had a hand in it, yes.

—Put his two cents in. But you gotta admit, Hilary stands out. Wouldn't work overtime, said the extra money didn't mean anything. Gets to work ten to nine, my salesmen go in, Hey, write this up, and what's the smart-ass answer? I'll get to it at 9:00. What kind of attitude is that? And another thing, what's with this -

—You're firing Hilary because -

—You're the head of Copy and Continuity.

—You want me to go in – Mr. Henderson, are you serious?

—You've said you wanted more responsibility. We're prepared to in-crease your salary, as of the next pay day. He named a figure, an amount substantially higher than what Mare now earned, and slightly more than what the other radio station offered. Later, she wondered if they knew her plans, and for several days questioned why she remained. —But to earn that means more work. You'd be on the board too, in a junior capa-city, and we'd send you on a few computer courses. We have to have an answer today. To all of this. And Hilary has to be let go. This morning.

—This increase covers part of Hilary's -

—Hilary goes regardless. These aren't thirty pieces of silver. You're go-ing to be in administration, so it's for what lies ahead. Now we'll get into that.

When Mare returned to Copy, unsure how she made it through the rest of the meeting, neither of her colleagues were there. Megan would be on her smoke break, and she had seen Hilary in a salesman's office. The tele-phones were quiet, as was the printer used by the sister stations to send in copy, leaving only ambient noise. In the silence she felt a headache swelling. She had chosen to stay, which meant following ugly orders. If she did not do it Henderson would, and the Lewis family did not like un-cooperative employees. Christ. To be on the board, and to start this way. She went over to Hilary's desk, unsure why, or else not conscious she sought guidance on what to do in her new role. No one could be seen coming down the hall. I'll say I was looking for copy, but my heart's pounding, Christ, I'm too young to have a heart attack, it's stress. Gingerly she rolled up the yellow backing sheet from Hilary's typewriter as if what was on it would be a sign. She read:

O My Servant!

Free thyself from the fetters of this world, and loose thy soul from the prison of self. Seize thy chance, for it will come to thee no more.

She read these words twice more, her throat constricting, without breathing, then rolled the sheet back down. Since May there had been comments, which she admitted sharing in, about Hilary's strange ideas and expressions. Her colleague joked and laughed, was nice, amenable, but at heart seemed more serious, too driven, now that she had the motivation to think about it. —I know I shouldn't have read it, it doesn't help me. Fetters, prison, my servant, what is it but a prayer. Not one I've heard. I just, like, read someone's mind, someone talking to – to God. On paper. Not private. Mare looked around, as if coming out of a daze, or arriving at the edge of a resolution, the headache's growth stalled, her stomach knotted. She intensely wished what was written there had not been displayed for anyone to find. —Everyone. Right in your face. It should be hidden, words like that. Maybe it was the accident, maybe something else, but Christ! it makes people uncomfortable. It'll be in my head when I fire – and I won't be able to stop thinking about it. Why'd you bring it up? What -

—Blessings, my child. Mare jumped in her seat. —Harvey! How long have you been – you scared the shit out of me.

—You looked deep in conversation.

—I wasn't talking to anyone.

—Saw your lips moving. Don't worry, I do it all the time. Didn't mean to catch you off guard there, Uncle Lou.

—But you didn't hear me.

—Not a word. Any more spots, is what I wanted to ask. Mitch's in there, he's eager to leave. Had a meeting this morning with Henry, and between you and me and the guy upstairs he's pretty ticked off. Heard you got the big call yourself.

—No, the other one.

—Is that so? I'm beginning to feel left out. You'd tell me if it was serious. Bob's okay, but Mr. L.'s another case. Meetings – hold on. Mitch, nothing here, you did a fine day's work in fifteen minutes. See his face? What was I – yes, I come out of them mumbling myself. I'd like to say I was praying but, ah, nothing so high-falutin'. You look a little white. Go for a walk around the building. Take a gander at the boss' new car.

—A new car?

—Daimler, I think. Special ordered. Olympia must have upped his bonuses, all those guys around last week.

—That car's probably worth a salary or two.

—More than we'll see in boxes.

—Maybe I'll take a look.

—Worth it. Anyhow, here's the copy. I'll just rise up like Lazarus, if my bones will let me, and get back to the nationals. Go and sin no more. Mare took the commercial scripts, closed the hatch, and crossed to the filing cabinet, too afraid to speak further with Harvey in case something slipped out. Why shouldn't he trust me. When'll they fire him? Some morning, like they do with anybody important. No one'll be around, his work life over before people come in. As for Hilary, who cares about an experiment? Talking to myself, out loud, Christ. Getting psyched up. Like I won't be thinking about that prison of self shit. Why wasn't that something you could laugh about, like Harvey's priest bit? Why was Hilary so damned serious? Not like a funeral, but it means something. You shouldn't be out in the open about it, I think. A line got crossed in, when, July? and is that what Bennett wanted to say? I can see why, kind of, yes, religion doesn't have any place here. Loose the soul, but on your own time, thanks! Keep it at home, or in a church, or wherever. I had enough evangelizing from my parents, and that we're-all-one crap, to last a lifetime! The door opened, letting in David Wilcox's This Side of Heaven from the hall speakers. Hilary regarded Mare, who paused in her filing. —You know you can hear those drawers slam all the way out there? It must have been some meeting.

—You heard me? Hilary nodded. —Come on, outside. Something to tell - to show you. From the bosses. They left for the parking lot, followed, thanks to a speaker attached to a corner of the building, by the same song that an agitated young man in a warehouse snapped off. —Loyola! Loyola! Are those I know you can hear me suits ready for Mr. Glenny yet because he's coming in ten minutes he said and can you answer me if they're ready or not? He called out they were bagged and waiting. —Well bring them in here, you think he wants to go into a packing room?

—It's all of ten feet, for -

—What did I say? Hang them there. You really have to do better than this, lately you've been out of it. Too many late nights and too much drinking? Never mind, it's your life, just smarten up. Starlene rose, knocking today's *Courier* to the floor, where it fell open on **MALL VIDEO TAPES ON PORN MARKET, COPS SUSPECTED**, the heel of her left shoe separating from the sole. —Look at that, get me the glue. Are you listening? Hello? He handed her the bottle from a nearby shelf. —What are you sitting around for? Do something.

—There's nothing -

—Got the stocklist mailed?

—to pack. I did that Monday. No, yesterday. Her stockinged foot, green nail polish showing through the pale hose, attracted his attention, especially the second toe, which was longer than the first. —So you need me to tell you what to do every minute or else you just sit there, how you get anything done's amazing. You've been like that since you started here, no ambition, no changing you as hard as I tried to encourage it so I gave up, you'll always be a slacker. What are you looking at?

—I was - nothing.

—Don't lie, you were looking at my foot, you weren't even listening to me now are you listening to me?

—Am I what?

—Loyola! What's your problem? You're a bit thick at the best of times, but for the last week or so you have gotten worse, am I right? You better snap out of it. And this glue, how old is it? Noon came and departed, the telephone rang, and up until 1:15 Loyola barely thought about whether Starlene's tongue had become sharper lately. Janet occupied his mind and heart, and ever since she had had her hair styled in a fashion reminiscent of his mother he experienced a troubling desire for her. —Because it suits my *face*, why else? ran her explanation. Each day intensified his feelings and, he could tell, hers as well. On Saturday she would leave for Vancouver to take up a new job, this time in television, but she did not ask him to decide what to do. Yet it could not be more plain that if he stayed in Bowmount for too long after she left irreparable damage would be done to their relationship. What the hell's here for me anyway? Dad's getting colder every day. But I love him. But I need my own life. Don't I deserve that, after all this time? Go to Vancouver? Leave for the big city and pack bigger boxes. No, there has to be more chances there. And to be with Janet. Every other woman's been as bad off as me. I know there's something between us, I know what's stopping me, us. Yeah, us, I'm sure, or else why would she do her hair that way and dress like she -

—Loyola! Stop your daydreaming! Can't you hear the bell? Honestly! It's not worth keeping you on these days. Come on, Mike's waiting, he doesn't have all day to -

—It's not worth taking your shit either. The thought came out, possibly despite himself. —What did you say? The bell rang again. How many rings before she was on me? One? Starlene smiled. —I didn't think you'd repeat it. Now -

—What are you, deaf as well as dumb? You heard the bell, you trying to tell me you never heard what I said?

—Why you little -

—Keep it to yourself. You've been hassling me too damn long. You'll have plenty of time to bitch later, people like you always do. Loyola surprised himself by getting through the off-loading of clothes without the usual anxiety. Indeed, he felt elation over removing the smile on her face. But she'll can me soon. She's furious, she's not saying anything while Mike's around and we're this busy. Now she knows how I've been feeling. Eat it, cunt, you deserve it. Choke on it. What gave me the balls to do that? I didn't plan it, but I'm so tired of her mouth, the last thing on my mind was Janet. And if she leaves me, if I let her go, what'll that mean? I can't, no matter how Dad and everyone'll take it. He looked through the glass separating his room from the stockroom and saw Starlene on the telephone. Hold on for a few more days, make her fire you, give me enough time to save some more money. She never thought I'd answer back. That I was human. You just wait, before I go you'll hear something else, kiwi slut. Pinstripe followed houndstooth, bird's eye, Prince of Wales check, dinner jacket and black trousers into a corner of the room, two boxes for posting this evening, the bulk waiting for tomorrow's pick up. For possibly the first time in his employment at Moscati-Mann Loyola worked cheerfully.

—Yes yes, I bloody well know what his rights are! but he's do you hear me so pleased with himself, he's whistling! I know, you said apply pressure and he'd crack, the jerk, but I can't afford it now we have shipments coming in this and next week. After that? I'm staying behind tonight to write up the ad for his replacement, someone normal who you can have a laugh with instead of wondering if he's going to do his job when he isn't looking down your dress or I swear at your feet. Yes my foot, today, like you did but from him it's – a fetish? That's gross, sick, and her eyes flicked suspiciously from the figure in the packing room to four pairs of unused shoes haphazardly lying under a chair next to her desk. —Anthony? It'll only mean paperwork but he has no life that's why his wife divorced him and he's no fan of Loyola's. Cause? It's just as easy to get him so fed up he quits. All right, all right, I'll calm down. Her right hand rested on the slightly moist lip of a mug which read **NEW ZEALANDERS DO IT UPSIDE DOWN**, what she regarded as a cute jokey gift from her new mate. —When will I see you? Make it 7:30 and here. That way I can get more work down, all these suits to bill. No one's here then, Anthony leaves at 6, you want to look at the returned suits? What? Starlene turned from the packing room, and her eyes intermittently looked through the narrow window that opened into the well between the walls of the buildings. The sun had disappeared, it had begun to rain, and she could see the water gradually darken the red bricks through how many shades before turning black, listening to suggestions as to what they could do in the stockroom all by themselves. —A camera? Then we'd what? We got a few coats, I could spread them out, and – yes yes. She set the handset down gently. —God, he's so different. And strong. Not like you, she whispered at the back of the young man energetically putting together a cardboard box. —I'll get back at you, soon.

Interchapter

Many things occurred, or intensified, over the next few days, and once the excitement passed Bowmountians would say that when the weather turned, oh, that first weekend in November, life grew nasty, though the lowliest citizens and the City Fathers were well aware that mid-October marked the climatic change. The Gallico scandal was revealed fully by journalists. It was named after a miner from ore-rich Scanlon Ridge who, visiting Bowmount for the first time in twenty years, stumbled on a sex scene in the Mall but fled the washroom unobserved, vowing never to return to the city again. Bulletins on each of the seven accused men, six of whom would be tried and convicted, were updated regularly. The seventh man, released on bail, locked himself in his garage with kerosene and matches, and the explosion was, in the words of local wits, Fred Rifkind's final house job. The investigation of the illicitly copied videotapes, discovered selling in Belgium, England and Japan as **Gallico Goes Off! 1, 2** and **3**, continued and would perhaps in time result in official reprimands and dismissals due to incompetence. The issue of Fr. Jerome Ryan and the revelations about certain brothers and nuns, as a consequence of his arrest, filled column space when either the policies of the Burke Administration, or Michael Plumb's plans for a sequel to the financially successful Pilgrim's Progress, with more towns (as yet unnamed) and more saints (not yet confirmed) to be included on next year's itinerary, did not.

The behaviour of the clergy garnered unwanted attention from a national talk radio program on CCII. Dr. Rory Quasten's November 6 broadcast began, —Good evening, everyone, good evening. Tonight . . . some listeners will not have read or heard that another of the priestly class, this time from Bowmount, has been charged with molestation and sexual abuse, but it will come as little surprise that the head of the Catholic Church in that province defends his cleric. And it's no surprise the Catholic Church refuses to apologize. The young boy's name can't be given out, but we understand that he's a regular little boy. Or he was, before this tragedy happened. Now . . . his life is ruined. One look at the Pope's pronouncements and encyclicals, those messages from the apostolic Mount Olympus, and you have to ask yourself, does he know his time is up? Our question tonight . . . shall the lamp of religion be abolished? You know the numbers, and we'll take calls right after these local announcements. When we come back you'll meet my guest, Michael Brown, a Vaticanologist. Stay tuned. You know there's always more with Rory.

Citizens found no relief from sex in the cultural pages of local papers or in the entertainment segment of news broadcasts. On the day of Quasten's show, Nadeen Sarkissian's new instalment opened to hostile, delighted and confounded reviews. **Jassing Mapplethorpe** shocked everyone, not least because it marked a departure from what one article called —The muffled conceptualism of the crushed exhaust pipe. The photographs, mostly in black-and-white, were immediate successes in the art world, giving rise to much debate, from the first day till well beyond the last, over the vital topics of composition, texture and lighting, leaving, in the gallery owner's words, —That subtext stuff for plebs. The various body parts used, belonging to Caucasian, Asian, Aboriginal and Afro-Canadian men, were highly stylized. Two complimentary photographs, blown up to considerable size, stood side by side. In the first, a white male with short blond hair and a thick golden moustache faced the camera. His eyes were closed and he wore a broad smile. Entering his left ear was a white swollen penis, which emerged from his right ear as circumcised and black, a strand of semen caught in mid-air as it dripped onto the shoulder. The Rapture (Between Friends) divided viewers in three camps, those who were convinced this was obscene, those who admired the layout, and those who did not know whether to laugh then or later. In contrast, next to it was an identical set-up, only this time the focus of the shot, a Eurasian woman, bore an expression mingling rage, powerlessness and despair. Everyday Life (The Working Girl), so the catalogue breathed —derides the patriarchal structures of dominance by men in straight and homosexual societies, where submission of women, their constant oppression, their role in life to be breeders or divas, is desired not least by the boy-culture juvenile minds find sexually potent. The revelation that Sarkissian was not a homophile disturbed many who assumed that the avant-garde always carried pink banners. Over the next few months denouncements of her work, past and present, started appearing in small magazines. From the first night most commentators focused on the photograph of the man, a model not present opening night, who became, unsurprisingly, known to his friends by a rather obvious slang term.

Sarkissian's Mapplethorpe chair proved highly controversial, and alarming to some. Actually an upended stool, the three thin legs widely separated, with wide rubber rings on each leg that could be adjusted for height, the chair was the centre of a dozen photographs. In the first, all one saw was the naked tattooed back of a beefy white male, his anus clearly penetrated by one leg. Further variations showed the same back joined by black and brown backs, each man having selected the length of penetration by moving the rings up or down, in a composition called West-South-East. The one-seater model featured in a single photograph was described by the catalogue as —meant for nights without a partner. A parallel series depicting females in identical postures bore titles such as Secretary Rape and Fascist Undermining Of Women.

Present at the opening, Sam caught remarks from some of the people who, in two days, would be at the show, **Religious icons for the 90s**, that included his painting. —That display, how'd she get these three guys to sit on that perverse thing in front of everybody? —See the Asian hunk, is he, Judas Priest I'm turned on. —Money. —He doesn't need that leg, he must get it every night. —Where's the nervy bitch who's co-opted - there she is! You! You! —Stool's a great idea. Connotation, hehe-heh. Just the word. —See that guy, dyed hair, he touched the - oh, his boyfriend. Lucky him, the old fart. —The people aren't going to understand this. So . . . —Is this government funded? —Cautious. I mean, *I* think it's great, but it's not for everybody. The wrong people, someone fresh off the farm wanders in, what the hell'll they think? —I hate it. —So? —No denying it's raw. —But the models are well done. —And what the fuck am I going to say? The *Courier*'s a family newspaper. Supposedly. —I got to tell you, this Sarkissian, remember her first show, you think this is all a phallic attack? —Not here, I know you're excited, but later. —Not then, but maybe. —So? — Misogynists hate women, but what's a woman who hates men? There's a word for that, isn't there? —She's Greek, right? —Greek Cypriot. —What's the diff? A Fury. —If there's a toilet we can sneak into . . . —And hates gays too. —You there! —I'm going to start taking this personally if she doesn't explain herself. —Read the catalogue, she says no world religion advocates homosexual love. What else do you need to know? —Great legs and ass on her. —Bitch! Wait till I get a word in her ear. —Maybe she's lesbian. —Might explain this, and the pipe show. —So. —You think it's a polemic? In conversations along a multitude of political, social and class lines a critical consensus on the artistry of the show slowly formed, one that respected extreme views if advanced by insiders. Those outside the clique who had their own interpretations were ignored, and this included Sam, who concentrated so intently on the images he did not notice Sarkissian standing next to him until she tapped his shoulder, drink in one hand, her eyes slightly glassy.

—Oh, hello! Most, ah -

—You don't like it. No, I know you don't. I knew you wouldn't. Painters, you're all the same. Or maybe the frankness of the sex frightens you.

—Wait now, I only – let me get a word out -

—So you can dump all over it.

—You sent me an invitation! I thought -

—Course I did, to show you what photography can do. But I've been looking at your face all screwed up as you went around. Maybe if I'd used some mute woman you wouldn't hear my models scream. It might appeal to you.

—That's low, why you'd bring her into this -

—Everyone knows, Sammy. She going to be there when your painting's shown? I've heard about it, about the models you used, the wonderful Godly Tynbourn, and her voice carried above much of the conversation in the immediate vicinity, —how he's rescued Christ from the Church. She stumbled while moving closer. —You're so passé. Topic, medium, philosophy -

—You think gay sex -

—You look at the catalogue? Didn't think so.

—If you -

—Your whole art is dead. See this? gesturing to a woman's contorted body, —That's the here and now. It's where society's at, not in paint, or in print, not in Jerusalem in 1 A.D. This, this is reality. All your metaphysical bullshit, it's like somebody said, the rainbow-coloured butt of a baboon. Never to be seen, just some gentleman's agreement that it's hidden but there.

—And what's so special about photography? A few reviewers took notes. —At least in paint you get texture. With you it's all vision, eyes only, one sense at the expense of others. Is that reality? It's not even representational! We smell and hear and feel, but this photograph, it's only surface.

—And the installation, those men you see using the chair -

—Sensationalism, that's what. You don't have a woman there because -

—Would that turn you on? You only see surface, you little worm, you pompous romantic.

—And you're nothing but a journalist! Postcards have the same quality! Deeka really influenced you, these are his ideas! That remark drew a hard blow from a clenched fist, which caused an uproar, and the two were separated. The show and the clash of opinions made excellent stories, and also good publicity for both artists, though such a consideration could not have been on their minds. The public spat amused those who could stomach the report on the show, particularly those familiar with both combatants. Alone in a downstairs room of Janssen's Funeral Home, Stan Miloz read the *Bowmount Courier*'s report, grateful for the diversion. This morning, the day after the show, he had again looked at Mr. Lonegin's body mutely, unable to come up with suitable words, devoid, he privately admitted, of one idea as to what he might wish for his dead father-in-law. Stan checked his watch, eager for the service to start. It would be a relief to have the days of mourning over with.

Duncan Lonegin had died on Sunday afternoon, alone in his study, of an unexpected heart attack. His wife came home to find him on the couch. Camilla and Stan were due to return from their honeymoon at the supper hour. The doctor said death had been painful but swift. Marian, with her new-found energy, arranged the funeral home, the service, and the burial in the Anglican cemetery, according to her husband's last wishes, providentially written down the day after the wedding. In Tupholme Street United Church, crowded with family and friends of the deceased, business associates and colleagues, Stan felt mixed feelings as the minister, Rev. I. William Müller, aggressively led the congregation through the rituals. The poor bastard, lying there like that ahead of his time. Jesus, he hadn't been that bad, was he? I coulda been nicer I suppose, but it ain't my fault he was boring. Going on about religion so much. Who did he think listened? Marian? But she's different now, and what happened there? He looked at his mother-in-law sitting next to her daughter, their grim expressions reasserting how physically alike they were. The minister's abrasive voice cut through these and other thoughts like an axe, and Stan found the dreary hymns a welcome relief. He never sang, certainly would not start with these unfamiliar pieces, such as Fairest Lord Jesus, and in this was not alone. It worked out that the United Church parishioners were seated in the centre aisles, with most of the Roman Catholics and others occupying the right and left wings. Only in How Great Thou Art did the three sections come together, and that occurred near the end.

In the middle lay the meditation, followed by the eulogy. The minister's delivery obliterated all personal thought, and Ivy found it difficult to concentrate on her friend's father. It was as though that was not allowed, as if the minister's burden was to remove everyone's involvement with the corpse lying in the coffin. His words were common, his ideas conventional, that death is but the stage to eternal life, that the soul survived the mere corporeal existence to join in unending celebration with God and the Lord Jesus Christ in divine unity. Hands jammed inside tired gray trousers, spectacles flashing under the lights, Reverend Müller rasped about the real meaning of Duncan Lonegin's passing, when in truth they had never met, and the meditation, with the substitution of appropriate details, could have been used for anyone. He had the grace to admit his unfamiliarity with the dead man, allowing Camilla in her eulogy to supply the personal element the family and friends required and deserved.

Among the mourners were some people from St. Finnian's, including Fr. Liam, temporarily assuming Fr. Jerome's role. He sat in the back, sang every song with ease in a pleasant baritone, and deliberately ignored glances and whispers about his presence, for he had come to pay tribute, on his own behalf, to a man he respected. Everything went well until Camilla reached a certain section of her eulogy. —My Dad was Roman Catholic, as all of you know, of St. Finnian's. But he didn't want his body to enter the temple of Sodom again. Those are his words. He didn't want to be interred in his parents' family plot, as he knew priests were buried in the same cemetery, priests who had been fornicators and paedophiles. This is what the Church represented for my Dad at the end. And not just for him, I know. He would want it said here today, in a place which he could turn to, that the human tragedy we're commemorating also embraces the living. Especially those of his generation who've been thrown out of the Church. Many mourners tsk-tsked at this, and Fr. Liam's complexion reddened. Ivy involuntarily shook her head, disappointed at her friend speaking like this at such a time.

The concluding portion of Camilla's eulogy – or speech, as Archbishop Mason classified it on hearing Fr. Liam's account – followed more traditional lines. She returned to her pew amid exclamations to the right and left. —Apostate. —You know she's been influenced by Marian. Hasn't set foot in St. Finnian's since her confirmation. —Attacking poor Fr. Jerome like that, in public, here. Here! —No wonder we Catholics don't have eulogies any more, if that's how people are going to get on. Eventually the body of Duncan Lonegin was lowered to rest during miserable weather, the wind howling, the rain seemingly coming not from above but from the side. People held their coats tightly shut, jammed their hats down, attempted to keep their useless umbrellas from flying away in the storm. Ursula remarked that the sight of the mourners at the cemetery struggling from the grave back to their cars, scrambling over the suddenly mucky ground that threatened to pull shoes off, put her in mind of the retreat from Moscow. Stan and Camilla agreed that it was best if Camilla stayed in her parents' house for a couple of days, since in the wake of the activity the silence would be hard on her mother. As she exited the car she placed a small key attached to a chain in Stan's hands. —No more. He nodded, pained and pleased that this game was over.

It was clear everyone had changed natures in the last month.

A *new cycle*

Tomorrow, Monday, November 13, he would not have to ride to work on the number nineteen or walk up Elephant Hill past the too-familiar Crucifix, and he would never see or listen to Starlene again. Why was it only now, early in the evening, that he realized how happy he felt? Why had the feeling waited? The north wind blowing patches of fog from Bowmount River could not spoil the mood as Loyola made his way to Central Street, Johnny's Bar and The Great Pan being two places he intended to visit tonight. Less than a week ago he had bought a ticket to Vancouver. His lease expired on the last day of the month and the intervening time would be spent packing or selling his belongings, temporarily storing what he wanted to keep at his father's. Tomorrow he would have to talk to his father, carefully choosing the words, because Mr. Holden had already commented on consanguinity and the unusual closeness of his son and niece. At least she didn't show up with that hairdo. He'd've flipped, and who needs that?

A fire engine swerved down the road, its siren echoing in the fog and down the long corridor of buildings housing restaurants, boutiques, and clothing stores. An ambulance blared in its wake. Dad would have a heart attack if he knew. Knew what? We haven't done a thing. If we're there, to-gether, maybe – how will it feel, to be, her underneath, and that picture? His resolution hardened, but also brought back Friday's fight with Star-lene. She had accused him of sloppy work, and what started as a lecture at 10:30 escalated to shouting within fifteen minutes. Half an hour later Loy-ola had his final wages and the paperwork in his hand and was shown the door by Anthony Coish. Numbed, he sat on a bench in the small park on Prospect Avenue. That cunt planned it. Loyola remembered as he walked that he had called her half a dozen names, and quoted the insults she had used on him, but as he crossed the street, pausing to look down at a news-paper headline that read **Joy Took Pleasure From Rape, Says Murderess**, he wondered if she had called him an honest-to-God mother-fucker. He preferred to dismiss this, imagine it was said, but he could not, not yet, because the word honest made it stick in his mind. He did not deny she said —You incestuous bastard, in front of a shocked Doug, with Anthony there fingering his moustache, letting one brown loafer fall off, slipping his foot back in, over and over. Right then he knew he had been deballed. Yes, Janet called once in a while, but how did Starlene know their closeness? There wasn't anything to know about, so who's she been talking to? Her last words also would be hard to forget. —Go have a fuck-fest with your family in British Columbia, and name why don't you the first two-headed freak after your mother! She left, slamming doors, vic-torious, though damaged by what he had said. Trapped in the middle of the intense brownness of the stockroom, the harsh smell of plastic, dust, and wool in his nose, caught by the disgusted looks of the two witnesses to his castration, his rich, passionate, layered, and secret world had be-come nothing more than a dirty grotesque fantasy.

Anthony stepped forward. —Starlene fired you somewhere in that ri-diculous thing. I was going to do it myself, the postal books are a mess, you can't write worth a bean. Customers ring me, they ring Toronto, com-plaining about the wrinkled clothes. It's about time she did something about you. Past time. Now she's gone off to have a little cry in her car, tee-hee-hee. Come with me. I want you out of my sight before noon.

A police car sped past, its blue and red lights illuminating a sign out-side Blair's Superette, Now In Season Moosebruger. Some teenager re-ar-ranged the letters, or did Blair spell it that way? But this is why I didn't feel good until now. My guts all over the floor, and how did she know? There's only one way. He noticed the fog had taken on an acrid smell and that it was warmer. Flecks of an unknown composition landed on his beige jacket, and grit irritated his eyes. The gutters were filling with wa-ter and flames stood out in the overcast sky. He hurried forward, sneakers squishing in the puddles, smoke now blocking out everything to the left and right, leaving visible only flames and lights. He began coughing, but kept going, tripping over hoses and running past police barricades. Calls for help and barked commands rang out from different directions, mingled with the noise of pressurized water, and at some point the chemical smell choked him. What's in that part of the street? A laundromat, Front Row Bleachers, a photo developer's, an art gallery, a used clothes place, what else? Would Moscati-Mann stink this way if I burned it down, with Starlene and Anthony in it?

An agonized yell from his left or right, —The Great Pan is dead!, startled him. Loyola took out the handkerchief his mother had always insisted he carry with him. He mopped his eyes and held the cloth over his mouth and nose. Sweat covered his body as he looked at the blazing restaurant. Years ago the only house he considered a home burned to the ground and he had watched helplessly as his mother appeared at the upper windows, unable to open them, and the flames blocked the stairs. Those flames were the same colours as the ones now reducing this building to ruins, the place where Janet had waited so often for him. Loyola lurched forward, racing towards what remained of The Great Pan, avoiding a policeman's reach, to work his way around the trucks, stopping only when he came upon the ambulance seen earlier. A stretcher was being carried to it. —My mother, is she there? —Who, son, who? —My mother, my – Janet. —No, this guy's one of the cooks. He went outside and just had a heart attack. Was your mother in there? —What happened? —A fault in the stove, goddamn Ukobach kitchens, three fires this season. Your mother, where – hey, son! Come back! Officer! In the commotion he slipped down an alley, rejoining Central Street at Fairview. A few house numbers further was Johnny's Bar, another police barricade a few feet beyond it. Trying not to cough, though his lungs felt heavy with ash and his mouth tasted terrible, Loyola made it inside, where Jules greeted him.

—Welcome, my fine young gadabout, you've been – what's this, you're – Johnny, water, quickly!

—He looks like he's been in a garbage pail. Basically. In a few minutes

Loyola had his voice back and Sylvie was shaking off his coat out on the sidewalk. Naturally, everyone knew about the fire, it was on the radio until Johnny, disgusted, put on music, but Loyola was congratulated on breaking through fascist lines, a boozy cheer issuing from Jack, Wes, and Jimmy. Jules ordered spirits and led him to a booth, narrowly missing Ivy's entrance. She ordered a Perrier. —Ivy, on this kind of night you need coffee. And he's not here yet. —Who? —Once the traffic gets moving again. Hey there, Pops, what can I get you? A paper landed on the bar and Ivy decided to move down one seat for the older man, accidentally bumping Bart, sitting with his back against the wall. —This, this is what he painted? He's a, he's a -

—Relax, Pops.

—But Jonathan, I've never seen anything more shocking. *The Carlyle-Bowmount Despatch*'s arts section was headlined **Christianity in tatters – local artist's vision**. —He sat here and told us – you, Bartholomew, you were there. He was doing God's work, painting the Holy Family, and this is the result? Is this true? Johnny nodded, placing Ivy's two drinks before her. —You saw it, Pops?

—Is that some kind of joke? It's disrespectful, a disgrace! I wouldn't show myself in there if I was paid. He lied to us, didn't he? He calls himself an artist? Bart sighed, moved his head out of the darkness, his eyes so red Ivy felt her own itch, and said, —Maybe he did. Maybe he did God's work. Who can tell?

—You'd say that? You felon! You were the one -

—Pops, knock that off, no trouble. I think Bart's just saying God works in mysterious ways his wonders to perform. Pops shook his stick at no one and everyone and finally Ivy. —And you, what do you think?.

—I haven't seen it.

—You don't need to see it to think. Read this and you can make up your own mind. The next time I see him I'll let him know what a foul thing he's done.

—Get it off your chest to Sam when he comes back to town on Thursday, he's visiting friends. Now, you want another drink?

—No, I'm going home. That young man said an art gallery was on fire? It should be the one where that abomination's hanging. When he left Ivy wanted to ask Johnny about the fuss, but he was serving Victor and someone else. Anxious to forget about Alistair's being late, Bart cleared his throat. —The painting, by Sam? He – do you mind?

—No, go ahead.

—It was a triptych. One picture of the Virgin Mary, another of Christ in the centre, and then Mary Magdalene. They were really large. Harry said they were magnificent, but that Sam needed Crisco. I guess you can mix that with paint. I don't know.

—Well I wouldn't know either -

—The opening was Wednesday. Sam had a good place in it, Harry said. Harry should be telling this, he was there. Johnny, where's Harry?

—Haven't seen him.

—What about Alistair?

—For the last time, no, he hasn't been around today neither.

—I wonder where -

—Maybe they're sipping margaritas together under palm trees, I wouldn't know. Yes, Jack, yes? Bart reddened further, something Ivy had thought impossible. —What was I saying? Do you find it hard to concentrate sometimes? Harry was invited to the opening. The painting was slashed.

—Somebody vandalized it? Bart shook his head. —Sam painted these things that'd make you weep, Harry told me, then, like a surgeon, made cuts here and there. Harry thought he'd gone mad – but Sam's smart, did you know that? – defacing the – and the girl was there with her parents, I think they're lovers. Sam and Judith, I mean. Bart checked his watch, looked at the door, took another sip of beer. —The catalogue said the painting was about, and I think Sam wrote this, the state of Christianity. Not that he doesn't believe in Christ, but -

—What's the name of the painting?

—<u>The Relics of Faith</u>. Sam cut out body parts, bits from the Crown of Thorns, the Cross too, and get this, he removed bones and hair from Mary

Magdalene, clothes from the Virgin Mary, and, and, I'm sorry, Christ's foreskin. Said these were kept in churches, villages, and were things the superstitious prayed to, no real belief in God any more from Christians, and that the Vatican had cut up the message of the Holy Family to suit their needs. We need a new message, he said. People there called it – you heard Pop. Mutilation, heresy, blasphemy. Sam says it illustrates the paganism of present-day Christians. They had to remove the painting – you hadn't heard any of this?

—I've been out of town for a few days. I only came back last night. You remember all that from . . .

—I have a good memory. Then someone threatened to wreck the gallery. The painting was shown two nights, now it's in a vault. The critics hated the whole show, said the concept was reactionary. They went after Sam for not painting Christ along traditional lines, making him look like a Titan, they even capitalized that, don't know why. Oversized.

—For the cutting.

—What?

—The figures would have to be big, so he could remove the pieces and keep them recognizable. And they aren't human, are they? They have to be larger than us, if you believe in them.

—I wouldn't know, I gave that up – I guess I never had it, spirituality.

—Maybe when you're older you'll think – I'm sorry, that's not my, sorry. I shouldn't even be saying that. She did not know why Bart was smiling. When he asked her if she really thought he would live much longer she had no reply. —It's all right, forget it. Here, there's who you're waiting for. Turning, she saw Phil enter with someone, and excused herself. Bart sat alone once more. Everyone's here but Alistair. Doesn't he know how humiliating it is for me to be seen waiting like this? Like my plans fell through. Plans? Get aholt of myself, when was the last time I had plans. Bart's weary eyes jumped from where Phil was introducing Ivy and Hilary, to the booth where Loyola sat scowling as he listened to Jules Deeka. Jack, Wes, and Jimmy were figuring out which civic holiday was better, the Carlyle Festival or Bowmount Day, and Victor and Johnny were comparing hockey teams. These and other groups emphasized his unique status. Once again he looked at the door, though it had not opened, trying not to check his watch. Alistair was rarely late. There had been no answer at his apartment this afternoon. Would knowing the time magically make him appear? Picking up the discarded paper Bart forced himself to concentrate on the stories, beginning with page one. This was a trick he often tried when waiting for someone. People always disturbed you when you were watching television or in the bathroom, so perhaps if he pretended to be involved in some activity they would pick that moment to call or come by. Despite the fact this trick seldom worked, he would read and wait for Alistair to show up, undoubtedly in the middle of an interesting news item.

At almost the same time, on a highway winding through one of the valleys surrounding Bowmount, authorities were at the site of a car accident. In the darkness the set faces turned blue red, blue red. —Car went off the road at a high speed into this tree. We have one corpse in the car, the passenger, and one on the ground.

—Who are these lovely people? asked a late arrival. The ambulance driver, Derek, looked away from his colleague to Brad. —What the hell you doing covering the death beat, thought you were in sports.

—CCII's fucking me around, giving me night shifts, weekends, road reports. Nice to see you. Been awhile. I was driving by and saw the lights.

—The cop's over there taking witness statements if you wanted to ask him anything.

—In a minute. How'd this happen, Derek?

—No seatbelts on either of them. That's why this guy's dead. Hurtled right through the windshield. Broken neck, instant death. The other guy was banged around in the car. Safety bag didn't do enough. They were both dead when we got here. We're as useless as tits on a bull.

—That's a lot of blood.

—The guy on the road here looks familiar. You're Mr. Reporter, you should know. Brad Dombrowski took a look and whistled. —Some story, huh? He nodded, his pen already writing. By the time he finished the policeman had come over. —Hey there, Mark, how's it hanging?

—Long and full, you bastard, what're you writing about us now?

—Just getting a look at the bodies. This guy's a someone. Anything to tell me about what went on, or who the other one is? The policeman considered this. —We haven't had the coroner out here yet. Derek, what're you still hanging around for? You and, what's your name -

—Vahid, Vahid -

—You two go over there for a minute, will you? The reporter and the policeman inspected the passenger side of the vehicle, its body bent almost in half by the force of the impact. —If that was an American car it wouldn't be in that shape. Or European. Foreigners.

—The passenger?

—No idea. Some guy. Tall. Can't find a wallet yet, but don't want to disturb anything. But I'm sure they were drinking. You can smell it on this one and there's a smashed rum bottle in the back. Brad asked to look inside. —Just don't touch anything. Here's a flashlight. The reporter looked away from the twisted body of a man partially covered in the remnants of blood-stained plastic, and spotted a cassette in the tape deck.

—Mark, mind doing a favour?

—It'll cost you. Not money, a good p.r. piece. We've had the shit kicked out of us lately with one thing and another. A couple of screw-ups and everyone gets tarred. Brad pointed to the pink-coloured cassette. —Atmosphere for my story. —Removing evidence, maybe. Could be serious. This is a big deal. Understood? Quick, before anyone else shows up. Your car. Nothing was written on the cassette but the label had a pattern of some sort. Brad played side one in his car. They heard bars of a song neither could name, some man singing about how the best day in his life was the day he kissed his girl good-bye. —Hold on. He played the other side and they heard unearthly sounds, over a bed of a piano and harps, with whistles in the background. The sounds were vaguely familiar. —Whales!

—What?

—Whales. Maybe they were listening to that when the car crashed.

—They must have been drunk, listening to that garbage. A couple of fairies?

—Wouldn't that be a story? But they died while listening to a relaxation tape.

—A what? Give it back, I'll put it back in their car.

—How's that for a deduction?

—Keep your day job. You think anyone'd crash a car because they were relaxed? Drunk, that's what they were.

—Don't rule it out. Thanks, Mark, I owe you.

—You do, and don't forget, we know where you live. In a quarter of an hour Brad was broadcasting on CCII over his cell phone with a short announcement about —a tragedy tonight that's claimed the life of one of Bowmount's most prominent men, whose identity, until next of kin have been notified, cannot be revealed. The car he was driving was travelling towards the City of Bowmount, on Valley View Highway, when it swerved off the road, in the words of one witness, and hit a tree. The body of the car buckled with such force that the tree is in danger of toppling over. The driver was thrown from the car. The other occupant, a man not yet identified, also not wearing a seatbelt, died on the scene. Police expect that it will be tomorrow when they will be able to publicly identify both men. CCII will be there when they do. From the Valley View Highway, this is Brad Dombrowski for CCII News.

An hour had passed and it was now 7:30 p.m. Many customers were leaving Johnny's Bar, and the owner nodded to each one, though he would have wished the crowd tonight had been less sombre. —Sylvie, it must be the weather. Look at all the boss faces on them. You know, he said in answer to her puzzled look, —the kind of worried face bosses have. Like me, I guess. She unobtrusively pointed at a threesome putting on their jackets. —Yeah, she looks happy, Phil too. He must have charm, though I sure as hell don't see it. Did Harry come in? I wonder where he is. But look at those two all hidden away, they're nothing but - goodnight, Vic, my bet's on the Habs. Trouble, the pair of them. To Sylvie, he continued, —Neither of 'em belong to the new place I start building come the new year.

—You told her, didn't you? My whole life exposed. How, why?

—Loyola, I made friends with your nemesis because you needed saving from that boiling sea. Look kindly on my final intercession before leaving this town that suffers from gigantism of the ego.

—What?

—I rescued you like I promised. It's an apology, too.

Recovered somewhat from being fired, Hilary talked to Phil as they waited for Ivy, who was in the washroom. Loud voices rose from a far corner of the bar. —And what did I find when I came back after my travels? You, rooted, stuck. What did I do? I let air into your stifling world.

—You came back the same person you were when you left. You think I've changed. Well, you stayed the same. You went travelling, you had all those talents, the degrees. What good are they? You're the disappointment! No big things from you, so don't start knocking me, Jesus.

—One independence day speech a year is enough, Loyola. You're as conventional as everyone else, expecting a man of learning to deliberately set himself aside from the herd. There's something to being discreet, do you know that? It's the average man, like the Frenchman said, who wants to stick out, an original man hides it.

—Talk like a normal guy then.

—Normal? If you want to ruin your life, go ahead, just acknowledge the psychology behind what you're doing, and don't pretend, least of all to me, that it's honest love. What is it with you, a cunt comes along and your head gets turned. You let Kate get to you about us, then you -

—And you and Nadeen, blowing up like that over her wanting -

—That voluble cum oddity, who cares about her? She didn't do badly out of me, look at that show, my ideas, mine. But let's get back to you, with your infantile obsession -

—My what? You crock of -

—Both of you, out, out of my bar, right now! Hear me? Don't come back until you can be civil. Johnny had come in at some point. Ivy witnessed the last part of the exchange, but it was less compelling than contemplating Phil and Hilary's closeness. They've such similar ideas about the world, it's like Phil's found something there, and that's what I'm looking for, isn't it? They have some rapport because of what Hilary has to share. I know Phil's been with women, but not now, he's on his own. God, he calls me and – he's younger, not as young as that guitar player, but young. Is it envy over what he and Hilary talk about? Phil nodded at her and she rose to join them as they stepped outside, where Johnny had moved Jules and Loyola in the hopes that the presence of policemen might calm them down.

—I hope you and your cousin have a good time together. She's sluttish, but a monogamous slut, I'll give her that. Don't you see you're throwing your life away for nothing more than a girl?

—A girl you wanted to fuck. Ivy flinched as if this was aimed at her and she recalled the details of the encounter at Winterton's. She felt, for the first time, Phil's arm around her shoulders. Did I shrink back, or did he move forward? Not so long ago, Ivy thought self-interrogation a way to anticipate future dialogues, helping her come up with quick responses. Now she wondered if it was solely the refuge of the lonely. She heard Loyola say, —What you're saying, you bastard, is that you're jealous. I've done something you'd never have the courage to do. It's, what, unconventional? Go on, mess with Starlene's head, get her to quit so she can join you in Paris where she thinks you'll take her. Lie to her. What kind of life is that? At least I'm not -

—You'll be in therapy in two years when you start to wilt every time she kisses you, and you finally understand you're humping a corpse. Loyola was quivering. —You broken down old man. You were never anything, and I was too stupid to see it. And you know what? You weren't going to be anything either. Just like me, only people expected better from you. So there is a difference between us. Jules jabbed at Loyola's chest without touching him. —If it was that, that, some rule of society broken, do you think I'd say anything? Me?

—Yes!

—You're regressing! Back to the womb you go! That's what I can't let you get away with. They argued as they made their way west, toward the fire, one a few steps behind the other.

—Ivy?

—I know. It's so . . .

—Like watching a car wreck. I didn't know they were like that. Amazing how people can hide out in the open. For a moment they were silent until Hilary spoke. —We have to get going, Phil. Ivy, you're invited too, you know. There'll be food there. Or we can drop you home, since your car's in the garage.

—Ivy and I can get a bite after. How does that sound? With everything we talked about, I didn't get a chance to ask how the trip went. You must be tired. She nodded. —Thanks. Thanks, Hilary. I need to get some air. I'll catch up. Phil smiled at her and slowly drew his arm away. —When you're ready. We're parked up there. She sank back against the rough brick wall of Johnny's Bar, closing her eyes. Tonight something previously unknown had been introduced to her life, and delving into it would not separate her from Phil, or so she hoped. There aren't any guarantees, yet I know he wants to be with me. We'll see. Voices to the right made her turn west, where Jules and Loyola, well down the road, yelled at each other, though what they said could not be discerned. She felt their dissension was almost as old as time. Beyond them, foul black smoke from The Great Pan fire mingled with the thickening fog lit by thin yellow-orange flames. The two figures receded until swallowed by shadows. Drawn by the heavenly scent from a nearby Persian restaurant further up Central Street, she turned east. Under a lamp at the corner of Fairview waited Phil, with Hilary unlocking car doors. In a moment he would ask her to join him, she could picture his smile, and what would she say? I feel we're equals, united, and isn't that absurd, to be convinced of that, in so short a time, when I'm only starting to know him? Ivy, go slow. But the old world she knew, containing her, Phil, and everyone else, had shivered to pieces, the wall supporting her had disappeared, and she had been freed to decide between what might be. —Ivy, he said, in a tone she knew would never be forgotten, —do you . . . would you like to come along? Ivy did not know. Until she did.

Jeff Bursey has had his plays performed in St. John's and Charlottetown, Canada; his short fiction has appeared in award-winning anthologies and journals; his first full-length fiction, the exploratory, critically acclaimed *Verbatim: A Novel* (2010), is set in the same city as *Mirrors on which dust has fallen*; and his reviews and academic articles have appeared in *Henry Miller: New Perspectives* (Bloomsbury), as well as in *American Book Review*, *Canadian Notes & Queries*, *Electronic Book Review*, *Numero Cinq*, *The Winnipeg Review*, and other places. His website is www.jeffbursey.com

Christopher WunderLee is the author of a novel, *Moore's Mythopoeia*; a novella, *The Loony: a novella of epic proportions*; a collection of short stories, *Visiting Hours*; and a book of poetry, *Kalopsia*. He lives in Seattle, Washington with his wife and two mutts.